TIME SIEGE

BOOKS BY WESLEY CHU

Time Salvager

The Lives of Tao

The Deaths of Tao

The Rebirths of Tao

The Rise of Io

TIME SIEGE

WESLEY CHU

TOR

A Tom Doherty Associates Book
New York

TIME SIEGE

Copyright © 2016 by Wesley Chu

A Tor Book
Published by Tom Doherty Associates, LLC
175 Fifth Avenue
New York, NY 10010

www.tor-forge.com

Tor® is a registered trademark of Tom Doherty Associates, LLC.

The Library of Congress Cataloging-in-Publication Data is available upon request.

ISBN 978-0-7653-7754-8 (hardcover)
ISBN 978-1-4668-5602-8 (e-book)

Our books may be purchased in bulk for promotional, educational, or business use. Please contact your local bookseller or the Macmillan Corporate and Premium Sales Department at 1-800-221-7945, extension 5442, or by e-mail at MacmillanSpecialMarkets@macmillan.com.

First Edition: July 2016

Printed in the United States of America

0 9 8 7 6 5 4 3 2 1

To my brother, Stephen,
and sister, Amy

ACKNOWLEDGMENTS

They say our childhood can be some of our most formative years, that it is those early memories and experiences which help define who we are. If that is true, then I owe a lot of me to my older brother, Stephen, and my younger sister, Amy.

I am the middle child, which is great, and by great I mean I don't have the responsibility of being the familial standard bearer who has to break in all the new clothes and drive the rest of us in his car, and I totally don't have to deal with being the baby and have all that attention thrusted upon me. Who needs that pressure, right?

My siblings have been with me through serious highs and hilarious lows. They stuck with me partially because someone needs to bail me out of trouble, but mainly because that's what brothers and sisters do.

Everything I learned about being a productive member of a post-apocalyptic zombie society I learned from them. Use the hot water before it's gone. Don't snitch. Share your toys. Don't share your hamsters. Never pick a fight with someone twice your size. You can build a wide assortment of weapons from common household items. And no matter what, you get your family's back even if they're wrong.

Also, your brother and sister will lie to you just for fun. Until I was seven years old, I believed my parents got me at a Sears Blue-Light Special. They don't sell kids at Blue-Light Specials! I checked. They will also challenge you to do things you would not do otherwise, like inhaling black pepper up your nose or wearing their makeup. And they do so because they're family, and I'm dumb.

My childhood was some of the best years of my life, and I always cherish the memories I share with them. As we grow older, we forge our own paths. We're separated by distance and time and children and publishing deadlines. Life will never be that simple or pure again. It only gets busier, more complex.

But I'll always remember that person who taught me how to ride a bike. I'll always remember seeing her walk for the first time. I'll always remember what it's like to have someone who has your back no matter what, even when you're wrong.

Especially when you're wrong.

To Stephen and Amy, this book is for you.

TIME SIEGE

ONE

THE SLOG

Roman struggled to keep his footing in the ankle-deep slog of the muddy riverbank. The tainted water, mixed with rubble, dirt, and debris, had been accumulating broken bits of the ruined city for centuries. The resulting mixture was a slow-moving speckled brown mush that folded over itself repeatedly as it flowed down the steep slope.

He slipped on a metal plate embedded in the goo and fell onto his belly, sliding several meters and losing whatever small progress he had made climbing up the hill. He spat out a mouthful of the gunk and cursed as a mushy tide swelled, rolling over and caking him in its grime.

Black abyss, he was going to smell like shit until his next shower. Unfortunately, his next hygiene maintenance wasn't scheduled until the morning after tomorrow. That meant he was going to stink like a latrine until then. Probably meant he was going to have to rack outside of quarters tonight as well.

Someone above him laughed. "Chaki, you bunking with Roman, right? Have fun."

Chaki's face appeared at the top of the hill as Roman tried to reclaim his footing. "Damn clumsy fodder. Stop playing in the mud. The collie's here."

Roman looked at the green metal plate that precipitated his fall and scowled. There were some letters on it in an archaic form of solar

English. He wiped the gunk off with his sleeve and read it slowly: NEW LONDON.

"Are we on the right continent?" he asked in a loud voice. "I thought we're on one of the Americas."

"What kind of a stupid question is that?" Renee called down.

"I don't know," Roman said. "This is my first tour on this planet. I just thought London was a city in Europe. Or was that Africa?"

Overhead, a gray box-shaped ship struggled to fly around the many obstructions to their position. On top of the hill, fallen poles, loose wires, hanging vines, and building fragments jutting up and out were scattered all over the landscape, often making it difficult for the collies—flying boxes not known for their maneuverability—to reach their landing zones.

They were near a river mouth, and the soft ground had sunk so much that many of the buildings on both sides of the river leaned in over the water until they formed a triangular roof above it. Several of these buildings looked ready to collapse and probably wouldn't stand much longer.

"Why are our extraction points always on top of hills?" Roman grumbled. "Why can't it just come down to us for once?"

He renewed his efforts, using his hands to claw his way up. His arms sunk elbow-deep into the muck, getting even more grime onto his now completely filthy uniform. Not that it mattered anymore; he couldn't get any dirtier.

Roman and the other half-dozen jackasses with him were just finishing an eight-hour patrol of a region southwest of the city of Boston. Surveillance had picked up movement from what could possibly be the wastelander tribe they had been searching for the past six months, and of course, his was the unlucky squad sent here to investigate.

The Cooperative Forces, or Co-op, was created after the failed attack on Boston to retrieve the temporal anomaly to fulfill the agency's contractual obligation to the megacorporation. It was supposed to be a joint operation by Valta and ChronoCom. However, those Valta assholes—their leader, Securitate Kuo, specifically—did not seem to know what "joint" meant. Almost all the heavy lifting was carried out by ChronoCom monitors, while Valta's troopers just sat on their collective asses. Kuo had even had the audacity to tell the lead monitors to their faces that the Valta troopers were too valuable to waste. Black abyss, everyone in the agency hated that woman.

Ever since they had cleared out all of Boston and realized that the savages had fled, the patrols had had to expand their search perimeters to include the areas surrounding the city. Now, Co-op troops were forced to blindly chase the hundreds of random energy signatures that popped up, in the hopes that one of them was the tribe of savages they were after.

Roman finally reached the top of the hill and was helped to his feet by Renee and Pau. Chronman Mong sniffed him irritably as he continued to eye the collie making its way to their position. "Next time, be more careful, fool. If the collie pilot insists we clean his ship, you're the fodder doing it, you hear?"

"Easy for you," Roman muttered. "Not every asshole gets exos to fly around."

Roman wouldn't have dared to say that aloud. Mong was a Tier-5, fresh out of the Academy, and like most chronmen, thought he was a big deal. If Roman had to guess, the guy was probably nineteen years old. Definitely green and inexperienced, but already as arrogant as a Tier-3. Still, even the lowest chronman outranked the most experienced monitor.

The squad brushed themselves off and waited as the collie lowered itself to the ground. Fortunately, this patrol had been uneventful, though part of him wished the damn savages would just show up so they could end this hellish mission working under those corporate Valta assholes.

"I can't wait to get transferred off-planet," he ranted. "I didn't sign up to escape from the hellhole on Naiaid to end up in an even worse hellhole on Earth."

A couple of the other monitors chuckled in agreement. Mong just sniffed and continued staring at the collie. No doubt the kid probably felt insulted having to patrol with a bunch of monitors instead of running time salvages, which was what chronmen were supposed to do. The collie landed with a splat in the mud, and the squad, exhausted and glad the day had ended without incident, made its way on board.

Mong looked Roman over and stuck his hand out. "Wipe yourself off first, damn it."

"Yes, chronman." Roman sighed. "Just give me a . . ."

His voice trailed off as a dark flash arced up into the air. He squinted and raised an arm just in time for the object to thud into his shoulder, the impact knocking him on his back once more into the mud. Roman groaned and stared in shock as a thick wooden shaft stuck out of his body. Another shaft sunk into the soft ground near his feet. He began to scream.

More spears rained down, bouncing off the collie's roof and sticking in the soft ground. There was a loud bang, and Chaki fell, clutching his leg. A blaster shot narrowly missed Renee. The rest of the squad scattered for cover, their wrist beams pointed outward at the ruins surrounding them.

A swarm of savages appeared, seemingly crawling out of every nook and cranny of the ruined buildings. They peppered Roman's squad with small-arms fire, ranging from thick spears to primitive firearms to blaster rifles. Mong activated his exo and launched into the air. Most of the enemy attacks bounced ineffectually off his shield.

"Defensive positions around the collie," he roared. "Renee, get Roman. Gouti, suppression fire on the building to the north."

Two kinetic coils appeared on both sides of Mong as if he had grown wings, and he barreled toward the main group of the charging savages head-on. The coils cut the savages down as he swept through them, knocking a score of them off their feet. He changed direction and shot upward along the nearest building. Redirecting the coils into the opened windows, the chronman began to pluck savages out and drop them down into the streets below.

Roman whimpered as rough hands grabbed his injured shoulder and hauled him to his feet. "Come on," Renee said, dragging him toward the collie's opened hatch. A savage charged at them from the left, only to fall to her wrist beam. Another came from their right, which Roman was just able to hit before the savage could bury a hatchet in his face. More came from every direction, forcing Renee to drop him halfway to the ship so she could engage them.

Roman fell onto a knee and held his right arm with his left to steady his trembling body. His nerves screamed as he forced his arm up to aim with the wrist beam. He hit an old-looking savage in the chest and took out another who didn't even look old enough to shave. That last one came perilously close to sticking him with another spear. He watched, dismayed, as the young savage fell at his feet.

An involuntary shudder coursed through his body. He had almost become dinner just now. At least that was the rumor among the monitors; these wasteland tribes were cannibals, and civilized people were a delicacy. He couldn't think of a worse way to go than roasting over a fire. He bet he tasted awful.

Gouti screamed at them from the collie's hatch, "Get your asses inside!"

Renee picked Roman up again and the two desperately tried to sprint to the collie. To his right, Baeth shot a charging savage point-blank in the stomach, then fell to a vicious club to the side of his face. Roman watched in horror as a savage woman towered over his squadmate, ready to strike the killing blow. It never came. *They must like their food alive when they cook them. Those bastards.* It was too late to help Baeth now. The rest of the squad converged on the collie. Chaki was limping badly while Gouti desperately tried to provide covering fire.

Mong was still flying through the air, acting as a battering ram and launching his body at groups of savages, trying to keep them at bay to buy time for the rest of the squad. Roman, himself a failed initiate at the Academy, had often seen chronmen and auditors in battle. Mong wasn't one of the more skilled exo-wielders, but he was getting the job done. Roman and Renee had almost fought their way to the waiting collie when it began to take off, jerking unsteadily into the air.

"We're not in yet!" Renee screamed, dropping Roman and sprinting toward the ship. It was too late. By the time she reached it, the collie was already five meters off the ground. Before it could speed away, something slammed into it, knocking it out of the air. It crashed to the ground on its side, almost crushing Renee and Roman as it slid down the slope. The two were just able to dive out of the way at the very last moment.

"Black abyss, no." Roman stared at a new figure floating in the air above him. It was the traitor, James Griffin-Mars. Before Roman could react, a coil wrapped around his feet, lifted him off the ground, and tossed him into the mud. Renee tried to flee down the hill but was pulled back and flung into the embankment next to him.

"Chronman." The traitor's voice echoed through the ruins. "Leave the Elfreth alone and face me."

When Mong, who was still busy tearing through scores of savages, didn't respond, the traitor shot forward in a streak of yellow and collided with the chronman. The two of them, exos flaring, slammed into the side of the hill, spewing mud and rocks into the air. A second later, they exploded out and crashed down at the bottom of the riverbank.

The men's coils were interlocked, but it wasn't difficult to tell who was winning. The traitor had the chronman wrapped in what looked like ten coils. Somehow, Mong was able to slip away and launch up into sky. Just as quickly, the traitor shot half a dozen coils after him. The chronman created four of his own coils to fend them off, but it was obvious the former Tier-1 was much more skilled than the Tier-5. The traitor's coils tied up Mong's coils, and then the remaining ones sunk into his shield and dragged him back down to earth. As much as Mong tried, he couldn't get away a second time.

"Go ahead, you abyss-plagued traitor," Mong spat. "Finish the job."

By this time, the rest of the savages—and they numbered in the dozens—had the monitors surrounded. Most of his squad were beaten up pretty badly. Baeth had suffered a concussion and was awake but woozy. Blood poured down Chaki's leg, and Roman still had this stinking spear sticking through his shoulder. Two of the savages were carrying an unconscious Renee up the embankment. The remaining monitors—Gouti and Pau—were being rounded up. A few second later, the pilot of the crashed collie was pulled out of the wreck and also joined the prisoners. Roman squeezed his eyes shut. This was when the savages would decide which one of them looked the most delicious.

Roman had been with ChronoCom for almost fifteen years, and nothing made the hair on the back of his neck stand up more than savagery, either from the pirates along the Ship Graveyard or the commies in Venus or these primitives here on Earth.

The traitor suspended Mong in the air. "Release your bands to me and I will spare you and your people."

"How about you go fuck yourself," Mong replied.

"Actually," Pau said, "that's not a bad trade."

The chronman shot him a glare. "Be quiet."

"Give him the stupid bands," Gouti said.

"Shut up, monitors," Mong snapped.

"Just give him the fucking bands!" Roman screamed.

The rest of the squad joined in with their pleas. Mong looked furious, but Roman didn't care. It was better to give up the stupid bands than become dinner. Chronman or not, this kid was risking their lives for no reason.

"Fine," Mong snarled. "You want the bands? Here you go."

He held his hands out, and with a snap, all his bands broke in two.

Roman's legs gave way and he collapsed to the ground. That fool. Now they were all going to be dinner. He felt his pants grow warm as he wet himself. This time, his body shook from fear instead of pain. He couldn't decide what was worse, being boiled alive or roasted over a fire.

He flirted with the idea of pulling the spear out of his body so he could bleed out. Roman gripped the shaft with his working arm and took a couple of deep breaths. He gritted his teeth and willed his arm to pull the spear through his body. The stupid thing wouldn't budge; his arms felt like noodles. He tried once more, and again, his hands felt so weak, he could barely hold the shaft, let alone budge the damn thing.

Roman just couldn't do it. He was too frightened to kill himself. That was why he had failed to tier at the Academy. He was good enough, everyone said so. He had surprised his teachers by failing. And now his stupid cowardice was going to get him killed in the worst way possible. His frustration and the tension in his body built up, begging for a release. Roman's arms shook as he stared at his own blood sliding down the shaft and dripping onto the ground. He did the only thing he could think of at this very moment. He began to bawl. All eyes turned to him as his sobs grew louder.

Pau leaned in to him. "Pull yourself together."

"Please . . . please don't eat me." Roman sniffed loudly. "I'll taste terrible."

A buzz spread through the crowd of savages. A few of them seemed to understand what he said and translated to those who didn't. A chorus of laughter erupted. Several of the savages began rubbing their bellies. An apple bounced off his head. Even the traitor was masking a smile.

The traitor floated Mong to the rest of the squad and picked up the broken bands, examining them one by one. He sighed and tossed them to the ground. "You're making my life a lot harder than it has to be."

Mong stuck his chin out defiantly. "Just get it over with and kill us."

"Speak for yourself," Gouti grumbled.

"If we had wanted you dead, you'd be dead," said James.

Roman looked over at the rest of his squad. He hadn't realized this at first, but it was true. All of them were alive, and it probably wasn't a coincidence. In fact, these savages took extra precautions, at the risk of their own lives, not to kill any of them. Why?

The traitor motioned to a group of savages standing nearby. "You have seven minutes. Get to work."

Roman watched open-mouthed as two dozen savages swarmed the collie, like burn ants over a corpse, and began to strip it bare. To his shock, they moved efficiently, as if they knew what they were doing. These were primitive savages. How could this be possible? However, within minutes, many of the collie's modules were dismantled. All that remained was its frame, engine, and structural components.

"Wrap it up," James said. "Co-op forces will be here any minute."

Just as quickly as they appeared, the savages disappeared back into the ruined city. The only one left was the traitor. He surveyed the sky and then the squad. "Your people will be here soon."

Mong looked confused. "Why not just kill us and be done with it?"

"Shut up before he changes his mind," Roman hissed.

The traitor studied Mong's face. "How many years out of the Academy, chronman?"

Mong hesitated before answering. "Five months."

The traitor nodded. "You use the exo well for a Tier-5. You'll make a fine chronman one day. Just make sure you live long enough to make a difference."

"Why are you letting us go?" asked Mong.

James sighed. "Because at the end of the day, you're just trying to do the right thing, and so am I." Then he shot into the air in a streak of yellow and was gone.

Five minutes later, a Valta Valkyrie appeared, followed by three collies. The area was soon flooded by monitors. Roman looked in the direction he had last seen the traitor as he and the rest of his squad were led to safety. This was the first time he had seen the traitor, this James Griffin-Mars. He had to admit he was surprised. All the intel had described the man as an unstable, greedy, self-serving lunatic. This man seemed anything but that. He glanced over at Mong, whose troubled face spoke volumes as well.

Roman crawled into the medical collie and was soon in the air. His last thought before he passed out was that now that he was injured, did he still have to wait two days to shower?

TWO

THE SITUATION

James watched from the mid-level of a nearby building as a small fleet of collies and Valta ships swarmed the battlefield where the Elfreth had just ambushed a squad of monitors. He took a quick inventory of the number of ships and personnel, the time it had taken them to arrive after the first shots were fired, and how large of a perimeter they maintained while executing the retrieval. The Co-op's response times were improving, though still not quick enough to catch the tribe during a raid.

Once he had finished gathering the necessary data, James headed to their temporary home, choosing to go on foot instead of risking being seen flying through New London at this hour. There was already a lot of heat in this region, and his exo would shine like a beacon in the black of night. With few tall buildings in this area still standing to provide cover, the less he used his exo, the better.

The Co-op was not proficient at guerrilla warfare, not like the wasteland tribes who had had centuries of experience executing hit-and-run raids. They had other overwhelming advantages, though, possessing vastly superior firepower and nearly infinite resources, while the Elfreth's already meager stock was fast withering away. Without Smitt's access to the chron database to calculate jumps, James was unable to jump to the past to resupply the tribe as he had done previously.

Not that he could jump right now anyway, even if they did have access. Grace Priestly, the Mother of Time, was adamant that his next one or two jumps would kill him. He had made too many jaunts to the past without taking the miasma regimens, the medical treatments necessary to combat lag sickness, the long-term degenerative illness caused by time travel. His body was too permanently damaged to risk another jump. This was a serious problem, because the Elfreth had depended on his salvaging for food, medicine, and equipment, especially now while on the run with the tribe unable to farm.

James stayed moving on foot, sipping the energy levels of his bands sparingly to avoid detection, using his exo in short bursts to leap through the streets and between the buildings. He circled west in a roundabout path in case he was being followed, until he eventually reached the ruins of Groton Space Port.

The space port, already half-submerged in the encroaching brown ocean, had been a major hub in the early days of interplanetary freight. When the Core Conflicts broke out at the turn of the twenty-fourth century, Groton Space Port was converted to a military installation and was one of the last surviving ports when the megacorporations from the Outer Rim planets arrived and laid siege to the planet. All that remained now were blown-out buildings and skeletons of ships from previous centuries. It was also the perfect hiding spot for the Elfreth's current project and their last hope for survival.

James landed on the wing of an old Publicae drone ship and hopped over onto the back of a Venetian heat absorber, then onto an old Earth-bound civilian carrier. The history of humanity's aviation continued to unfold as he crisscrossed the watery graveyard. The brown ocean currents had invaded the airstrip long ago, and now some of the crafts were uprooted from their final resting places and being carried away by the dense, heavy waves of the polluted ocean. They banged against other crafts, rocking back and forth as the slow-moving tide flooded and ebbed.

He reached one of the few still-intact construction hangars built on a hill and entered, promptly coming face-to-face with three guardians wielding high-powered blaster rifles. He nodded as the lead lookout, Mhairi, waved him through. He was getting better at remembering their names; it was something Elise had stressed he should do, claiming it made him a more integral part of the tribe.

At first, he resisted. A short memory was useful for a chronman. After all, while salvaging, he interacted with thousands of people who were already dead. Remembering their names meant they would linger with him even after the salvage was completed. Even while at the agency, he rarely bothered remembering names outside of auditors and administrators. Chronmen and monitors came and went. What was the point of getting to know anyone?

In many ways, it was the same with the Elfreth. There were so many in the tribe, and he had little confidence that any of them would survive this war with the Co-op, so why remember names? Why give them this power over him?

For Elise, though, he made an effort. Every time he met someone he did not recognize, especially the guardians and the food staff, he took a few extra seconds to recite their names into memory. At first, he thought it a waste of time. Slowly, those names and faces began to connect. Every subsequent time he would see someone whose name he remembered, he found himself waving at them and inquiring about their day. Bit by bit, he learned more, until he actually considered a few of them acquaintances. This, in turn, made them less wary of him. When Pon, one of the first guardians he had befriended, died at the hands of the Co-op, he felt an immediate sadness and pain. These were something he rarely allowed himself to feel. They also reminded him why he didn't like remembering names.

James glanced to the side, and saw the group of hallucinations that always seemed close by. They had been less vocal as of late. The ghosts of Grace and the Nazi soldier still hung around, though they mostly stayed in the background and argued with each other. Sometimes, he would catch them shooting angry accusatory glances his way. In the Nazi soldier's case, James wished he knew the boy's name; calling him "Nazi soldier" or "fucking fascist" was getting old. He almost had to concentrate to notice them anymore.

The ghost of Sasha was different. She usually kept to herself, but was always watching him, as if judging his every move. Sometimes, he would wake in the middle of the night and find her standing in the corner, just staring at him. It was unnerving. The few times he tried to engage her, she just shook her head sadly, or disapprovingly—he couldn't quite tell which. He waved at her as he passed; something he couldn't help but do when he was alone. She never waved back.

James didn't understand why she was there at all. The real Sasha was alive again. He had risked his life making one last jump to retrieve his dead sister from the Mnemosyne Station, the refugee camp she had gone missing from twenty years ago. Grace had warned him back then against jumping, but as far as he was concerned, it was the best thing he had ever done in his miserable life.

He reached an elevated platform in the hangar where Chawr and his friends were busy working on their latest creation. When James and Elise had first joined the Elfreth, an argument had precipitated Chawr and his friends wanting to break from the tribe. They were young, strong, and felt they could do better on their own than burdened with the many elderly and weak. James had convinced the young man to stay, and Chawr and his crew had asked James to teach them how to work on his collie.

He had agreed to mentor them, and now he couldn't be prouder. Over the months, the crew, now calling themselves the flyguards, had become indispensable to the tribe. They looked his way as his boots clanged on the metal steps up to the platform. They waved enthusiastically and joked among themselves as they dug through their latest haul from the collie they had stripped earlier today.

"Did we get what we need?" he asked.

Hory held up part of a cockpit console. Bria did the same with a cooling coil, but it was Chawr who picked up the crown jewel of their loot: the stealth module. ChronoCom collies were the most advanced stealth ships in the solar system. Since the agency wasn't military, they relied on this advanced technology, developed during the Publicae Age, to avoid getting into battles.

James shot Chawr a thumbs-up and looked at the metal monstrosity to his right. Ever since his own collie had been shot out of the sky during the attack on Boston, the tribe had been busy trying to get him spaceborne again. They had been unsuccessful at stealing existing Co-op ships—they were too heavily guarded and secured—so instead, the Elfreth did what they did best: stole what they could and salvaged from wreckages.

The end result was a mutant insect-like collie assembled from the bodies of five separate ships destroyed in battle. It was four times the size of a standard collie, had three cockpits, and had to be powered by six separate engines. The dozens of window panels on the starboard side made it look like it had spider eyes. The center piloting cockpit jutted out near the top in an odd off-angled direction. The port side was just two standard collie bodies welded together.

When Elise first saw the thing, she couldn't stop laughing and named the ship *Drunk Engineering*, saying it was a veritable Frankenstein. *Drunk Engineering* hit a little too close to home, but the name *Frankenstein* took. Now, the Elfreth's new flagship *Frankenstein* was ready for its maiden voyage into space as soon as they installed the stealth module.

James would be lying if he said he wasn't worried about the *Frankenstein*'s space-worthiness. The ship had only logged fifteen hours over the Atlantic Ocean, and the modified shield arm was fairly new, so he had minimal confidence in the ship's structural integrity. He would also be the first to admit his technical knowledge of ships was poor. Thank the abyss they had Grace Priestly to help with his deficiencies.

He looked over at the flyguards monkeying around with the parts. The kids who had assembled and welded her together weren't exactly trained engineers. Still, it should work. Collies were legendary in their sturdiness and ease of maintenance, their modular nature allowing their parts to be easily assembled and replaced. What's the worst that could go wrong? James chose not to answer that question.

He felt a presence behind him, and a pair of arms wrapped around his waist. A soft body pressed against his back, and a head burrowed forward from under his armpit. Elise's familiar scent filled his nostrils, and the nagging anxiety he always felt when she wasn't close by faded. He leaned his head down and kissed her.

Grace Priestly, the High Scion of the Technology Isolationists, appeared on the other side of him. She put her hands on her hips and shook her head. "The scouts said you spared those ChronoCom monitors. Why? They won't grow a conscience just because you are merciful."

James grunted. "Mercy has nothing to do with it. I know the agency. They aren't enthusiastic about wasting resources on this operation. They're sending their worst units: old and green monitors and low-tiered chronmen. If we start killing them en masse, Director Young will have a change of heart and start sending better-trained troops, then we'll really have no chance. Remember, winning for the Elfreth isn't defeating the Co-op.

That's not possible. The only way we'll all come out of this alive is if we outlast them. They need to tire of searching for us. And we need to do this with as few casualties to the ChronoCom forces as possible."

"And Valta?" Grace asked.

"To hell with them," said James. "Those we kill as many as possible."

There was a loud clatter, and the three of them turned their attention back to the collie, where the flyguards were moving the stolen parts over for assembly to the *Frankenstein*. Chawr cursed at the crew as they powered up a laser welder to install the final pieces. Grace winced at the sloppy measurements the tribesmen made as they prepared to cut.

"You're really flying into space in that death trap?" Elise asked.

"Sometimes, pet," Grace added, "your bravery and stupidity still amaze me."

James moved his arms around both their shoulders and squeezed. "I've done dumber things before. Not much, but dumber." He turned to his left and looked at Grace. "As soon as we get the module installed and tested out, you're coming with me."

"If my life is going to depend on this contraption," said Grace. "I'd better tell these fools how to do the work properly." She grumbled something about how the dead and the stupid went hand in hand and hobbled toward the flyguards.

When he had first brought the Mother of Time to the present, she was already one of the greatest physicists to have ever lived. Within the short time she had spent here, she had also become a biologist to match Elise, as well as a master engineer. When Grace found out what he was trying to do, she personally took over construction of the collie and made sure this hodgepodge of dead ship parts would actually get them where they were trying to go. That was the real reason James had some semblance of confidence in the mutant collie. However, it was obvious Grace couldn't care less about aesthetics. The *Frankenstein* was downright ugly.

James watched them work for a few minutes longer before he and Elise left for the Elfreth's main living quarters. The evening meal was just beginning, and the lines for the children and the elderly were forming all the way out of the room and into the hallway. There were several calls of "Oldest" as they passed, and even a few "Elder" for James.

He fought the urge to ask her to skip eating in the public hall and spend some time alone. He was leaving tonight. Who knew when or if he would ever return. However, James also knew better. Elise was taking her new role as Oldest of the Elfreth very seriously, especially now that their numbers had swelled and morale was low.

The tribe needed their leader among them. He stayed silent, but kept at her side as she walked among the people—her people now—stopping by each group to exchange words of encouragement and comfort. He was amazed at how she remembered everyone's name, and how she was able to relate to each person as if they were close friends. Mostly, she just listened supportively as they voiced their concerns and fears.

That daily routine took up most of the night, and she was always the last to eat and exhausted by the time they had finished making the rounds and sat down. He held her tightly as she closed her eyes and took a few moments to compose herself.

"I don't know how long I can keep lying to them," she said, her voice soft. "I keep telling them everything's going to be all right, but I know it's not."

"It will be," he said, though he didn't quite believe it himself. "Look, maybe I shouldn't go."

She shook her head. "We've gone over this. You know you have to."

"Maybe I can delay the trip. We're barely staying one step ahead of the Co-op as it is. If they find you and I'm not here—"

She cut him off. "It won't make any difference, James. If they find us, we're all dead anyway, whether you're here or not." She caressed his face. "We'll be fine. Just get what we need and return safely."

He shook his head. "It's not a good time."

"It'll never be a good time. Besides . . ." Her voice softened as a small figure ran up to them. "There's more at stake."

"James!" Sasha bounced up to them and threw her arms around his neck.

His little sister leaned to the other side and gave Elise a peck on the cheek. She didn't like kissing him because of his beard. It made her itchy, she said. He was all right with that. Her overly enthusiastic hugs were a fine consolation.

The fact that his sister was alive again was a miracle. She was still a child, ten years old now, but alive. He had stolen her away from Mnemosyne Station after the battle at the Farming Towers. It was the last jump he had made, possibly the last he'd ever make. That was perfectly fine by him. Sasha was the one thing in his life that made him proud to have walked the path of a chronman. However, in saving her from death, he might have subjected her to a worse fate.

Sasha coughed and wiped her mouth. She was getting sicker and sicker. Within days of arriving in Boston, his young and frail sister became ill. Unlike Elise, who had a healthy immune system from a lifetime on Earth, Sasha had spent her entire life in artificial environments, and her body wasn't prepared for Earth's toxicity.

At first, he had tried to protect her with his atmos, thinking he could wean her off it over time. But as the Co-op continued to hunt them, forcing them deeper underground, power became scarcer, and they no longer had the energy levels to spare to keep the atmos band on at full strength, so she had to make do with a lower level of protection. It didn't help, or at least it wasn't enough.

Now, even though she was eating more regularly and moving about more than she ever did back when they were in the squalor of Mnemosyne Station, she looked weaker and thinner than ever. No one knew what it was, not even Grace.

None of the doctors on Earth were willing to help her. In the present, most doctors were trained and indentured to the corporations. To acquire the services of one would require authorization from the indenturing corporation, and that was something Valta made sure was denied to all of the tribes in this region. He could try to kidnap a doctor, but that would incur the wrath of the indenturing corporation, which would be almost as bad as their current war with the Co-op. That left him only one place to seek help. Unfortunately, that required a ship and would take him far away from Elise and the tribe. He had no choice; his sister's life depended on it.

Sasha coughed again, and her entire body shook. She wiped her mouth and James noticed blood on her sleeves. He felt his hands tremble as he fought the urge to squeeze her tightly to him. That wasn't going to help. He opened his mouth to comfort her and no words came out. His mind was paralyzed. He had never felt so helpless in his life.

Elise exchanged worried looks with him. She took out a rag and wiped the little girl's hands. "Sasha," she said in a calm voice. "Why don't you let your brother and me finish our dinner. We'll be up in the quarters in a little bit. We'll make a fire, and you and I can finish the alphabet and numbers.

Sasha made a face. "James is leaving tonight. Can't we just spend time together as a family?"

Elise smiled. "Of course we can, hon, but just tonight. You start studying again first thing tomorrow, all right? My lab assistant needs to know how to read."

Sasha gave them both one more hug before running off. As soon as she was out of sight, Elise turned and cupped his face in her hands. "You go up to space and you figure out how to save our girl. I don't care what it takes. Do you hear me?"

He nodded.

"Good, no more talk about staying to look after me and the Elfreth. We're going to be fine. Just come back to me as soon as you can."

THREE

OLDEST

Elise Kim stood at the water's edge and looked out to the horizon, where the black ocean and dark sky met. The last glimmer of the *Frankenstein*'s multicolored exhaust signatures had just disappeared into the thick layer of low-hanging clouds. James and Grace had cobbled the ship's engines from a couple of collies and a Valta Valkyrie attack ship. From what Elise could tell, it had taken a significant amount of tinkering to get everything balanced. She was shocked the damn thing flew at all, considering how glued and bubble-gummed the contraption was, and even more so that they were actually brave enough to take it into space. Brave or stupid. Then again, Elise was from the late twenty-first century; space travel had still been in its toddler stage then, and mankind hadn't colonized the solar system yet. Everything about where they were going was amazing to her.

She waited until the last glimmer of *Frankenstein* was gone. She looked up at the vast expanse of the sky, feeling more alone than she had in recent memory. Both James and Grace were gone, her rock and her wisdom, for Gaia knew how long. She had no one left on Earth she could lean on for support or advice, and a whole bunch of people who expected her to lead them. Elise was terrified.

"Please come back to me. Both of you." She could barely hear her whisper over the crashing of the waves against the shore.

There was a soft crunching of boots behind her. Rima stood waiting respectfully until Elise looked her way. "Oldest, the tribe is gathered and ready to depart. Oldest Franwil says we are already running short on time if we wish to cross the Long Island Sound by sunup. She warns that Moma is due soon and may not last the duration of the journey. War Chief Eriao says scouts report several bands of Neverwheres lurking upriver along the Thames half a day to a day out. He expects a raid and asks we be gone before they descend upon us."

Elise wished they could spend a few more days at Groton. This had been the most restful time the tribe had had in months. Still, with the Co-op close by and the Neverwheres encroaching, staying at the space port was too risky.

The Elfreth had run into the Neverwhere tribe while passing through New London. The vicious bastards had been hounding them ever since. Elise had thought the Elfreth had lost them when they holed up in Groton to finish building the *Frankenstein*. She glanced back up toward the sky. Not a moment too soon, she guessed.

It was probably for the best. They had hung around this place almost two weeks now, far longer than any other time since they had fled the Farming Towers in Boston. Couple that with the *Frankenstein* launch, whose maiden voyage, if it did not go fully smoothly, would raise who knew how many alerts tonight. They could only hope the stealth systems on the collie functioned properly. In either case, best not stick around to find out.

Elise checked her AI band. Sunrise was four hours away. They should have already left by now. Using the skypath highway to cross the thirty-kilometer Long Island Sound was dangerous. On the elevated road some three hundred meters up in the air, the Elfreth would be exposed not only to enemy patrols, but to Earth's harsh elements. If just one enemy patrol spotted them, there would be no more Elfreth tribe by dawn. However, it was the only direct overland path they could find that went all the way to their destination. Most of the roads in this area, a veritable swampland so close to the ocean, were impassable.

She turned to Rima, who was awaiting instructions with a chalkboard in hand. "Let's get this show on the road. Tell Eriao to have guardians five hundred meters ahead of the main group. Once our people are half-way up the ramp, we pace as fast as the tribe can go. Where is Oldest Franwil?"

"She is with the kowrus."

"Tell her we will have to hope for the best for Moma."

Elise watched as Rima scribbled furiously on her chalkboard in short-hand and then sprinted away. The girl had grown up since they first met less than a year ago. For one thing, Elise used to have to look down at her when they spoke. Rima must have hit her growth spurt, because she was now half a head taller than Elise. That wasn't saying much, since Elise's nickname on the badminton team had been Low-Hanging Fruit, and yes, it had been ripe with double entendres. Secondary school girls could be bitches. Elise still felt a little self-conscious when she had to speak with the entire tribe and barely reached the neck of most people.

Rima had matured mentally as well, having been forced to grow up quickly over the past few months. When they first met, she had been an illiterate wild child who only knew how to hunt, fight, and cause the elders headaches. Elise had tapped into the girl's potential, taught her basic math, and cultivated in her a love for reading. In a short while, under both Grace's and Elise's tutelage, she became one of the most literate people in the tribe. Who knew what Rima could have become if she had grown up in a more enlightened time. It wasn't too late, not if Elise had a say in the girl's future.

Elise walked to the foot of the ramp and followed the road with her eyes as it inclined and disappeared into the fog. A few minutes later, she heard gravel crackling behind her. She watched as the front of the caravan passed, the group of vanguards followed by hundreds of men, women, and children. The sound of their footsteps, little pitter-patters, became louder. The creaking of wooden axles and wheels grinding on the road soon joined the chorus. Farm animals came next—several dozen cows, a flock of chickens, followed by pigs, goats, and kowru, a genetically engineered fast-reproducing cross between brahman and giant rabbits bred during the early twenty-fourth century. Oldest Franwil was with this group, watching over some of the flock. She pointed at Moma, the very pregnant kowru, and held up five fingers. Elise nodded. They would have to cart the mare soon.

ChronoCom and Valta had returned the week after their attack on the Farming Towers with forces ten times larger than the one Levin Javier-Oberon, the former high auditor of Earth, had led against them. Instead of another battle, they came upon an abandoned settlement. By that time, the Elfreth had packed up and gone deep underground, hiding inside Boston's maze of buildings and old transit systems.

Elise had initially hoped that they could wait out the Co-op as the enemy scoured the ruins for them. She had underestimated their resolve. The Co-op hunkered down and began to systematically wipe out all the other tribes that lived there. Boston became a graveyard and a prison within a few short days. Dozens of ill-prepared tribes who had survived hundreds of years of famine, pestilence, and disease in the harshest of lands were decimated by a genocidal onslaught. The Co-op was undiscerning as to who fell into their crosshairs. Elise, feeling the guilt of bringing so much death to these people, had ordered the Elfreth to take in all refugees, swelling their numbers from the original three hundred to nearly a thousand.

The fighting became a slow bleeding game of cat and mouse as the Co-op hunted the Elfreth and the tribes sprung ambushes to pick off the invaders one by one. Eventually, James and Eriao convinced her that they couldn't win this fight, and that their only chance was to flee the city.

It was a tough call, but Elise had reluctantly agreed. The weight of her responsibility to her people sometimes made it difficult to breathe. Every victory felt slight, every defeat crushing, and every mistake magnified. But for some reason she couldn't quite fathom, the tribe continued to look to her for guidance. Why did these people still have faith in her?

The past few months had been hard, and the Elfreth's long list of problems grew daily. Now on the run and completely nomadic, the tribe was unable to farm. They were also too large and unwieldy, having been joined by several smaller groups caught in the conflict. While that made them stronger than most other wastelander tribes, it also made hiding difficult. The tribe had been resolving this by splitting into small orga-nized bands and never staying in one place for more than a few days. However, they were constantly encroaching on other tribes' territories. Most of their skirmishes were with them rather than with the real enemy. A thousand tribesmen was also a lot of mouths to feed. With winter on the horizon and the joint forces of Valta and ChronoCom con-tinually on their heels, the Elfreth faced the real threat of starvation.

The rest of the Elfreth continued streaming out from the darkness, merging into one long caravan as they got onto the ramp. The parade continued as small groups of the Elfreth—Elise had organized the groups to be self-sustaining in case they were separated—began to make the slow climb up to the skypath highway. A few waved at her, and some who had only recently joined the tribe bowed. She muttered each of their names as they passed, trying to remember as many of their faces as possible. So many people, so many needs. She waited until the last of the main body passed before starting her own journey up the ramp.

Elise joined a group of new tribesmen. The people here were formerly known as the Acquina, a small tribe that had lived down the river from the Farming Towers before the invasion. She shared a few friendly words with Lia, their former Brightest, before picking up her pace to catch up to the next small group. There, she spoke with a group of older Elfreth, with some of whom she had shared duties tending to the crops on top of the Farming Towers back in their home. Most of them embraced and encouraged Elise, nearly moving her to tears. She missed those simpler days.

She continued up the parade, taking advantage of this long walk to get to know her people again. There was a group of nomads who had joined just last week now serving as scouts for the guardians. She spent a part of the walk being scolded by some of the older kitchen staff about food stocks; not that they were low—everyone knew that—but they needed to spend more time foraging for sapphire fruit, a spice that preserved meat and vegetables from spoiling. Elise assured them that she'd look into it.

Next, she gave an encouraging pep talk to a group of children who by now were used to being fugitives. That broke her heart. She spent a few minutes longer than she had to, telling them a story about her time in the twentieth-first century, now commonly referred to as the Golden Age of Humanity. She watched their eyes get big as they soaked in every word.

"And you'll bring those days back, Oldest?" a little girl asked.

"Of course we will, child." It was a straight-up lie, but hope was one of the few things Elise could offer these people in abundance. As far as she was concerned, hope was as nourishing to these children as food, even if it was a lie. Especially if it was a lie.

She continued moving up the line and was particularly grateful when the highway leveled off. She checked the time: three hours until sunrise, and then several more days' journey to the dreaded Mist Isle, a place so dangerous, it almost wiped out the Elfreth when they first passed through generations ago. Now she was leading them back to it.

Elise hoped to Gaia she was making the right call. In any case, the decision was made, and for better or worse, the Elfreth were heading west. She looked up at the sky, where a gap between the clouds had revealed thousands of stars. Her rock and her sage had left her alone down here. All she had to rely on now was her own judgment, and that scared her more than anything else in the world.

FOUR

Kuo

Senior Securitate Kuo Masaki-Europa of the Valta Corporation's Special Operations Division floated a hundred meters in the air above what looked like an antique-ships graveyard. An assortment of primitive-looking crafts, some half submerged, littered the field. According to Ewa, her second in command, this space port hadn't been searched because it had been completely underwater up until a month ago.

Below her, a trio of Valta hounds skulked inside the buildings, supported by forty ChronoCom monitors and Valta troopers. Surveillance had captured a strange blip exhibiting both Valta and ChronoCom ship signatures less than three days ago. The blip had disappeared shortly after. As a precaution, the hound pack—Valta's elite field scouts—was deployed to investigate. They called for the monitor backup shortly after, when they detected a large mass of people coming in from the north.

Large groups of savages on the move was rare among these ruins. The hounds felt there was a good chance these were whom the Co-op were searching for. Out of curiosity and the need for exercise, Kuo had decided to accompany the assault team. She had to give it to the temporal anomaly scientist and her tribe of savages, this project had taken far longer than expected, to the point it had come to the attention of Valta's Board of Directors. This was not the type of recognition she wanted within the megacorporation.

"This is Hound Two," a voice crackled through her comm module. "Inside a hangar. Located stacks of cannibalized ship parts. Recognize part of a collie hull."

That ship signature was not a fluke after all. What were the savages up to? What could they possibly want with a ship, especially with her fleet of Valkyries blockading the region?

"Hound One reporting," another voice joined in. "Located living quarters. The hearth is cold, but has recent signs of use. Probably a day, no more than two. A large group of people was here recently. By the waste levels, estimate several hundred, if not more."

"Verify their identity," she said. "Find which direction they went."

"It'll take time to scour the grounds," Hound One replied. "The rising tide will be problematic."

Kuo checked her AI module. The tide would rise two meters within the next hour. She cursed. This was the closest they had gotten in months. The savages had been cunning, hiding among this filth, keeping themselves just one step ahead of the Co-op. They leveraged the terrain well and employed hit-and-run tactics to steal supplies.

"Hound Three here. I have movement in hangar grid nine!" There was a scream, and then static.

"All Co-op converge on nine." Kuo pulled up the map of the area in her AI module and located grid nine. She launched herself north to the edge of the space port and landed in front of a large hangar with massive double doors. She powered on her exo and created a thick white trunk. Using it as a bludgeon, she slammed it against one of the doors and knocked it off its hinges.

A barrage of small-arms fire struck her shield, sparking the electrified white sphere protecting her. She expanded the field and flew into the hangar, the white-bluish tint of her exo illuminating the room. She saw a dozen figures slinking back into the shadows. Hot red flashes of energy beams, mixed with antique projectile weapons, bounced against her shield.

Kuo focused on one of the energy streams coming from behind a stack of containers. She shot the trunk—as thick as she was tall—straight into the source of the weapon fire. The resulting impact exploded containers and bodies into the air and knocked over a portion of the wall.

Ocean water rushed in from the outside, sweeping savages, water, and rubble across the room. Another cluster of shots hit her from the right, and she swung the trunk down, killing her assailant instantly. The rest of the savages had seen enough and tried to flee. Kuo punched several with the trunk, easily breaking bones and crushing skulls.

She extended the trunk until it covered the length of the room and then swept it in a full circle. The remaining walls collapsed, and the entire building fell on top of everyone inside. A moment later, Kuo shot back up into the air and watched as the savages fled.

By this time, the plodding monitors had arrived, swarming around the stragglers who hadn't been quick enough to escape. The ones still trying were cut down by the Valta troopers guarding the perimeter. The entire area around the destroyed building was reduced to a chaotic melee.

Kuo chose not to engage any further. Her exo wasn't designed for precision, and the savages were too intermingled with the monitors to safely target. Her relationship with Director Young was strained as it was. She would rather not have to add friendly fire to his list of grievances.

She saw a small mass of the savages waist-deep in the brown ocean, retreating into a building on the far side of the field. "Save a few to interrogate," she broadcasted, and launched toward them, covering the hundred meters within a second. She landed on the roof of the building and shot a trunk straight down. Tweaking the current of her exo, she wrapped the entire building in her field and electrocuted all the living things inside. Her levels dropped precariously from that maneuver, but not enough for her to care. These savages had killed a Valta operative. In her eyes, this was unforgivable.

"Find Hound Three's body," she ordered as she headed back to where the bulk of the monitors were rounding up the survivors.

The monitors had captured forty savages and killed about three times that number. Her own casualties numbered twelve monitors and the hound.

"This is Hound Two," a voice crackled. "You should see this, Senior Securitate."

"On my way." A few minutes later, Kuo arrived at the hangar to see scattered collie components littering the floor. The savages had been busy. It looked like they had been building a ship of sorts. That must be what set off that alert that attracted her hounds. Were they trying to escape by air even with a Valta blockade over the region? She found her answer when the hound led her to a stack of discarded parts off to the side.

She scoffed; of course. They were after collie stealth modules. This information fell in line with the recent reports of the savages ambushing only the monitor patrols. That must mean they'd succeeded in scavenging a working mod. Kuo suppressed her irritation. This complicated things. It also posed new questions. What did the savages intend to do with a stealth ship? Surely they wouldn't be able to ferry their entire tribe away without being caught. Where were they going, then? Did the fugitive and the temporal anomaly plan to escape on their own and abandon the savages? Possible, but unlikely. By all indications, the anomaly was rather attached to the tribe.

Kuo waited for the rest of her forces on the ground to complete their survey of the space port. There was entirely too much ground to cover and too few forces to do the job. Chances were, much of the evidence had already washed away with the tide. All they had to show for the night's work were three dozen prisoners who ended up not even being who they were after.

This tribe that had been hiding the anomaly had been incredibly resourceful in keeping their movements a secret. In the past six months, even while the Co-op had rounded up thousands of these savages to question, only a handful—less than five confirmed—had been Elfreth. In every single case, these savages had chewed a poisonous weed that killed them before Kuo's people could torture them for the truth. In fact, the only reason they knew that three of the five were Elfreth was because they found the weed on their corpses after the fact.

Ewa landed next to her a short while later. "The grounds are cleared, Senior. At this point, we believe the targeted tribe has escaped our blockade through the skypaths."

Kuo pulled up the map of the region on her AI module. "The land south of here, called the Long Island, is mostly flooded and uninhabitable. If they continue down the skypath, it banks west toward . . ."

". . . the Mist Isle," Ewa finished.

Kuo gritted her teeth. If that was the case, and the savages were able to reach the island, then her project had just become exponentially more difficult. She hardly had enough personnel as it was. If the Co-op had to open a new front onto the Mist Isle, then she would need to double, possibly triple her current resources.

"Prep a Valkyrie," she ordered.

"Yes, Senior. Destination?"

"Chicago. We'll need more monitors. Many more, and if that fool Young denies me, I'm going to skin him alive. While I'm gone, recanvass this region. I want around-the-clock sorties sent south and westward originating from this location."

Ewa hesitated. "South to the ocean. How far west? Our Valkyrie rotations are already near capacity."

"All the way to the Mist Isle."

FIVE

THE WRECK

The two monsters met in the heart of a debris field littered with centuries of twisted wrecks deep inside the Ship Graveyard. James stared through the *Frankenstein*'s small window slit as it pulled closer to the corpse of the famed and briefly-feared *CP Godzilla*. The monstrosity was so large, James lost sight of the stars. A few minutes later, the collie entered one of the huge tears on the *Godzilla*'s body and proceeded through a dark tunnel deeper into its bowels.

Grace poked her head next to James and made a face at the hundreds of protruding jagged metal edges pointing at them like teeth.

"Impressive, isn't it?" he said.

"An impressive waste, you mean," she scoffed. "I bet this stupidity was the idea of some politician with a Napoleon complex."

"What's a Napoleon?"

Grace looked him up and down, and smirked.

The *Godzilla*, named after some mythical monster in human lore, was the largest ship ever built. Commissioned during the height of the Core Conflicts, it was the Core Planets' solution to bringing an end to the devastating war that had dragged on for nearly fifty years, taking a billion lives. It was supposed to be a ship so powerful and imposing that no faction would dare wage war against them ever again. Its design and silhouette were echoed like that of a monster or demon from the old Greek legends. It was heralded as the ship to end all wars.

The *Godzilla*'s supremacy in space had lasted a full half battle. During its first and only fight, the Outer Rim fleet realized that it was literally impossible to miss hitting the gigantic ship. They focused their fire on certain critical areas and, like a human being, once the ship's internal organs failed, the rest of the whole soon followed. The damage in certain critical systems cascaded to others and, as the battle wore on, the *Godzilla* became a crippled sow, too injured to fight effectively, yet too large to retreat. The original builders were right about one thing; it did usher in a new era of peace, though not the way they had imagined.

The war ended six months later once news of the *Godzilla*'s destruction reached the rest of the solar system. The resources consumed to build the behemoth had bankrupted the Core Planets, not only in terms of raw materials and manpower but also of spirit and resolve.

Now, almost two hundred years later in 2512, the corpse of the *Godzilla* had found a second life. The ship was so large that, even destroyed, most of its body was still intact. Nestled deep inside the Ship Graveyard, where no government or corporation ruled, it had become a haven for pirates, smugglers, and factions who wished to stay outside of corporate and planetary laws. Dozens of small thriving colonies now lived inside its body in isolated compartments that could still sustain environments.

James noted several large menacing guns trained on them as they passed. He had been here a few times, though never on ChronoCom work. The Wreck Colonies, as they were known, had formed a loose coalition government and forbade any time salvaging on the *Godzilla*. James could understand why. The ecosystem of the Wreck Colonies was at the mercy of a slowly-decaying ship constantly being bombarded by debris and the corpses of other ships. Any small ripple in the chronostream could be devastating to *Godzilla*'s current occupants.

"To the hideous-looking vessel," a voice drawled over the comm, "We found five separate ship signatures on you: three from ChronoCom, one from Valta, and one from Europa Planetary. All of them are disallowed here at Bulk's Head, or the rest of the Wreck, for that matter. You're either lost or you suck at masking your shit. In any case, prepare to get blown out into space for being stupid. Goodbye."

James rushed to the console and slammed a fist on the comm button. "Bulk's Head, this is the independent Earth vessel *Frankenstein*. We do not belong to any of those entities. Ship signatures are from cannibalized vessel parts. Please verify and do not shoot. We are here on business."

There was a long pause. James fixated on the antiship cannons trailing them as the seconds ticked by. At this range, one blast would blow them into dust. Hell, with the way the ship was welded together, a hard kick to the hull would probably knock a few panels loose.

Minutes ticked by as the collie hovered right in front of a cannon's muzzle. They waited to see if it'd charge up and incinerate them to cosmic ash. James wiped the sweat off his brow. He had his exo powered all the way up, ready to shield Grace for an escape, but he doubted that'd do much good. He looked over at Grace, who by this time had gotten bored staring at the big gun and had gone to the storage bin to get a snack. The old woman had already cheated death once. What did she care about another brush with it?

Finally, after James was almost sure they were going to just get blown up, the voice came back. "You guys got the scratch for payment?"

"We do," James replied.

"Good. You're in Dock Wu. As a precaution because of your multibanned signatures, we're going to search you. Exit your"—there was a chuckle—"craft with your hands up, register your weapons and bands, and declare your cargo. If you don't plan to do any of the above, save us the hassle by telling us now so we can blast you. Otherwise, you'll just piss us off and it'll just get worse. By the way, have your bribes ready. There'll be five of us."

"Loud and clear," James said, releasing the bands on his wrist and laying them out on the bench.

A blue light flashed in the darkness, followed by another farther down the tunnel and another after curving around the bend. James steered the unwieldy collie after the lights, letting the trail of blue beacons guide them through the maze. Along the way, he noticed several more hidden cannons locked in on their ship. This maze was the first of the Bulk's Head colony's defenses. There were many stories about corporation police chasing pirates into the maze, only to get lost and never come out again.

After a dozen twists and turns, they finally reached what looked like a dead end. James turned the collie to the right and floated into an expansive cargo hold. A large bay door on the left wall halfway down the room swung inward, and a beam of light flooded them from the opening.

James moved the lumbering *Frankenstein* into the space. Once parked, he waited for the door to close and for the yellow light to turn blue, indicating recompression of the room. He signaled for Grace to follow him as he opened the hatch and stepped outside. He inhaled, noting how much of a struggle it was to take a full breath. He had forgotten how difficult it was to breathe in some of these artificial atmospheres, which often had only a fraction of Earth's oxygen levels. Grace was having an especially difficult time catching her breath as her nearly hundred-year-old body struggled to acclimate to the environment.

They waited at the base of the *Frankenstein*'s ramp, hands raised behind their heads. A group of men in patchwork clothing, looking more likely to rob them than anything, rushed in with guns raised. They moved in an organized fashion as three of them kept watch over James and Grace while the other two searched the collie. The three men roughed up James, pushing him around while patting down his clothing and rummaging through his pockets. They gave Grace decidedly lighter treatment when she shot them a stern look. The former High Scion had an uncanny ability to sometimes put people—even thugs—on their best behavior.

Eventually, after the men had finished combing the ship and taken their bribes, James and Grace were allowed to go into the next room, where they had to pay their security fee, an exception fee, hangar service fees, five disavowed fees, and last, a you-look-like-trouble fee just so they could continue in.

Grace fumed as she checked their scratch. "Isn't the whole point of being autonomous from government that you don't have to pay exorbitant taxes?"

James grinned. "Funny. You just called it a tax. Let's just call it what it is: a bribe to a bunch of greedy assholes." One of the guards overheard and glared. "Sorry, no offense," James added, not really meaning it.

The guard shrugged. "None taken. We *are* a bunch of greedy assholes, and we'll be right here to take your exit bribe when you leave."

They exited the hangar and entered the main residential levels of Bulk's Head. Other than the fact that it was inside the dead hulk of a ship and controlled by pirates, the colony seemed almost like any other, except for the fact that everyone they came across was armed to the teeth. This particular colony was under the protection of the Puck Pirates, one of the larger and more dangerous pirate conglomerates in the solar system. Few corporations or governments were willing to incur their wrath. It was almost never worth the hassle.

Bulk's Head was one of the larger travel hubs in the Wreck, so most people paid them little attention, though a few did give Grace a second glance. Not many people survived to her age in places like this, though the glances probably had more to do with the fact that she carried herself like the High Scion of the Technology Isolationists instead of just an old woman walking through the crowded halls of a pirate den. James reminded himself he'd have to have a talk with her about this soon, lest one of these bandits decide she must be someone worth robbing or kidnapping.

"Is it going to be a problem that you have a sizable price on your head?" Grace asked when he threw back his hood.

"That's one of the few things I don't worry about here." James chuckled. "Bounty hunting is one of the few laws they strictly enforce. Most of the guys here have prices on their head. If they were to allow it, the Wreck would implode within a matter of hours."

James felt safe as they crossed the different levels, passing the merchant district, slavers' quarters, import markets, and made their way through the busy passageways to the residential levels. He didn't completely let his guard down, though. Crime was still high, and people often disappeared in the middle of the night. The bounty on James's head was large enough that it could tempt someone to risk Puck Pirate justice. Greed made men foolish and reckless.

The two rented a small one-room residence just big enough to sit together without having to crawl over each other, yet not large enough for both to sleep at the same time once the bunk was lowered. The room's oxygen usage would also be an issue. Each residence was allocated a certain amount of air every day. Anything past that would incur overage charges.

"I do not understand." Grace frowned when he explained it to her. "Why is air so expensive, and wouldn't air just flow inside once you open the door?"

"Air has to be constantly recycled and filtered in the colonies, especially older places like this that constantly leak." James pointed at the dim blue lights lining the door. "Sensors at the door measure oxygen intake and count it against our allocation. We pay daily penalties for going over."

"I studied the Wreck's economy on our way here," said Grace. "It's large enough that there are opportunities for points of entry, but small enough to be manipulated. It'll be a fun puzzle to solve. I should be up and running in no time."

James headed out the door. "I'll start getting a lay of the land on a possible salvager. Maybe I can find a doctor, an ex-chronman, or an illegal jumper."

"Keep an eye out for an access hack as well," she yelled after him. "And stay away from the bars."

James looked up and down the rusted and warped hallways and randomly picked a direction to stroll to get to know his new environment. Familiarity with his surroundings would be important in case things went bad, and if Grace's plan to manipulate the market succeeded, they might make some enemies. He hoped she knew what she was doing. He stopped himself. Of course she did. Grace always knew what she was doing, and in this case, she had to. Their success depended on her.

It had been months since James had last walked among civilized people in the present, if he could call pirates and smugglers civilized. The place was surprisingly clean for a pirates' den, though to be honest, after living underground in the ruins of wasted cities, any place seemed clean. Still, Bulk's Head struck him as pretty civilized, up until he rounded the corner and saw a corpse decaying in a back alley.

He continued on, first mapping out the paths near their residence to make sure they had multiple routes to the *Frankenstein* if they needed to make a quick escape. Then he toured the main halls and different sections of the colony, mentally categorizing the vibe of each place, making sure to mark down points that might prove useful.

He continued upstream against the busy crowds, getting bumped constantly at intersections. It had been a while since he last was in a space station. Funny, he didn't remember ever having to deal with this before. Then he realized: he was no longer of the tier. For so long, he had taken for granted the aura of fear surrounding chronmen. Now, no one gave him space when he walked down the halls; no one paid him any deference. For once, he was as invisible as he had always wished to be when he was a chronman. He was just like everyone else, a commoner. A nobody.

And he hated it.

More and more people shoved past him, pinballing him into others who reciprocated by pushing him into even more people. James resisted the urge to lash out. He took a breath, remembered his new place in the world, and followed the flow of traffic. The more he explored the colony, the more depressed and suffocated he felt. The place reminded him of a mixture of Himalia and Mnemosyne Station, two of his least favorite places in the world. Though in truth, most stations these days looked like this.

Before he realized where the crowds had taken him, he found himself in front of one of the colony's many seedy bars: the Drink Anomaly. Of course he would end up here. The temptation was strong. If he was smart, he would keep walking. Grace had found one of his liquor stashes in the hold one night on the way to the Wreck and berated him so loudly her voice echoed across the entire ship. She had thrown Sasha's name at him over and over again, bludgeoning him with her sickness.

The thought of his sister gave him pause and filled him with a mixture of relief, anxiety, and guilt. Relief that she was back in his life and that he could finally let go of the guilt that had plagued him for the past twenty years. It was accompanied, however, by the crushing anxiety and burden of parenthood, knowing her safety and wellness was once again in his hands. He had failed her the first time; he didn't think he could survive failing her again. For twenty years, all he had cared about was himself. Now, alongside his concern for Elise, it was almost too much pressure to bear.

"Pull yourself together," he growled. "You've faced sun raiders and Plutonian cannibals. Taking care of the two women should be far easier."

It wasn't, though, at least it didn't feel that way. Black abyss, he needed a drink. The ghosts of the Nazi soldier and Sasha were standing on either side of the bar entrance. His sister's eyes bored into him and seemed to disapprove of what she saw. She looked away.

The Nazi soldier whistled. "First time away, and that's all you can think of. I would think her death and twenty years of guilt would make you a better brother."

"That's not true," James protested. "I need to go inside to find her a doctor."

"You only think that."

"Fuck you, you little fascist," James snapped, not taking his eyes off his sister.

"You know, I have a name."

"Yeah? What is it, Nazi?"

"You should have asked before you killed me." The Nazi soldier laughed and turned to Sasha. "Come on, girl, your brother doesn't care about you. He just wants the bottle."

"No, that's not why I'm going in," James protested. "And don't talk to my sister." He stopped. Of course that was why. He couldn't lie to himself. He was getting pulled by the lure of the alcohol. He had been trying his best not to drink. Promised Elise, promised Sasha, promised himself. Yet here he was, at his first opportunity away from his loved ones, heading straight into a bar.

He looked down at the hallucination of his sister still standing there as if guarding the entrance. No, she was guarding him from the bar. James swallowed and felt his mouth go dry. He forced himself to turn away and stagger down the hallway, each step taking more effort than the previous. Finally, after what felt like walking in triple gravity, he turned the corner and leaned against the wall. His brow was drenched in sweat and his hands shook uncontrollably.

He took a few deep breaths and tried to refocus his mind. Focus on what his real purpose was here on Bulk's Head. He was here to help to save Sasha, the real Sasha, not this hallucination in his sick mind. She was alive now and back with Elise on Earth. He looked back around the corner and saw the neon-lit sign of the bar entrance. Below, the ghost of his sister stood, staring at him. Always staring.

James turned away with fresh resolve and walked in the opposite direction. He had a job to do here. He had a time traveler and a doctor to find. For Sasha. It was time to get to work.

SIX

MIST ISLE

The dark figures disturbed the haze in ones and twos, slicing through the black and gray roiling fog that permanently blanketed the region. The numbers of bodies appearing and disappearing increased, followed by the growing sounds of thousands of footsteps. Mist swirled around the silhouettes, dancing in circles as if alive until it eventually lost its form. A few moments later, it was as if the procession had never come through.

Elise tilted her head to the side and stared at a metal sign hanging off only one corner of a leaning pole: BROOKLYN BRIDGE, with an arrow pointing to the top left corner of the sign. Behind it, an ominous structure full of wires and beams and stone poked through the fog.

It had taken almost a week for the Elfreth to move down the skypath highway across the Long Island Sound, down the length of the peninsula, through the mostly-submerged Hamptons, then west down the lower Suffolk path until they reached the outskirts of New York City. It took another day to navigate through Queens, but now they stood on the east side of the East River entering the dreaded Mist Isle, better known during her time period as Manhattan.

Today was the first day they entered the haze, originally created by a frequency EMP bomb, dropped during the Core Conflicts in the middle of the twenty-fourth century. The lingering effects of the bomb now manifested as an unnatural, permanent fog. It prevented all frequencies from penetrating inside or out, effectively creating a surveillance and communications dead zone. It would hamper the Elfreth, but would completely mask them from the Co-op as well. A more than fair trade-off, and a necessary one.

A shriek pulled Elise's gaze out into the ocean. She saw a tall dark object in the distance, a lone broken tower rising up from the water just to the south of the island. A dense flock of large creatures shaped like pterodactyls circled above it, their high-pitched cries piercing the otherwise quiet night. There seemed to be a nest of some sort at the top of the jagged point. Something about the building pulled at her memory.

She squinted at the flying creature. Some idiot hadn't brought back dinosaurs, had they? Who knew. Elise had been in 2512 for less than a year and she had already seen things more terrifying than she could possibly have dreamed existed, from humanoid snakes to packs of seemingly intelligent lions to centipede bears; the geneticists of the future must have gone to town with mutations. It made the twenty-first-century biologist in her nauseous.

Elise studied the lonely building again and then realized why its shape seemed so familiar. It was a decapitated statue of a woman with one arm raised, cut off at the elbow. She could see a hole through the body of the statue where its heart would be.

"Give me your tired, your poor, your huddled masses yearning to breathe free." The words came out so softly Elise almost didn't realize she had said them. They were from another time, long past and probably forgotten, except perhaps saved on some chron database server somewhere. There was meaning behind those words, a spirit of generosity and community. Words that no longer had a place.

She shivered as a gust blew in from the south, pushing such a thick bank of fog over the Statue of Liberty that it disappeared. It came in so quickly, everything around Elise darkened several shades in a blink of an eye, as if a cover were pulled over the world. It was strange, this fog. When the wind blew, she could see the mist move, yet it didn't move. Then she realized that there were two layers of fog here, one that reacted to the air, and one that ignored it completely. The scientist in her wanted to investigate further, but the Oldest in her had more urgent matters on her mind.

In the distance, thunder rumbled first from the west, then the east, and then all around, as if each of the clouds loaded with acid rain and lightning were echoing in a chorus. The crackling increased, soon followed by lightning dancing horizontally across the sky, streaking from heavy cloud to heavy cloud. The storm would be upon them soon, and when it was, it would be unforgiving. The world she lived in now didn't know how to treat its inhabitants in any other way.

A shadow appeared through the mist until she could just make out Rima's face. "Oldest, the last of the tribe is gathering at the base of the bridge. Eriao says we are too exposed and recommends we cross tonight or find shelter. However, Oldest Franwil demands a pause."

Elise gave the Statue of Liberty one last sorrowful look. "Stay standing as long as you can, old girl." She turned to Rima, who stood waiting with a chalkboard in hand. "We camp for the night on this side of the river. Tell Eriao to find an open area closed off on at least two sides, either by the river or a building. Two-hundred-meter perimeter guard. Why does Franwil need a pause?"

Rima scribbled furiously on her chalkboard and nodded. "The Oldest is with the kowrus. Moma is giving birth now."

Elise sighed. Another problem to deal with. "Take me to her," she said, following the girl back to camp. They passed the team of guardians watching the rear and continued up the length of the procession, turning in to a side street near the front. Elise found the herd of kowrus mewing in an open field just off the main road, attended to by half a dozen women. Oldest Franwil was elbow-deep inside the pregnant mare. Sasha was by her side, trying to soothe the struggling animal. The girl was often at Franwil's side now that Grace and James were out traipsing through space.

The old woman looked up and shook her head. "She cannot be moved. The foal needs to be turned and delivered. Leave us if you must."

Elise scanned the area. They were completely exposed out here, standing just off a main street that saw heavy traffic. Thank Gaia the fog obstructed the views of most of the natives living in the nearby buildings, especially with both Franwil and Sasha here. A raid right now would be upon them before they even knew it was coming. If something happened to James's sister . . . Elise shuddered; she couldn't even finish that thought.

A kowru was a valuable animal, and the pack was critical to the tribe's survival. The problem with this species was it had an extreme

pack mentality. If one of them couldn't move, the entire herd would refuse to leave. That meant they had to deliver the foal soon or risk losing
the entire herd.

Elise had delivered her first foal as an intern at the Prin Ridge Ranch
in Montana as a teenager, before she learned how to drive. She wiped her
hands and rolled up her sleeves. "Allow me, Oldest. Rima, tell Eriao to
bring a team of guardians. Sasha, we need more clean water. Boil some
now."

A team of guardians arrived a few minutes later and took up position
around them. Elise was grateful for the additional security. For the next
hour, they coaxed and comforted the mare. The stress of their journey
must have made it particularly difficult for the expecting mother.

The now-blazing fire nearby had to be a beacon to every predator
within a kilometer. No sooner had the foal been delivered and taken its
first step, One Huang—"One" being the title for a guardian who commands a team—pushed for them to leave. He barked out several orders
and stamped out the fire. "Apologies for rushing you, Oldest, but the tribe
encountered raiders from two directions. We are skirmishing with the
ones to the north now. Another tribe previously undetected is moving in
from the east. I must take you to safety."

Hastily, she picked up the newborn foal and carried it in her arms.
The guardians closed rank around her and sprinted toward the encampment. Gunfire erupted around them, kicking up stones and dirt, the
popping sounds bouncing between the buildings and lingering in the air.
To her right, one of the guardians fell and came up limping. Another had
to help carry him to safety.

Elise looked to her left and checked on Oldest Franwil. A burly man
was carrying the elderly woman as if she were a child. A long spear
landed a few meters to their side, sticking up from the ground. More
echoes of small-arms fire bounced in the air. A rain of arrows dropped
nearby. Another guardian took one to the arm, but she didn't lose a step.
Fortunately, the rest of them reached the encampment unscathed.

A minute later, they had entered the defensive barricades erected by
the wagons and vehicles. The guardians swooped and corralled Franwil
into a large tent. Elise was pleased that her pulse had quickened only
slightly.

"My, how this future changes a person," she murmured, taking a deep breath. If something like this had happened a year ago, she would have suffered a heart attack by now. Now these dangers felt like nothing more than an irritating part of her new reality. She looked down at the foal still in her arms. Well, not everything in the world had changed. She ordered Sasha to fetch a blanket to swaddle it.

She looked over at Rima. "What about the mother?"

"Moma is being well cared for," she replied. "Do not worry, Oldest, we're not leaving something as valuable as a kowru unattended. If you'll excuse me, I wish to join the guardians and help beat back the raiders." She bowed and hurried out of the tent. The girl still had some wild child left in her. Elise prayed for her safety.

In the distance, the popping sounds increased and the shouting grew louder. The fighting did not seem like it would end anytime soon. Elise got up to make the rounds and see to the rest of the tribe. It seemed that most had made it here without too much trouble.

Elise checked the individual groups huddled around small fires. The constant threats of attack were wearing the Elfreth down. Back in Boston, the Elfreth only had to worry about the Co-op. All the tribes had a shared history after generations of coexistence would unite to fight a common enemy. Now they were in foreign lands. Their enemy was the Co-op as well as every other wastelander tribe that believed their territory was being infringed upon. Everyone was their enemy. How many fronts could the Elfreth face before it broke them?

Elise peered out the tent cover into the sky. "Hurry home, James, or there might not be anything for you to come back to."

SEVEN

BULK'S HEAD

Locating black market salvagers was a delicate task. Folks in this business didn't advertise their trade and hated inquisitive strangers. ChronoCom hunted illegal time salvagers relentlessly, so those who prospered in this field were either very skilled, highly secretive, or protected by a powerful organization. Usually, it was all three.

The death rate of black market time salvaging was extraordinarily high, often a factor of ten higher than chronmen. Chronmen spent five years at the Academy and were supported by the full weight and technology of the agency. Even then, their odds of surviving past their first year were only around 70 percent. Seventy percent of illegal salvagers, usually rusks hoping to earn quick scratch, did not survive their first year.

And if the job didn't kill them, the auditors usually would. Unskilled salvagers left behind traceable ripples. Those footprints were all an auditor needed to track down exactly what had happened and correlate it with events in the present. Illegal salvagers might get away with a few jumps, but eventually, auditors would catch up to them. The ones who did survive and prosper were usually Academy-trained operatives, often former chronmen within the higher three tiers. They were the ones who were not only skilled in combat, but also familiar with the agency's systems and methodologies, and usually still had contacts within the agency to obtain a steady supply of miasma.The only way to buy access to these skilled black market salvagers was to work underground connections and bribe for the information, which for a newcomer at Bulk's Head was expensive.

It took James days of futilely working on rumors and leads before he got his first break. Word of his inquiries must have spread after the way he threw scratch around at several different establishments. Eventually, on the morning of their tenth day at Bulk's Head, he received a hit. A boy approached him as he was sitting alone at the Drink Anomaly and held out his hand. The boy, likely no older than ten or twelve, demanded James buy him dinner. When James refused, the boy told him that naming a collie *Collie* was stupid and lazy and that James better buy him a meal. James signaled to the waitress and bought the boy all he could eat and drink for the rest of the night.

That bit of information could mean only one thing. Only a few people were aware that James's old collie—the one that was destroyed by ChronoCom when they attacked the Farming Towers—was named *Collie*. It had been a running joke among some of his tier.

He watched as the boy ate his fill and got drunk off two drinks. Before the boy passed out, he handed James a piece of paper. On it was an address. It took only a few more minutes of asking around to find out that this address was located in the Puck Pirate section of the colony. Well, James did want to attract a salvager's attention. It seemed he had attracted the biggest one.

James finished his drink and looked at the young courier passed out on the table. He debated whether he should leave the boy there. If he was lucky, he would wake up with a splitting headache tomorrow. If he wasn't, he might wake up without a kidney.

Feeling parental, James grabbed the back of the shirt and hauled him to his feet. "Let's get out of here, kid."

He smacked the the boy a few times to rouse him and then escorted him out of the bar. They walked all the way across Bulk's Head until the boy's head cleared a bit. James honestly wasn't sure where the Puck Pirate section was, so he had the boy lead him there. When they arrived, he bought the boy a bag of water and sent him on his way.

James was accosted by three security guards as soon as he neared the Puck Pirate security zone. When he provided his credentials, he was blindfolded and led around for another ten minutes. He had a sense that they were descending to the lower levels after having made dozens of turns.

They could be walking him out to an airlock for all he knew. Finally, they took his blindfold off, and he found himself standing in front of an ornate metal door at the far end of a long hallway.

He inhaled; the air here was much cleaner than that in most of Bulk's Head. An important or rich person must live here. The guards spoke with someone through a comm next to the door, and then it clicked opened. James was greeted by a familiar face.

Hubbs had been two years from earning out from ChronoCom when he was caught smuggling miasma regimens to the Puck Pirates on the side. When the monitors tried to take him in, he killed three squads and a Tier-3—he was a Tier-1, after all—and then fled to Bulk's Head, far enough from ChronoCom's grasp not to make it worth their while to get him back. He had been running the Puck Pirates' salvaging operations ever since. Currently, he was hovering at number nine on Chrono-Com's most wanted list.

"Black abyss, James fucking Griffin-Mars," Hubbs exclaimed as he waved James into his extravagant quarters. "I thought you were dead until you started poking around my neck of space. Poked a giant in the eye by now or something. You always were a little broodier than the rest of us. Heard about your split with the agency. Rumor has it you broke a few time laws."

No sooner did James walk ten steps into the room than he found two burly men on either side of him. He didn't miss a beat as he eyed both men up and down, making note of the weapons in their hands. One had a close-range ion hand cannon and the other an exo-chain.

"Are these guys really necessary?" asked James.

Hubbs shrugged. "You know how it is, can't trust anyone these days, can we? You blue with this?"

"Blue," James replied.

Exo-chains were the bane of exo wielders, and moderately rare due to the fact that exos were expensive and not common in regular armies. Once an exo-chain was attached, it prevented the wielder from activating his exo. If the exo was already on, it prevented the creation of new coils and leashed the wielder to the chain's length.

James didn't trust Hubbs to be completely unarmed, but he had little choice in the matter, especially since he was here for a favor.

The exo-chain, a red lasso made of energy, struck his body with a jolt and latched onto him. Hubbs, holding on to the handle, led him into a small waiting room. He signaled for James to sit on a settee and walked to a small bar on one end of the room. He took out a decanter and two glasses. "Whiskey drinker, right?"

A shudder coursed through James as his body suddenly tightened. His mouth dried up and he found himself having trouble formulating words. One drink could very easily slip into a binge. He shook his head. "I'm on the job."

Hubbs paused and then looked back at James. At his hands in particular. He nodded. "I appreciate a man who can keep them separate." He poured himself a glass of a dark red liquid and brought a glass of water to James. He sat down on the couch opposite him and leaned back. "What can I do for you? Looking for work? I run a top-notch operation. We can always use another Tier-1."

"I'm actually recruiting."

Hubbs looked surprised. "A couple months out of the agency and already growing an operation? Color me impressed. Didn't think you had the entrepreneurial chops. Funny, thought I would have heard of a new player in this exclusive market."

"I'm not working the market." James mulled over the next thing he was going to say. "I need things salvaged."

"Why don't you just do it your . . ." Hubbs stopped. "You miasmaed out, didn't you? How badly?"

"Next jump, perhaps. The one after, definitely."

"I see." There was an awkward silence, and then Hubbs slapped his knees with his hands enthusiastically. "Very well then, a client. Even better. Tell me what you're after and I can give you a quote. Can't guarantee I'll be the one jumping, though. I am expensive."

James took a deep breath. This was the part where he expected to get thrown out of the room. "That's the thing, Hubbs. I'm not hiring. I'm recruiting for a cause."

He told the ex-chronman as much of the story as possible without giving away the details, glossing over Elise and Sasha and focusing on how they might be able to cure the Earth Plague. He watered down the conflict with the Co-op and avoided telling Hubbs how little resources the Elfreth actually had, especially that they couldn't keep a salvager on retainer. Instead, he tried to appeal to Hubbs's concern for humanity's greater good. Hubbs was already wealthy. What could he acquire to fulfill his life even more? Why not fight for a cause? Why not create a legacy that would outlive him?

James knew early into his pitch that he had failed. He watched as Hubbs's eyes glazed over and his face seemed to melt. James continued anyway, the words tumbling out of his mouth faster and faster. "When we succeed," James concluded, "you will go down in the chronostream as one of the most important and influential people in history. What do you think?"

There was a pregnant pause. Hubbs didn't move from his spot. He didn't reach for his drink. He didn't even seem to be breathing. He just stared at James good and long before he finally spoke. His words didn't inspire any confidence.

"James Griffin-Mars." Hubbs smacked his lips as if rolling the name in his mouth. "I have killed men for wasting less time than you did just now." He put up a finger. "Well, this explains why you have that massive bounty on your head. I haven't seen anyone debut on the bounty list that high since someone offed the CEO of Burning Storm. I didn't think the rumors were true, about you breaking the first Time Law, but it seems I was wrong to believe that you couldn't be that stupid."

James opened his mouth to respond when Hubbs silenced him with a hand and picked up the exo-chain. "I'm talking and you're not going to interrupt. In fact, you're done talking. The smart thing to do right now is to hand you over to ChronoCom and collect that fat reward, except for the fact that the one on my head is still larger than yours, so collecting the bounty could get awkward.

"You're toxic, James Griffin-Mars, and your being here puts the colony at risk. But because we have history—I still remember what you did covering for me on Venus—I'm not going to turn you in or kick you out of the colony. Not yet. You've got thirty days to finish your business at Bulk's Head. That should be plenty of time for every other salvager here to turn you down, and that's what's going to happen once you pitch your moronic cause. After those thirty days, you're gone, understand?"

James nodded.

"Now get the fuck out of here. Forget you ever saw me. One more thing," he called after James as the two burly men led him out the door.

"Don't cause any problems in my backyard. You get only one strike here in Bulk's Head."

James was unceremoniously hustled out of the Puck Pirate section of the colony with a warning to never return. That meeting pretty much went exactly as he'd expected. The illegal salvagers, especially, had long abandoned the moral directives ChronoCom professed in saving humanity. It was a lost cause, but one he had to embrace.

He returned to their quarters and found Grace Priestly busy with her own project. She looked up from her work as he walked in, downtrodden. She nodded when he told her how the meeting went. "Shot down by the Puck Pirates' main salvager? Might as well flame out starting at the top. Maybe one of the smaller operators will see the nobility of our quest."

James snorted. "I doubt it. The whole meeting was pretty humiliating."

She shrugged. "The Puck Pirates' salvager was never going to say yes to you anyway. He just wanted to know what you were doing here on Bulk's Head, probably wanted to make sure you weren't trying to muscle in on his business. Now that he knows you're on a quixotic quest that's doomed to fail, he'll probably just leave you alone."

"Now that you put it that way, I somehow feel even worse," he grumbled. "What's a quixotic quest?"

She smirked. "You are, James."

He walked over to her table and looked at the fast-scrolling vid. "How is your new criminal empire doing?"

"Fantastic." She beamed, rubbing her hands together. She was clearly having too much fun at the moment. "I have a large deal in the works between three parties for a chron database access hack. Playing them off against each other at the moment."

As one of the brightest minds in history, she had quickly become the scourge of the information market on Bulk's Head. Since Grace started with only few contacts and assets to barter with, she began by brokering small deals. A tech needed a V1 apropros extender, a collector wanted a twenty-second-century organic portrait, a mercenary needed repairs on his flak armor, and a smuggler needed a way to sneak into Europa Orbital Port, and Grace would somehow tie all of these clients together so everyone got what they needed. All for a small fee, of course.

In under a week, she moved up to bigger and more lucrative projects: business mergers and classified information, and even brokered a kidnapping exchange. In a frighteningly short span of time, she somehow managed to worm her way deep into the highly volatile and lucrative underground trade network and grow a fair-sized information brokerage within the colony.

"For now, I have some information to expedite your search." Two messages appeared in his AI band. "Someone owed me a favor and provided me lists of salvagers and doctors for you to hit up. Pay them a visit and see if any would consider helping our cause."

James went over the lists of nineteen salvagers and forty doctors and cross-referenced them with the list of Bulk's Head alliances he was cobbling together. Seventeen of the doctors were indentured to various crime syndicates or gangs. They would be protected and off-limits.

That left just a few independents. He had to persuade them to accept what limited scratch they had to come pay Sasha a visit on Earth. James was not beneath kidnapping them outright, though that was a sordid business. Kidnapping skilled technical and medical labor was considered one of the more heinous crimes in the solar system. James wasn't ready to go that far yet. However, for Sasha, he was starting to consider it.

Grace also sent him an updated figure of how much scratch he had to work with. He grimaced. "That's it?"

"I need the rest for cash flow. You need scratch to make scratch," she said defensively. "When I'm done getting what I need, you can use the rest."

James spent the remainder of the day visiting three salvagers and seven of the doctors on the list, confirming they weren't interested in coming to Earth. The cheapest doctor quoted five times the scratch he was allocated, and the salvagers didn't even bother asking a price. Most just laughed, some even harder when he tried to appeal to their humanity. One of the salvagers threatened to kill him for being too stupid to live.

James spent over an hour with the last doctor, at one point simultaneously pleading and threatening to get the poor man to come to Earth, half promising riches and half making death threats. He couldn't help it. His sister's life was on the line, and no one seemed to care a whit about it.

By evening, he was so frustrated, he wanted to break something. Disheartened, he dragged his exhausted body back to the residence. This was a fool's errand, one that kept him away from Elise and Sasha. That's where he belonged, not here in the middle of the Ship Graveyard begging criminals to join a hopeless cause.

He stood outside the door to their residence and thought about telling Grace just that. They should just abort this. They both should be somewhere else. He should be at home protecting his loved ones. She should be working on the cure to the Earth Plague. He worked up the courage to tell her to pack up and walked in the door.

Grace hadn't moved from the table. She saw the look on his face when he stormed inside and focused her attention back on the vid. "You look exhausted. Get some sleep."

"Grace," he began. "We should reconsider——"

"Pet." Eyes still glued to the screen, she pointed at the bed. "The answer is no. You still have the majority of the salvagers and doctors to talk to."

"We're wasting our time here."

She tore her gaze away from the screen and spoke to him in a measured tone, as if talking to a child. "The TIs have a saying: before making decisions of consequence, count the stars. Why don't you do that first thing in the morning?"

"I don't know what that means."

"It means get some rest and do your damn job, for space's sake." She stood up and folded her arms. "James, I'm speaking to you as the High Scion right now. Call it a day and get some rest. You'll have better luck tomorrow."

"Yes, Grace."

"Call me High Scion. I'm revoking your first-name privileges until you stop sniveling."

James sighed and went to bed.

EIGHT

REINFORCEMENTS

Kuo stood behind the windowpane and looked down at the masses milling on the Chicago streets just north of ChronoCom's Earth Central campus. The dense crowds were immense, almost frightening for someone from Europa and used to the limited and comforting, controlled environments of the civilized colonies on the Outer Rims. She fixated on one of the large intersections, six lanes by six, and watched in bemusement as the logjam of pedestrians, vehicles, and beasts of burden waged a war of inches.

The worst part of what she saw below was that there were millions of people in the city, and not one of them was relevant. These weren't Valta's demographics. Market research had calculated that only 6 percent of Earth's consumers had anything more than a four-times-removed association with any of the megacorp's bottom line. In other words, Kuo had very little business here on this disgusting planet, and she couldn't wait to get off Earth as soon as possible.

The past week, while she had been at Earth Central, Kuo, for some reason, had found herself gravitating to this office and staring at the chaotic activity outside, at the same time fascinated and horrified by the planet of her species' origin. The director had the best view in the building. He had gotten so used to her coming and going that he didn't even bother addressing her anymore.

"Director," she remarked, still studying the traffic jam trying to untwine itself. "Why do you allow this to continue?"

Young Hobson-Luna, the high director of ChronoCom on Earth, looked up from the book he was buried in. "Allow what to happen, Securitate?" He got up from his chair and hobbled next to her, his twisted leg dragging behind him, slightly off balance because of his amputated arm. He followed her gaze to the churning streets below. "Why do we allow traffic?"

Kuo pointed down at the mess below and then up at the heavy skyway traffic of flying vehicles in similar lanes coming in and out of the city. She gestured at the gray and brown wind, visible to the naked eye, blowing past the window. "This planet is a mess and has been for six hundred years. Look at the waste. Unforgivable. Yet, you let it continue. If ChronoCom is truly interested in preserving resources for humanity's survival, the first thing you should do is declare martial law on the planet, quarantine the savages, and allocate the remaining resources for optimal use."

"You mean turn Earth into a supply depot for the megacorporations?" Young answered dryly. "Unbridled capitalism poses similar threats."

Kuo scoffed and walked to Young's cabinet to help herself to his liquor. She poured two glasses of red wine and handed one over to him. She held it up and waited until he clinked glasses and took a sip. Even someone dosed with an antidote beforehand would have just a slight hesitation in drinking poison. It was human nature. Not that she distrusted the man. However, coming from the world of cutthroat corporatism, old habits died hard. In this case, the director passed.

She raised her glass in a toast and sipped. "Humanity is at a precipice. Like it or not, the corporations are the only thing staving off extinction. It's been proven again and again throughout history that governments are not up to the task."

"What would Valta do if they were in the agency's place as the only authority of Earth?" asked Young.

"Now is the time to act decisively, Director. You might consider those dirty masses outside people; I consider them the greatest waste of resources in the solar system. A person is either a contributor to or a burden on society. Waste in this time and age is a sin. It must be eliminated."

"So you would commit genocide?"

"Don't be absurd." Kuo shook her head. "Valta does not waste. We're not monsters. The corporation is practical and recognizes that there is skill and talent among the population. We simply have to sort the wheat from the chaff. The rest will be shorn in order to allow the greater good to survive."

"And how do you intend to judge who is worthy of survival?" asked Young, his eyes glinting. He looked down at his broken body. "I assume I would get culled with the rest of the trash?"

Kuo rolled her eyes. "Please, Director, you insult us. You obviously have not met our CEO. Zu Wen-Europa has been wheelchair-bound since he was four years old. Your experience, leadership, and wise decision making"—she emphasized the last three words—"are what makes you worthy. Otherwise, yes, there is little reason to have you around."

"Thank you for deeming me of some value." He bowed, making an elaborate but comical gesture with his bent, one-sided body.

The sarcasm wasn't lost on Kuo. As much as she enjoyed making her point, she knew better than to continue digging at the high director of ChronoCom. He was more useful as an ally, for now.

"Down to business then, shall we?" She placed the wineglass on his desk and sat down. "I ordered more monitors for the next phase of my project. Why has this not happened yet?"

"Yes, about that," Young said, taking a seat opposite her. "I put that on hold until we can have a discussion. You don't requisition a tenth of my available monitor ranks without speaking with me first."

"Good," Kuo said. "Now that we've spoken, when will the five hundred monitors be ready?"

"What do you intend to use them for?" he asked.

"Does it matter?"

There was a long silence. Young spoke in a slow, measured tone. "ChronoCom is not your supply depot either, Securitate."

"We're owed this support, Director."

"You were owed five hundred monitors and support personnel, which you were given."

"Now I need more."

"Not with the way you're deploying them, you don't. Why are the casualties so far eighty percent ChronoCom personnel? You are abusing this relationship."

"I am leveraging the resources available to me in the most efficient way possible." She shrugged. "I brought highly skilled, specialized operatives for the project. Your monitors and newly raised chronmen are less skilled and more expendable."

For a second, Kuo thought the director had found a backbone. Young leaned forward, and, pressing his good hand down on the desk, rose to his feet. His eyes flashed, and he looked as if he was going to say or do something interesting. Kuo almost activated her exo. Almost. After a few seconds of intensity, the broken administrator she had come to know became whom she thought he was.

"ChronoCom did not sign on to take the brunt of this operation. We acknowledge what is contractually due, but we expect compensation to cover our costs and resources."

"I will take that up with Liaison Sourn," she said, letting a small smile appear on her face. "I'm heading back to the field, Director. My hounds believe they have located the temporal anomaly near the Mist Isle. Give me what I need, and we will be off your hands soon enough."

Young sighed. "Very well. This is the last time, Kuo."

She finished the rest of her wine and stood. No use in letting it go to waste. It was an excellent twenty-third-century Triton vintage. She placed the glass on his desk and nodded. "Valta reinforcements are arriving in three days. Please see to it that they are transferred to my location. As soon as I receive both, I can finish this project."

Kuo left Young's office and passed by several agency personnel as she exited the building. She ignored them, but was aware that all their eyes were glued to her as she passed. Every single one of them would probably stab her in the back, given the chance. She was, without a doubt, hated by everyone in ChronoCom. The trial of Levin Javier-Oberon, one of the more popular planetary high auditors in recent memory, had seen to that.

That was all fine by Kuo. The little agency, for now, was nothing more than a tool, a subcontractor the megacorporation leveraged to accomplish its goals. Their opinions meant nothing to her. The only ones that mattered were those of her superiors and of Valta's Board of Directors.

In the end, no matter what anyone else said, Kuo knew that she was on the side of good. She followed the highest calling in the solar system: profit, market share, and, ultimately, the survival of mankind. Many of the ignorant might think Valta was only looking out for its own interests, and they wouldn't be mistaken. What they didn't realize was that greater good and corporate interests had to be aligned in order to accomplish the monumental tasks humanity needed to stave off extinction.

Corporations just needed the proper incentives. They were the key to saving the species from itself, and the way to engage and encourage them to do so was to make saving humanity profitable, because in the end, companies were owned by shareholders and short-term gains were what mattered to them, not long-term intangible needs.

Some called it greed, others selfishness. Kuo considered it leveraging humanity's greatest strength. The drive for wealth and success was the one virtue humanity had exhibited throughout history, and the one trait that had consistently pushed humanity to excel. The origins of the collective needs must begin with innate base self-desires. It was this desire to accumulate wealth and power that would save all of mankind.

In the past, humanity had tried to be altruistic in accomplishing its goals; it had rarely been successful. From common interests to religious righteousness to philosophical logic, humans throughout history had rarely ever accomplished anything worthwhile without significant self-interest as their source of motivation. Now, in these dire times, it was humanity's greatest advocates—the megacorporations that specialized in accumulating wealth—that would lead them from the brink of extinction.

A few minutes later, Kuo arrived at the Geras Towers at the south side of Earth Central's campus, which housed corporate dignitaries and guests. She noted the four troopers manning the entrance and the additional one at the lift. Neither the agency nor the megacorp was taking any chances with the Valta delegation residing here.

Ever since the trial several months back, tensions between the two camps had been high. Reports from Boston had only worsened relationships between the rank and file. It had gotten to the point that Sourn had insisted all ChronoCom personnel be banned from Geras Tower unless expressly invited, thus replacing the monitors with Valta's troopers.

She found Sourn in the top-floor suite and waited respectfully at the entrance. The vice president of Earth operations and liaison to the Board of Directors stood in the middle of an open room, surrounded by a dozen giant floating heads. She recognized four from the Board of Directors: Camminsol, the vice president of Jupiter operations; Bodard, the transit chief; Meadors, the second-fleet admiral; Damian, the inner-region finance master.

The last was the one to worry about. At the end of the day, no matter the position, it was always the finance lords of the corporation who dictated policy. The news she brought with her was not going to help matters any. Sourn glanced her way and acknowledged her with a slight nod.

Kuo walked down to the end of the hall and waited. The view from this window was of the massive lake just east of the city. In the distance, a never-ending storm brewed over the brown waters, sucking up the muck until it created funnels that randomly meandered the breadth of the lake's surface. She saw easily seven or eight of those funnels just writhing within eye-shot.

Lightning came down intermittently, several bolts striking one of the many rods dispersed across the lake that harnessed nature's destructive energy to power the city. She followed the path of one of the brown funnels as it headed toward land. It reached approximately a hundred meters from shore before a sonic boom dispersed it.

She had asked about these land defenses when she first arrived. The sonic emitters spanned the entire length of the shore. At first, these funnels, a product of the planet's increasingly violent weather patterns, were thought to be anomalies. Over time, though, they became regular occurrences. Prior to the sonic emitters' installation, the funnels were wreaking havoc along every coastal city on the planet, to the point that several of the smaller cities were abandoned.

Kuo shook her head. So many checks and balances. Nature had turned on her own children, choking its remnants in this cesspool. Everywhere humans lived, they fought a high-cost battle to survive. It should be a clue for those remaining on this planet—somewhere around two billion— that they were no longer welcome. It was foolish to think otherwise.

The intelligent and efficient thing to do would be to start over. Recategorize the planet as a hostile environment and outlaw habitation. Eliminate the local denizens and transfer the ones worth saving to the efficient and highly-regulated colonies throughout the rest of the solar system.

Then, the megacorporations should harvest the remaining resources—Earth was still the greatest repository in the solar system—to ensure humanity's survival.

"Senior Securitate Kuo, Liaison Sourn will see you now," a woman's pleasant voice chirped inside her head.

Kuo tore her gaze from the hypnotic destruction of the lake and strolled into the next room. Sourn was still talking to one of the floating heads—Damian by the looks of it—when she came in. The image disappeared, and Sourn motioned for a hover chair to approach her.

He gestured for her to sit. "How goes the mission to locate the temporal anomaly, Kuo?"

Kuo bowed and sat down. "It goes, Liaison. Unfortunately, she was able to escape our grasp and disappear outside the ruins of Boston. We have expanded our search perimeters to cover the entire region."

She had submitted weekly statuses since the project started. However, she knew Sourn, a climber within Valta who had eyes on a board chairmanship one day, wouldn't have bothered reading it and wanted just the condensed information. If she performed well under him, he would take her with him, hopefully straight off this backwater planet. If not, his disapproval could mean a career stranded here on Earth.

"The director is asking for reimbursement for the requisition of five hundred extra monitors," she continued.

"Not an unreasonable request, especially after seeing your deployment schematics." Sourn shook his head. "Young has already complained to me about how you are using his monitors. Really, Securitate. Did you have to be that obvious?"

Kuo bristled. Of course the old man had. Why else would he have had the gall to outright ignore her request for more monitors? Which left one more thing . . .

"Liaison, I must inquire: At what point is locating this temporal anomaly a negative return on investment for Valta? She is valuable as a scientist with subject matter expertise on the Nutris machines we've retrieved, yes, but the resource expenditure has been significant, and Valta having to rely on a nonprofit entity such as ChronoCom"—Kuo clicked her tongue disapprovingly—"has been limiting and problematic. Furthermore, due to the nonprofit's bureaucracy and inefficiency, she was allowed to escape, and we now believe she could be hidden on the Mist

Isle. Locating the subject will be a costly affair. I have a difficult time estimating the feasibility and justification of continuing this project."

Sourn waited until she finished. He ran his index finger and thumb along his chin as if he were stroking an imaginary beard. A small smile broke on his face. "Your analysis is correct, Kuo. This project is now already a negative return for Valta, even with ChronoCom doing the brunt of the heavy lifting. Regardless, we proceed as planned. Valta considers our arrangement with this nonprofit a moral imperative."

"I don't understand," she said.

He pointed at her. "Let's say the temporal anomaly—this scientist— escapes us, and we allow ChronoCom to renege or renegotiate the terms of the agreement due to their failure, and they negotiate to credit us whatever they think they owe us in salvage. What happens next time?"

"Take the lessons learned from the experience and don't make the same mistakes. My first recommendation would be that Valta lead the project from the outset."

Sourn nodded. "That lesson is already learned regardless. What happens the next time we purchase service from the agency and they fail to deliver?"

"We just have to—"

"There won't be a next time," he snapped. "Because there won't be a 'this time' either. This is the problem with nonprofits. Like governments and all other inefficient public entities, they are far too often allowed to fail without consequence. Well, we are holding them accountable. I have already informed the entire board that we will deliver this temporal anomaly because it is what we're owed. And you will deliver, Kuo. You're not returning to Europa until this job is completed. See to it."

That was it right there. That was the real reason. Sourn had promised the delivery of this scientist to the board. Failure was no longer an option. Kuo involuntarily clenched a fist. "Yes, Liaison." She bowed.

"One more thing, Kuo," he said as she was about to leave the room. "Even the troop distributions. I don't want to hear another complaint from that cripple about how we're abusing his resources. A healthy business relationship should be built on fairness and trust, after all."

NINE

BREAKING POINT

Grace Priestly had flat-out lied. James's luck wasn't better the next day, or the day after that. In fact, every day for the next two weeks was worse than the last as he went down the list of salvagers and doctors, begging and pleading for help. Regardless of profession, everyone was telling him no, and each time it felt like a punch in the gut.

None of the doctors would even entertain the notion of making the trip to Earth. Some turned him down less cruelly than others, but the result was all the same. They didn't care that it was his sister, or that she was a child and possibly dying. All they saw was how much he had to offer.

To be honest, James didn't blame them. He was asking a doctor to abandon his practice to come to Earth just to treat Sasha. Bringing Sasha here was out of the question. A pirate's den was no place for a ten-year-old. He shuddered at the thought of her falling into the hands of slavers and deviants. He could have brought his sister here and stayed for her treatment, but that would have meant leaving Elise back on Earth for abyss knew how long. That was not a risk he was willing to take.

No, he had to find a doctor who was willing to treat her on Earth, perhaps appealing to someone's heart, or sense of adventure, or even a doctor who owed money and needed a change of scenery. By this time, James didn't care. However, he had no such luck and hadn't come across a generous- or desperate-enough soul to consider this sort of arrangement.

He had even less luck tracking down a willing salvager. Every single one was a hardened mercenary. None cared a whit about his quest to cure Earth and openly scoffed at what he could offer. By this time, Grace had earned enough to pay for a couple of salvages, but not enough to make a real difference to the Elfreth.

Grace had already told him what she would do with the rest of their funds if he failed to recruit a salvager. If it came down to supplying the Elfreth or finding Sasha a doctor, he knew which direction she would choose. She had already earmarked large portions for supplies to last the tribe through the winter, and the rest to purchase much-needed equipment for their research to cure the Earth Plague. All this just made him more desperate.

James was returning from his latest rejection, the last on the list of salvagers. He was at a dead end, having exhausted all his options in Bulk's Head. He was frustrated and had given up on this colony of assholes. He wasn't giving up on Sasha, though, and was already formulating another plan. If he couldn't bring a doctor to her, perhaps he could smuggle her to one of the more civilized colonies, like Titan or Europa or Ganymede, or even that dump Rhea. He would have to abandon her there, but at least she would be seen to. Corporate-owned colonies didn't starve children. He could find her again in a few years. The very thought of this plan broke his heart and made him want to throw up, but he was running out of options.

"James," Grace's voice popped into his head. "Any luck with the Festa Triad's salvager?"

"No." That one word must have conveyed how defeated he felt.

Grace, however, did not coddle people. "I can tell you're moping, so stop it. I think I have something. Sending the information to you now."

A message appeared in his AI band, pointing to an address in a run-down, industrial lower section on the fringe of the colony. He pulled up the data: Roft Hess-Mimas. Supposedly a Tier-4.

"I've never heard of this guy," he thought to Grace. "Where did you come by this information? Who is he?"

"I was brokering a batch of tach blades when one of my partners asked if you were looking for a cheap salvager. Said he heard secondhand of a man dropping in for a week to pick up a miasma regimen shipment. Said he's hard up for work and willing to operate on the low."

James stopped in the middle of the hallway and stared at the message floating inside his head. "Have you verified the information?"

"Not much to verify. The man is due to depart on a shuttle first thing tomorrow. That I did check out."

James cursed. He hated going in blind. He was a long-lived chronman exactly because he didn't jump into situations without vetting every detail. However, if this ex-chronman really was willing to work for cheap and was leaving the next day, then he had to risk it.

"I'm on my way." James turned down a side hallway and made his way toward the main stairwells leading to the lower levels. He checked his bands, noting that his exo was powered just under 50 percent. That should be sufficient if a problem arose.

Bulk's Head's constabulary was surprisingly professional and efficient, considering they were policing a pirates' den. Perhaps especially because they were policing a pirates' den.

Firearms were illegal in all of the Wreck colonies. Discharging a weapon in a hundreds-years-old spaceship was extremely dangerous. An unlucky shot could cause a terrible explosion or leak precious air, water, or some other life-sustaining resource. This made melee weapons—knives, clubs, and other undetectable weapons—popular choices. James himself carried an old-fashioned retractable baton in his back pocket.

The crowds became sparser the lower he got, until he was the only person continuing down a dimly-lit stairwell. He continued down a narrow hallway that became so dark, many of the tributary corridors faded to black. Only a few lonely flickering white lights kept the complete blackness at bay.

The air was thinning, too. He must be reaching the edge of the colony. James activated his atmos and took a full breath. He had to be careful. One wrong turn, one mistakenly opened door, and he could be sucked into space.

The address to the residence was a run-down respiratory chamber, one of the many complex automated courier systems used throughout the ship. The Core Planets had liked to model their ship terminology after human physiology for some reason. That practice had begun and died with them. The room was long and narrow, with just enough space for two people to stand back-to-back to work and long enough he couldn't see the wall on the other end. There were two dozen small orange lights scattered on both walls, illuminating the room like candles. He took a step inside.

"State your name." The voice came from the far end of the room.

"James Griffin-Mars. You're Roft Hess-Mimas, a Tier-4? What year at the Academy? Where were you stationed?"

There were fewer than four thousand chronmen in the solar system. James didn't know all of them, especially the newer ones, but it was a small community.

"I'm asking the questions here. You need me. I don't need you. What job are you after?"

"That's not what I heard," James said. He took a step forward. "Let's discuss this. It's a series of jobs—"

"Stay right there. Release your bands and we'll talk. You can put them back on after we're done here.

James hesitated. No chronman worth his salt, former or not, would ever tell another to release his bands unless they were fighting. Before he could activate his exo, a flash and a shock struck him, binding a reddish string of energy around his waist. James found himself unable to activate his exo.

The exo-chain's glow illuminated the rest of the room, revealing three figures on the far end—one sitting in a chair, and two standing to his side. One of the three figures charged and clocked him across the side of the face with a hard object. Fortunately, James had a split second to react and rolled with the hit. It spun him around, and he crashed to the floor.

"Release your bands or I'll bash your head in," she snarled, swinging a metal pipe downward.

"Don't kill him," a voice said behind her. "We can't get the bands then."

James swung his head to the side just as the pipe thunked against the floor. He kicked out, taking one of her legs from under her, and rolled to his feet. He was immediately tackled by another individual—this time a scrawny man with powered gauntlets. A punch to the gut sucked the wind out of him, and he doubled over. Another strike to his chin almost knocked him out. James fell backward until his back slammed against the wall panel. A second later, Scrawny's shoulder rammed into his gut.

"Release your bands, asshole, and we'll let you live."

James's consciousness ebbed in and out. He took another glancing hit to the side of the face, managing to partially dodge the blow. He raised both hands and slapped Scrawny in the ears and then put him in a head-lock. James threw his free elbow down on Scrawny's back until he forced the guy to his knees. Out of the corner of his eye, he saw the woman fly at him again. He caught her arm as she swung the club. James spun to the left and threw both of his assailants onto the ground.

"Who do you think you're dealing with?" he snarled, his anger boil-ing over. His frustrations from the past weeks overcame him as he turned on the figure holding onto his exo-chain. The man pulled out a pistol and fired. The beam of light went wide left, but seared James's left arm, spinning him around. James continued charging, ducking under-neath another shot before he pounced on top of the man. Two quick looping punches on the crown of his head folded the man in a crum-pled heap. The handle to the exo-chain dropped to the ground and pow-ered off.

James powered on his exo and shot coils from his body, wrapping them around his assailants and lifting them up into the air. Two of them were unconscious; one moaned softy. The three of them looked like nothing more than thieves.

"Please," the one still conscious, the woman, begged. "Don't kill us. We're just trying hock some gear for food and air. We'll leave the col-ony. We won't bother anyone anymore. I promise!"

James was unsure what to do with them. A quick squeeze of the coils would end them. They deserved it. Who knew how many people they had entrapped with this scheme. Still, he was tired of all this killing. These shits were young, barely in their twenties, probably get-ting by the only way they could. They got their hands on the exo-chain and decided it was going to pave their way. He saw a lot of himself in them.

He looked at the exo-chain lying on the ground, and for a second con-sidered confiscating it to sell. He picked it up and examined its condi-tion. It was a moderately valuable piece of tech. Then he noticed how worn it looked and wondered how many people this gang had entrapped with it. There was blood on this thing. He created an additional coil and smashed it.

"I'm sending your prints and images to the Puck Pirates," he said. "I don't know what they're going to do with this information once they receive it. I'm sure you don't either. You might want to reconsider your scheme at Bulk's Head."

James dropped the broken fragments of the exo-chain on the ground and stormed out of the room. He made the long walk back up the main stairwell in silence. His face ached in several places, and the laser burn on his shoulder stung. It had been a closer call than he cared to admit. Anyone semi-competent would have been able to finish him off three-versus-one once he got caught in the exo-chain.

He was angry at himself. He should have known better. The old James would have for sure. He had gotten desperate. These three punks had probably scouted him out, knowing that he was making the rounds. They probably sent the information to Grace right after his last rejection to entrap him. If he had been anyone else, a Tier-3 or lower, they would have succeeded. Probably forced him to give up his bands and then jettisoned him out into space, never to be seen again.

Deflated, James dragged his exhausted and hurt body back up to the main levels and made his way to the residence. He had been up nearly twenty hours now, working fervently to find solutions to his many problems before hitting that dead end. Well, it seemed the end was in sight now, and he had still made no headway. It was over. He had failed.

The longer he was away from Earth, the likelier it was that something was going to happen to Elise and Sasha. He just needed to go home. It made him feel slightly guilty that the fight with the three hooligans had felt good. He was so frustrated recently that he had been itching to break something. Break someone.

He passed the now-familiar hallway leading to the Drink Anomaly, and the neon sign blinking pink, bathing the area in its sugary glow. He stopped and stared. Of all the times he had needed a drink and forced himself to keep walking, this was the time he might actually deserve one.

"The past is already dead," a soft voice whispered.

He stood there and watched the patrons walk in and out. The alcohol inside beckoned him. He felt his body pulled toward the bar as if there were a powerful magnet in there, and his skin had turned to metal. James almost felt himself lifted off his feet as he stumbled forward.

The hallucination of Sasha stood next to the entrance and folded her arms in front of her chest. She seethed. James avoided looking at her. If he couldn't see her, she didn't exist, right? She didn't exist anyway. The real Sasha was on Earth. Alive. As he entered the Drink Anomaly, he saw Sasha leave her post and stomp around the corner.

"The past is already dead."

That damn voice. Where was it coming from? James entered the main room of the bar, and the sounds of the crowd drowned out the whisper in his head. It was packed. Brightly-garbed pleasure boys and girls were sprinkled among dozens of surly-looking patrons. James felt energized and alive again as every step took him closer to what his body needed.

The bartender walked by James a few times as he waited at the counter. The first few passes, the bartender must have appraised James's clothing and decided he wasn't worth paying too much attention to. Then he proceeded to ignore him for the next twenty minutes. James felt an itch crawling up his neck as he tried to stave off the shaking in his hands. Finally, the bartender, taking his time wiping the counter, looked his way. "What will it be, my friend?"

That once-familiar phrase, something he often heard in his head while on jobs, stunned James as if he were splashed by a bucket of cold water. Waves of grief long-suppressed washed over him, and he felt stabbing pain rend his chest. He hadn't realized how much he had missed hearing those words until someone else spoke them. The bartender had to be from Proteus, the same moon colony that Smitt came from.

James's vision blurred and he wiped his eyes. "Whiskey. Make it a good year."

One drink. That's all it would be. One drink to wipe away all of today's rejections and failures. Tomorrow, he would start anew. Let this one drink clear his mind. He promised. That's all he would be here for.

"I knew you couldn't survive without me." That voice again.

A tin cup appeared almost instantaneously, and then the bartender was gone, moving over to serve another patron. James stared at the cup sitting on the counter. He felt his throat dry in anticipation. Every nerve in his body screamed at him to pick it up and inhale the alcohol inside. He put both hands on the cup and pressed down, forcing it to stay on the counter. He was squeezing so hard its sides began to dent. He felt the urge to lift it again and throw its contents back in one smooth motion. Just one wouldn't hurt, would it?

He looked back at the bartender chatting with another patron and stopped. The man's face had changed. Perhaps it was the light reflecting off his complexion. Perhaps it was his slightly familiar-sounding accent. Then the man's features seemed to wash off his face, as if it were a paint mod erasing itself, except what was hidden behind it was someone familiar. He forced himself to look away and scan the crowd, trying to keep his shaking hands from being noticed.

"You all right there, my friend?" the bartender returned and asked. He even sounded familiar.

James inhaled and turned back toward the counter. The bartender's face was normal again, unfamiliar. James picked up the whiskey and lifted it to his mouth. His hands were shaking so badly he had slopped half of it out of the cup. He felt himself lean toward the left, almost falling off the stool. He was just tired. The stress. Problems stacking on top of problems.

"I shouldn't be here," he muttered desperately over and over again. "Shouldn't be here. Shouldn't be here. Need to get out of here."

The voice whispered, "We're both right here, where we're supposed to be."

James slammed the cup down on the counter and stormed out. Pushing his way through the crowd, he headed straight for the residence, knocking aside anyone who got in his way. All the voices nearby sounded like insects buzzing, and the room swayed at an odd angle, the right corners turning into parallelograms. He stumbled into the residence and collapsed onto the bed. Fortunately, Grace wasn't there at the moment. He wouldn't have been able to explain what was going on right now.

"I just need to get some sleep," he mumbled.

He had been under a lot of stress lately. It had been a while since he had felt this sort of pressure. Sleep would do some good. He crawled under the sheets. His body shook uncontrollably, and he felt chilled to the bone as he huddled in a fetal position under the blankets. A few seconds later, a drowsiness washed over him. James wiped his brow; it was wet. He felt the hairs on the back of his neck rise, and a cool breeze brushed his cheek. That shouldn't be possible. Then, he closed his eyes and suddenly felt very cold.

TEN

MY FRIEND

James Griffin-Mars shivered as he stood watch on Outpost U-B at the northern edge of the ChronoCom Academy grounds on Tethys. The Outpost was nothing more than a rectangular shelter with four walls, a roof, and a trickle charger that barely had enough levels to keep one band charging at a time, let alone an oxygen band, heat band, comm band, and AI band. Not only that, James had to reserve enough of the charge to power his water purifier, ration utility, and in the end, put enough power into the rover to truck his way back to the Academy two hundred kilometers to the south.

This was all part of the box test, the fifth that James had had to survive in five years and one of the most difficult of the tier curriculum. Each year, the test got a little harder, the resources a little more scarce, and the stay in the box a little longer.

This last time, James had to survive twenty days off five days' rations and water. It was a difficult test, but one designed for the initiates to succeed if they managed their meager resources wisely. However, most people failed, with over 90 percent requiring extraction before the twentieth day. The fatality rate hovered around 19 percent.

So far this year, none in his class had succeeded in passing the fifth box test; James was intent on being the first. He was near the end, having survived eighteen days, but was risking failure. He had miscalculated some of his earlier metrics and was scrimping on some of his levels, trying to play catch-up. Right now, he was barely surviving by turning the levels of his oxygen band only high enough for labored breathing, and his heat band just warm enough not to go into hypothermia. However, in doing so, he had let the levels of his comm and AI band lapse so he wouldn't be able to call for help if he were to concede the test, nor could the Academy administrators track his life signs. It was foolish, but James would rather go all out to pass the test than have his odds of success diminished by those level-guzzling safety nets.

Lying on the hard floor of the outpost, shivering and barely conscious, James stared out the porthole at the almost painfully bright reflective icy surface of the moon. Two more days. Forty-eight more hours. The rover required sixteen hours of charge to cover that distance. His oxygen band needed fourteen more to sustain this level of breathing. His heat band . . . James felt his consciousness leave him as he closed his eyes and embraced the darkness.

"Wake up, James."

He opened his eyes. The frozen plains of Tethys were still there. Bright, uniform, white. Barren. Except now, there was a small black speck in the distance. He couldn't tell what it was. A vehicle? Hallucination? God, for all he knew.

"It's not God. You're not dead yet, my friend."

James rolled off his side onto his back and sat up. To his left, Smitt sat on the floor with his back against the wall, chewing on a ration bar. James hoped to the abyss that wasn't one of his. If Smitt had decided to munch on his food, James was going to kick his ass. He had only five left, barely enough to survive the next two days and the return trip to the Academy.

He sat up and felt the room sway. He took a long, slow, labored breath. "What are you doing here, Smitt? If the admins notice you're here, I'll get disqualified. I'm not taking the damn test again because you're bored for company. I swear—"

"Relax, James." His best friend chuckled. "No one knows I'm here. You powered down your AI band, remember? That was stupid, by the way."

"I need every edge I can get." James palmed the wall with both hands and got onto unsteady feet. He looked out the window again. The black speck was still there, growing larger. He turned around and stepped over Smitt on the way to the wash basin. The small container had a fifth of a liter of purified water. James drank a third of that, letting the water sit in his mouth for a good thirty counts before letting it slide down his throat. He took another deep breath.

He turned back to face Smitt. "I can't talk too long. I don't have the oxygen to waste. You can't stay here either." He paused. "How did you get here, anyway?"

Smitt hopped onto his feet and wiped his hands, scattering the crumbs of the ration bar on the floor. He had always had been a messy eater, though James thought it was cruel to be so wasteful in front of him while he was testing. Smitt walked over and picked up the rest of the water and guzzled it down before James could stop him.

"Ah," he said, smacking his lips. "Nothing like cool refreshing ice water to wash down a lunch made from recycled plastics."

James stared at the empty container, stunned. "You just drank the rest of my water." He considered putting his hands around his best friend's throat and choking the life out of him.

"No, my friend. You only think so. Look again." Smitt pointed at the empty container in his hand.

Smitt's words slapped James in the face. He looked down. The water had refilled. How was this possible? "What did you . . . ?" He stared at his friend. Funny, Smitt looked much older than he remembered. They were at the Academy. Smitt would be about nineteen right now. *Would be. No, he is.* James noticed Smitt's arms. He wasn't wearing any bands. How was he surviving out here? What was going on?

Then he remembered. This test was a long time ago. A lot had happened since then. James did survive this test. He became a chronman. "Smitt . . ." He looked back at his friend. "You . . . you died."

Smitt shook his head. "I'm sorry we never made it to Europa together."

"You're not actually here. Neither of us are. You never were." James looked around the room. "No, you were." He walked over to the wall with the porthole. The black speck was distinguishable now. It was a rover speeding along the plains, getting larger and kicking up a trail of ice dust as it approached the outpost. He turned back and looked at Smitt. "The real you is there, aren't you? You're coming to check up on me."

Smitt walked up next to James and looked out the window. "You didn't call in for six checkpoints and your AI band was down for the last two days. The admins assumed, and very accurately, I might add, that you were probably conserving levels and that you were willing to risk retrieval in order to finish the test. They were right, you brave, fucking idiot. Those assholes were applauding your gutsy call even as they wagered among themselves if you were going to survive. I said to abyss with it and came to check up on you."

James closed his eyes and dug into his past. So many buried memories, so many that he wanted to forget. This wasn't one of them. But he had forgotten. Why? He looked up at his best friend. "I had failed."

Smitt nodded. "I probably got to you four to five hours before your levels gave out. You were already unconscious for abyss knows how long. I brought you back to the Academy."

"You got reprimanded for coming out here," James said.

Smitt grinned. "Screw them. You lived."

But Smitt didn't. Kuo killed him for helping James. He knew the risks, but James was selfish. If James had truly cared for Smitt the way his friend had cared for him, James would have cut off all contact with Smitt once he had become a fugitive. Instead, Smitt risked his life helping James inside ChronoCom and paid the ultimate price.

James felt his throat catch as Smitt patted him on the back and headed toward the exit. "Take care of yourself, my friend. Don't let my death go to waste, and when I say that, I mean don't avenge me." He opened the door and stepped out, closing it behind him.

James ran to the window and saw Smitt's figure disappear into the distance, seemingly fading into the air the farther he walked from the outpost. A second later, the rover zipped past the porthole. James heard the door slam open and saw a much-younger-looking Smitt run into the room.

"James," he squeaked in a high-pitched voice. "Fuck, you're unconscious. Damn stubborn idiot. I knew you'd pull something like this . . . Snap out of it!" He slapped the unconscious James. "Come on, don't you die on me and leave me to fend for myself, you asshole. I knew you couldn't survive without me." Smitt slapped him again. "Wake up!"

James opened his eyes just in time to see Grace hovering over him, her pruned hands held up in the air.

"I'm up, I'm up," he said.

She brought her hand down on the side of his cheek, ringing his ears. She hit him so hard she nursed her hand afterward. "I knew your head was as hard as a rock."

"What did you do that for?" He grimaced, rubbing the side of his face.

"You woke me up with your flailing and yelling. And because I wanted to." She bared her teeth in a wicked grin. She noted the sweat pouring down his brow and dabbed him with a rag. "Hallucinations again?"

Grace moved out of his way as he sat up and swung his legs over the side of the bed. He buried his head in his hands and took a deep breath. He hadn't thought about Smitt too often over the last six months. To be honest, he had had other things on his mind with Sasha back in his life and the Co-op hunting them down. However, that moment with the bartender had triggered something.

At first, he thought he just missed his best friend, his only friend, really, over the past twenty years. It was more than that, though, he realized, as the feeling lingered and grew. It wasn't just because he missed Smitt; it was because James had never buried him. He had never properly said goodbye. His relationship with Smitt felt unresolved.

So many things pulled at him: Sasha, Elise, the Elfreth, the Co-op, the drinking, and now the ghost of his friend. He was a man trying to tread water as waves crashed over him. Every time he thought he could take a breath, a new weight came and dragged him underwater again. He felt as if he were going to crack. James stood up and walked to the door. He knew of only one way to relieve the pressure.

"Where are you going?" Grace asked sharply.

He didn't look back as he opened the door and stormed out. "I just need to go for a walk."

"Don't you think about . . ."

James didn't hear the rest as he raced down the hallway. He didn't consciously know where he was going, but his body knew, as if somehow that would fool his psyche, or his consciousness. He moved quickly down two levels to the pleasure lair, the lowest main floor in Bulk's Head, ignoring the catcalls from the local brothels and the music playing from the discos and lounges.

He found himself standing in front of a small dinky bar nestled in the far corner of one of the seedier corridors of Bulk's Head. He didn't know how he had found this place; he certainly hadn't been here before. A small

LED sign blinked the word "Moonshined" in bright purple letters. It was dark inside. He peered through the only window next to the door and saw that this little shithole was long and narrow, with barely anything more than a counter and a row of stools. Definitely not an establishment people went to, to socialize. As far as he could tell, there was no one inside. It was perfect.

James slid the heavy rusted door open and walked in, surprising the bartender, a large homely woman with the front half of her hair shaved and the back in a long queue ponytail. She must be from Larissa, one of the more backwater colonies of Neptune, home of a colony of Chinese descendants who preached blood purity.

He sat on the first stool, and to his credit, second-guessed his decision before opening his mouth. He killed any resistance inside him quickly. "Whiskey. I don't care what kind." A plastic cup appeared on the counter and the bartender sloppily poured him a shot. He grabbed the bottle before she could take it away. "Leave it."

James held the plastic cup almost reverently. He noticed his shaking hands as he brought it to his lips. Something in him was screaming. That small voice; barely perceptible, like a tiny buzzing in his ear.

"Fuck it," he muttered, and threw the contents back.

The bad whiskey burned his throat and made his chest tighten. He felt his body physically react as this calming sensation washed over him. He felt like he was in control again, that all the shit he's had to deal with this past year wasn't drowning him, tearing him apart piece by piece. He poured himself another drink and closed his eyes, letting the harsh burn of the alcohol wash through his body. Like a purifying fire, it dulled the pain.

"You're supposed to report to the Hops before you make your way here," a familiar voice quipped.

James sprayed his drink all over the counter. He ended up coughing in fits as he tried to catch his breath. It couldn't be. He squeezed his eyes shut and took several deep breaths. When he opened them, he stared straight ahead at the shelf of bottles. He had only had two drinks. He had to get ahold of himself. He looked to his left.

Smitt was sitting on the stool next to him. He tsked at the bottle. "If you're going to fall off the wagon, at least do it with good swill. Mark the occasion. I bet they make that crap somewhere in the back room."

James didn't know the details of what had happened to his former handler. All he knew was that the Valta securitate had tortured him. According to Levin, Smitt didn't give anything away. To the end, his friend had stayed loyal and had paid the price for it by dying at Kuo's hands. James clenched his fist and turned back to the bottle. Smitt wasn't supposed to be here. He was dead. Why did all the dead things in his life keep coming back? "The past is already dead," he muttered.

"You only think that, my friend," said Smitt, leaning into James and plucking the bottle from the counter to pour himself a drink. James looked over and saw Smitt holding the plastic cup and examining it under the dirty yellow light. He shook his head. "What I wouldn't give for real glass." He handed the cup to his left, where Sasha, sitting next to him, took it. Before James could stop her, she put the plastic cup of whiskey to her mouth and drank it.

"Eucch, gross." She grimaced, and stared James straight in the eyes. "You broke your promise to drink this icky stuff."

"Sasha," James whispered. "What are you . . . You shouldn't be here."

Smitt patted James on the shoulder. It felt as real as if his friend were sitting right next to him. "You only think that, James. We're both right here, where we're supposed to be."

He offered James the bottle. James took it, and this time, he didn't bother using the cup.

ELEVEN

DOWNTOWN JUNGLE

When Elise was in secondary school, the badminton team had elected her captain, because she was the most popular girl on the squad and the only one nobody hated. She had won Ms. Congeniality the year before at the spring formal. By the end of the season, the entire team had turned against her, and she had quit badminton altogether. Elise had learned a valuable lesson from her time as captain of a strong-minded competitive group of girls swinging rackets at little birdies at extreme velocities. Unfortunately, it wasn't how to be a better leader.

Elise realized at that time that she hated leading anything that wasn't furry with four legs, and that she never wanted to do it ever again. That was why when the Elfreth had made her an Oldest alongside Franwil, she felt this terrible sense of foreboding doom. Less than a year into the job, her trepidation had only worsened, especially as the Elfreth crossed the Brooklyn Bridge into the Mist Isle.

Downtown Manhattan was populated by thousands of territorial tribes that fiercely protected the floors they occupied, and none of them was particularly happy with a large group barging in on their turf and occupying their buildings. She had sent envoys to negotiate treaties with them, and to explain their plight and intentions. Most of the time, her people returned empty-handed. A couple of times, they didn't come back at all.

Whatever wasn't occupied by the native Mist Isle tribes, nature claimed. Sometimes, it was just a few floors, other times, entire buildings, but as the Elfreth moved deeper into the island, they often had to cut through thick vegetation thriving inside the buildings. What once had been offices, condominiums, warehouses, and factories were now jungles and tribal lands, nests for cat-like predators and other variety of subhuman species. Sometimes, especially on the lower levels, it was flowing rivers and waterfalls.

Finally, desperate to find shelter from the elements and get deeper into the jungle of buildings that appeared more structurally sound, Elise made the difficult decision to order the Elfreth to force their way into the nearest intact building. The tribe was able to occupy two lower floors of one of the gigantic skyscrapers along the shore of the East River. Their hold on the floors was tenuous at best. Just to maintain the perimeter required dozens of guardians to stand watch at all times.

Elise stood at the barricaded entrance to the west stairwell and watched as six guardians pushed back a group of raiders that had come in from one of the floors above. The incursions were coming from every side.

Nature had also turned on them for invading its space. Sometimes, the raiders came in the form of aggressive packs of wild animals or strange humanoid creatures. Everything living here seemed instinctively trained to kill and was very good at doing so. The attacks came at all times, during the night, during the day, sometimes in single groups, sometimes several at once. Elise actually witnessed two sets of raiders fighting each other for the privilege of raiding the Elfreth. It was insane.

Sometimes the attackers came in twos and threes, other times in packs of fifty. Rarely were the forces large enough to truly threaten the Elfreth, but by the end of the first week, the entire tribe was physically and mentally drained.

"Pino is hurt, and his team is exhausted," she said, grabbing Rima by the shoulder. "Get backups in to replace them. Tell Eriao to assemble another team to deploy into the rotation. In fact, tell him we need shorter rotations."

"But Oldest—"

"I don't care if that means more shifts. People need to rest."

Elise watched the girl run off to carry out her orders. With their short-wave-comm units no longer working in this mist, the Elfreth had resorted to using couriers. With the amount of work on Elsie's plate, that meant she was running Rima ragged. At this rate, she might need to get a few more assistants.

She stepped aside as replacements relieved poor Pino's team. Three of his six guardians had suffered injuries. The barricade, erected from furniture, metal drums, and chunks of walls, had saved them from the worst of it, but they came out of their shift with several minor cuts and ugly bruises.

Elise looked out the window up at the rest of the city. Manhattan looked so different from 2097. She remembered being there just a few weeks before her assignment on the Nutris Platform. It felt like an eternity ago.

A thunderstorm brewed overhead, though it was too hazy outside to actually see the clouds above. Thick sheets of brown water ran over the building and the streets below. Swaths of water poured through the uncovered windows, seeping into the floor and creating streams that flowed the length of the hallways. The street below was completely submerged in the brown muck they called an ocean in the present, no doubt courtesy of the steadily rising water levels and Earth Plague that covered the rest of the planet.

Above them, the city seemed to go up forever. Manhattan had built upon itself, adding more and more floors. The building they were in was originally only thirty floors. Now it was over 120. It was as if they had stacked several buildings on top of each other.

Hundreds of bridges connected the buildings together at different floors, making the entire city look like a chaotic three-dimensional spiderweb. It was these corridors that all the denizens of the downtown traveled through. Right now, just occupying two floors, the Elfreth had to guard two main entrances, four bridges, and six stairwells.

Sasha came running up to her. "Elise, Oldest Franwil needs you downstairs."

Elise gave the barricade one last look before leaving. Now she knew why Franwil, the former leader's wife and the logical candidate to lead the Elfreth, had refused to take the mantle. Putting out one fire after another was exhausting.

"Oldest Elise," Franwil said, even before she stepped foot into the main room. "Our supplies of grain are low. We will need to send another expedition to hunt again. Also, we have used up the last of our quaro seeds. Those will need to be traded for once your chronman returns."

Elise noticed the change of expression in Franwil's eyes. *If* the chronman returns. Elise bit her lips. If he didn't, they were all doomed. The list went on and on. By the time Franwil was done, Elise had a headache. More mouths to feed, no place to farm, and under siege from all sides. On top of all of this, she had a cure to find for the Earth Plague.

"Oldest Elise," Pino called, limping hurriedly into the room. "The Five Pointers are attacking the southeastern stairwell and have broken into the hallways. Ramoc is asking for reinforcements."

"Damn it!" Everything was falling apart. Elise reacted quickly. "Sasha, wake the Fenwicks tribe to shore the line. Rima, run to the north side and tell the guards at the stairwells there to watch their rear. Make sure they maintain their positions." She turned back to Pino. "I'll be along shortly."

Franwil walked up to Elise and put a hand on her shoulder. "You haven't slept in two days. The rest of the guardians can take care of it. You're no use to the Elfreth, nor are you closer to finding a cure for the planet, if you die fighting on the barricades."

Elise let out a deep breath. Franwil was right. It wasn't like she was much use to them during the battles anyway. Still, it was what Qawol, the tribe's former leader, had done. She learned early on that being a leader was not only making the right decisions, but being there to inspire those who follow you.

"I'll stay safe," she replied, signaling to Pino to lead the way.

Elise was also one of the few who wore a wrist beam. She had tried to pass it on to another of the guardians who would put it to better use, but James would have none of that, saying there was no chance he would let her ever walk anywhere unarmed. She lightly touched the six bands on her wrist before following several Elfreth to the upper level. Over the past few months, she had gotten adept at using the wrist beams. The very violence she used to loathe she now depended on far too often.

She joined a small group of guardians and made her way to where the fighting had spilled into the hallways and individual rooms. This building used to be a residential high-rise, so there were dozens of smaller rooms. After the Elfreth plugged the breach, they would have to clear each room out one by one.

Right as her group reached the upper level, they swept into a fire-fight. A stream of Pointers met them head-on, trying to push them off the floor. Elise dropped one with a careful shot to the chest and pulled back, being careful to stay out of melee range. The rest of the Elfreth took up a defensive position near the center of the room and began to push outward. Elise directed the guardians to where they were needed, much like Qawol used to. To be honest, she had no idea what in Gaia she was doing, but it was what they expected of her, so she tried her best.

It took them until sundown to push the Pointers back up the stair-well and clear the rest of the floor. The final count was six dead and five times that number injured. The raiders had also managed to steal several crates of food and a cache of ammo.

Elise reminded herself to tell Eriao to keep more guards on the stor-age rooms. This was the second time in as many days that the raiders were able break past the barricades and steal supplies. The Elfreth were weak-ening. Every day, there were a few more injured and a little less food. If something didn't change soon, the tribe wouldn't survive the year.

Franwil met her at the entrance to the stairs. She gave the area a glance and threw on her wrap, ordering the group of men and women to lay out cots. As Elise went to get help, the Oldest stopped her.

"You, to bed, girl," she said sternly. Then she was gone, walking to the west side of the floor, barking orders as she went.

Elise waited a beat until the Oldest was out of sight. Then she rolled up her sleeves and went to the east side of the building to help set up tri-age there. It was going to be a long night caring for the injured.

"Oldest," Rima called, running up to her. "Mangil says the tide is mov-ing in and flooding the lower floor."

Elise cursed. This was the last thing they needed. If the bottom floor was lost, that meant the Elfreth had only one floor under their control. It wasn't enough space.

"Get the stockpiles moved to a dry place! Pull all our people up. In-form Eriao that we no longer have a bottom escape route and to double the guards to the upstairs stairwells and to the bridge. Tell him to meet me at the northwest stairwell. Hurry, before we lose everything!"

Instead of tending to the wounded, she headed to the topmost barri-cade, where the Five Pointers and the Elfreth stared each other down across a double-wide set of stairs. Elise pushed her way past the guards and studied the dozen armed Pointers staring back.

"Tell your chief I wish to speak with him." Her voice echoed up the stairwell.

A few seconds later, one of them responded, "The King tells you to come up if you want to hear his words."

The King, huh? Someone had an ego. She felt rough hands on her shoulder. "Don't even think about it, Oldest," Eriao whispered behind her. "These people are not to be trusted."

"The ground floor is flooding," she whispered back. "Can we fight our way through?"

"Yes, but it will be difficult. The Five Pointers is a large tribe."

Elise looked at the sharp stakes angled down at them. Not just difficult, but bloody. Behind her, two teams of guardians came into the stairwell. They were soon followed by more Pointers joining the already-crowded stairs from above.

"How about the other stairwells?" she asked.

"All able-bodied guardians are in place," Eriao said. "We just need one of the groups to break through and hold the entrances to the Pointer floors. The rest of our people can reroute up that path then."

"Other options?"

"We can fight our way up or cross one of the bridges to the next building."

"What is across the bridge?"

"A dense and wild jungle. It will be hard going to cut our way through."

The group of Pointers above them began to bang the floor with their weapons in unison, echoing beats all around the walls. Several hurled insults down at them. Someone threw a rock that would have hit Elise if Eriao hasn't pulled her back. The ones behind her barked orders for the guardians to remain calm. The tension increased as the two groups reared at each other.

"Your will, Oldest?" Eriao said, positioning himself in front of her. He held a spear in one hand and a pistol in the other.

Elise could feel the violence lingering in the air. Did she want to order her people to attack another tribe? They were supposed to be fighting the Co-op, not each other. The Elfreth were the ones who were encroaching on the Pointers' territory to begin with.

"You should retreat to safety," Eriao said, leading Elise by the arm. "This is no place for the Oldest."

Someone above threw a spear that clattered against the back wall. Someone on her side threw one back, bouncing it harmlessly against the barricade. Men and women shouted up and down at each other as the space between the two groups shrank. Long spears jabbed downward at them, daring them to get closer. She felt helpless as her guardians moved up the stairs.

"Stop!" she yelled.

No one paid any attention to her. She grabbed Eriao by the collar and screamed in his ear, "Pull back!"

"Oldest?" For a second, he looked uncertain, as if he were going to disobey her order. Then he nodded. He turned toward the two teams. "Back to the bottom of the stairs. Inform the other stairwells."

Elise signaled Rima closer. "Tell Franwil we're packing and crossing the bridge. We leave tonight."

"It might not be better there, Oldest," Eriao warned.

"It can't be worse than this," she replied. Elise didn't know if standing down was the right call. She just knew that attacking definitely felt wrong. In any case, she was the Oldest, and this was her decision to make. She only hoped that it was the right one.

TWELVE

A Solution

James felt a thump on his face; he chose to ignore it. A few more followed, but they felt distant and light. He stayed within this colorless womb, floating in blissful awareness of being unconscious. In the distance, he could hear the buzzing of voices, soft, irritating, but easily ignored. He couldn't feel a thing. The numbness, he relished it. He had somehow lost all sense of time in here as well, wherever here was. It was ironic, he thought, to have that happen. He had spent his entire career, most of his life, in fact, keeping track of time. Now that he had let go and stopped worrying about it, he felt so free.

He hiccupped and suddenly had trouble taking in a breath. That was strange; he shouldn't be breathing at all. However, as he continued to choke, his sense of time returned. He could tick the seconds that he was drowning. His body spasmed and he woke.

James opened his eyes and saw a steady stream of water pouring onto his face like a waterfall. It went into cavities it had no right to go up and he sat up choking and coughing. He waved his hand up to ward the water away. Instead, the downpour came down even harder.

"Cut it out," he sputtered.

He stood up and slipped, falling back into the shower and banging his already-throbbing head against the wall. With a growl, he reached up and grabbed the first thing his fingers got close to, which in this case, was the front of someone's shirt. His eyes focused and he saw a grizzled-looking thug holding him down. They were trying to drown him! James clawed at the man's arms and face desperately, but was too weak to buck him off.

His would-be killer looked to the side. "You want me to keep going?"

"I guess you should let him up," a voice replied. Wait, that sounded like Grace.

The water spout stopped, and rough hands hauled him to his feet. He wiped his eyes with his wet sleeve and tried to stand, slipping once more as he shivered in the freezing water. Someone threw a towel at his face.

"Is there anything else, ma'am?" the thug asked.

"That will be all, Mr. Jae. Thank you for your assistance, and please give my regards to Mr. Hubbs. For your troubles."

"Yes, madam."

A few seconds later, Grace and James were alone in their residence. She looked livid. "A bunch of Puck Pirates, led by a snot of a man who called himself Hubbs, dropped you off unceremoniously at our doorsteps. He muttered some nonsense about using up your one strike, and that we had until the end of the week." She put her hands on her hips. "Tell me he isn't saying what I think he's saying."

James nodded glumly, though inside he was relieved. That meant Grace had no choice now but to agree to go home. "Guess we're wrapping it up."

She saw through him, as she always did. "You'd like that, wouldn't you? Well, for once you didn't fully screw things up. Something interesting fell in my lap."

"Is it an Orion cruiser ladened with Titan sources? Otherwise, I think we're up the abyss with our options."

Grace smirked. "Remember that chron database access hack I was playing those three bids on? Well, one backed out. One abruptly left the colony last night—something about being involved with a string of exo-chain robberies. The last, now without any competition, is trying to lowball the price. The seller is pissed and just wants to get it off his hands without losing scratch. It's a pretty good deal, so I decided to buy it for our own uses."

"That really doesn't help us," James replied. "Read-only access hacks are uncommon, but it's finding a salvager who can run the jobs that's the hard part."

"That's where you're wrong," Grace said. She sat down in the chair on the other end of the room. He could tell when she was exceptionally proud of herself, which she actually was quite often. Usually she deserved it, though. "I had a client come to me the other day. A particularly unpleasant gentleman. He was on leave from his job and wanted a bulk supply of various narcotics to distribute when he returned to his place of employment."

Grace paused as James stripped off his wet clothes. She leered, and all of a sudden, he was her pet back on the *High Marker* again.

Blushing, he turned his back to her and pulled out a set of dry clothing. "Go on."

"Well, pet," she purred. "I arranged for the sale of the narcotics and as I was making sure it couldn't get traced back to me, I found out that my client is a prison guard on Nereid. Something about all this rang a bell. I couldn't quite put my finger on it."

A memory nagged at James as well. Then he realized what she was getting at. He spun around. "No!"

Grace had a wicked grin on her face. "Yes, James. Yes."

"I'm putting my foot down. There has to be another way."

She shrugged. "You can put your foot down if it makes you feel better, pet. There is no other option, especially now that you've gotten us kicked out of Bulk's Head. In fact, since I've already spent most of our scratch purchasing the access hack, the plan's already in motion. The guard's transport is leaving in two days, which gives us just enough time. I paid to have him followed. Here's what we're going to do."

James stomped and dragged his feet a couple of times as he emphasized his displeasure with Grace's plan, but, as always, it was useless. Eventually, he resorted to just saying no over and over again until Grace mentioned Sasha and promised to find a doctor from the past who could help her. Reluctantly, he capitulated.

A few hours later, after he had sobered up, he found himself back in the Drink Anomaly, staring at a large individual sitting in a corner booth. He still hated the idea, but Grace had bashed his head in with her logic and twisted his heart with shame. In the end, he realized it was a good plan—their only plan, really—no matter what his personal feelings were for this.

The guard was drinking hakash, a mineral-based liquor popular with the outer colonies. James couldn't stand the stuff; to him, it tasted like dirt. James ordered a hakash of his own and brought it to the man's table.

He slid into the bench across from the guy and studied his target. He was older, large and heavyset, the kind of guy who would need to pay for two seats on a transport. He also looked hard as metal. The multiple scars on his head told James he had a history of violence. The way his eyes shifted constantly told James even more.

The big man wore a gray meshed body-conforming uniform that adjusted to its wearer. James wondered how intelligent the clothing was. Probably not too much, considering how low-tech the guy's job was. Still, it was something he'd have to take into consideration. No bands on his wrists, no firearm, either, but he had a holstered melee weapon, a pain stick or an electro jag knife.

The guy didn't react when James invaded his space. He simply took another sip of his hakash and studied James, a potential new threat. He didn't try to act friendly or puff his chest out. James appreciated the honesty. The two men sat in silence, waiting for the other to make the first move.

After a few minutes, the gray-uniformed man must have noticed that James hadn't touched his drink yet. His body noticeably relaxed, and he downed the rest of his hakash. He placed the empty cup off to the side and leaned back as James pushed his forward. The guy sniffed his newly acquired drink, lifted it up momentarily toward James, and then took a sip. James appreciated that sign of respect as well. He sort of liked the guy. Pity.

Once the big man put the cup down, he nodded. "Son? Nephew? Lover?"

"Son," James replied.

"Name?"

"Let me buy you another drink first."

For the next few hours, James chatted the man up. His name was Raets. He was a veteran of the Crimean Conflicts of 2502 and 2507, both times on the losing side, which was pretty interesting, because picking the losing side twice in a five-sided war required the wrong kind of extraordinary luck. It could also mean outcomes meant little in Raets's financial decisions. He was a mercenary in the truest sense.

Raets took up security after the contract expired, resorting to more lucrative work escorting low-level wealthy who could afford only one or two guards. Those were generally the most dangerous of security assignments, since the lone bodyguard was usually the first mark to take out in any hit. He left that line of work in 2510 after a string of attacks by the Saturn's Ring Bandits left his employer airlocked out into space and him held prisoner for two months. When the security company refused to pay his ransom, the Ring Bandits made an arrangement with him directly. Now he worked as a guard for the Amazon Corporation.

Raets wouldn't go into details what that arrangement was, but James had a pretty good idea. The Ring Bandits were one of the largest and most active pirate groups, rivaling the Puck Pirates. They had tens of thousands of men operating throughout the solar system, and thousands rotting throughout the penal colonies. No doubt he worked guard for the Ring Bandits more than he worked for Amazon. He had taken leave for the past month to make his annual visit to his family on Mars and was on his way back to Nereid. He was scheduled to hop on the next supply freighter departing for the penal colony.

By the time the Drink Anomaly closed for the night, one hour before it was to reopen for the morning, James had studied his target nonstop for almost four hours. He believed he could talk the same way Raets did, imitate his mannerisms, and use the same vocal tics the man used. James's paint band had long finished copying the man's features. All he needed to do now was acquire the small details, the nuances that made Guard Raets, Raets.

They were kicked out of the bar and walked together down the corridor to the general residents' quarter, James trailing just a few steps behind the unsteady Raets. The big man held his liquor relatively well, considering how much he drank. James had sent him nine hakashes and who knew how many he had drunk before James arrived. Raets favored his right leg slightly and had a tendency to swing his arms when he walked. He also tended to hug the wall, which was fairly typical of someone working security.

Raets side-eyed him as they stopped in front of his residence unit. "Why are you following me? I don't fuck men in case you're wondering."

"Just making sure you get home all right, friend," James said. "After all, you're my contact to my son. Can't let anything happen to you, now can I?"

Raets's eyes narrowed. "You never told me the name of your boy. What do you want exactly? Something smuggled in? A letter? Look, jackass, give me a name and tell me what you want to give him."

James shrugged. "The package is large. I'm sure it'll cost me significant scratch, but I'm sure it'll be worth your while. Can we arrange a time tomorrow for me to show you?"

Raets's eyes narrowed. "Hang on a second."

He opened the door to his residence and disappeared inside. A second later, James doubled over as something hard rammed into his abdomen. The initial pain from being stabbed gave way to even more pain as volts of electricity coursed through his body, sending him stumbling backward. Raets charged out of the dark residence, holding a pain stick in his hand. He brought it down on James's crown, knocking him down to the ground.

"You almost had me going, jackass," Raets said. "Then I realized you actually don't give a shit about anyone in prison. Let me give you a piece of advice. Next time you try to pull a con like this, the first thing you do is ask about your son's welfare. Shit like how's he doing? Is he eating enough? Is he anyone's bitch? Whose cock is he sucking?"

Raets kicked James in the stomach, hard enough to bounce his entire body off the ground. James's head smashed against the far wall as the pain stick clipped him behind the ear. "Otherwise, it comes across like you don't give any shits. Who do you work for? Internal affairs? For Amazon? Did the warden send you?" The pain stick flew at him again. This time, James brought his forearm up just in time.

The impact jolted his entire body; he hoped he hadn't broken a bone. For a second, he considered powering on his exo, but he refrained. It hadn't come to that yet. Bulk's Head security would detect the exo within seconds in this residential area. If security came sweeping down on them, he could lose the mark. The risk of being detected was far too high. Also, a small part of him was still hoping he wouldn't have to kill Raets. The man was technically innocent, though with each passing blow, James was starting to care less about that.

Raets swung the pain stick again, no doubt intending to finish this one-sided affair and crack James's head open. James swung his head to the side at the last second just as the stick came crashing down, striking the grating hard enough to chip metal. He grabbed Raets's arm and yanked, pulling the man off balance. With both hands on the man's wrist, James leveraged himself to his feet, and the two struggled for control of the pain stick.

Raets was strong; far stronger than James. The two banged back and forth along the walls. Without his exo, James didn't have the strength to just pry the pain stick away. Raets must have noticed.

"You're painted up, jackass," Raets snarled. "That or you are weak."

He swung to his left and threw James into the wall. Then he swung right and did the same to the opposite wall. Sensing James's grip slacken, Raets lifted his arm up and threw it down, trying to slam him onto the ground. Instead, James got his feet under him planted against the wall and pushed off, barreling them both into Raets's residence.

Off balance, Raets pivoted right and tried to swing him off. James's body destroyed two levels of shelves and swept the contents off a third. He swung his legs around and managed to scissor Raets's head between them. He squeezed them together as he clung to Raets's arms. The big man, mouth full of James's thigh, roared and charged, smashing him into the wall.

James thought he heard a rib pop, but kept pushing his legs together. Raets smashed him into the wall two more times before he began to weaken. Finally, after what seemed like an eternity, he dropped to one knee, and the two of them crashed onto the floor. The big man continued to paw at James's legs until he finally went limp.

Gasping for breath, James pulled himself from underneath Raets. He stumbled forward and closed the door before anyone walked by. The neighbors had most definitely heard the ruckus, but in this sort of place, no one stuck their head out and asked for trouble. By the time he got back to the unconscious man and checked his pulse, Raets was already stirring. The last thing James wanted to do now was go another three rounds with the giant. For a second, James considered just killing him. It would be merciful and painless. It was also tactically the right decision.

James wrapped his hands around Raets's neck. A quick twist would end it. He stopped himself from following through. The guy, no matter how crooked or bad, was just trying to get by.

"Black abyss," he muttered. "You're losing your edge."

That wasn't quite true. He was in denial. He had lost it months ago. A year ago, he wouldn't have cared whether or not he killed Raets, that Tier-5 Mong or those monitors. Now, he just couldn't stomach it anymore.

James unhooked his cryo band and linked it around Raets's wrist. Within a few seconds, the big man was snoring lightly. He took the next hour combing through the apartment and stripping Raets of his uniform. Using the real thing would give him a lot more flexibility if needed. When he was finished, he left the residence, giving Raets one last look. The cryo band would have enough power to keep him asleep and sustained for two weeks. That should be long enough for James to get to Nereid and finish the job.

"Sleep tight, big guy," he said, hurrying back to the studio.

He found Grace packing when he returned to their residence.

"You look like shit," Grace said. "At least more than usual."

"Hello to you as well."

"Did you find what you needed?" Grace asked.

He held up Raets's duffel bag. "I leave in two days. Wait for me at the Kuiper Belt. I've already put in the exact coordinates in the *Frankenstein*. Are you sure you'll be all right piloting her?"

"Really, James? Did you just ask the Mother of Time if she could pilot a vessel she designed and built?" she scoffed. "I'm sure I'll be fine."

James had his doubts. The *Frankenstein* was difficult to control, built from a hodgepodge of ships not known for their maneuverability. "I guess we're set then."

Grace smirked and tsked mockingly. "Oh pet, I always knew if you didn't change your ways, you'd end up in prison."

THIRTEEN

339

Inmate 339 walked through the narrow passageway, his eyes alert and constantly scanning the shadowed crevices on both sides. His feet felt every uneven bump and groove of the etched stone, worn down by years of daily traffic. He had been walking—bouncing, more like, in this reduced gravity—through the lower subsections of the prison, known as the dungeon, for the better part of an hour now.

630 and 461 trailed a few steps behind in a single file. 630 could competently watch his back but 461 would be worthless in these cramped quarters. He was here more as a visual deterrent than anything else. Maybe they could avoid the song and dance altogether for once. Probably not, though. Things didn't work like that here in Amazon Penal Colony 3.

The small group turned the corner and continued down a steep slope. These tunnels ran deep throughout Nereid. The penal colony carved a way to wherever the mining was best. A string of dim lights lined the ceiling of the pathway, spaced every forty or so meters, just bright enough to tell 339 what was directly in front of him, but not much more. If someone was trying to ambush him, this would be the place to do it. This was the world he lived in now.

Along the way, he passed a cluster of other inmates using energy picks to chip away the dense top layers to where the low-grade mineral deposits or gas pockets lay. The junk inside the moon wasn't worth much, but for the Amazon Corporation, which was in the prison business anyway, the side venture of putting their convicted slaves to work was just an added bonus. It also kept the sheep too tired to cause trouble.

339 saw a body lay crumpled in a heap at the end of one of the excavated grooves. He signaled to the other two and waited until they took up positions on either side of him. He bent and rolled the body over. It was still warm, if barely. The pulse was weak. Irritated, 339 glared at the half-dozen men hacking away at the rock. "506 is still alive. Why hasn't he been taken to an aid station?"

The nearest inmate didn't even bother looking his way. "Good riddance. Old man was holding us back. On his last leg anyway. Besides, our cart's only half full. Not gonna lose a day's worth of digging and get half rations for his sorry ass."

339 stood. "All of you, pack your shit and move him to an aid station. Now."

Most of this gang of workers ignored him. The Amazon guards never wandered down here. With the way the penal colony was set up, supervision wasn't really necessary. You did what you were told, starved, or were jettisoned out into space. Other than that, the inmates ran their own hierarchy.

"When did they start promoting inmates to guards?" One of the inmates shrugged. "You can take your orders and kiss——"

The man next to him grabbed his shoulder and spun him around. The loudmouth swallowed his words, looking more worried than frightened. "Oh, didn't realize it was you. Come on, lads. Pack it up."

In less than a minute, the entire group had gathered their gear and loaded the unconscious man onto the cart. 339 checked the body again before they began pushing it back up the passage. He took out his pack of heater cigs and handed one to each of the workers. "Each of you take this, and give one to 506 when he wakes. If he pulls through, you'll get a quarter ration as well."

The loudmouth shook his head. "Don't sweat it, 339. I know I owe you. I'll see to the old geezer." He managed to look ashamed.

339 watched them until they reached the end of the corridor and turned the corner. He turned back to his two guys. "Let's go."

630 grinned. "More polite than a small-dicked guard with a pain stick."

339 grunted and gestured for them to follow. Time was running out.

Hopefully it wasn't too late. The three of them continued deeper under-ground past several more clusters of inmates until they reached the far end of the tributaries, where the smooth walls gave way to more natural jagged edges. They left the last of the ceiling lights behind as they de-scended into the mine.

This was the farthest reach of the prison, almost an hour's walk from the main colony. The air down here was the hardest to breathe, the tem-perature always near freezing, and if someone was injured this far out, the odds of them making it back for help were slim. 339 should know; he had been one of them just six months ago.

Inmates who died down here sometimes weren't found for weeks. The fodders were always sent down, with the odds of them surviving the first month less than half. The longer they were tenured or the better they worked, the closer they were allowed to mine near the penal colony. The small group proceeded to one of the more recently excavated tunnels. The cart tracks ended a hundred meters in, and the walls were all virgin.

"Split up. Three-hundred-step limit. Don't engage," he ordered, point-ing to the two side tunnels on the right.

The three of them spread out, moving through the darkness with their shoulder mounts the only source of light. He heard the other men call out intermittently.

"Sixteen steps."

"Twelve steps."

His fellows continued to call out, their voices bouncing around the walls, fading the farther away they got. Within two minutes, 339 found himself alone. Most inmates hated the tributary tunnels. The blackness down here often was suffocating and easily disoriented the senses. For 339, who spent the majority of his life working in zero gravity, the wide expanse of space wasn't too dissimilar from this darkness. In both cases, a person had to turn off or filter out the senses that weren't necessary so that he could focus on what was important. Otherwise, their environment—either the terrifying vastness of space or the crushing darkness of a tunnel deep underground—threatened to overwhelm.

The one thing Inmate 339 couldn't turn off was his mind, and in these dark winding tunnels, there wasn't much else to do but put one foot in front of the other, and think. Thinking was often the enemy. A man could drive himself crazy thinking about all the mistakes he had made in his life. Many had after spending prolonged periods of time down here.

339 shook his head. This was his lot now, his penance for his morality. The best way he could honor it was to make the most of it. Those bastards thought they could take everything from him. They had tried and almost succeeded. He almost lost it the first few days down here. Then he remembered who he was. What he was. That was something no one could take. Which was why he was down here right now.

Behind him, he heard it. A bell. Two rings, followed by a pause, and then another ring. Clear and precise. One of his guys had found what they were looking for. 339 hurried back, moving in the darkness more haphazardly than he should have been, occasionally stubbing his toe in his thin plastic shoes and stumbling over sudden changes in the elevation.

By the time he got back to the main tributary tunnel, both 630 and 461 were waiting for him. 461, with the bell in his hand, signaled for them to follow. He led them down the second tunnel on the right, which angled to an upward climb before flattening out into a long passageway.

"How many, and are we too late?" 339 asked.

461 shook his head. "Looked like five or six Apexes and three fodders."

"Must have taken a while to drag them all the way there," 630 added.

A few minutes later, they heard the rhythmic sound of fists pounding flesh, a smack and thud that echoed against the hard rock walls. It was followed by groans and laughter, and then more thuds.

339 and his companions rounded the corner and came upon a group of inmates beating on three others. They must have just started, since only one was unconscious while the other two were curled up in fetal positions as the bullies towering over them rained down blows.

339 had had to deal with this when he first arrived as well. Except when it happened, it was seven of the Apexes against just two. 339 killed two that day and sent three others to the infirmary. The fodder fighting alongside him didn't make it. That was the day his legend here at the penal colony was born.

He coughed.

Half of the Apexes taking a break from the beat-down looked his way. One of them stopped, but the other three kept going.

"Guess we're done here." He recognized 793's voice. He was the ringleader among them, and incidentally one of the men 339 had sent to the infirmary that day.

793's group sauntered past 339 as if nothing were the matter. These beatings, known as welcome parties, were a weekly occurrence, something that happened every time a new shipment of inmates came in. This was how the Apexes maintained their control and fear over the eastern blocks of Colony 3. Most of the time, 339 was too late to stop them. By the time he found out about one and made it down here, the beatings were done, and the only thing left to do was pick up the broken bodies of the new inmates and drag them to the infirmary. This time, he was almost too late. Almost.

He stuck his hand into 793's chest as the guy tried to pass him. "This is the last time."

793 batted it away. "Whatever, suck-space. Just because you're some ex-cop doesn't mean you own the place. You stop us when you find us."

Before he could take another step, 339 leaned forward, collapsed his arm, and threw an elbow that shattered the man's cheekbone. 793 continued to flip in circles as he flew backward in the light gravity.

339 saw a flash to the side and juked left as a body came crashing toward him. One of his hands grabbed a forearm and the other, a part of a shirt, and he spun downward, throwing the Apex in a circular motion until his momentum carried him straight up. 339 let go and watched as the man slammed into the ceiling.

Another came at him. This time, the inmate had a metal shank, which he swung in wide arcs. These guys obviously weren't the Apex's best. 339 caught his wrist and bent it at an awkward angle until the Apex dropped the shank. 339 slammed the inmate's face down onto the ground and finished him off with a kick to the jaw.

Still another attacked. This time, 630 and 461 took care of the Apex. 630 pinned him down while fat 461 sat on top of him. 339 looked at the remaining two Apexes huddling in fear. "Pick up your trash and take them back to your boss. Tell 881 that if I find out about one more of these incidents, I'll take your entire crew out."

He kept the quivering bullies under his steely gaze as they struggled to drag their four companions out of the room. Good thing gravity was light here, though he was willing to bet those four were going to have pretty bad scrapes and cuts by the time they woke up. Not to mention the broken bones he had probably given two of them.

He pointed at the two new inmates slowly getting to their feet. "Help those two back. I'll take care of the last."

339 walked over to the unconscious inmate and shined his light on his face. It was a mess of blood and dirt covered by thin wisps of gray hair. The man's cheeks were hollow, his skin crackly. Though he was saved this time, 339 feared this man's tenure on Nereid wouldn't be long. He bent over and checked the body. Nothing was broken. Then he got onto a knee and tapped the man gently on the face.

"You're safe now," he said. He watched as the man's eyes fluttered open and recoiled at the sight of 339. The fodder tried to scramble away. 339 held up his hands up. "Easy, friend. The Apexes are gone now." He stood up and offered his hand. "What's your number?"

The older man reluctantly accepted it and got up. "I'm Bonner. I'm not supposed to be here. They said I planned my wife's death. It isn't true. I was already an executive on Europa. Why would I wish to harm her? It's a terrible mistake. I love my wife. I would never do anything to harm her."

339 waited until the man got the rambling out of his system. It was common occurrence here. Every single one of the fodders felt the need to spout their innocence to the first person willing to listen.

When the elderly man had talked himself out, 339 shrugged. "I don't care, friend. One thing I do know is that no one gets sent to Nereid without deserving it. Now, what's your number?"

"I told you. It's—"

"In the penal colony, we go by our numbers. We're dead to the outside world, and they're dead to us. I'm 339."

The fodder looked miserable as he tried to recall his number. "I'm . . . I think I'm 552."

"All right then, 552, you have a long walk ahead of you. If you miss evening rations, you're not eating until the new shift."

He helped the new inmate turn on his shoulder-mounted light, and guarded his eyes with his hands when the fodder shined the light at his face.

552 gave a start. "You look familiar. Have we met? What's your name?"

It wasn't a surprise to 339 that the man might have seen him before. After all, his face at one point was plastered on all the vids throughout the solar system. And though only six months had passed, it felt like a lifetime ago. Several of the inmates had mentioned it before, though none had ever identified him. He would prefer to keep it that way.

339 turned around and beckoned 552 to follow. "Let's go."

The elderly man hobbled after him, leaning against one of the walls for support. "No. Your face. Your voice. I remember now."

For a moment, 339 considered acknowledging it. It was a name he had not spoken since the day he stepped foot on Nereid. Maybe it would bring a little of his former self back, a little of his old life. It would be good to remember that he had not always been just a number.

No, the past was dead. This was who he was now.

He turned to face the elderly man. "My name is 339. Get moving."

FOURTEEN

AGGRESSION

At dawn, the Co-op massed their forces along the northern shore of the Harlem River. Six days ago, a hound pack had caught scent of the savages passing through a section called Richmond Hill during a random patrol. They had managed to obtain visual confirmation of the temporal anomaly's savages and followed them all the way west until they lost track of them in a densely populated area called Queens. Their last sighting indicated the savages were heading directly west into the Mist Isle.

At the time, Kuo did not have the resources to invade the island. With the nature of the EMP cloud, they would be without modern surveillance or communications, and would have to operate in low visibility. The bomb that was dropped on the city during the final days of the Core Conflicts had only been used once, and its lingering effects haunted the island to this day.

The heavy concentration of savages in this area was problematic as well. She had had insufficient manpower to deal with such a large force until recently. Now that Young had given her the five hundred monitors she requested and Valta had added an equal number of troopers, the Co-op was finally ready to conquer the island and root out the anomaly. Kuo stood on the roof of a mid-rise on the edge of shore and looked across the water at the mysterious and shrouded Mist Isle. She could just make out the faint outlines of the buildings as a bubble of thick gray fog enveloped the island.

Her forces would have to move carefully. Manhattan was a three-dimensional maze of dense skyscrapers connected by stairs and bridges that spanned upward for hundreds of meters.

There were far too many nooks and crannies and holes for this temporal anomaly to hide in the isle. She intended to establish a foothold at the northern end of the isle and then sweep south, taking territory, floor by floor, building by building, block by block. Couple that with the Valkyrie fleet blockading the island, it should only be a matter of time before they flushed the temporal anomaly and her tribe out of hiding.

Kuo signaled to Ewa standing next to her. "Commence the attack."

That would be the last order her invading forces would receive until evening. With the EMP fog, all her units were autonomous, having co-ordinated tactical plans the night before. This meant there would be little room for making battlefield adjustments, but she doubted that would be necessary. They were fighting savages, after all.

A few minutes later, an attack force of three hundred leapt across the Harlem River while her ground forces moved across a bridge once known as the Broadway. Today's objective was to capture a foothold down to Dyckman Street. Once secured, supplies would be ferried in to establish a base of operations.

The first of her forces hit the northernmost skyscraper, a building with eighty floors and nine bridges connecting to adjacent structures. By her scouts' estimations, thirty tribes could be living in this building, and there could be as many as two thousand savages to root out. Her troopers and monitors would be constantly surrounded and outnumbered, especially the deeper they penetrated into this dense urban jungle. There was little room for finesse. The Co-op would have to come down on these savages like a hammer and flush them out of their holes.

Her vanguard had no sooner landed on the other side of the harbor than they came under attack. Small-arms fire peppered them from the building. The previously-black windows lit up with yellow bursts of light followed by the sounds of projectile and energy blasts. An explosion erupted off to the side, sending a plume of smoke into the air.

White and blue fields lit the ground and air as Valta troopers engaged the enemy, her ground forces charging into the building through the lower level while those with flight capabilities entered through the windows higher up. Several new explosions signaled the Valkyries and collies joining to the fray. At the same time, several squads of monitors were dropped via collies onto the connecting bridges to secure proper choke points.

"Send second wave," Kuo ordered. "Tell the Valkyries to be careful with their incendiaries. I want all the structures intact. Detain all savage leaders for questioning at the 218th and Ninth facility."

"Yes, Senior." A field of white expanded around Ewa and she took off. Kuo followed suit, launching across the harbor and skimming the side of the building. Behind her, two other securitates followed closely. She barreled into one of the open windows and caught a group of savages while they were trying to fend off troopers coming up from the lower levels.

Three securitates—Valta's elite special ops in full combat exos— against a bunch of subhuman primitives was overkill, but Kuo never did believe in fair odds. A group of the stupid subhumans, some barefoot and dressed in dirty rags, charged her wielding sticks. Kuo stared in contempt as their primitive weapons bounced off her shield. She let a burly man through, dodged the club he swung, and cracked his knees with a well-placed kick. She let another with a sharpened stick charge in. This time, she plucked the weapon right out of his hands—the boy seemed hardly older than a teenager. She reversed the weapon and jammed it into his stomach.

The three of them continued cutting through the enemy's ranks with their thick trunks, smashing a dozen at a time, flinging them across the room, and sometimes through the walls and out of the building. Within a minute of their entry onto the floor, with the chaos they sowed, the savages broke rank and abandoned their positions to flee upstairs. Once the floor was fully secured, any remaining survivors they caught would be taken to the holding pen to await interrogation. Then her forces would repeat the carnage the next floor up, leveling any defense the inhabitants tried to erect.

By the end of the first day, all objectives had been achieved, and the Co-op had established two kilometers of inroads onto the island. The enemy's casualties numbered in the thousands, while the Co-op had lost thirteen. Not all of the savages had fled the captured territories yet. It would take several more hours before they could all be rooted out.

Reports from her hounds began to trickle in. Word of the attack had already reached the tribes to the south. Many were already in full retreat, panicked and fleeing deeper into the island. The chaos sown by just one day was already sending fear and upheaval ahead of their arrival.

Kuo stood on one of the large balconies of a recently captured build-ing and studied the map of the island. There was so much area to cover and she had so few forces. She already predicted the Co-op would en-counter containment issues. Still, she was loath to ask for more re-sources. She looked down at a large open space below where several of her troop pods were corralling a sizable tribe that had recently surren-dered. An idea occurred to her.

She stepped off the balcony and plummeted thirty stories down to the ground below. Half of the street was drowning in water as the tide washed in. This area would be completely submerged by nightfall. She landed with a loud crash onto the cement, sending a ring of air and water outward. Dozens of savages near her pulled away, covering their faces as if fearful of meeting her gaze. She must seem like a god to these mud-dwellers.

Kuo sniffed at her surroundings and increased her atmos levels. During combat situations, she liked to keep those settings low. Atmos dulled many of the senses that were important during combat. She once saw a trainee suffer life-threatening injuries when he had his atmos on full and burned away all his levels because he did not realize he was standing in front of a plasma fire.

She walked into the building and entered a large room that spanned the length and width of the entire floor. It was filled with prisoners sit-ting on their knees lined up in rows. There must have been several hun-dred of these savages trussed up with their hands behind their backs, heads bowed and despondent. Many looked injured; others were lying prone on the floor, either dead or nearly so. Dozens of monitors patrolled their lines, making sure none of the savages acted up or tried to escape. On the far end, savages were being yanked from the lines and dragged up-stairs to the interrogation rooms.

Kuo scowled. What a waste of resources. She saw Ewa directing the troopers and signaled for her to approach. "Find me the leader of this tribe and bring him to me."

Ewa nodded and relayed her orders, and soon, her troopers were bark-ing her commands down the line for the terrified tribesmen to bring

forth their leader. In short order, two of her troopers produced an older-
looking savage with skin more ornately decorated than that of the others.
His face was bloodied and lumpy, a mass of purple flesh dangling off his
skull, and his body was gashed in a dozen places. He seemed hardly able
to stay sitting up. His eyes were alert, though.

Ewa led them upstairs two flights, turning down a long narrow hallway flanked by several smaller rooms. They entered a windowed corner
office with a table and chair in the center. Her troopers grabbed the man
by the arms and pushed him inside. The man fell onto his knees and rolled
onto his back.

"You are this tribe's leader?" Kuo began, towering over him.

He struggled to his feet and bowed. "I can tell by your presence that
you are a chief. I am Principal Holic of the Northwoods tribe occupying
the Heights Block. Formerly." He said the last word without a hint of sarcasm. "These are my people you have captured and now call your own."

Kuo glanced at the tentacles of swirling haze poking into the window
and then back at the principal. "You will be my mouth to your Northwoods. Tell them that we will generously provide food and shelter. In return, they will become productive members of our species by earning
their keep. Their keep will be to perform duties and tasks as I see necessary. If your tribe does what is required, once I have what we need, they
will be free to go. What do you say, Principal?"

Holic took a step back and spat. "You intend to use me to enslave my
people."

"I intend to use you to provide the wisdom your people so desperately
need right now," she said. "My generous offer is immediately rescinded if
there is any insubordination. Disobeying an order is death. Striking one
of my people is death. Understand?"

"Fed and sheltered with our building and our food." Holic shook his
head. "I will not tell my people to bend the knee. The Northwoods are
of no use to you. Please leave us in peace."

The insolence and arrogance of this savage. She wrapped a trunk
around his neck and picked him up until his feet dangled off the floor.
Holic's tattooed face turned red under the layer of grime on his body.
His arms and legs flailed, overturning the chair as he pawed at the thick
translucent strand of energy choking the life out of him. She lifted him
higher until his head was almost touching the ceiling, and then she

dissolved the trunk. He fell, splitting the table in half as he collapsed to the floor. A groan escaped his lips as his chest heaved.

Kuo was impressed at his resiliency. Most spaceborn with their long and brittle bones would have broken something at that high of a drop at this gravity. These savages were hardy, if anything. They would have to be to survive in this abyss-plagued environment. Maybe Valta could put them to better use than extermination. Cheap, sturdy labor was difficult to come by.

Kuo pulled the chair up and sat down in front of Holic. "I believe everything and everyone has value, Principal. Humanity is at a precipice, and as much as I am loathe to admit it, you and your people are still humans. Therefore, I give you an opportunity to help save our race. Help us, be productive, and your people will live. Otherwise, you are all just waste. What do you choose, Principal Holic?"

"Even if I give the command," he said, "my tribe will not follow my words."

"Be more convincing," she said. "Do you want your Northwoods to survive? They will listen to their principal, will they not?"

The principal hesitated, and then he gave her a tilt of his head. "We cannot speak more." Holic turned and sprinted toward the window. He leaped out, a foolish suicide attempt that was immediately stopped by Ewa as she wrapped a trunk around his waist.

"No," Kuo said. "He is a stubborn animal. If he wishes to serve his people no more, honor that request."

Kuo created her own trunk and cut Ewa's off. She leaned out the window and watched as the principal of the Northwoods plummeted to his death. She turned and walked out of the room. "Find the second in command of that tribe and tell him he's their new principal. Relay my orders for him to give to his tribe. If he refuses, send him the way of his predecessor and then find the third. Also, question these Northwoods about the temporal anomaly. It seems news travels fast on the Mist Isle. Someone is bound to have information about her or her tribe's whereabouts."

"How do we do that?" Ewa asked.

Kuo shrugged. "They're savages. Beat it out of them."

Ewa leaned in. "Senior, most of these savages have nothing to do with the temporal anomaly or those we hunt. Perhaps we could find an alternative way of retrieving the information we need, possibly some incentives: food, or offers for resettlement."

Kuo stared Ewa down. "You think I'm being cruel."

Ewa hesitated. "I'm just seeking options, Senior. Surely we can budget or at least request allocation from the corporation . . ."

Kuo stared Ewa down. "Valta is fighting a multifront war against half a dozen corporations. At stake is not only market share and profits, but humanity's survival. Every day, we are all forced to make difficult decisions with dwindling resources. Do you really want to justify a large expense on a horde of nonproductive savages when those resources could be better used on the front line?"

Her second-in-command looked away. "Of course not. I just . . ."

Kuo shook her head. "You think I'm being cruel but the solar system is slowly starving, Ewa. I'm simply a realist. We need strong people to make the hard and difficult decisions. We are the only thing that stands between humanity and extinction. I have to be cruel because the alternative is worse. Now, do you have a problem with my order, Securitate?"

Ewa bowed. "No, Senior. It will be as you ordered."

FIFTEEN

NEREID

The heart of Penal Colony 3 on Nereid was the commune. It was where all the inmates gathered to socialize, where they had their meals, where the wardens provided instructions, and where most of the murders happened. Contrary to its name, there was never anything communal about it. The commune was probably the most dangerous place in the colony.

Considering how little oversight the prison had, 339 was surprised by how few murders actually occured. Part of it was because the inmates generally governed themselves, having naturally formed a social hierarchy for mutual protection and order. The other part was due to the Amazon Corporation's controversial use of poison as a form of punishment.

Punishments at the penal colony consisted of differing levels of poison. A minor infraction resulted in a mild poison that left the inmate weak and debilitated for a few days. Usually, if an inmate had friends and a gang to watch his back, he would come out of the punishment with just a few days of stomach pains and bad cramps. Without support, the inmate would suffer a few days of beatings in his weakened state. More severe crimes were punished with deadlier poisons, sometimes resulting in blindness or loss of limbs.

339 found it interesting that violence and murder weren't heavily penalized, the wardens caring little for human life. What usually led to minor punishments was failure to mine ore, process gas, or perform other

work. Mid-level penalties were given for inconveniencing the guards. The most severe penalties were for insurrection, which led to the inmates' organs being harvested for sale on the organ market.

That evening, during their last few hours of freedom before all the lights shut off and the gates locked down, 339 and the rest of the inmates loyal to him gathered around the northwestern corner of the commune. It was a daily routine for all the inmates to come together for their only meal. There were slightly over four thousand inmates in Colony 3, and all of them were now crammed into a small space designed for no more than three thousand.

The inmates were divided by their loyalties and alliances, each gang falling into its natural hierarchal location with allied gangs sitting close to one another. Strength in numbers, especially when it came to mealtime. Hunger befell the new inmate who did not pledge his loyalty or make friends quickly.

The four corners of the commune were the most desirable, as they afforded any gang the most defensible positions. Currently, 339's People and 881's Apexes, the two largest gangs, were positioned in opposite corners.

The People's rise as one of the dominant gangs was unprecedented. By far the newest power in the ongoing gang wars, the People was only a few months old, and filled with the groupless, weak, and bullied. It was a merger of every single unwanted inmate previously deemed unworthy of a gang. Fortunately, there were many of them.

339 had gathered them all together shortly after his arrival. Within a few weeks, they had coalesced into a cohesive unit with enough numbers and discipline to protect themselves. Within two months, they were able to stake a corner. Now, all other gangs were allied with either the People or the Apexes.

339 watched as those near him ate their dinner, a combination of watery gruel and grainy seeds. 506, the unconscious prisoner he had found the other day, had indeed pulled through. True to his word, 339 had awarded the workers who had brought the man in a quarter ration out of his own meals. He would go hungry tonight, but it was nothing he wasn't used to. If he had to guess, in his six months here on Nereid, he had not eaten every one in five days.

He looked across the room at the Apexes. They were bigger men, better fighters, more savage, and their boss, 881, was a skilled and charismatic leader in his own right. However, the People had more numbers and allies, and new inmates flocked to them daily. 881 was aware that he was losing ground as the scales slowly tipped in the People's favor. 339 feared that war would break soon, one that he knew the People would lose.

As if by some mental connection, 881 glanced his way and their eyes locked. 339 saw the skin around his eyes wrinkle and clench. He felt the man's hatred, suffocating in its weight. His heart twisted in his chest, and he momentarily felt a deep sense of loss. He looked away. It shamed him, for no matter what he did, he would have to break a pledge to keep another.

The lights on the ceiling dimmed twice and the inmates began to disperse. Lockdown came fifteen minutes later. The guards in Colony 3 did not bother making sure inmates were in their cells. Once lockdown occurred, everyone was trapped in whatever room they were in. All heat and oxygen generators in the common areas were shut off. Those caught outside of living quarters would be forced to endure a night of freezing cold or thin air, or both.

The gangs broke up into smaller packs as everyone made their way to their individual blocks and cells. Since the guards didn't bother to check who stayed where, inmates were allowed to switch rooms. Most of the People had taken to Block San, though they would need to expand to Block Si soon.

339 did a quick head count as his people filed through the tight corridors, keeping an eye on members of the more unfriendly gangs that passed too close. Scuffles could break out from the slightest nudges, and the walk back to the cells was treacherous, often leading to shanks in the back. Sometimes, careless inmates would suddenly find themselves alone and cut off from allies. 339 had already survived three such attempts.

An Apex approached. Both 630 and 461, standing guard nearby, intercepted him. The unfriendly raised his hands and sleeves, and did a slow spin as they searched him for hidden weapons. 630 nodded to 339, and he nodded back.

"You owe us for three, Peeps," the Apex whispered. "881 wants you to know we're going to carve it out of your flock. You can't be everywhere, query?"

339 ignored the threat. "You just tell 881 to remember that the fodders are now under my protection. Every single soul that comes through
Hell's Gate. Understand?"

The Apex leaned in. "881 knows you won't fight him. He knows if he
starts, he'll finish. Says you're a little bitch. We all know, coward."

630 lunged for the Apex, but 339 held up a hand. "If you're finished,
dog, go back to your master."

It wasn't news; everyone in Colony 3 knew it, though only 339 and 881
knew why. The three times the two had come face-to-face during full-
scale brawls, he had refused to engage the other boss. Emboldened, 881
had simply become more aggressive, crueler. In every one of those fights,
the People had lost ground and had to retreat. One day, 339 would not be
given the option to retreat, and he would probably die for it.

He watched as the Apex wandered back to his side of the room, then
he turned to 461. "Call all the captains to my cell. We need to meet."

Thirteen minutes later, eleven other men huddled inside 339's four-
bunk room, sitting elbow-to-elbow on the beds and taking up every inch
on the sides as he stood in the center.

"The Apexes are baiting us now. War will soon follow," he said, pacing up and down the narrow aisle. I want riot training for every member
once every three nights. We're not going to win one-on-ones, but we'll
win in gang fights. 630, organize a rotation of standing heavies ready to
move during the day."

630 scribbled on a piece of cloth with charcoal. "Arm them from the
stockpiles?"

339 shook his head. "Not yet. We want the guards on our side."

"Our boys will be at a disadvantage," 461 said.

"The guards have mostly been neutral so far," 339 said. "We don't arm
up until they pick a side."

"Still sounds risky, boss." 630 frowned.

339 tapped his finger on his chin as he paced. Men would die from
this decision. Still, he wanted to win wars, not battles. "We go with numbers for now. I want minimum six gang chains fifty meters apart during
digs in the dungeon. Closest gang to the commune allocates one man to
alert the rest of the People. No fodders go unattended from now on. Get
three for one at all times."

Two hours into their planning, a loud crack of metal clanged through the otherwise silent block. 339 put a hand to his lips and stilled his men. There were too many to hide, so why bother? It was unusual for the guards to come at this hour. Either something was wrong or someone was getting punished. No good news ever came in the dead of night.

The gang sat quietly as another banging on the gate echoed across the expanse of the outer hallway. The sound of approaching footsteps added to the chorus. 339 closed his eyes and listened, though something inside him already knew that whoever it was, was coming straight to this cell.

A moment later, a shadowy figure in a guard uniform appeared outside his gate. His shoulder-mounted light turned on and he scanned the dozen souls inside the cell. 339 recognized the guard, one of the more dangerous ones who usually allied with the Apexes. A small wave of worry washed over him.

"Guardsman Raets," he said with a small bow. "What can we do for you?"

The guardsman touched his hand to the control band on his wrist and the gate swung open. A small alarm rang inside 339's head. Something was wrong here. None of the guards would ever dare wander into a block without backup, let alone come into a cell with a dozen inmates. This was a high-security prison full of hardened criminals.

Raets walked as if he had no worries. "Get out. All of you," he said in a deadpan voice.

"The air is off in the hallway," 630 said.

Raets shrugged. "This won't take long. You'll live."

339 stuck his hand out and motioned for them to stay. "It's late, Guardsman Raets. What do you want?"

"I won't repeat myself, inmates," Guardsman Raets spoke again, his voice soft. "Stand aside."

"You're not Raets, are you?" 339 said. "What are you, an assassin?"

Immediately, 339's captains all jumped off the bunks and made a wall between him and the fake guard. 461 slipped to the back and blocked the gate. His men's loyalty touched 339. A few months ago, these ragtag fodders only looked out for themselves. The only thing they cared about was how they could avoid the violence and gangs, to dig for more minerals so they could eat just one more meal, and to survive one more morning in this hellhole. Now, there was a wall of them standing between him and an assassin. The warmth that welled in him felt greater than any heater cig could.

Then 339 noticed a familiar faint translucent yellow glow surround the impostor guardsman. "Get back," he cried.

It was too late. A sudden force expanded from the impostor, and 339's captains flew backward, slamming into the bunks and the walls. 102, the oldest of his captains, lunged at the assassin, only to stop in midair. He squawked as he floated, rotating onto his back as he flailed his arms and legs.

339 was a dead man. This assassin was skilled with an exo, not some inmate punk who had just happened to get his hands on a set of bands. In fact, everyone in this cell was as good as dead.

"Everybody stay down." 339 pushed 630 back to the ground as the man tried to get up, then put his hands behind his head. 102, still rotating like an errant satellite, floated out of his way as 339 stepped up to the assassin. "Let the rest of the men go. I'm your mark."

The assassin scanned the rest of the room, looking unworried and almost bored. "Still the same righteous bastard. Prison hasn't dulled that sharp stick up your ass."

The assassin's face began to erase itself. First, the skin tones faded and the colors began to swim together. Then the lines across his face unraveled, un-drawing until there was nothing more than a blank canvas on his face. Then the flesh tone dispersed, revealing a sharp face, pronounced nose, and short unruly hair matted to his head. The only thing different was that he was now dark. Much darker.

339 was surprised. This was the last person he expected to see. A series of emotions surged through him. Some relief, some curiosity, but mostly anger. He clenched his fist. "What are you doing here? Come back to finish the job?"

"I'm not here to kill you," the man replied. "I wish I was. On the contrary, Levin Javier-Oberon, I'm here to break you out. Earth needs you."

SIXTEEN

REUNITED

James could really use a damn drink right about now. The journey to Nereid from Bulk's Head had been particularly rough. Who would have thought taking a beating from Raets would have been the highlight of his week?

After acquiring the guardsman's identity and hopping on the transport, it had taken him two days to reach Appolonia Trading Station orbiting Neptune before transferring to Nereid the next day. Add another day to locate Penal Colony 3, two more to embed himself as a guard, and then one more to locate the right prisoner. Now, the guy that James had made this incredibly long and dull journey to retrieve was telling him he didn't feel like leaving. For some insane reason beyond comprehension, Levin was actually giving him shit for trying to break him out of jail.

Black abyss, his mouth was parched. Just the thought of a drink—preferably something from the Luxe Empire—right now made his skin itch. James's wits and patience were near their end. For the life of him, he couldn't figure out why the fool wasn't jumping at the opportunity to leave Nereid. James had just assumed that he would break down into big fat tears of relief once he showed up. Well, maybe not tears. Levin Javier-Oberon was still an auditor.

"Look, maybe I'm not being clear," he said, gnashing his teeth. "I came a long way to break you out of the worst prison in the entire solar system. If you don't want to come then you're an idiot."

One of Levin's toadies raised his hand. "Boss, I don't know what the abyss is going on, but if this guy is here to bust you out of Nereid, God, do it. Go. Take the chance."

Levin turned to his man. "It's not as simple as that. I have oaths to keep, not only to you men, but to someone else as well. I can't break them."

"Boss," another one of his guys added. "I'm an old lifer. Nereid is my fourth stint in prison and the hole I'll die in. In all my miserable years, there's been few good, clean guys, and you're one of them. One of the last decent fucks in the universe. I owe you more in the two months I've known you than anyone I knew my entire life, including my mother, so if this asshole here wants to break you out, oath to us or not, take it. Get the fuck out of here, boss!" Several of the captains around him nodded.

The news that 339 was not only ex-ChronoCom, but an auditor of the ninth chain, came as a shock but not too big a surprise to his men. They all said they knew something about him was special. James had to give it to the guy: only here a few months and already treated like a messiah.

"You should listen to them," James said. "In fact, I can't even believe we're having this discussion. Are you space sick or something?"

Levin dug in. "I chose to come to Nereid to atone for my crimes. I don't have much these days except my integrity."

Flabbergasted, James clenched his fist and his jaws and every part of his body in between, and had to physically will himself not to punch the wall. "Here's what I'm going to do," he said finally. "I'm going to step out of the cell for five minutes. You finish up whatever you have to do with your guys, and then I'm going to come back and blast a fucking hole in that wall behind you, and then we're going to leave."

Without waiting for an answer, James stomped out of the cell. He rounded the corner into the corridor and took a deep breath. Convincing an ex-auditor doing a life sentence in the worst shithole in the solar system to leave was supposed to be the easiest part of this job. The guy should be offering to name his firstborn after him. Of course, things were never that easy, not that breaking in here was easy to begin with, but to actually have the job fall apart because the guy *wanted* to stay in prison . . .

A guttural noise crawled up his throat. It killed him that this ingrate was what was keeping him away from Elise and Sasha. It had taken less coaxing from Elise to make him leave her. It had taken his little ten-year-old sister telling him to stop being a concrete-head to get him to fly across the solar system. Now, the only thing keeping him from returning to the two most important people in his life was this asshole dragging his heels.

"I should just kidnap him and force him to freedom." No, James knew that wouldn't work. A guy like Levin was all principle. Probably would rather die than be forced to do something. That could be arranged. No, the Elfreth need him; Elise needed him. Levin had to be persuaded to come willingly. It was the only way.

James buried his head in his hands. "Black abyss, I need a drink." Those men were whispering animatedly inside the cell, probably either figuring out how to steal his bands or to tell him to get lost. Well, good luck to them.

"Time's up," he said and walked back in. "How do you want to play this?"

Levin didn't look like he was packed and ready to go. In fact, he was sitting on the bed looking more relaxed than ever. He pointed at the bunk bed across from him. "Have a seat, James. Rest of you, please wait outside."

James kept his sights on Levin as one by one, his eleven men filed out until they were all alone. Levin pointed at the empty bed again.

"I'll stand," James said. "I'm not staying here long."

"How long have you been here in the penal colony?" Levin asked.

"Long enough to know you're running half the joint. Impressive, though not a surprise, really."

"You know what will happen if I leave, right? My boys will get butchered."

James shrugged. "So? This is a prison. Butchering happens."

"I've made promises. I can't just leave them like this."

James had a bad feeling about what his former superior was about to say next. "Look, we don't have time for this. I'm not going to stay here and help you muscle a prison war. Not to mention the amount of heat it'll bring. I'll have Amazon military here within days. On top of that—"

Levin shook his head. "I don't want you to fight this war. I want you to help me prevent it altogether. You do this one thing for me, it'll allow me keep all my promises and save these poor souls."

"What do you care about a bunch of convicts? You're Levin, High Auditor of the ninth chain. Hardass."

"Former High Auditor, and I've come to care since I became one of them. That and I don't break promises."

"This isn't a negotiation. We . . ." In his head, James heard Elise and Grace, and Oldest Franwil, for that matter, berating him. Bitters make poor lures. It wouldn't hurt to hear him out. He exhaled, resigned. "What do you want?"

"I want to take someone else with me when we go."

James reluctantly nodded. "It complicates things, but can be arranged. Let the lucky lad know he got a ticket out of hell and let's get out of here."

"He's not in this block."

That threw James off. "Isn't Block San the People's block?"

"It is." Levin stood up and beckoned James to follow him. James extended his atmos over Levin and they headed into the darkened corridors toward the main hub connecting all the blocks. Outside, the rest of his men lounged in the hallways, watching James warily. Levin told them to wait in his cell until morning, and then he and James made their way to the hub gates. He pointed through the small window across the communal hub to the gate at the far end. "The guy we need to get is there."

James pulled the schematics of the prison in his AI band. He frowned. "My intel says that's Block Ba, the Apex quarters."

Levin looked at James, a small smile cracking his lips. "That's right. If you want me to go with you, we need to take the leader of the Apexes with us."

Levin had to be screwing with him.

"Get outta here. You're kidding, right?" he asked. "He's the last guy you want to watch your back."

"Like you said; what's escaping from Nereid worth to a convict?"

This complicated James's plans. It was one thing for the man to bring a loyal underling, probably someone Levin could control. Bringing a total stranger could cause problems. The man could stab them in the back or betray them for a pardon.

He shook his head. "Too risky. It's a long flight back to Earth. That guy could just murder us in our sleep."

"Let me worry about him," Levin said. "That's the deal. We bring their leader with us and I'll cooperate."

With almost any other person, James would have refused. However, no matter how much he hated Levin's guts, he knew the man kept his word. He nodded. "All right."

"Good. What's our escape plan?"

James shrugged. "Yeah, about that. We'll need to work something else out. I wasn't expecting to transport three."

His original escape plan literally entailed blowing through one of the exterior walls and carrying both of them out into space to the *Franken-stein,* waiting for them within the nearby Kuiper Belt. However, his bands didn't have enough levels remaining to carry three that distance, at least without a little help. They would need to board a ship to take them at least part of the way.

"We'll address that once we get everyone on board," Levin said. "Open the gates. Let's go visit the Apexes."

James bristled at being ordered around. He had never taken to Levin's authority, even when he was the subordinate. Now that he was here to rescue the man, he took to it even less. It was something they were going to have to work out if they were to coexist. Still, he dutifully did as ordered and opened the gates.

He put Raets's paint job back on him, just on the off chance they ran into another guard wandering the halls. The two walked in silence in the darkness, navigating the quiet rooms, opening and closing the gates through James's control band as they traversed the sprawling facility, past the fabricating shop, through the processing plant into the commune. It took them twenty minutes of winding paths and a dozen flights of steep stairs before they reached Block Ba on the opposite end of Penal Colony 3. It was located in the lowest level of colony, converted as a late add-on when the prison had become overcrowded. It was also the farthest from the rest of the other colony, offering the residents here the most privacy.

"That was like descending a steep mountain," James said. "It must be a hellish trek after a day in the mines. Why would anyone want to live so far away from the rest of the colony?"

"Block Ba used to be an old storeroom next to the heat generators. Even turned off, the corridors and shared rooms in the block stay relatively warm."

They reached the large double gates of the block at the end of a large ramp. James activated Raets's control band, and the gates slid outward, with the sound of chains clinking together. The two of them walked into the block and stopped. All the inmates were already in the shared space, awake and waiting for them.

James took a step back. Why were they out of their cells? The two of them were outnumbered two hundred-to-one. Even with his bands, it would be a difficult fight.

"Stand behind me," he said.

"That's the second reason," Levin added. "There's no cells here. It's one large room. The Apexes are better coordinated than all the other groups because they aren't separated like the rest of us."

The front line of Apexes moved closer to the gate, some with metal rods and shanks in hand and others yawning and trying to figure out what the commotion was about. When they noticed Levin standing behind James, they all became alert. A few shouts of warnings later, the entire room seemed ready to lynch them, despite James still wearing the guardsman uniform. Possibly in spite of it, for all he knew. The crowd was getting ugly.

"Back off," James barked, pushing Levin into the hallway.

The first of the Apexes got within arm's reach. James gave him a sharp kick to the abdomen and sent him tumbling into three others. Another came from his blind side. He sidestepped a clumsy swing and elbowed the man in the throat. Still another got closer. This time, Levin stepped in, took the man's knees from under him, and then tossed him onto the ground, bowling over a group of Apexes. This only enraged them more, and they surged forward.

"Stop!" a voice rang over the snarls of the ugly mob.

Immediately, the unruly crowd pulled back and parted ways down the center. James took the moment to assess the Apexes. He noted how well-trained they were, disciplined, like a military force. Every single man here was larger than everyone in that cell with Levin. In a gang war, it seemed the People were indeed doomed to fail.

"339, what are you doing here?" A shadowy figured appeared from the crowd. "Looking for death? Or you, Raets, Looking to curry favor from the Apexes by delivering him to us?"

It was probably better James kept as much space as possible between the Apexes and Levin. Once they got their hands on him, James doubted he could get him back in one piece. He took a step forward. "Amazon guardsman orders. You will not touch this man. Tell your boss to call off his dogs or there will be consequences. We need to speak with 881."

The figure stepped up to James, looking momentarily confused. "What the abyss is wrong with you, Raets? You don't recognize me? Nobody tells the Apexes what to do in my block, not even the guards."

James should have figured the man was 881 by the way his men treated him so deferentially. Still, he didn't have time for this.

"We need to talk."

"There's nothing to talk about."

"Yes there is, Cole," Levin said, stepping up next to him. "It's time we address our differences, nephew."

Chatter swept through the Apexes at this revelation. James looked at Levin in surprise, his unusual request now finally making sense. He remembered Cole, an unimpressive Tier-4 who had fled to the past. It was quite a large scandal among the tiers at the time for the blood relative of an auditor to desert. Levin himself had to go back and bring his nephew to justice.

At the sound of his actual name being used, Cole flew into a rage and charged his uncle. By now, James had had enough. He powered on his exo and lifted the man by the front of his shirt, yanking him upward off his feet. The other Apexes around him scattered backward.

"You got someone with bands to kill me?" Cole snarled as he dangled in the air.

"Why does every criminal here think I'm trying to kill them?" James said, exasperated.

"What else do you think happens in a penal colony?" Levin said. He walked up to his nephew, narrowly dodging a kick, and looked up. "If I wanted to kill you, Cole, I would have done it months ago. Are you ready to talk?"

Realizing how outgunned he was with James there, Cole nodded. James dropped him unceremoniously on the ground and kept his face stony when the inmate popped back up to his feet and glared at him.

"Who are you?" he asked.

James dropped his paint job.

Cole gave him a sidelong glance and then focused his attention back on Levin. "You were less ugly as Raets. What do you assholes want?"

Levin looked at the crowd of Apexes standing around and turned his back to them. "Let's talk outside in the hall."

"Step out so you two can get me alone?" Cole sputtered. "I don't—."

"He's got an exo on, Cole," Levin said. "Do you really think it matters?"

The Apex leader's eyes panned back and forth between them until he finally, reluctantly agreed. He followed them out to the top of the stairs, close enough for the Apexes to still keep sight of their leader, but far enough away that they couldn't hear what they were talking about.

"You got two minutes," Cole said, keeping as far away from James as possible. As if that would make a difference.

"I'm breaking Levin out of Nereid," James said.

"And I want you to come with me," Levin finished.

It took a few seconds for those words to sink in. Cole's expression morphed from anger to shock to realization and finally to hope. Then he turned back into his angry, suspicious self. "Why? What's in it for him if I come with you?"

James threw up his arms. "You, too? What is wrong with your entire family?"

"I get nothing for your release, except peace of mind," Levin said. "I'm making amends to your mother, and to you."

"I wouldn't even be here if it wasn't for you," Cole spat.

James placed himself between the two men. "I couldn't care less about your stupid family feud. The offer is there. Are you coming or would you rather rot on Nereid for the rest of your life?"

Levin was strangely silent, pensive, failing to make eye contact with either of them. James could see the pain on his face as he waited for Cole to answer. There was a quiet desperation to him that seemed foreign on that face. James realized then just how painful sending his nephew to prison must have been for Levin.

Cole, on the other hand, looked conflicted. He knew this was probably his only opportunity to leave Nereid. However, it would make him beholden to the man who had put him there. He had held on to his pride and anger for so long that it was difficult for him to give Levin an inch, even if it was freedom being offered.

In the end though, his better judgment won out. "Fine, I'm in. When do we leave?"

Levin and James exchanged glances. "Day after tomorrow when the supply ship comes," James said. "We'll need a distraction."

SEVENTEEN

THE ALL GALAXY

The larger tribe descended upon the smaller, unsuspecting tribe just as it was crossing the fifth level over the triple-wide Allen and Canal Street crossing. A thunderous crash echoed between the buildings as the rear of the smaller tribe was smashed by the larger group. As those on the bridge tried to flee across it, more from the larger tribe appeared on the other end, cutting off their escape.

Many of those trapped were not warriors, and the few who fought back were easily overwhelmed. The ensuing battle couldn't even be called that as the tribe on the bridge, caught in the crossfire, was cut down indiscriminately, even as many threw their weapons down and raised their hands. Surrender wasn't much of an option in the Mist Isle. A series of explosions—low-grade incendiaries—erupted at the center of the bridge, sending men, women, and children flying through the air. Many were swept off the bridge and plummeted to their deaths five stories down.

Within seconds, the attack was over. Dozens of bodies littered the bridge as the victors picked through the corpses for spoils. Anything valuable remaining—technology, food, survivors—was distributed among the larger tribe. Arguments and scuffles broke out between the victors fighting over the spoils. Some got into heated arguments over gear and new slaves and had to be forcibly separated. Two men from each side fought over a high-tech rifle. Two women argued over a young man.

"Oldest, we must leave. They are too close." Eriao pulled Elise back from the window. The massacre that had unfolded below had frozen her in place. She would have thrown up the contents of her stomach if there had been anything in it.

Elise's heart pounded in her chest as she looked back at the long line of Elfreth huddled close to the floor. This particular attack had hit too close to the main body of the tribe. It was the same tribe that had been stalking them the past few days. The Gazzys, as they called themselves, were nothing more than pillaging marauders who wouldn't even speak to them. They were vicious cannibals who preyed upon the weak.

These small-scale melees were nonstop down at the lower levels of the Isle. The fighting over spoils and floors was intense, and the hundreds of small tribes fed upon each other as they strived to grow large and strong enough to take over the higher floors, where there was enough light to farm and where there were fewer bridges and passageways connecting the buildings to defend.

Everyone was exhausted, having been on the run for days, not staying in place for more than a few hours at a time. Her decision to avoid conflict with the other tribes had proven costly. They had not been able to find a suitable space and were now transient outcasts. There were few promising floors on the lower levels and the ones that were dry and defensible were already occupied and heavily entrenched. No one was in the mood to share.

Several of the elders openly questioned her decision not to physically take the floors they needed, though none dared defy Franwil and Eriao. For now, those two still supported Elise, but the war chief's patience was running thin. Elise pulled out an old map of Manhattan and looked at their position. Many of the buildings had changed since the time of the map's printing in 2233, but it was the best they had. She peered out the window at one of the largest buildings farther down the block, taking note of the dozen sky bridges running from it.

"We go two floors up and cross the street west." She traced her finger along the map. "Then down four floors heading north until we hit that series of high-rises."

She handed the map to Eriao, who studied the route she had laid out. "West is a triple-wide, at least a hundred fifty meters. With our numbers, we risk being exposed for too long. You saw what happened to those poor bastards back there. What were they thinking, trying to cross at street level at this time? We should continue north first and then cut across under the cover of night once the street narrows."

Elise frowned. "I was hoping to hit the business district. The buildings there are tall and thick. We have a better chance of finding quality shelter there."

Eriao looked doubtful. "Larger buildings are more coveted. We'll find stronger and better-armed tribes in those spaces. The towers further north are more modest with smaller tribes who might be willing to negotiate, or at least allow us to pass unmolested." He handed the map back to her. "In either case, it will be better if we force our way through weaker tribes than the stronger ones."

"Fine, we head north," she said reluctantly.

The rest of the Elfreth packed up and moved, the guardians taking position at the front and back of the long caravan. She watched as the herd of kowru passed, especially noting the foal that clung to Moma at all times. The poor thing had to be carried up the stairs and had never seen grass before. It saddened her to think that these ruins and this constant struggle were all it knew.

The Elfreth continued north, going up and down several floors until they reached a bridge that crossed over to the next building. They usually had to wade through jungle-like wilderness or encountered other tribes protecting their territories. The majority of those tribes preferred to just let them pass rather than fight, but some would try to extract tolls from the Elfreth.

This was where Elise drew the line. In most cases, she was able to talk them out of this blackmail. In two, she had resorted to intimidating them with the Elfreths' cache of advanced weapons. One or two blasts of her wrist beam or powered rifle, and insinuating that they had plenty more where that came from, was enough to get their way.

By dusk, they had reached the All Galaxy Tower on Broadway and Nineteenth Street. Elise remembered hearing about this place in 2097. Back in her time, most countries competed with each other either through sports or building exotic buildings. The All Galaxy was the Democratic Union's hat into that arena. She had seen mock-ups and holographs of the proposed tower, but they had just laid the foundation when James had whisked her away to the present.

Now, as she stood at the bridge connecting to it, she had to admit;

even abandoned and run-down, the thing looked impressive. This building was huge, massive. It wasn't so much that the All Galaxy Tower was
tall; it wasn't. It was just really wide, taking up several square city blocks.
According to the map, the building's edges touched Fifth to Park ave-
nues wide and Nineteenth to Twenty-second streets long.

She stared open-mouthed as the skyscraper stretched up and disappeared into the fog. The building wasn't exactly short either—a hundred floors or so, though definitely not the tallest in Manhattan. Also to
her surprise, most of the outer-wall window panels seemed intact, which
meant those living inside were not only receiving the sun for crops, but
also were sheltered from the elements. Elise felt a jab of envy at the inhabitants of the giant tower. After weeks of slogging through rain and
being constantly battered by wind that swept through porous buildings,
just the thought of having walls was amazing.

Elise's eyes lingered on the building until she realized that the Elfreth
procession had stopped three-quarters across the long sky bridge connecting to the All Galaxy. She broke into a trot and saw Eriao organizing the
guardians in the front. "What's going on?" she asked when she got to
him.

Eriao pointed at the entrance to the tower at what initially looked like
a mound of junk blocking their way. On closer inspection, she realized it
was a purposely-made barricade spanning the width of the bridge. On
top of a makeshift parapet, rows of armed people stood ready to repel
them. From what she could tell, most of their defense seemed low-tech,
but they were entrenched enough that it could cause a problem, especially
since the Elfreth would have to charge the length of the bridge.

Eriao gestured at parts of the barricade. "Oldest, most of the barricade is made from concrete and metal. We will not be able to tear it
down easily."

"It looks like it's been there awhile," she added, pointing at a set of
rusty metal double doors built directly in its center.

"Should we turn back?"

Elise studied the people standing on top of it waiting for them. They
were an assortment of men and women, some young, some elderly. Many
were fit and well-armed, others injured and holding spears; all looked
determined to not let the Elfreth pass. Perhaps they should just turn
back.

She looked back down the bridge toward the building from where they had come. Turning around wouldn't solve their problems. There was nothing for them back there. This place, this All Galaxy Tower, looked like the best chance for the Elfreth to find a place to settle. Her people were exhausted, some half-dead on their feet. They had to stop running. Elise gritted her teeth. She had gotten them into this situation. She would get them out.

Elise walked toward the barricade, shrugging off Eriao when he tried to hold her back. Her heart hammered in her chest as she saw the dozens of weapons, all pointed at her. "We come in peace. I wish to speak with your leader, your chief," she said in a loud, slow, clear voice. She inhaled and exhaled with each step, half expecting to hear a bang and something rip through her guts at any moment.

She waited as the people standing on the parapet above her chattered among themselves. Her gaze fell upon a young man who holstered his rifle and locked in on her. She noticed a small red light moving up her chest to her face. These people had some advanced weapons after all. She continued forward, one slow step after another.

"This is Flatirons land," a woman's voice called out. "None enters. Go around."

"Please." Elise no longer cared about keeping the desperation out of her voice. "We are willing to offer a trade for sanctuary in your building."

"The Flatirons have fallen for this ruse before," the voice replied. "We will not again."

"We can't go back the way we came. There are those chasing us."

"Then you bring them to our building if we let you pass."

"I beg you." Elise took a step forward.

The ground at her feet kicked up dust, causing her to start. She threw her hands straight up in the air, her sleeves falling down to her shoulders and exposing her arms. They shook as she tried her best to fight back the tears. If this other tribe saw the Elfreth's leader panic, what would they think about the rest of her people? Some leader she had turned out to be.

"Leave," the woman's voice repeated. The dust in front of Elise kicked up again.

Elise took a step back. "Can we at least talk this over?"

"No. My next shot will be through your heart."

Resigned, Elise turned and walked back toward the tribe. She hadn't made up her mind yet whether they should attack the barricade or not. It would be bloody. Did they have a choice, though? How long could they keep this up?

"Wait," a new voice rang from behind the barricade. It was a man's voice this time. Older, more frail.

Elise realized that the word, while still being translated through her comm band, wasn't from the common language these wastelander tribes used. It was Solar English. The new speaker had been to the outside world.

She turned around and waited. There was a long pause. Elise kept her hands held up above her head. She forced herself to keep looking straight and not back at the Elfreth twenty meters behind her. If they wanted to kill her right now, there was little her people could do to stop it. After what felt like an eternity, to the point Elise was beginning to get bored, the metal door in the barricade swung open, revealing a darkened room behind it.

"You may enter. Only you."

Elise took a step forward, and her legs almost buckled. She looked back at the Elfreth. Both Eriao and Rima were shaking their heads furiously, gesturing for her to backtrack toward them. She tried to take another step forward, and found that her leg was refusing to lift off the ground.

A middle-aged woman stepped out from the barricade and walked hesitantly toward Elise. She stopped just in front of her and bowed gracefully, almost in a curtsy. Elise tried to return the gesture but looked awkward trying to imitate that motion.

"I am Harre, the Teacher's sister," she said. "I will stand in your place until you return."

Elise looked at the distance from here to the barricade, and then back at the Elfreth, who seemed so much farther away. It hardly seemed like a fair trade-off. However, this small gesture was more than she had thought she would receive. It gave her a small boost of courage.

"Thank you," she said.

She forced herself not to look back again as she walked through the double doors into the darkness behind the barricade. Immediately, weapons surrounded her on either side. Several narrow beams of light focused on her. Shadows danced around her, prodding her forward. A path in front of her opened as they herded her a third of the way down the length of the building, through a massive wide-open hall with ceilings three stories tall. This looked like it was once a lobby, or a warehouse. It actually reminded her of those old train terminals from before her time. It was gigantic. Cracked marble ran up and down the walls and torches were spaced evenly down the hallway, giving her a perspective on how expansive this building was.

A woman wielding a rifle stepped into one of the lights and pointed at a door to the side. "Go."

It was the same woman who had spoken with her earlier at the barricade. Her left arm and shoulder were bandaged tightly with rags, and she had red burn marks all over her body. Elise looked to both sides of the woman and realized that many surrounding her had suffered similar injuries. Pitched battles had been waged here lately. No wonder they were suspicious of strangers.

Elise stepped into the small room and found a roaring fireplace in front of two wingback chairs. On the left, a wrinkled man with long gray hair and a beard to match sat staring up at her. He motioned to the other chair. "Sit. I am Teacher Crowe of the Flatirons. You are standing in my home. Allow me to offer you a seat."

Elise was thankful that she got to sit. Her legs were Jell-O right now, and it helped calm her shaking. If she really was going to negotiate, it might help to not be quaking in her shoes the entire time.

"Thank you for speaking with me," she said. "We were on our way north. My people just need a place to rest. Your tower seems spacious and sheltered. I ask that you consider—"

"In a moment, we will speak more of that," Crowe said, cutting her off. "You wield chronman bands."

Elise held up her arms. "You know what these are?"

"I do. In fact, I recognized many of the weapons your warriors wield. Why not simply blast your way through us?"

"I meant it when I said we were peaceful," Elise said.

The old man nodded. "You are not from around here. You speak our language through your bands." This teacher, it seemed, knew a lot of the outside world.

She nodded. "I've joined my tribe recently."

"Yet you lead them."

"It's complicated."

"Tell me, what other technology do you possess?"

It was an opening, at least. Elise took a deep breath and began negotiations.

Two hours later, an exhausted and relieved Elise left the center doors of the barricade and approached the Elfreth. By this time, Eriao had lined the Elfreth up only a few meters away from where Harre stood, and had them ready to attack at a moment's notice. The woman's face drained of tension when she saw Elise come out.

"That took longer than I thought," she said.

"Your brother asks a lot of questions."

"The Teacher is not actually my brother." Harre shrugged, a wry smile on her face as she retreated back into the barricades.

"What happened?" Franwil demanded.

"It is night, and the jungles are awakening. We need to get off this bridge immediately and find shelter," Eriao said. "The tribe is ready to go. We might be able to take the north portion of the building southwest of here. I'll send scouts there to locate a safe place to set up camp."

"No." Elise pointed at the entrance. "We go in."

"How much do we have to pay for passage through their building?" he asked.

"We're not passing through," Elise said. "I negotiated for food and two floors on the upper level. The Flatirons own the entire building from this floor up."

"How is that possible?" Rima asked. "Do they have that many in the tribe?"

Elise shook her head. "They're a large tribe, slightly larger than us, but not much. They destroyed all the connecting passages above and guard this floor like a fortress. They use the above floors for farming, much like we did with the Farming Towers back in Boston."

"Why are they letting us in, then?" Eriao asked.

Elise pointed at several of the crates being carried by the Elfreth. "Bring seventeen of the medical supply crates, including all the equipment for treating burns, and leave them in the hallway. They're no longer ours. Also, hand over thirty powered blaster rifles with chargers."

"Oldest," Eriao said, alarmed. "That is a high price to pay."

She sighed. "I know, but we need the respite."

Franwil nodded. "It is a high price, but worthwhile if we have found a safe haven where the Co-op and those other wastelander dogs cannot nip at our heels, even for a little while. I trust that you and their teacher came to a good permanent accommodation?"

Elise sighed. "Accommodation, yes. A permanent one, no. We're only allowed to stay for ten days."

EIGHTEEN

Riot

For the second time in less than a year, that bastard James Griffin-Mars had turned Levin's life upside down. It was becoming a habit, though Levin was hard-pressed to argue that breaking out of prison wasn't going to be an improvement. He guessed it'd have to depend what was waiting for him outside.

The main reason it took so long to plan the riot to distract the guards wasn't actually because starting a two-sided riot took planning, it was because the Apex and the People had to negotiate the terms for the fight. In the end, the best Levin could do was ensure that neither side would use weapons and that the riot would end as soon as they were gone. He hated himself for abandoning the People. The two groups also committed to keeping the peace, though that promise was probably only good up until Levin and Cole got off-moon. He had had to try, though.

"I don't want to hear it," 461 said, shaking his head when Levin tried to apologize to him personally. "I don't want to hear about your ass abandoning us or not keeping your promise. If you get a ticket out of here, you take it. That goes for any of the boys. Have to be an idiot not to."

"They're good men," Levin said. "Keep them safe. As long as you stick together, you'll be all right."

"Don't worry about us in the clink, free man," 461 replied. "Someone out there thinks you're valuable enough to bust out. You just make sure you do what you set out to do."

"I'll come back for all of you someday," Levin said.

461 smirked. "Don't make another promise you can't keep, boss."

Levin put a hand on 461's shoulder. "We'll meet again, my friend." The men he led, he didn't know who they were before they came to Nereid, but he knew who they were now. These were good people. People worth redeeming. He stuck out his hand. "Levin Javier-Oberon."

"Pardon, boss?"

"That's my name. Each of us, we're more than just numbers. I think it's time we remember that."

461 hesitated, and then shook Levin's hand. "Iro Bami-Earth."

"From Earth?" Levin said, surprised.

Iro nodded. "The Colorado underground colonies, actually. It's why my skin is as pale as a spaceborn. Got pinched when I was young robbing a food corporation's delivery transport. Was starving. Accidentally killed a guard when I hit him." He looked down at his beefy hands. "Didn't mean to. I was big even as a kid."

Levin understood. He had no doubt several of these people's stories were similar. Times were hard, and it brought desperation out of those who might not have committed any crimes otherwise. Funny, he hadn't thought this way before he came to Nereid. The penal colony had reformed him, but not in the way it had intended.

The riot erupted after the meal that night. It began with a wink, a nod, and then a hard right cross from 461 that intentionally missed one of the Apex captains. With tensions on both sides boiling over, it didn't take much for the staged fracas to turn into a real one.

Levin watched the chaos unfold. Watched as several of his people were bloodied, and as the violence spread from inmate to inmate like wildfire. Soon, the entire commune was a battlefield. James, still with Raets's paint over him, pretended to try to quell the riot. He made a pretty good show of it, using the big man's arms to pull the inmates apart and knock them on the ground. Then, Cole dove off one of the dining tables and jumped on top of him. More of the Apexes followed suit until he was buried beneath an avalanche of bodies.

That set off all the guards. Usually, when fights broke out, the prison guards were content to spectate. If it got bad, they usually would just vacuum out the air until the prisoners passed out. However, if one of their own was in trouble, the others would soon come down in full force.

Standing in the midst of the fracas, James made his presence known as he pretended to be in serious trouble. He shrieked for backup at the top of his lungs as he made wide clumsy swings at the inmates surrounding him. The inmates had been instructed not to touch him, but some of them must not have gotten the memo. Those unfortunate fools who took it too far—all Apexes, as far as Levin could tell—were handled by James with extreme prejudice, which made the scene only more realistic.

From a professional auditor viewpoint, if Levin were grading James's performance, he would have said the ex-chronman was overacting a little. The guy James was impersonating looked entirely too amateur, and the way he pitched the screaming was a bit too frantic. He was also beating the inmates who got close too efficiently. A regular guard wouldn't have had his skill, and his actions should reflect that. Also, a real guard in this situation wouldn't have had the breath to keep shouting this loud while fighting at the same time. To be perfectly frank, Levin was disappointed in this Tier-1's performance. Not that it mattered. Not anymore.

James did his job, though. The penal colony guards must have raised the alarm, because a few minutes later, the two double-door entrances on both sides slammed open and several rows of guards, clad in riot gear four shields wide, charged into the commune. They barreled into the crowd of prisoners locked in step, indiscriminately swinging their pain sticks.

The inmates were ready for them. No sooner had the doors opened and the guards streamed out than the inmates stopped fighting each other and turned on them. The guards weren't ready for the coordinated attack and were pushed off to the side, away from the entrance. The rest of the inmates charged through the security doors. They were met by another locked double door at the far end of the corridor and pounded at it futilely.

James, still painted as Raets, appeared next to Levin. They signaled to Cole, and together, the three of them pushed their way to the front of the crowd. "Stand back," he said, pulling the men next to the door away from it.

Levin nodded at James, who approached the door and placed his hands on it. A yellow glow leaped from his palms and blew the doors outward, ripping the panels off their frame and flinging them into another group of guards on the other side. The mob surged forward. James signaled to

Levin and Cole, and together, they broke away from the main crowd, moving down a side corridor and up through a maintenance stairwell.

"Do you know where we're going?" Cole asked.

James pointed at his head. "Mapped it out the day I got here. Let's go. We can hijack one of the transports before Amazon security arrives."

Cole stopped. "That's suicide. We can't outrun anything with a transport. They'll blow us out of space."

"Shut up and keep moving," James growled, hurrying them along. The sounds of the fighting faded as they continued to the surface. Six flights up, they ran into four guards positioned at the hangar doors. James held up a hand and, with a kinetic swing, swept all four aside and slammed them into the walls. "Keep watch," he said, as he used his exo to pry open the thick bay doors.

Cole ran to one of the unconscious guards and picked up a rifle. He walked over to the next unconscious guard and jabbed the barrel into the man's forehead. Levin knocked his arm away as the rifle discharged harmlessly into the air.

"Stop! What are you doing?" Levin said, spinning him around and grabbing the front of his shirt.

Cole pushed Levin backward and pointed the rifle at his chest. The two froze. "I should," Cole said, his voice low. "It would serve you right. You sent me to this hellhole, your own flesh and blood."

Levin held his ground and gave his nephew a resigned gaze. "Is this how you really want this to end? Do it, then."

"I wouldn't do that if I were you," James said, his focus still on the doors. "Levin's a bastard, but he's the only reason you're getting off this rock, boy."

For a second, Cole looked like he was going to pull the trigger anyway. Instead, he spat and pointed his rifle down the hallway. "It's not over between us."

Levin picked up one of the other rifles and took position next to him. "I doubt it ever will be. We're family."

"I have no family."

"Your mother disagrees."

"You should have just left me in the Ming Dynasty—"

"Will you two just shut up?" James snapped, looking their way and rolling his eyes. "I swear, if you guys keep this up, I will just cryo both your asses until we get to Earth." The bay doors began to creak as James's exo pried them apart. A second later, the doors were forced open just wide enough for each man to slip through sideways. "Come on."

Levin slipped into the massive hangar first, followed by Cole, and then James. Right away, a barrage of weapon fire hammered the bay doors. Levin grabbed Cole just as the man came through the crack and pulled him to the ground. They scrambled behind a stack of metal containers.

"Exo on the far wall," he called as James appeared last through the door.

At least three guards were converging on them. The guard with the exo floated in the air, a green glow surrounding him. It was a security exo specializing in crowd control. Levin had fought against these before, though he wasn't sure if James had had the experience.

"The exo is powered for multiple coils," he called out.

"Don't worry about me. Get that ship up and running," James said, launching into the air and putting himself between the exo guard and the transport.

The last thing Levin saw before turning away from the battle was thirty thin strings of coils leap out of the guard and shoot toward James. In response, James summoned ten or so of his own yellow coils and moved to intercept.

Levin pulled Cole to the hatch of the transport. "Take out the guards. Keep them off James."

Cole moved to the belly of the craft and engaged the three guards, taking one of them down as they ran toward the ship. Levin entered the transport and got to work. It was an old Valiant model, easily three hundred years old. Simple and slow, but efficient and reliable, basically a giant flying container with a tiny engine. They weren't going to get very far in this tub. Cole wasn't wrong earlier about James needing more than a ship to escape the penal colony. He hoped James had a better plan than to try to escape in this thing.

Levin ran the length of the box-shaped transport into the tiny cockpit. Outside the three front slits of windows, he could see flashes of green and yellow lighting up the room. Those green coils were everywhere, seemingly filling up the entire hangar. He hoped James could pull this off. The ex-chronman could take care of himself, but who knew what shape he was in after having spent so much time as a fugitive.

Levin got to work on the transport's startup sequence. The good thing about cheap, reliable ships was that they were as basic as they came. Besides fairly simple navigation and a minimal shielding system, the rest of the ship was nothing more than thrusters, steering, and life support, something Levin could have built while an initiate at the Academy. There wasn't even artificial gravity or central heat; the cockpit was outfitted with only an electrical heater. Basically, this thing was a miserable ride. However, it's simplicity made it a cinch to start. Within a few seconds, the rear thrusters had rumbled to life.

Levin ran back to the container side of the ship and shouted down at Cole, "Get in here and close the hatch." He ran back to the cockpit and looked out the window. Those green coils were still everywhere, and there wasn't a hint of yellow at all. Levin couldn't see the fight outside clearly, but he worried that James might actually be losing.

Well, nothing could be done for him now. If James survived, they had a chance. If he didn't, then they were all as good as dead. That green exo guard could easily drag and ground the transport, though even if they managed to escape the hangar, they wouldn't get very far.

It had been years since Levin had had to pilot a ship, and this damn thing was wide as a star base and responded just about as well as one. He lifted the transport up and maneuvered it—if one could call driving this ship that—to the center of the hangar. He nearly careened into another ship as he turned it toward the exit. The turning speed of this thing was painful. The transport rumbled forward, floating across the length of the hangar slowly to the launch-way. James must still be fighting, since green coils hadn't pulled the ship back to the ground.

Levin felt every second tick by as the transport made it past the air shield of the hangar to the runway outside. As the ship made the final turn, his heart fell. The exterior bay door was closed. He checked his console for weapons; there were none. The shield arms of the transport were barely strong enough to take a solar flare, let alone crash through those external hangar doors. They were trapped.

Off to the side, he saw a flare of yellow, and then James streaked toward the exterior door. He must have not only survived the fight, he must have knocked the guard out of play. James motioned for Levin to hold and began working on the door.

Levin felt his palms sweat as James flitted from the right bay door to the left. This was taking too long. He was surprised the hangar wasn't being flooded with more guards; the riot must still be taking most of their attention. He silently thanked the People again. He'd keep his promise to his men somehow. One day.

Eventually, James was able to crack the mechanism locking the doors shut and push them open. As soon as he flew into the transport, Levin punched the ship and took off. A few minutes later, in a very rough ride, they cleared Nereid and were shooting off into the blackness of space. Twenty short minutes later, the radar began to blip.

"Two incoming Amazon drone ships on intercept within ten minutes," said Levin.

Cole leaned over the console and looked over at James, panicked. "What's your plan now, chronman?"

James muttered, "We'll cut it close. I hope this tub bought us enough distance for my exo levels to last us the rest of the way. How far are we from the Kuiper Belt?"

"Not close enough to make it before those drones come," said Levin.

"We don't need to be. Set a heading for the opposite direction." James signaled for them to follow him. "Let's go." He threw his atmos over Levin and Cole and carried them off the ship. Floating in space, they watched as the transport continued its casual path away. James pulled the two men in close and shot toward the Kuiper Belt.

"Stay close and quiet," he ordered. "I'm going to power down and we'll wait them out. Attack drones shouldn't have powerful enough sensors to find us, but you never know."

No sooner had James lowered his atmos than the three of them felt the cold creep of space wash over them. The ex-chronman was maintaining just the minimum levels to keep them alive, but not much else. Breathing became more labored as the three clung to each other for warmth. Levin was starting to feel his consciousness fade by the time James finally raised the levels.

"Now what?" Cole grumbled. "We're trapped out here without a ship on the fringe of Neptune. What the abyss do we do now?"

James gave him a flat stare. "I'm a Tier-1, boy. I always have a plan."

NINETEEN

THE DOCTOR

James almost had to eat his words. It took the *Frankenstein* much longer than anticipated to find them in the Kuiper Belt. By the time he caught sight of it, moving sporadically toward them, his levels were down to eight percent and he was starting to doubt that they were going to make it.

When the *Frankenstein* came into view, James nearly whooped for joy, except that his throat was so dry he could get only a squeak out. Their little band of jailbreaks had spent over two days floating in space waiting for Grace to find them. In order to conserve energy, James had kept his bands powered to a bare minimum. The three of them spent many long hours of breathing hard and freezing their asses off. None of them had eaten, and they were all experiencing severe hunger pains. For some reason, and James took full responsibility for this, none of them had thought to pack food. Fortunately, Levin had had the foresight to bring a canteen of water; that had been their only sustenance.

Needless to say, tempers were short.

Cole squinted. "Is that a ship or a magnetic meteor that passed through a junk heap?"

"It's your ride home, you little prick," James huffed. As far as he was concerned, the only people allowed to laugh at it were the people who had built it. He checked his levels: they should make it in time; he hoped they made it in time. That was, assuming Grace was able to pilot the *Frankenstein* to their position. He watched as it maneuvered around an asteroid, making an arc that was too wide. It just managed to stop right before it hit another asteroid, make a slow pivot, and then speed toward them.

The *Frankenstein* nearly collided into them when it finally reached their location. James had to move the group out of its way, lest they get smashed. They got into the ship through the hatch with what James estimated was less than thirty minutes of levels to spare on his bands. Maybe an hour if he had jettisoned that punk Cole.

He had decided early during their time sharing body heat that he detested the young ex-chronman, which shouldn't have been surprising, since he was Levin's flesh and blood. The two apples must have grown from the same branch. If anything, Cole was an even bigger asshole than his uncle. He had a chip on his shoulder and was unpleasant to be around. At least with Levin, you knew what you were getting with his arrogant sense of righteousness. Cole was just an angry young man who faulted anyone and everyone for his problems, and generally was only looking out for himself. The boy could not be trusted.

The three of them stumbled out of the compression chamber and collapsed onto the deck of the collie, sucking in air as they tried to regain feeling in their frozen fingers and toes. James rolled onto his back and squeezed his eyes shut, trying to will the splitting brain freeze out of his head. His vision was blurry, but he could tell Grace was huffing down at him.

"This tub handles like a nightmare!" she yelled, nudging him with her foot.

"Great to see you, too." He sat up, groaning. The three of them had taken to staying as still as possible to conserve energy, and now his joints were protesting their intended use. "I told you to get some practice before I left, but you said you were going to be fine."

"I was fine," she snapped, "until I had to move this unwieldy cow around a sea of flying rocks."

"You mean there's more to flying a ship then plotting courses and going straight?" James allowed a grin to appear on his face.

Grace looked like she was about to hit him, but then she threw her arms around him. "I didn't think I was going to make it in time."

Her show of affection and concern surprised him. James sat there awkwardly, unsure of how to react. Her body was shaking; she must have been really worried. He reached up and patted her on the back. "There, there."

Grace pulled away and the High Scion was back in an instant. "Don't patronize me, pet. Just because you've seen me naked doesn't mean we're on equal footing. I'm still the——"

"Wait, what?" Levin exclaimed, looking indignant. "You slept with her? You sacrilegious bastard."

"It was for a job," James muttered in a low voice.

"Best he's ever had," Grace said smugly. She looked over at Cole. "Who's the boy?"

Cole stood up. "Who are you calling a boy, old hag?"

Levin got to his feet and bristled. "Watch your mouth around the Mother of Time." He turned to Grace. "Apologies. This is my nephew, Cole."

Grace looked Cole up and down. "You two were in prison together? Certain habits must run in your family."

"You could say that," Levin said dryly.

Cole's eyes widened at the mention of the Mother of Time, and he looked her up and down as well. Then, with a shrug, he walked to the back and to find the food locker. A few seconds later, he appeared with an armful of rations. He gave them all a sullen scowl and then went into one of the side rooms.

"That young man could use some manners, or a spanking," Grace observed.

"Prison obviously didn't help with rehabilitation," said James.

"It's been a difficult few months for him," said Levin.

"Not for you though, right, Levin? You haven't changed a bit," said James.

Grace waved them both off. "Let's get down to business. Levin, you have me to thank for your freedom."

Levin stood up. "Thank you for saving us, Mother of Time."

"Don't thank me yet. I intend to put you to good use. You are going to be our new salvager."

"From auditor to pirate salvager," Levin mused. "This story just gets better and better."

"Not a pirate but a crusader. You are being recruited by those of us who wish to cure the Earth Plague and save the planet."

"It's still illegal jumps, no matter how rosy you're painting the picture."

"Hardly. Pirating is much more profitable. This will be more rewarding."

"Can I say no?"

"Of course you can. James can also throw you out off the ship, but neither of you boys will do such things, will you? You need us as much as we need you. You have an inherent desire to keep the chaos at bay. You want a cause to believe in and fight for. You thought ChronoCom was your tool to maintaining that order, but then you looked under the hood. That's the real reason you chose to go to prison, wasn't it? You didn't want to be part of the corruption. Let us provide you with purpose again."

Levin grunted. "All you had to do was say no. I already assumed this is what you were breaking me out for."

"Good. I'm glad we're on the same page, because you're jumping as soon as we reach Venus next week."

Levin shrugged. "All right then."

"You've already found a mark?" James asked.

Grace nodded. "I've been putting that chron database access hack to good use. Found just the candidate for us. I actually knew of the old man. One of the best inventors to have ever lived. He was a great military inventor, a creative genius, and a mediocre doctor."

James frowned. "How does that make him a good candidate if he's a garbage doctor?"

"There's a lot of variables involved in determining jumps," Grace said. "You know that. With the time frame we're working with, I found someone who was dying roughly around Venus's current orbit and rotation, one we can detour to on the way back to Earth. He'll be a good pick because he will also be useful to Elise's research as well as the Elfreth. And he's a doctor. The only catch is that he's just not a very good one."

"Wait a minute," said Levin. "You want me to pick up a person?"

"This is my sister we're talking about," James said. "I'd prefer we skip all the other accolades and focus on the doctor part of the equation."

Grace scoffed. "Well, he's who we're retrieving, unless you want to spend sixty hours querying the damn chron database to find a better subject. Be my guest."

"Stop," said Levin.

"He really is our best choice?" James pressed.

"He's our only choice," said Grace. "Trust me, pet, he'll be fine. This will all work out for the best."

"Fine, I trust you." James turned to Levin. "I hope you're not too rusty."

Levin moved in between them and put his hands out. "I'm not doing this jump."

Both of them looked at him quizzically.

"What happened to not saying no?" James asked.

"I will bend my morals for this higher goal and salvage for you, but I will not break the Time Laws, especially the first one. That's where I draw the line. I won't bring anyone back from the past."

Grace's hands curled into claws and she scratched the air in frustration. "Always those fucking Time Laws. I wrote those damn things. Can everyone stop throwing that shit back into my face?"

"What good are you, then?" James grabbed Levin by the collar and pushed him up against the wall. "My sister is sick, you asshole. You're going to help me cure her, or you will find yourself on the other side of that airlock."

Levin's face didn't change, and he kept his hands folded in front of his chest. "Don't threaten me, James. It didn't work when you were a chronman. It won't work now." He looked over at Grace. "You want me to do your dirty work? Fine, but it'll be on my terms. Take it or leave it."

"We'll take it," Grace said. "Let him go, James. We'll find someone else."

"You said he was our only choice."

"He is, but we'll find another way."

Something in James snapped. After weeks of not being able to find a doctor, and then being offered this glimmer of hope, only to have it thrown away, his frustration boiled over and he slammed his fist against the wall, sending a reverberating ring across the entire ship. He forced himself to step away from Levin before he did something permanent that he might regret in the future.

After twenty years of grief and guilt, the universe had given his sister back to him, only to force him to watch her slowly waste away. James felt like the entire world was against him, was mocking him. Well, fuck the universe. Screw them all; he wasn't going to stand by and let it happen. Not again. He'd die before they took his sister from him again.

James inhaled, held his breath, and slowly let the air escape through his nostrils. He turned and looked at them both. "I'll go."

"You can't. You'll die," said Grace. "I won't allow it."

"I'm not needed anymore." He gestured at Levin. "You have your salvager now. I'm expendable."

She shook her head. "You're not expendable. What about Elise? You're going to abandon her in the present?"

That hurt him. James had promised to protect Elise no matter what. She was the one person in his life other than his family whom he ever loved. However, Elise had the Elfreth now. She had Grace and now Levin and others to watch over her. Sasha had James. She'd always had only him, ever since their mother had died. He had let her down once; he wasn't going to let it happen again.

"My mind is made up," he said. "I can't think of a worthier way to sacrifice my life. If I make it back, then great. If I don't, then it's in a higher power's hands. Please watch over my sister."

Grace shot Levin a glare. "And you're going to let this happen?"

Levin's expression did not change. "Every man must make decisions in his life that defines who he is and what he stands for, even if it costs him everything. I have already done so." He walked toward the back supply room, and stopped just as he was about to pass James. Levin put a hand on James's shoulder. "You do what you must. I will do the same. Godspeed."

TWENTY

FIRST ALLIES

Two more days.

Elise couldn't sleep, which should have been weird, because she was always bone-weary these days. The past eight days had been a godsend for the Elfreth. The Flatirons had given them two floors of the All Galaxy Tower, and the tribe had taken full advantage of the respite to recover from their long journey. However, with the knowledge that they had to be back on the road soon, it had been anything but restful for Elise.

As the Oldest, she still had a million things to do every day: managing the daily issues of the tribe, checking to see if her research was still intact, making sure Sasha wasn't getting any worse. The weight of the world seemed to rest on her small shoulders, and Elise was just getting tired of trying to hold everything up.

Two more days.

She tossed and turned on a tattered, lumpy couch in an old office. In forty-eight hours, the Flatirons wanted them gone. Tomorrow was going to be a busy and sad day. The Elfreth would have to start packing again. It was a shame.

The two tribes had gotten along fairly well, though most of the time, the Elfreth were quarantined to the floors given them. The entrances were guarded at all times, though after a few days, the Flatirons relaxed their vigilance and began to trade goods and mingle.

She had initially hoped that this growing trust would allow her to negotiate with Teacher Crowe to let them stay a few more days, but so far, he had been adamant about enforcing their ten-day stay. She didn't blame him. One extension could lead to another, and before anyone realized, it could become a permanent stay, and the Flatirons were not willing to double the size of their population out of charity, even though they had more than enough space on the upper floors. The Mist Isle tribes jealously guarded their territories.

She pulled the thin blanket over her head as the guardian on watch banged the nightstick, letting the rest of the tribe know not only the time but that they were being watched over. It might not make as much sense to keep watch now that they slept within the safety of the walls of the All Galaxy Tower, but Franwil insisted they keep as many of their traditions as possible. Elise agreed. Especially with their current state, their past was the only thing they could cling to. Who knew what the future was going to bring.

Sounds of stomping and shouting came from the lower level. Elise's quarters were near the stairwell at what used to be a set of elevator banks, so sound was often carried far up the shaft. She turned over. This was the second time these late-night noises had occurred. Was something going on down there?

It was times like this she missed James at her side. She prayed to Gaia he was all right. What was that man up to? Was he on his way back to her now? She squeezed her eyes shut and thought of his face; that scruffy face of his. One of these days, she would have to ask Grace to reinvent an electric shaver. That was what she was going to ask for, for Christmas. Well, whenever that was. No one seemed to know what date it was anymore.

The shouting below got louder. Elise sighed and sat up. It wasn't like she was getting much sleep anyway. She got off the couch, threw on her shoes, and made her way to the stairwell.

She knocked on the stairwell door. "It's Elise."

The door swung open and she greeted Nayad, the Flatirons fight, as their warriors were known, who was guarding the Elfreth's entrance. Right now, she was more doorman than guard. The first few days, she had guarded the Elfreth vigilantly, wearing full body armor and carrying an old shotgun. Now, she wore a loose shirt and pants, and the shotgun leaned against the wall.

"Oldest." Nayad bowed. "Is there something I may help you with?"

"What's all that racket downstairs?" she asked.

"A raid against the building. This time on the east." She shook her head. "In all my years as a fight, I have not seen so many raids."

Elise was puzzled. "Another? How many times do you get raided?"

"Almost nightly. Entire tribes. They have increased in frequency lately. Wait, you cannot go there right now. It's too dangerous."

Nayad called after Elise as she took off down twenty-two flights of stairs to the thirty-fourth floor, where all the barricades and bridges connected to the building, and aptly named the barricade floor. When she exited the stairwell, her mouth dropped. The entire floor was alive with activity. There was a makeshift triage in the center of an open area—the actual infirmary was one level higher—and armed people dashing back and forth down the main hall. On the north end, a cluster of them huddled at the base of the barricade. She also saw several Flatirons sprint toward the east.

Elise grabbed a boy carrying a stack of spears. "What's going on?" she asked.

"Double raid," he replied, and then ran off.

"Double . . ." Elise turned and sprinted toward Teacher Crowe's office. She found Crowe surrounded by his group of closest advisers hunched over a ripped blueprint of the building. The guard manning the door blocked her way, but she could hear the Teacher speaking.

The attack was coordinated. It had hit the north side first, pulling the guards' attention away from the other barricades. Then it had hit one of the east bridges fifteen minutes later. The second attack had broken through and taken much effort to push back. Casualties were high.

Elise seized this chance. "Teacher Crowe."

One of the military leaders, a mean one who was adamantly against extending the Elfreth's stay, noticed her standing at the door and scowled. He stalked toward her and slammed the door in her face.

Outraged, Elise banged her small fist on the thick wooden frame. There was a loud crash to the side, and she saw a few of the Flatirons fights on the parapet of the north barricade fall off. More ran to reinforce the faltering forces. She hammered on the door more insistently. The door opened and the scowling jerk who had shut it in her face caught her wrist as her fist flew toward him.

"The Flatirons are busy, floor vulture." That was the derogatory term used in the downtown area for the tribes who did not live or hold any floors in the buildings.

"Don't touch me, asshole," she snapped, trying to pull away.

"Let the Oldest in, Maanx, and show some manners."

"Yes, Teacher." Maanx reluctantly stood to the side.

Crowe's advisers parted ways as she hurried in. "You're under attack on two fronts, and your casualties are climbing."

"That news was not worthy of interrupting our planning, Oldest," Crowe said with an entirely straight face.

"Let me send in the Elfreth guardians."

"Teacher," Maanx said, "The street vultures should not be with weapons on our floors! They cannot be trusted."

"Look at what you're facing, Crowe," she said. "If you don't get backup and you lose containment of the barricades, you could lose the floor. You lose the floor, you might lose the entire building."

Crowe leaned toward Maanx, and the two had a heated whispered discussion. He turned to Elise. "We will allow fifty of your guardians to assist with the east barricade. How many more days are you asking to stay for this help?"

She was tempted to ask for another week. Instead, she took a risk. "Let's call it a freebie this time around."

He nodded. "Maanx will go with you."

Elise sprinted out of the room and made her way back up the stairs with Crowe's military officer at her side. She had a hard time keeping up with him as he took the stairs three steps at a time. His face wore a perpetual scowl. She reminded herself that the young man had influence over the Flatirons' leader. Elise was huffing and puffing by the time they reached the first Elfreth floor. Nayad got out of their way as Elise went to pull the door open. She had opened it just a smidgeon when Maanx slammed it shut again.

"I don't trust you, street vulture," he said in a low voice. "Do not try anything. My fights will be watching your guardians. Do not try anything wicked and evil."

By this time, Elise wasn't sure if the Flatirons just spoke weirdly or the comm band was translating things wrong. In either case, she wasn't going to give this guy the satisfaction of talking crap.

"Without our help," she replied coolly, "you might not have many fights left to watch over us. Get out of my way so I can gather my guardians."

Elise yanked the door harder than she had intended and hurried inside. "Guardians, up!" Her chest swelled with pride when twenty guardians seemingly appeared out of thin air. The past six months of trials had hardened the tribe's defenders. "I need thirty more volunteers to help the Flatirons defend the All Galaxy," she called out. A few moments later, sixty or so more guardians had assembled.

She turned to lead them downstairs when Maanx blocked the door. "Only fifty."

"Fifty with me," she called, not taking her eyes off the young man.

"You count as one," Maanx added.

"Stupid fool," she muttered under her breath. She probably shouldn't be going down with the guardians but there was no way she was going to let this jackass order around or abuse any of her people. No, just like Oldest Qawol had when he sent his people to battle, Elise was going to be right there standing alongside them. She reduced her numbers to forty-nine exactly and followed Maanx as he led them down to the besieged barricade.

By the time they reached that part of the floor, the fighting had spread to both eastern barricades. Elise watched open-mouthed as twenty or so defenders struggled to hold back what looked like five or six times their number. This wasn't a raid; this was an all-out attack. She looked over at the other bridge that was just a little ways down the hall. It wasn't in much better shape.

Elise pointed at the farther barricade. "We'll split up my people, half on each side."

"No, you street vultures stay together so I can keep an eye on you."

"Oh, for Gaia's sake, you idiot," she screamed. "Look at who's attacking you on the other side. Those are the people you should be worried about!"

Maanx hesitated, and finally nodded. "You stay here. I'll take half to the other barricade."

Elise divvied up her teams and urged them forward. She tried to join them on top of the parapet, but was held back by one of the older guardians. When she tried to follow anyway, he threatened to assign someone to babysit and keep her out of danger.

She felt useless watching from a safe distance. Her aim with her wrist beam was too poor to effectively shoot any of the attackers that were able to scale the barricade onto the parapet, and she was too worried about hitting her own people to even try. In the end, she realized that everyone would have been better off if she had just stayed upstairs. No, that wasn't true. At least that Maanx guy had someone to keep him in check.

The fighting continued for another hour. When it was all over, her tired and exhausted guardians dragged themselves alongside the even wearier fights. They retreated shoulder to shoulder as one unit down the barricades. They were replaced by other fights that, to be honest, weren't in much better shape than the ones who had just fought. They were just a little more rested. She took a quick inventory of her people and was thankful that there were no casualties, though over half had suffered injuries of some sort. One man had broken his leg falling off the parapet.

Maanx barked orders to the replacements filtering in. It was then that she realized that he wasn't actually scowling at her. That was just the expression he always wore. He turned and their eyes met, and he gave her an ever-so-slight nod. Then he went back to yelling at his people. Well, the fact that he didn't even bring up escorting her straight back to the Elfreth floors was progress. It was small, but she'd take it.

Elise directed her people to the infirmary one floor up and sent a runner to retrieve some of the medical supplies from her tribe's own stash. She stayed there for the next few hours until the growling of her stomach could no longer be ignored, and one of the nurses told her that she had already missed lunch.

Elise went up sixteen levels to the dining floor, which was the only floor where the tribes were allowed to mingle and trade. Out of the corner of her eye, she saw Crowe speaking with the food staff. She caught him looking her way, and then he focused back on whatever he was doing. Elise did her best to keep her cool. If the guy was going to say, do, or offer something, he'd do it on his own time. The last thing she wanted was to look desperate, no matter how much so she actually was.

She got the dregs of some sort of soup and sat down, staring at the bowl. She was so tired right now, she could just face-plant and drown in the broth, then she reminded herself that there were a dozen of her people bleeding on the floor downstairs. At least she had been able to walk up here on her own. They were the ones who had sacrificed, and for what?

Elise finished her meager meal alone and snuck one final peek at where she had last seen Crowe. He was no longer there. She swallowed her disappointment and stood up, ready to head back downstairs to the infirmary.

"Oldest, I did not want to disturb your meal," an old man's voice said from behind her.

Elise closed her eyes and held the relief back from showing on her face as she turned. "Please, Teacher, any time."

"My son says your people fought bravely, that perhaps the defense of the eastern walls might have been more difficult without you."

"Your son . . . Maanx?" Elise couldn't hide her surprise. "The sour one?"

"He trusts little, but means well." Crowe paused. "He is also loathe to offer praise, something I fear he learned from his father. He has had a difficult childhood."

"He seems like an upstanding young man," she lied. "Is there something I can help you with, Teacher?"

"I have an offer for you, Oldest. As you can see, the raids lately have increased not only in size but frequency, mostly from the north. We do not know why this is happening, but my people are struggling to hold our building. I would like to offer to share resources in return for shared work."

"What's the work?" Elise asked.

"Your guardians on the north and east walls. In return, you are welcome to stay."

Those were the two most often under attack, but Elise had seen the rest of the Flatirons' defenders. They needed some time off the front line to recover, and she knew she was buying Crowe's goodwill if she accepted. More importantly, she could tell he knew that as well.

"The Elfreth will need more floors. Also no more guards and locks. If you are to trust us with your safety, then you are to trust us as we have you."

Crowe looked thoughtful. "Within limits. You are still our guests, subject to our laws. Your tribe's labor is your own, not ours."

"But we are still our own tribe. Your stores are yours and ours are ours," she said. "We also must be allowed to plant and farm on unused floors."

Crowe nodded and offered his hand. "If you stay that long, they are yours within reason."

She shook it. The fact that he didn't disagree to their farming the upper floors gave her hope that he was offering a long-term stay. She kept her smile small as she went over a few minor details with him, but inside, Elise was ecstatic. For the first time in months, she finally saw a glimmer of hope.

TWENTY-ONE

TITUS

Are you sure you weren't sent by those pea-brained shits at the Praetorian society to give old Titus one last tug of the beard before he goes off on his final Light Burst?"

Titus 2.3, Grand Juror of Darkside Prime, having lived a 155 Venusian years, was the oldest man on all of Venus. He was also the foremost inventor of his generation and once considered the second-brightest mind of the century. Once, meaning he had just recently been bumped down to third by some upstart nineteen-year-old little girl named Priestly from those crazy Technology Isolationists. Go figure those jerk-offs couldn't wait a week and spare him the news of his demotion until after he'd already been fried to a crisp.

Supposedly, this Grace girl had a once-in-a-thousand-years mind. Bah, that's what they had said about Titus when he was young. A thousand years didn't count for much any more, did it? Still, he had held on to that title for most of his life, so he was content to let the child bear the burden of brilliance. Titus was pretty tired of being the smartest guy at every party anyway.

The stranger blocking his path to his honorary Light Burst shuttle craned his head back and looked up at the tip of the needle-shaped ship, slated to take off in the next ten minutes. The two stood at an impasse on the platform even as the Light Burst thrusters smoked, and it began its preignition sequence. Titus really should be buckled in by now. Five kilo-meters away, watching safely in their observation tower, Titus's family, friends, and peers were all waiting for him to commit suicide.

"I assure you, Grand Juror, as great of an honor as being granted the Light Burst voyage is, flying into the sun is probably one of the worst ways a person could die. As soon as your heat shields—"

"I know what happens, boy. I designed this flaming contraption. It's Venusian tradition to send us old shits off this way. Blaze of fucking glory," Titus huffed. "I've taken four life extensions already. That's a record, by the way. Most granted any Venusian, and frankly, my damn back's too tired to hold me up anymore. I've done more than anyone in three life-times, and if those dumb jerk-offs want to push me out now, well, I don't have the energy to argue."

"Your mind is still as sharp as ever, Titus."

"Address me as Grand Juror, boy. I've earned the title."

"As you wish, Grand Juror. I am here to offer you an opportunity to continue your work."

"Are you sure you're not from the Praetorian?"

"I assure you I am not, Grand Juror. If you do not believe me, then by all means step into the Light Burst and be on your way. I won't stop you. However, my scans have confirmed that you are still healthy and may live for several more years. If you wish to put those to good use, then you should come with me."

Titus hesitated. He had already said goodbye to his husband and two wives. He had held court for his grandchildren and played with his great-grandchildren one last time, making sure they all realized he wasn't returning from this voyage. The boys at the Praetorian Society had thrown him a grand party. They had even given him a prostitute, though Titus didn't know what he was flaming supposed to do with the young thing without hurting himself.

Everything felt pretty final. Sometimes, an old guy just has to recog-nize the end credits when they roll by. Still, the opportunity this stranger presented was interesting. After all, a couple of more years were nothing to sneeze at. It had only taken him two to invent the reflective rad shields everyone on the colony currently wore. That achievement had earned him his invitation to the Praetorian. There was also the matter of tradition.

Isn't this what he was supposed to do as an elder honored citizen of Venus? What if word got out that he skipped out on his own Light Burst? It would be a scandal! How could his familial clan—

"Excuse me, Grand Juror, time is running out. The Light Burst is going to take off in the next six minutes. I need to be away from the blast radius when it does. Regardless, you need to be on that ship or with me."

"Don't rush me, boy," Titus snapped. "Do you know who I am?"

"Yes, Grand Juror, you are—"

"I was being facetious, you little flaming punk. This is a big decision to make. I don't like being rushed. Where are we going anyway?"

"A place that needs your skills and intelligence. A place where you can continue to do good. So can I assume you will come?"

"Assume all you want. I'm still thinking. How did you get past security anyway? You know, I designed this entire launch bay. Call it professional curiosity, so in my next life, I can build a better system to keep creepy assholes like you out. This is a private party."

"Your two honor guards at the door do not know I am here."

"Really? Guards! Get your lazy asses in here."

The stranger sighed. "I really wish you hadn't done that."

The two red-clad Venusian Royal Honor Guards came running into the room, both carrying their battery tridents. Their insect-like armor, more ceremonial than functional, of that jackass Novein's worthless design aesthetic, no less, was modeled after a type of old Earth beetle that used to be worshiped as a god. The two men, however, were elite warriors specifically chosen by the Praetorians to honor Titus 2.3's Light Burst.

"Stand aside, Grand Juror," one of the guards said, leveling his battery trident at the stranger.

For a second, Titus feared that the stranger would use him as a human shield and that he would die at the base of his own Light Burst ship before even getting the chance to kill himself properly. That would have just been a final indignation. To his pleasant surprise, though, the stranger did not stop Titus from waddling off to the side to safety. The honor guard who had spoken aimed his battery trident and fired a lightning arc at the stranger. The stranger tilted just a couple of centimeters to his left and let the arc shoot harmlessly past his head.

"You have really good reflexes," Titus observed, admittedly enter-tained.

The second honor guard charged in closer and fired his trident as well. Titus's chest puffed up a little. He recognized one of his babies. It was a kinesis spear, one of his later inventions, which could wrap a kinetic field around an object and manipulate it. He watched as the blue field shot out and enveloped the stranger. Then, to his surprise, nothing happened. The field that was supposed to surround the guy just popped like a bubble.

"You must have a defective spear," Titus commented, his face turning a little red. His mouth dropped when a strange yellow crackle of energy leaped out of the stranger. At first, it looked like the battery trident had malfunctioned and was causing energy feedback, then Titus realized the stranger was surrounded by a nearly translucent field of yellow light.

The kinesis spear exploded in the honor guard's hands, and then the stranger seemed to have somehow teleported, or moved really, really fast, next to the guard. There was a clumsy exchange, and the honor guard flew into the air and slammed into the wall on the far side of the silo.

The remaining guard fired again; this time, his lightning arc hit the stranger square in the chest, but the blue arc harmlessly fragmented into thousands of pieces off the stranger's yellow field. A similar yellow surge followed, and an invisible force struck the honor guard, cracking his chest-plate in half. The impact slammed the guard into one of the railings.

The stranger turned to Titus. "I'm sorry that had to happen, Grand Juror. If you do not wish to come with me, I will not force you."

Titus, a lifelong pacifist, harrumphed. "You young men, always think-ing with your dicks and biceps. All right, now you've really piqued my curiosity. If I go with you, what's my guarantee what you're offering is true?"

"Would you like a cyanide pill before we leave? If you change your mind, you are free to still commit suicide."

Titus looked as the Light Burst began its final sequence. Sixty seconds until they were both burned to a crisp. It was too late to get away and too late to get into the rocket. It was the story of his life, always taking too long to make decisions.

On one hand, that's why he never got his proper due, and why he was only considered the second-best mind of his generation. He was much smarter than Novein, that hack. The only reason Novein always got the credit was because he knew how to work their peers at the Praetorian. He was also always first to market, decisive, and admittedly had better taste. That was why he was ranked first while Titus was always the brides-maid. Analysis paralysis was what his second wife called it. On the other hand, his careful decision-making had allowed him to live this long. Well, except in this case, where his indecision was going to kill them both.

"Oh, fine," he grumbled. "Though I flaming think it's too late . . ."

In a split second, the stranger grabbed Titus and cradled him close to his body. Just as the rocket ignited, the stranger and Titus launched up the tube, as if they had their own invisible rockets strapped to their asses. They shot straight through the launch opening and cleared the planet.

A few minutes later, in the black depths of space, Titus and the stranger watched as a spark of light erupted from Venus's surface, leaving a thin yellow trail. They floated for twenty minutes, watching his coffin dis-appear toward the sun.

"Like watching my own damn funeral," Titus grumbled.

"A spectacular event, Grand Juror," the stranger said.

"Now what? Why are we still floating here? It's making me dizzy. Makes me want to shit my pants. Where are we going next?" He paused. "How are you doing this?"

The stranger smiled for the first time. "Please stand by. We will need to wait until we are cleared to jump back."

"Go figure. You hurry me up and make me wait. How flaming rude. What do you mean, jump, anyway? Where are we going?"

"To the future."

Titus wasn't surprised. He had surmised as much when he saw all the stranger's powers. "Holy hell. I knew it! Talk about burying the lead. You know, boy, you should have opened with that line. I'd have hopped in your sack right away if you hadn't beaten around the bush and wasted my time. I look forward to the medical developments that will make my life more bearable."

"Apologies, Grand Juror, there isn't a cure for old age."

"Fuck." Titus paused. "Is the future at least nice? Like a utopian paradise?"

The stranger shook his head. "I hate to disappoint you."

"Flaming fuck. I might as well have stayed in the rocket, then."

"Would you like your cyanide pill now or when we get there?"

There was a bright yellow flash. Followed by intense pain. And then noth-ing. A few seconds later, James woke up to a voice screaming in his head as he stared at the abandoned Venusian colonies against the planet's an-gry red landscape. His skin burned from the intense heat of the sun, yet at the same time, he felt a bone-shaking chill spread through his body. He looked to his left and saw Titus floating next to him.

The old man's skin was rigid, and he had a look of panic frozen on his face. It was then James realized that he had fallen unconscious and that the atmos was off. Quickly, he willed it back on and enveloped both of them, raising the temperatures and pumping air into their protective bubble.

"For space's sake, James, answer me, damn it!"

"I'm here, Grace," he thought back.

"You goddamned flat-lined when you jumped back," she said.

"How long was I out?"

"Just a few seconds. Hang on. We're picking you up."

James checked Titus's pulse; at least the old man was still breathing, though his pulse was weak. He was lucky. The Grand Juror probably would not have survived much longer. James took a deep breath and promptly threw up. A splitting pain erupted in his head, pounding him like a ham-mer on a melon, threatening to splatter the contents of his brain next to the contents of his stomach. He hunched over and watched as the bile floated away and congealed on the wall of the perfect sphere surround-ing him and Elise's newest recruit.

He could really use a drink. He remembered he had snuck a small flask of whiskey from the Drink Anomaly on board while packing the ship. It wasn't much, but it was something, especially since that last jump seemed to have twisted his insides something fierce.

In the distance, he saw a small two-color spark approach. Then he looked down at his wet shirt and the contents of his lunch floating inside his atmos shield. How embarrassing. At least the wait for his ride wouldn't be too long. He was fortunate that Grace had taken precautions and had outfitted him with an emergency life support band on the chance that this might occurr, which of course it did. Otherwise, both he and Titus would be dead right now. She would never have let him live it down.

The pink was coming back to Titus's old crackly face, and he seemed to be breathing normally again. He was curled up in a fetal position, as if encapsulated in a womb and rotating like a planet without a care in the world. He was even starting to snore in the otherwise dead of space. It was almost cute.

The past hour had been traumatic for the old man, and he had complained and corrected James every step of the way until nap time. James already knew he was going to be a handful. That was the problem with gathering some of the greatest minds in one place. You also ended up with the biggest egos, and every one of them was used to being in charge. Well, Titus was Elise and Grace's headache now. They wanted a master inventor and fabricator, they got one. As long as he was a good enough doctor for Sasha, James couldn't care less about the rest.

"How's the old geezer doing?" Grace asked as the bulky transport came to a stop alongside him.

"Still alive, if that's what you're asking," he said, maneuvering to the rear hatch and floating inside.

"Take him to the bunk," Grace told Levin. Then she walked up to James and checked his vitals. "That's it, James. Never again. Next time you jump, you will die," she snapped. "You were already playing against the house on this one. You will not make it back, and then you'll be useless to all of us. Promise me on Elise's and Sasha's life."

He nodded. "This is it."

"Get some rest. I want to observe your life signs for a few hours."

"I need to pilot the ship back to Earth."

"That wasn't a request. Levin can take care of that."

James nodded and stumbled into the crew quarters. He was met by Smitt's ghost, who whistled as he looked at the unconscious Titus. "What the heck, right? Once you break the one Time Law no one dares breaks, who cares if you break it a few more times, right?"

James tried to ignore him. At least he was only being haunted by someone who was actually dead now, unlike Sasha and Grace.

"Come on, my friend." Smitt grinned. "The past is already dead. A person cannot simply un-die."

"Don't you have anything better to do?" he grumbled.

"You'd think so," Smitt replied.

"Your brain patterns are spiking, James. I told you to get some rest," Grace spoke inside his head through his comm band. "Are you talking to your phantoms again?"

"Just one." James hadn't told her about Smitt yet. He wasn't sure he should. This one felt different. He went into the back room and lay down on one of the lower bunks. His body hurt all over. Just as he was drifting off to sleep, he remembered the flask of whiskey hidden in the storage locker. It called to him. For a second, passing out felt like the better plan. Instead, James dragged his exhausted body out of bed and snuck next door.

TWENTY-TWO

ADMINISTRATIVE TASKS

The Co-op completed the takeover of another building, a large 133-story high-rise with twenty-three bridges connecting to adjacent buildings along 125th Street. The building served as a central hub to many of the other blocks in the Harlem region of the island. By the hounds' estimations, there were nearly four thousand inhabitants in just that building alone. The density of savages was increasing, but Kuo's forces had become more efficient, more adept at capturing and subjugating. Already, they had conquered a quarter of the island, encountering hardly any resistance as they steadily moved down its length.

Kuo, standing on the 114th floor on the south end of the building, looked down at a large jungle clearing a few blocks to the south. The haze was light this morning, allowing several hundred meters of visibility. The EMP fog had proven more problematic than she had anticipated. With limited numbers and no modern means of communication, her forces initially had problems maintaining their control over many of the blocks they had taken over. Sometimes, as little as two days after her troopers had cleared an entire building, another savage tribe would wander in, forcing her people to reclear it. There was simply too much area, horizontally and vertically, for the resources she had at hand.

Kuo found the solution to this problem in leveraging the thousands of savages they had captured. Uprooted from their homes with no place to stay, these doe-eyed primitives seemed to have lost all hope and direction. She was doing them a service by offering employment as indentured servants. In her eyes, she was elevating these wallowing primitives to civilized standards.

It hadn't taken much to convert them. Kill a few to instill fear among the rabble. Find someone with a semblance of authority who could keep them in line. Relay your commands and make sure they were followed. If any of the savages acted up, kill a few more. Then you fed them. Within a few days, all of the defeated tribes had fallen in step with the new order.

In the case of the Northwoods, Ewa had had to kill over a dozen of their leaders before she found someone who agreed to follow orders and keep the rest of them in line. In the weeks since, the Co-op had steadily increased its presence, taking over building after building. It had now indentured over a hundred savage tribes. Some were as small as twenty while others numbered nearly a thousand. With these additions, the Co-op was able to stabilize its holdings and make steady gains as Kuo's forces gobbled up block after block of the Mist Isle.

The original plan was to assign the stronger of the savages to menial labor, use the children as couriers, and to put the weak and old on watch. The last group was strategically placed at every building entrance and intersections dividing the blocks already conquered and the ones the Co-op hadn't cleared yet. If there was any disturbance, those on watch would tell the children, who would run and report it to a nearby monitor outpost. This setup was primitive, but it should have worked if everyone had done their job.

The first week of managing this system, however, had been a disaster. Her operations suffered from these savages' poor work ethic. They had no sense of responsibility or employment. Many times, her people caught them shirking their duties, sleeping on the job, or even wandering off from their posts. Usually, Kuo wouldn't have tolerated such insubordination, but as much as she hated to admit it, she needed them. She needed twice the number she had now to hold the line across the entire island as they continued south. Her reinforcements weren't enough.

Kuo blamed herself for this oversight. The savages didn't know better. They had descended from generations of takers and leeches and wanted the welfare—shelter and food—but didn't want to work for it. All this required the monitors and troopers to vigilantly manage the savages, which defeated the purpose of having indentured servants to begin with.

It took her a few days to come up with a solution. She found it in the past, after studying the economic models of the Neptune Divinities and even further back in a tiny totalitarian regime known as North Korea. It was a sound short-term strategy that would pay dividends.

Kuo walked to an open courtyard where the survivors of three tribes were being corralled and divided into laborers, watchers, and couriers. It was a large group, numbering nearly two thousand. She found Ewa consorting with a group of troopers and pulled her aside. "How many troopers and Valta personnel do we need to administer this many new savages?"

"Nearly seventy percent of our active hours, Senior," Ewa said. "At least for two days until they get under control and organized, then it'll require almost fifty percent to keep all the indentured in line and doing their job."

"This is inefficient and unacceptable. It will completely stall our offensive."

Ewa nodded. "The blocks we control grow by the day. It is difficult enough maintaining an offensive line with only two thousand combat personnel. We're acquiring buildings too quickly, and do not have enough ground personnel to cover them. Furthermore, we've received scattered reports of activity to the north, so we're utilizing even more resources patrolling blocks we've already conquered."

Kuo fumed. Maintaining momentum was important. She could see her entire offensive flounder under its own weight, otherwise. "The further south we move, the denser these buildings become. The only way we can sustain this pace is to change requirements. Lower squad readiness strength from eighty percent to fifty. These savages are nothing. Half-strength is all we need. Otherwise, we risk getting bogged down as an occupying force. I want the shocker pods moving at all times."

"That doesn't address the problems with the indentured or maintaining the integrity of the watch line," Ewa said. "Fifty percent are needed just to force the savages to do their job. We don't have enough resources to do both."

"Perhaps we are approaching it from the wrong angle, then," Kuo said. "I have a new idea. This group of freshly acquired savages will be our test case. We put the healthy ones to work performing menial labor and maintaining the watch line. We hold the weak and the elderly in holding pens. If the healthy ones do not properly perform their duties, we punish their loved ones."

"Hostages, Senior?" said Ewa.

"Motivation," Kuo replied. "For good service. In return, we clothe, feed, and house their people. This would solve two problems at once, since it requires less personnel to guard the old and weak." She pointed at the sullen group of prisoners huddled in the middle of the room, broken and bloodied from the day's fighting. "Here are your new orders, Securitate. Group all the savages by their family units: fathers, mothers, children, and then split them. The able on the left and the weak on the right. Set them to their duties with the understanding that their evaluation is performance-based and that the health of their families rests upon their fulfillment of their responsibilities."

"Yes, Senior."

Kuo stepped to the side while Ewa carried out her orders. The room became filled with sobs and cries and screams as the monitors pulled children from parents, wives from husbands. A few of them tried to resist, only to be beaten into submission. This process continued for nearly thirty minutes as the thousands were divided into two groups. It became apparent early on, though, that a third group had to be formed.

A large percentage, nearly half of the savages here, had no significant links to be accountable for. After the recent battles, many of the healthy and able savages had died. Many others had fled, leaving behind those who couldn't follow. Ewa ended up dividing those without personal connections into this third group, and it was the largest one by far. She approached Kuo when it was done. "What should we do with these, Senior?"

That was something Kuo hadn't considered. The wastelanders here had already proven themselves unreliable without proper motivation. Giving them positions of responsibility was out of the question. Keeping them out of charity even more so. Kuo walked to the bridge to the adjacent building and looked across at the darkened entrance.

A hundred meters down, where the bridge connected, a wall of bricks and garbage was being piled up, a barricade of sorts. The primitives actually thought it would make a difference. Most of the savage tribes had tried to do something of this nature every time the Co-op invaded a new building. It must be the way they were used to fighting each other.

It usually took her forces less than five minutes to punch through, though it was often the most dangerous part of the attack. Nearly half of their casualties so far had come from insertion points. It gave her another idea.

Kuo pointed at the building adjacent to them, the next on their list to attack. "The hounds estimate there are at least the same number of savages in the next building as there were here. When we took this building, they were entrenched, waiting for us. The next building will be even more difficult, and the one after that still more so. Instead of fighting them for every inch, let's soften them up a bit before we send our own forces in."

"I don't understand."

Kuo pointed at the third group. "We will not waste anything or anyone. Drive all these unattached prisoners into the adjacent buildings and have them spread word of our arrival. Sow terror among those who think they can stand up to us. Who knows, perhaps those savages will just surrender without us even firing a shot. In the worst case, the primitives will have to deal with a refugee crisis, either by killing them or housing them. It will sap their resources and their resolve. In any case, it will be out of our hands."

Ewa nodded. "I will tell the troopers to drive them out."

Kuo watched as the orders were relayed across the room. The prisoners looked dazed as they were brought to their feet and corralled toward the bridge.

Kuo rolled her eyes. "Ewa, when I say drive them out, I meant like this." She activated her exo and created a large white trunk. She trotted to the near end of the group and smashed it into them, sending bodies flying into the other bodies.

The savages in the group milled around at first, confused and unsure if they were supposed to stay still or run. They had been guaranteed safety and food as long as they surrendered. Now, wavering between fighting back and obeying, their natural instincts won out.

Kuo pressed on, pushing them forward with her trunk and attacking anyone who got too close. To her left, Ewa did the same. To her right, the monitors followed her lead, though with decidedly less enthusiasm and effectiveness. In a few seconds, it became a stampede as that third group of savages fled across the bridge, scurrying like rodents away from a flood, out toward the entrance of the next building over.

"Hold," Kuo said at the base of the bridge. "Don't let them back."

Already, chaos was unfolding as the defenders of the barricade in the other building met the fleeing prisoners with weapons drawn. The few who tried to turn back were met with wrist beams and exo trunks. The bridge became a death trap as the panicked savages were unable to move forward or back. Inevitably, most were trampled under the weight of the mob.

"Urge them forward," Kuo instructed, and watched as the monitors advanced.

The pressure built as the prisoners surged forward, finally overrunning the defensive barricade in the next building. Like a pressure valve bursting open, the fleeing and panicked prisoners spilled over and a full-blown riot broke out.

Satisfied, Kuo signaled for the monitors to stop their advance. "Maintain position here until nightfall." She signaled to Ewa. "Let them stir up chaos for two hours. As soon as the tired defenders think they have everything under control, we roll in. This will be our tactic going forward. From this point on, we will use these prisoners as our vanguard."

As Kuo left the room, her second hurriedly followed and called after her. "Excuse me, Senior?"

"What is it?"

"I don't want to speak out of turn . . ."

"You are my second and have earned your worth several times over. Out with it."

Ewa gestured at the crowd huddled in one corner. "You're asking that we corral them like fodder. These savages might not be earners, but they are still human."

"And you propose we care for them simply because they are? What value do they provide us, or to humanity as a whole?"

Her second stopped. "I'm just saying there are thousands of these savages here on the island. We can't just treat them all like expendable animals."

Kuo scanned the room at the large group of corralled savages. "Do you know," she said softly, "where I was born, Ewa?"

Ewa frowned. "Your surname says you're from Europa, doesn't it?"

"That was changed when I was young. I was actually born on Rhea."

Kuo's second looked surprised. "The failed socialist state?"

"My family fled to Europa and bribed the refugee administrators in order to avoid the stigma attached to our colony. But yes, I grew up there right as it was falling apart. I had a front-row seat to one of humanity's worst social experiments." She looked at Ewa. "You look surprised."

"I apologize for asking, Senior." Her second in command bowed. "You are just one of the last people I would ever consider having a socialist upbringing."

Kuo looked as if she had just eaten something distasteful. "My father, a noted habitat architect, was recruited by the government to design module additions for Rhea. The colony had attracted many skilled minds as potential colonists with promises of equality and easy living. For a while, it worked. The provisional government provided for all our needs. Eventually. though, there were too many nonproductive people to support, and too few of worth doing work. I still remember the inevitable food riots and module gangs taking over and hoarding oxygen shipments. The colony fell under its own dead weight, and like most, it was the takers who continued to take."

"Did your family make it out?" Ewa asked.

"They did. All except my father, who, to his dying day, was working hard to keep the colony functioning, even as the mobs tore into his module and rerouted the life support systems from his building." Kuo pointed at the huddled crowd. "I was young, but I remember. In the end, the mobs, those people of little value who did not contribute to humanity, they looked a lot like them." She turned to Ewa. "Just remember, Securitate. It does not take much dead weight to sink an entire ship. If we do not cut them away quickly, they will drag us all down." Kuo began to walk out of the room.

"I'm sorry about your father," Ewa called after her.

Kuo did not bother to look back. "Don't be. He was a foolish man with foolish ideas."

TWENTY-THREE

NEW HOME

The Elfreth were finally able to do the one thing that had been previously impossible: unpack. There was something therapeutic about being able to take their belongings out from storage and set them out. For the first time in months, they were no longer transients. The cooks were able to set up a kitchen. The teachers were able to choose a room and schedule school again. Even the farm animals were given an entire floor so they could graze freely on the wild vegetation that grew on the higher levels. Best of all, the Elfreth had a home again. Elise, Franwil, and the rest of the elders suddenly had to become city planners and unpack the entire tribe across the three floors the Flatirons had allocated them.

One of the first things they had to concern themselves with was planting new crops. The farmers were given nine floors on the upper levels, that received enough sun during the day to farm. Replenishing their blood corn, glow shrooms, and crippling weeds stores would be important to the tribe's continuing survival. Fortunately, almost all of the crops being planted were fast-growing, some sprouting and ready to harvest in as little as a week.

The Flatirons must have decided to trust them, because the morning after Elise and Crowe came to an agreement, all their restrictions disappeared. She no longer felt like they were living in a prison. Instead, they were given the run of the entire building and the freedom to mingle with the Flatirons, though both sides still mostly stayed with their own. The two tribes would need more time to get better acquainted.

By the end of the first week, as Elise walked through the three newly-established floors of living quarters, she could already feel the sense of community returning to the Elfreth. The bulk of the tribe lived on the fifty-seventh floor, dubbed Middle Village. The floor used to be an office, a massive cubicle farm with rows of walled offices on the sides. It took a little planning and more than a bit of mediation between quarreling families angling for the best spaces, but eventually, everyone was allocated a place of their own. They even put up street names so people knew how to navigate the maze of corridors.

The cooks had set up their kitchen on the north side of the fifty-sixth floor, called the Lower Village. The guardians made the south end of that floor their headquarters. The newly-erected blacksmith's hearth shared the same fire sources as the kitchen on the northeast side, and the entire west side was reserved for food storage.

The Upper Village, on the fifty-eighth floor, was more open. The Elfreth converted a series of small rooms on the northwest end into a school. Shops, vendors, and services quickly filled out the rest of the floor. By the end of the week, a thriving market had sprung up, and Elise could hear the friendly chatter of tribesmen living their lives again.

Elise even had a corner office to call her own. It amused her, because she always thought she'd have to move into an office when she was too old to pilot a mechanoid or handle the physically taxing work of a field biologist. Instead, she had earned it by somehow getting saddled with the head honcho job for a tribe of future earth primitives. Go figure.

The most important thing she had to take care of was the tribe's responsibility for guarding the northern and eastern barricades. Elise had promised Crowe that the Elfreth would completely take care of all four barricades on those sides. Their tenure in the All Galaxy depended on whether they kept their end of the bargain. She spent the bulk of her time with Eriao working out a barricade rotation, making sure a system was in place to make sure all her guardians knew their roles and had emergency contingency plans.

Elise also scheduled daily meetings with Crowe to make sure the two of them stayed on the same page. At first, she worried that she was annoying him; some of his closest advisers resented the Elfreth and her access to him. The teacher did not seem to mind, though; at least, he always smiled when he saw her.

The attacks, especially on the north side, had become a constant issue. It was strange, because most of the attacks seemed random and came from an assortment of tribes. Sometimes, it was a deliberate and planned organized assault by hard raiders intent on stealing supplies. Other times, it was an unfortunate group who just happened to be trying to move south. Rarely was a tribe foolish enough to attack them more than once. There was little rhyme or reason to why so many different groups were hitting them.

For Elise, it was especially difficult because many of those tribes trying to break through the barricades were just like the Elfreth had been two weeks ago. It seemed unfair to fight and turn them away. It bothered many of her guardians as well as they repelled wave after wave of raiders. There was no way the Flatirons could have held the entire building—all eight barricades—under this constant pressure, considering each barricade was hit at least once a day, the northern ones sometimes three. How did they hold the floor before without the Elfreth to support them? Disturbed, she went to speak with Crowe in his residence.

The teacher was stoking a small fire and speaking to a group of children when she came. He noticed her at the door and smiled. Elise waited until he was done telling his story, listening as he narrated the Flatirons' history to them in a song. The Flatirons had originated in Niagara and had fled when the Great Lakes overflowed. They wandered the region for a generation, turning into a warring tribe that pillaged as they went. It was a dark time for the world, and even darker for their tribe. It wasn't until after they entered Mist Isle and took possession of the All Galaxy Tower that they had domesticated and changed from a savage raiding tribe to farmers.

When Crowe was done with the story, he ushered the children out and beamed at Elise. "Another report, Oldest? We had one just a few hours ago. I am starting to think you simply enjoy my company."

"Always, Teacher." Elise took a seat opposite Crowe near the fire. "The raids on the building have been nonstop. My guardians say they've repelled a dozen this week alone. I'm running four shifts as it is. How were the Flatirons able to manage this?"

Crowe shook his head. "These are troubling times, Oldest. These frequent attacks are a new occurrence, they've only increased in the past few weeks. Our building is well-known among these blocks. Attacks were rare before, sometimes less than a few times a season. At one point, I feared my people were becoming too lax. Now I fear there are too few to hold the barricades."

"How did you know to choose to trust us out of all the other tribes?" she asked.

"Two reasons." He chuckled. "First, you asked. In the Mist Isle, it is a rare thing for a wandering tribe to wield words before the spear. The world is dangerous. In the many years I have been Teacher, only a few others have asked before attacking. Second, to be truthful, we had little choice. The Elfreth are almost as numerous as the Flatirons, and many of our fights are injured. If you had chosen to attack that night, I doubt we would have held the wall. When I saw the bands on your wrists, I knew you could be a formidable foe. I had no choice but to attempt peace first. I am glad I did. The Flatirons are grateful that you are helping share this burden."

"We are stronger together," she agreed.

It was a strange coincidence that these raids were increasing just as the Elfreth had come to the Mist Isle. Elise had a nagging feeling that they were related; she desperately hoped not. Coming here had been her decision. If the Elfreth had somehow led the Co-op here and they were the ones causing this upheaval, then the blame lay directly at her feet. That meant the Elfreth were taking advantage of the Flatirons' desperation over something they themselves had caused. That did not sit well with her.

"Oldest," Rima said, barging into the room. "A voom approaches from the south."

Panic seized her as she stood up. She had desperately hoped for a few months of peace from the Co-op, if not years. More important, was it a routine patrol or an attack? If it was an attack, the Elfreth were in no position to leave. They were as good as dead.

"Gather the guardians," she said. "How in Gaia did they find us so fast?"

"No, Oldest," Rima said. "The flyguards have been holed up in a place on the other side of the river outside the fog waiting for signals from the *Frankenstein*. Early this morning, Bria had run back to report that they made contact." She smiled. "Oldest Grace and Elder James have returned. They've pass through one of the underwater tunnels to the island and are landing on the balcony on the seventy-third floor."

The next few moments were a blur. All Elise could recall was being exceedingly out of breath as she sprinted up thirty flights of steps and dove into James's arms.

TWENTY-FOUR

FAMILY UNIT

James's eyes fluttered open and he looked at the blemished off-white ceiling in Elise's quarters. This must have been an office in a previous incarnation. There were white square frames running left and right, up and down, making a grid of sorts. Half of the flimsy panels were missing, and the rest disintegrated when touched. The black-and-white contrasts formed patterns and shapes of creatures if you stared at them from different angles. Sort of like clouds. Or dreams.

He felt strangely alone, in a pleasant way, although he wasn't the only person in bed. He realized it was because he hadn't dreamed last night, which was often the case when Elise was close by. His hallucinations also tended to stay away whenever she was near, as if somehow she warded him from them. Now that he thought about it, he hadn't seen any of the hallucinations lately, other than the new one. Where had they gone? Like wild animals, did hallucinations go off someplace quiet to die?

He heard the sound of soft breathing and glanced down to his left. Elise shifted, her arm draped around his chest as she nestled against him. Her head rested on his shoulder, and both their chests seem to expand and contrast synchronously. James brushed a wayward strand of hair from her face and caressed her cheek. The red hair she had had when they first met had long since given way to her natural black.

She loved that red and had vowed to one day find a dye. James would love her just the same if she had no hair, but he kept an eye out for it whenever he bartered for supplies. Hair dye was a rare commodity in the present. Once, he had brought back red paint. She laughed and said she adored him for trying. Those words alone were worth the effort.

James slowly shifted his body upward so the back of his head rested against the wall. They were lying on an old mattress with a dozen pillows on one end. When the Elfreth had learned that people in Elise's time slept on such soft things, they made a point of bringing her every single fluffy thing they found. Personally, James, who was used to sleeping on hard floors, couldn't stand sleeping on these things. Elise, however, really liked the pillows, so James made do.

She murmured something and clutched him harder, and then fell back asleep. They had had a late night together yesterday, first catching up as a family with Sasha, then making desperate love on this mattress and holding each other long into the night, watching the strange tentacles of fog that curled in through the windows and cracks.

In the distance, he could hear the guard tapping a nightstick against the floor, letting the rest of the tribe know they were being watched over. It was peaceful, almost too much so. James didn't trust silence, not after what he'd seen. Still, he wouldn't leave the bed and wake Elise. Franwil had pulled him aside last night and told him that Elise was barely getting four hours of sleep a night. The pressure of leadership and managing the Elfreth's move from Boston to New York had been trying. He felt that sharp but familiar sting of guilt for leaving her at such a crucial time.

The banging of the nightstick stopped abruptly. It was somewhere around its thirty-something tap already, meaning it was almost dawn. Something had to be wrong. Maybe they were being attacked, or someone had found an intruder or a wild animal had snuck through the stairwells. It could be any number of things. James tried to crawl out of bed without waking Elise.

To his surprise, Elise grabbed his arms and held him down. "We have guardians, James. They'll handle it."

"It could be another tribe trying to steal our supplies or . . ."

Her grip on his arm tightened and she opened her eyes. "My people have been getting by while you were away. They'll get by now that you're back. We don't need you here to save us. I, however, need you to stay here and hold me."

And that was that. James noted that she had called the Elfreth her people. She had finally accepted her role as their leader, something that was very much in doubt when he had left her. A little smile appeared on his face as he recalled her first days in the present. That Elise and the one lying now in his arms were two completely different people. It saddened him that she had lost a little of her innocence and exuberance, but she was also so much more now.

For the next hour, he cheerfully surrendered himself to the Oldest. The two drifted in and out of sleep together, holding each other until the last taps of the nightstick ended. They were the most peaceful moments James had had in months.

The dim light that managed to pierce the morning haze was just shining through the window when Sasha poked her head in the doorway, reminding him that he had additional responsibilities. She wandered to the bed and pulled on the blanket. "Why are you two still in bed? Oldest Franwil says that those who rise after the sun are doomed to bathe in darkness."

"I don't even know what that means," he grumbled, guilted into getting up. He was sort of a parent now, and wanted to set a good example. He gave Elise a peck on the mouth and slipped out from under the covers.

"It means you stink." Elise yawned and opened her eyes. Her gaze moved to Sasha and then back to him. "It's warm under the blanket. The Oldest here is making an executive decision to just roll with taking a bath in the dark." She turned over and went back to sleep.

James stood up and stretched, feeling his weary joints creak and pop. He felt a sharp pain just to the right of his heart. He moved his fingers along his chest and pressed on it, feeling his nerves cry out. He had first felt this pain shortly after he retrieved Titus. It had started with an ache at the base of his neck, but had since manifested all over his body, small sharp stabs or pain that came and went randomly. He took a few deep breaths until the pain passed.

"Well, are you coming?" Sasha said. "The day is wasting away."

James threw on his clothes and walked with Sasha from their corner room on the fifty-seventh floor down to the dining floor. He put an arm around her shoulder and pulled her in close. "You staying out of trouble while I was gone?" he asked good-naturedly. "Kept up with your studies?"

She nodded vigorously. "I kept my promise. I can count almost has high as Rima now. Did you keep yours?"

He hesitated. She already knew him far too well. He knelt down in front of her and held her hand. "I'm not going to be perfect, but your brother is trying very hard."

She gave him a flat look, her mouth puckering to the left. James took on a properly chastised look as his ten-year-old sister judged him for his crimes. Finally, she nodded. "I forgive you this time, James."

"Thank you, Sasha."

"But I won't always, so don't push it."

"You're learning all the wrong lessons from Franwil," he muttered as the two continued downstairs. A large number of people from both tribes were already in the dining area when they joined the breakfast queue. The Flatirons had their own dining hall, but more and more of them were coming here for meals. It wasn't surprising, really; the Elfreth had much better cooks.

He had brought up the fact that the Flatirons were using up their supplies, but Elise didn't seem to mind. In fact, she was going out of her way to offer up the Elfreth's resources to the other tribe. It seemed her plan to win hearts and minds was working, though it was a costly strategy. There were so many mouths to feed.

James and Sasha got in line with the rest of the tribe. When Mowcka, one of the Elfreth serving the meals, beckoned for him and Sasha to cut to the front, he shook his head. As an elder, he technically had the right to skip to the front, but he had learned early in chronman days how using privilege isolated a person from the common people. He had spent so much effort on getting the Elfreth to accept him because it was so important to Elise. The last thing he wanted to do now was place himself apart from the others. He already had enough of that in his life.

The two of them sat down and James listened as Sasha carried on about the day she was going to have. She seemed excited about everything, though considering the life they had lived on Mnemosyne Station and then on the run from the Co-op, he wasn't surprised. As difficult as living in the wastelands with the Elfreth was, it was a peaceful haven compared to the hell the two of them had endured after their mother died.

"What will you do now that Oldest Grace is back?" he asked. "Will Oldest Franwil have to share you? Everyone seems to love you."

Sasha beamed. "I like learning from both of them. They teach me very different things. Oldest Grace has me help organize the lab with Elise while Oldest Franwil is teaching me how to take care of all of the tribe's animals."

"Which one do you enjoy working for more?"

"They're different, James. Elise says one day, I'll need to know both things so I can help the people of Earth get better."

She continued chattering as they ate breakfast. James hardly said a word and just enjoyed hearing his little sister bounce from subject to subject. She was still young, and to his surprise, her life up until now had not killed her optimism. If anything, it seemed it had actually grown since he had brought her to the present.

A little while later, Levin and Cole came down. Cole went straight toward the front of the line while Levin, seeing James and Sasha sitting by themselves, walked over to them. James reminded himself that his little sister was present. He flashed the ex-auditor a smile. "Morning, Levin. I hear Grace is already putting you to work. Leaving for your first jump today?" He turned to his sister. "Sasha, I believe Titus, the new doctor who is supposed to make you feel better, is expecting you at the infirmary. Why don't you head down there? I'll be along shortly after I talk to our newest addition to the tribe."

Sasha nodded and waved at Levin as she got up. "Welcome to the Elfreth, Mr. Levin." Then she was gone.

As usual, Levin skipped the pleasantries. "Grace has already scheduled me for a jump this week, two the next, and three more after that."

"Welcome to time salvaging without rules."

"These wasteland savages do not have any miasma regimens."

"We don't have running water, either, in case you were wondering, and I suggest you temper who you call savages."

Levin glanced around the room and at least had the decency to lower his voice. He sat down at the table on the other side of James. "At the pace the Mother of Time is pushing, I'll miasma out like you in a year."

"You're looking past surviving a year, all things considered? When did you get so optimistic?"

"Don't get smart with me, James," Levin snapped. "This is untenable, and you know it."

James shrugged and picked at his food. He had to give it to the Elf-reth. The quality of their food had improved by leaps and bounds since he and Elise had arrived, though considering most of the tribe had been eating bugs, rodents, and plants that could shred a person's insides if not cooked correctly, there was very little place to go but up. "Look," he said, spearing a small piece of meat with a sharpened stick and sticking it into his mouth, "we tried for months to find black-market miasma regimens. You were responsible for getting my guy inside ChronoCom killed. The guy who was our friend, if I may add."

That was still a sore point for James. He knew it was misplaced blame, that he was transferring his anger to the ex-auditor from that Valta secu-ritate Kuo, the actual murderer, but James couldn't help it; Smitt was an open wound. His scowl was joined by Levin's as they sat opposite each other, both looking as if they were sucking on something sour.

"I'm sorry," James said, lowering his head. "That was unkind. If you say you did everything you could to prevent his death, I believe you." He motioned at the long line now forming all the way out the door. "Why don't you get some food before you leave for your jump?"

Levin looked down at James's plate and shook his head. "Water and dry rations will do. It's been a while since I've done this. I'd rather work off food I know won't make me throw up." He got up to leave.

"Levin," James called as the ex-auditor got up to leave. He stuck his hand out. "Good luck."

Levin looked down at James's extended hand, gave him just the slight-est of nods, and then left the room.

A little while later, James went down to the thirty-fifth floor to the building's infirmary. He heard Titus yelling and cursing from somewhere on the floor and followed the voice. He found the good doctor examin-ing Sasha on a wooden table. Oldest Franwil, her face painted with worry, was there as well. Titus 2.3 saw James walk into the room and turned on him.

"You!" He jabbed James once in the chest with a finger and held out his opened palm. "Hand me that cyanide pill."

"Excuse me?" James was taken aback. "If you're thinking about using that on my sister, I'm going to throw you off the building."

"Not for her, you flaming dimwit," Titus snapped. "For me! I had to sleep in a dirty and dank room last night. This ass hasn't slept on such a hard surface in half a century. If I had known we'd all be living like cave-men in the future, I'd have just stayed in my Light Burst and burned up in a blaze of flaming glory."

"His residence won't be ready until tomorrow," Franwil said. "And his list of demands is both long and impossible to fulfill."

Titus's face darkened. "I'm not asking for much. Just a few things com-mensurate to my rank as a Grand Juror and member of the Praetorian Society."

"There hasn't been a Praetorian Society in over a hundred years, Titus," said James.

"Call me Grand Juror, boy. Get me some flaming pillows at least. I won't tolerate another night like the last."

"Can we talk about home furnishings later?" James retorted. "Have you examined Sasha?"

The Grand Juror gave him one last scowl and then turned to his sister. Surprisingly, his demeanor changed immediately as he began to ask her questions, check her symptoms, and measure her vitals. This crass old, angry man treated Sasha warmly and with humor, once even making her giggle.

For the next fifteen minutes, James stood at the back and watched like a worried parent as Titus ran a battery of tests. When Titus was done, he complimented Sasha on how brave she was and then sent her out of the room. Once she was gone, he turned his attention back to James and became the asshole Grand Juror again.

Titus jotted a few notes on a piece of bloodcorn husk and handed it to James. "Find this or the future caveman equivalent of this. It should bring down her fever and cough."

"I'll see what I can do," James said, looking the list over. It was too bad Levin and Grace had just left. If they had just another few days to research, they might have been able to locate some of the medicine on this list for their next jump. "Do you know what's wrong with her?"

"Possibly," he replied. "I believe it may be a variant of Terravira mono-nucleosis though I can't be sure without running some more tests. It commonly affects young people and was just becoming a problem on Earth during my time. The symptoms are similar, but I can't be sure. Terravira mononucleosis was never a problem on any of the colonies. I'm going to need to get her blood checked, and I don't mean with leeches or whatever you medieval barbarians use."

"Can you cure her?"

"Don't press me," Titus snapped. He surveyed the infirmary. "I haven't had a chance to look this place over. I'll take a complete inventory of this dump today and make a list of things we need. I think the little girl will be all right. That is, if we get her on medication and treatment before she gets any weaker. For now, make sure her sleeping quarters are cleaned and washed."

"Thank you, Titus." James breathed, a wave of relief washing over him.

"You can thank me by getting me some flaming pillows for my sore ass," Titus said. "I'm serious. Get on it. I want something soft to sleep on tonight."

"That I think I can swing." James grinned. Elise had so many, she wouldn't miss giving a few to the old man. "Anything else?"

"Yeah, that Grace girl I met this morning. Kind of my age, a little younger. Gray hair, statuesque, gorgeous." Titus leaned in. "Is she single?"

TWENTY-FIVE

RIDING A BICYCLE

Levin stood in front of the uneven reflective metal and studied his own face. It had been months since he had last seen his reflection, since before his incarceration on Nereid, in fact. He didn't recognize the man staring back at him, though part of that could have been the dull, uneven surface elongating his neck and bloating his head. Or perhaps it was the way the dim light softened his features to the point he could barely make out his nose, let alone smaller details. Whoever it was, it wasn't Levin Javier-Oberon.

"You've been staring at yourself for twenty minutes now," Grace said, sitting in the pilot seat. "Any longer, and you're going to burn a hole through the hull." She glanced up and frowned. With a slightly exaggerated effort, she got up and walked over to him, grabbed his hand and led him to the bench. "You're nervous."

He could feel his face redden. "It's been less than a year since my last jump, but after Nereid, that feels like a lifetime ago." He looked down at the bands around his arms. They still felt foreign to him. Black abyss, everything did. When a guy experienced nothing but deprivation in a pit of humanity's worst, it tended to consume his entire being, leaving no room for whatever he was before. Now that he was back in the light, if he could call it that, he was having trouble adjusting to his previous life.

Levin looked up at Grace. And then there was the Mother of Time. He had all but worshiped her during his tenure at ChronoCom. This woman was responsible for humanity's survival more than any other per-son in history. Without time salvaging, mankind would have gone ex-tinct by now.

He must have been staring, because Grace rolled her eyes and put a hand on his cheek and pushed his face to the side. "Stop looking at me like you want to fuck me. You're far too ugly for my taste. The Mother of Time has to maintain some sort of standards, even around here."

That earned a little smile from Levin. The Mother of Time's sexual ap-petite was legendary. He had originally thought everything he had learned about her at the Academy was grossly exaggerated, the truth stretched into tall tales over the centuries. In this particular case, it seems it had all been true.

"You're doing it again, Auditor."

"Sorry, Mother of Time."

"Call me Grace. My TI days are long over."

"Call me Levin. So are my ChronoCom days."

A small light told them they had arrived at the planned coordinates. The two of them moved to the front of the collie and looked out the win-dow as the sun blazed brightly off the starboard side of the ship. Grace pointed at a vid hanging off the ceiling and tapped a black space near the left side. "You want to be three hundred meters west of here in exactly four minutes. I'll initiate the jump. Remember, you have nineteen min-utes before the *Blackwood* falls into the sun. Be out of the ship by that time. Do you understand? You have zero latitude here. One more second and you'll become Titus's substitute as a sacrifice to the sun god."

Levin nodded. Back when he was a chronman, a stash-and-grab like this was easy, something he was doing in his Tier-4 days. Right now, though, his stomach was in knots, and he felt like he was running his very first salvage.

She patted him on the back as he prepared to leave. "Kick those jitters and show me what one of the highest operatives in my agency can do."

It was a silly statement, but it worked. Levin stood up a little straighter and felt a small boost of courage. This woman knew how to push all his right buttons. Who was he kidding? Grace Priestly probably knew how to push everyone's.

Levin powered on his exo and atmos, double-checked the collie's in-terior life supports, and opened the hatch doors. He launched himself toward the marker Grace had designated through his AI band. Behind him, the sun blazed angrily, so large it eclipsed all of black space. His atmos, rad band, and exo were all working hard to keep him from being burned to a crisp, but even so, he could subconsciously feel the heat searing his back.

"How are you doing?" Grace's voice popped into his head.

"Just like riding a bike," he replied.

"Do they still have bikes in the twenty-sixth century?" she asked.

"No, but one of the first classes we took at the Academy was how to pilot all forms of primitive vehicles. That includes horses, cars, and bicycles."

"What about aircrafts?"

"That's the second class."

"You're near the jump point, Levin. Going in four, three, two . . ."

Everything turned yellow and Levin felt a vibration wash over him. It was a familiar shock to his body, an old lover stirring buried feelings of nostalgia over something long forgotten. When the yellow faded, and the stars obscuring his vision blinked away, he saw a long, thin cylindrical ship barreling into him. He didn't have time to adjust his exo before he bounced off the hull and spun away. It took him a few seconds to recover and pull out of the spin. He studied it as the wayward craft spun out of control on two axes.

"Couldn't have given me more than half a second to get acclimated?" he growled.

"I told you I'm precise. You have sixteen minutes. Prioritize weapons, batteries, and food. According to the *Blackwood*'s last distress calls, the power grid had blown out, so avoid engineering altogether."

Levin sped to the moving ship and latched on to the exterior hull. Immediately, the sun and the black space began to spin in seemingly random patterns as he joined the ship's rotations. He created four coils and kept two glued to the surface as he made his way to the hatch midway down the ship. It was a pretty standard design for twenty-second-century freighters, and he felt fairly confident he could navigate its interior with relative ease. Within a few seconds, he cut through the outer hatch and worked his way through to the compression chamber past the inner door to the ship's main quarters.

Fortunately, the ship's artificial gravity still held. He stood in the middle of a long hallway that spanned a hundred meters on both sides. To his left, he heard yelling. His AI band alerted him to medium radiation emanating from the right, though it was nothing his rad band couldn't handle. Levin took off down the right corridor. Running in the ship felt strange, as if each step felt heavier or lighter than the previous. The artificial gravity must be unstable and probably close to giving out. He had to hurry. Once it gave, considering how badly this ship was out of control, things could get dicey.

"Second door to your right. Should be a cargo hold. Just grab everything."

Levin blew through the double doors and entered a large room with cube containers stacked all the way up to the ceiling. In the center of the room, a group of men and women huddled in a circle, holding hands and praying fervently. They gaped at him as he strolled in and looked around.

"Seems I have company," he thought to Grace.

"A couple of Neptune Divinities. I would consider it a personal favor if you tell them the High Scion says hello and then kill them."

"A little bloodthirsty, Mother of Time? They're going to die anyway."

"You have no idea the pain and suffering these bastards put the TIs through."

"Who in the Holy Heavens are you?" one of the Neptune Divinities demanded, standing up.

Fortunately, he seemed unarmed, or Levin would have had to do something about it. He ignored the man and opened his netherstore container. "Don't mind me," he said. "Really. Keep praying."

The man took a few steps toward him and raised his arm. By now, the rest of the Neptune Divinities had noticed him as well. A woman got up and ran for the door out of the corner of his eye. The rest surrounded him.

"I wouldn't do that if I were you," Levin said. He created half a dozen kinetic coils and began to cut the bindings holding the cargo in place. Several of the Neptune Divinities gasped as he lifted a dozen containers at once and arranged them into a single file. Then he expanded his netherstore and floated the containers in as if down a conveyor belt. More cries of alarm from the Neptune Divinities followed. Their cargo seemed to float and disappear into thin air.

One of the men made the foolish decision of trying to stop him. He charged Levin's exo shield and bounced off it as if he had hit a wall, knocking himself unconscious. The rest of the group attacked, trying to surround and disrupt his work. Irritated, Levin created a long coil and swept them to the side and pinned them to the wall.

"The most efficient thing to do is to just kill them."

"Please, Mother of Time. Let me do my work."

Levin ignored the cries of the struggling Neptune Divinities as he gobbled up stack after stack of containers. By the time he was done, his netherstore was twenty-six containers burdened and its levels had dipped to 64 percent. He checked his status: thirteen minutes remaining. He turned to exit the room and ran into a group of armed soldiers manning the door.

"Oh, for abyss's sake," he growled.

"I told you," Grace said. "Should have listened to me. Like James, you'll learn in time that I am always right."

The squad opened fired, pinging Levin with gauss projectiles, popular in this time period. His levels plummeted 10 percent just from the initial barrage. He swore: he had forgotten that the type of exos the agency used were notoriously inefficient when it came to gauss weaponry. He dove to the side and aimed six coils at the squad of four, smashing them backward and into the corridor wall outside.

"Get moving, Auditor. You're wasting time, and levels, for that matter. The hit you just took could have held another three tons in the netherstore."

"I'm a little out of practice."

Levin charged forward without exo-enhanced speed, deciding to conserve his levels for the rest of the job unless he absolutely needed to use them. Two of the guards in the hallway were unconscious and the other two were just picking themselves off the floor. Levin grabbed the one closest to him by the collar and yanked him headfirst into the wall. He stepped up to the second and kicked him in the face.

He continued down to the next cargo hold and took a look inside. It was loaded with dozens of warheads. He skipped it. The warheads could be converted to power sources, but he doubted the wasteland savages had the technology to do so. The third hold contained long-term ship rations. He upended those quickly into his netherstore. His levels were dropping fast. Levin continued on through the holds, grabbing pallets of clothing in one room, and finding water filtration systems in another.

His levels were nearing 30 percent when Grace spoke up. "Wait. Back-track to that previous room."

Levin ducked back into a large room near the back. It was a garage filled with several vehicles, transports, and combat crafts. "What of it? We can't use any of these."

"Grab that machine in the left corner."

"The scout mechanoid? Why?"

"Just do as I say. You'll have to unload some of your stores to hold it. Hurry, you have only four minutes left."

Grumbling, Levin opened his netherstore and unloaded some of the containers of clothing and arms. He eyeballed the weight of the eight-legged mechanoid with the human upper and top, and then lifted it up. It was surprisingly lighter than he had thought, though still pushing the containment field of his netherstore perilously close to its limit.

"You're going to need to unload more. Your levels are at thirteen percent."

Levin dropped the mechanoid again and removed a few of the food-stuff containers.

"Not the food!"

"Too late, Mother of Time."

He picked the mechanoid up again and dropped it in. His netherstore capacity filled to a hundred and his levels dropped to 6 percent. He was heading toward the exit of the ship when the gravity gave out. Several of the crafts in the garage broke free from their restraints and slid across the room. Levin was unprepared as a tank-like vehicle slammed into him. He barely got his exo up in time before it crushed him into the wall.

Dozens of floating objects began to career around the room, bouncing off walls and smashing anything that got in their way. A transport craft collided with the tank-like vehicle and exploded, spewing shrapnel and burning debris all over the room. A cascade of smaller explosions followed.

"Auditor, get out of there. You're at eighteen minutes. If you're not out in the next forty-seven seconds, you're going to fall into the sun."

"Can I jump back right now?"

"No. It's far too dangerous considering the ship's trajectory and spin. Get out and stabilize in open space first."

"Easier said than done."

"I thought you were supposed to be good. I will be very put out if you die on your first jump, Auditor. Do not disappoint me."

Additional pressure and a critic. Great, just what Levin needed. To die on his first jump after getting thrown out of ChronoCom and breaking out of prison would be humiliating. He narrowly dodged a fiery metal beam soaked in oil that speared into the wall behind him. He oriented himself and powered on his exo, ready to punch a hole through the ship's outer hull. Then he realized he didn't have enough levels. The only way he could get out was the way he had come in.

Ducking and pushing aside wreckage all the way, Levin shot himself down the length of the main corridor, having to fight off the bodies and debris flying at him. A woman with desperation on her face clutched at him as she flew past. He pushed her face out of his mind. It was a look he had seen thousands of times before. A good chronman had to have a short memory. It was the ones who didn't who ended up poking a gas giant in the eye.

He checked the time: thirty seconds until nineteen minutes. He wasn't going to make it. He had to try. Levin continued up the main corridor, dodging the stream of objects. Gravity had now completely abandoned the ship, its out-of-control rotation creating pressure and forces that moved every which way. Levin felt like a pinball.

Fifteen seconds.

He wasn't going to make it. What a way to go. Dying in a sun was probably the most painful death he could think of. It would be a torturous few seconds before his body burned into a crisp, his fluids evaporating in a flash once the ship around him melted and his exo and atmos shields give way.

The timer had already hit the twenty-minute mark when he reached the hatch. His levels were down to 3 percent. Even if he got out of the ship now, chances were, his levels were too far down for him to survive the trip back to the collie. Still, he had to try.

Levin punched out of the ship and was temporarily blinded by the sun's brightness. Using his AI band to show him the way, he shot himself toward the designated jump point. Even then, he knew he wasn't going to make it. He checked his levels one last time; less than 1 percent. It was over. The jump would consume the rest of his levels and then the sun would burn him up.

"Let no one say that Levin Javier-Oberon did not fight to the last," he said, closing his eyes.

The black space in front of him began to glow yellow. There was a flash and then an upturn of his stomach, and before he knew it, the ugly collie was floating right in front of him. Levin pushed the nausea down into his gut and shot himself into the hatch. A few seconds later, the nether-store container was hooked up to the collie and he collapsed on a hard metal bunk, heaving and sweating.

Grace's upside-down head appeared. "I told you not to miss that nineteen-minute mark."

"Your times are off," he huffed, picking himself off the bunk.

She gave him a condescending smirk. "I'm never off. I padded them. I knew you were going to be a little incompetent the first time back."

"I'm a little rusty."

"Same thing, Auditor." She felt his forehead and then checked the readings on the wall panel of the collie. "Your atmos failed before we picked you up. Your rad band managed to ward off most of the radiation, but you didn't come out completely unscathed. Fortunately, I have a rad tank you can soak in back at the All Galaxy. Until then, I recommend you rest."

"I'm fine, Mother of Time."

"I didn't ask you how you were, Auditor. I don't know why chronmen are always so hard of hearing." Before he could say another word, she activated his cryo band and Levin felt darkness sweep over him.

TWENTY-SIX

THE CARROT OR THE STICK

Elise sighed in resignation as she made a loop around the rooms that now held the key to saving the entire planet. The new lab, on the seventy-ninth floor, was easily ten times the size of her old one back at the Farming Towers, but not nearly as nice. Actually, it was downright filthy in here, but it was one of the least damaged parts of the tower. She sniffed the air; it would probably take her a week before she could get this place clean enough to work in.

Not that she had been putting many hours into her work recently. Elise had been pretty delinquent researching the cure for the Earth Plague, though she gave herself a pass, albeit just a temporary one. Being on the run tended to have that effect. The upheaval of the past several months had not only halted any progress, it had probably set her back a little. Hopefully just a little. She would prioritize her work here now that things had settled. It was the most important thing she could do for the people.

She went to the racks of testing beds that housed the various strains of the Earth Plague. Right now, six of the beds, mostly old aquariums the children of the tribe had scrounged up from an old pet store and repurposed for her use, were intact. A few had suffered cracks from the long journey from Boston, but it wasn't anything a little duct tape couldn't fix. Four hundred years in the future, duct tape was still king. The remaining containers were an assortment of old pots and plasticware, which was appropriate, since the vast majority of her actual science equipment consisted of kitchen utensils.

She was making headway toward a cure, albeit slowly. Even now, samples LL and R3 showed promise. Bacteria levels in those two had stabilized, with decomposition of organic matter functioning as it should before the fungal taint's infection. This formula worked only on a very specific strain of the plague. It would be useless against the dozens of other identified strains of the plague. Whatever the cure was would have to be synthesized to work on the entire family of the fungus or possibly be adaptive to hundreds of different variants.

That would require the bacterial sequencer James had stolen from the Nutris Platform. Unfortunately, they were no closer to locating the machine than when she had first arrived. In fact, he had dropped the ball completely on it. Not that she could blame him. The two of them had been running and reacting for so long now they'd hardly had the chance to do any of the work that was really important. Like him finding the bacterial sequencer. Or her actually working on a cure.

Elise worried that so much of their plan hinged upon retrieving the machine. She had originally hoped that Grace and Titus could just reinvent or build new machines to duplicate what they needed. However, genius only went so far. Their specialties were too far from this field of work to bridge the technology and knowledge gap. As brilliant as they were, the work on the Nutris Platform was cutting-edge. It would take several years for them to get caught up, years neither of them had. The one time James had tried to retrieve a scientist who might have been able to reengineer the machine, he had failed.

Still, Titus 2.3 was fitting right in and had already proven his usefulness ten times over. Within the first couple of days of his arrival, he had dug up the Elfreth's stash of solar panels and hooked them up to part of the building's existing grid, meaning Elise could plug something into a socket in her lab and it would actually work. The power was limited to certain floors, and she had to prioritize its use carefully, but it still made a huge difference. The electronic equipment she had been forced to work without for the past several months was coming back online.

He also got the water purifiers working in the kitchen two days ago, and he and Grace were designing a working elevator and an analog telephone network for the building. When news of what they were working on reached the tribes, the Elfreth and the Flatirons practically deified the two old geniuses, and they both reveled in the attention.

Rima appeared at the door. "Oldest Elise, Oldest Grace and the new chronman are returning. Chawr says they should be arriving on the landing deck soon."

"Did Grace give a time?"

"Yes, Oldest. She said seven-zero-nine."

Elise pointed at the working digital clock—the only one in the entire building that she was aware of. "How long until they arrive?"

Rima scrunched her face as she worked on the math. She almost used her fingers until a disapproving glance from Elise made her put them behind her back.

"Seventeen minutes. No, seven," she said finally.

Elise nodded and waved her away. The only way the girl was ever going to reach her full potential was if she stopped treating time and measurements in approximations. She got up and walked over to the south-facing window. It was dark outside, and the mist tonight was heavy, so there wasn't much to see. However, a few minutes later, she saw a beam of light slowly swimming in the darkness just above the waterline. The *Frankenstein* weaved lazily between buildings, ducking under bridges, getting closer and closer to the All Galaxy. Between the EMP fog and its anti-detection abilities, the collie should be safe from the Co-op's surveillance, which constantly blanketed the region, but it was best to be careful anyway.

Elise left her lab and went down to the landing deck on the seventy-third floor, bounding down the stairs two and three at a time. The deck was the highest of three large open areas in the building and the largest of the Elfreth's storage floors. If for some reason the Elfreth and Flatirons lost the lower levels, the seventy-second floor would be the last line of defense.

This was their first salvage in months. What if something had gone wrong? What if the jump had failed? What if something had happened to Levin? So much depended on the former auditor providing them with a steady source of supplies. She didn't realize she was holding her breath until she saw Grace and Levin unloading their haul from the netherstore container and dividing it into parcels for the children to move to storage.

Levin's eyes met hers as she walked by, and her body shuddered involuntarily. She had been avoiding him ever since he had arrived; the incident of the battle at the top of the Farming Towers was still the stuff of her nightmares. Elise pushed those thoughts away. That was all in the past. Things were different now. She turned her attention to the pile of containers and equipment appearing out of midair and let some of her tightly-wound nerves loosen. She hadn't realized just how dependent the Elfreth were on James's salvages until he couldn't run them anymore. "Did everything go all right?" she asked.

Grace nodded. "The auditor here almost fried in the sun, but he'll be around for at least another jump."

"I'm out of practice," Levin said.

"I'm glad," Elise said, still unable to look him in the eye. "This will really help the tribe."

The ex-auditor looked unconvinced as he took out a crate of dried rations and gave it to one of the children to run down to the kitchen. "We need to acquire some miasma," he said flatly. "Otherwise, I'll burn out like James within months."

"We've tried," Elise said. "It's not easy to find."

"Try harder."

Grace walked over to Elise and took her hand. "Come here, girl. We have a present for you."

The Mother of Time led her to the other end of the balcony, where the collie was parked. Elise rounded the corner behind a pallet of supplies and squealed. There, next to a stack of metal drums and an array of solar panels, was Charlotte, or at least the cousin of the beloved mechanoid she had lost back in 2097. It was all she could do to not jump up and down in excitement.

"She's beautiful," she exclaimed, throwing her arms around Grace.

Grace squawked at the sudden show of affection and awkwardly accepted her embrace. Elise approached the mechanoid and touched one of its eight legs. It was sleek, its skin a dark cobalt that seemed to shimmer and change depending on the angle of the light. Its limbs were much thinner than Charlotte's back in 2097, almost impossibly long, considering its size. She tested her weight on one of its legs and then climbed to its human-shaped torso. Her fingers ran up the side of the headpiece until she felt a small indention. She pressed it and the front upper torso of the mechanoid opened, splitting outward from the middle.

She grinned and turned to Grace. "It's definitely a more advanced version of Charlotte, but a lot of it is the same. I'm going to name her Aranea."

Grace nodded. "Don't try to take her out for a spin yet. Titus and I will need to clear the security protocols, reprogram, and check functionalities first. The last thing we need is for the savior of Earth to lose control of her new toy and plummet off a building to her death. It's over a century more advanced than the ones you're used to, and it's a military vehicle, so it's probably weaponized."

Elise held her hands up. "You got it, Grandma. I promise I won't play with it until you give me the go-ahead. I'm so excited. Thank you, thank you!"

She hugged the Mother of Time again. Charlotte was one of the biggest things she missed from her time. Sure, clean air, good food, and controlled room temperatures were great too, but piloting her mechanoid had been one of her greatest joys. With all the bad things happening lately, this little spot of good news was exactly what she needed.

"Thank the auditor," Grace said. "He's the one who risked his life to retrieve it for you."

Elise went back to the other side of the roof where Levin had just finished divvying up the salvage. She bit her lip, forced her eyes to lock onto his face, and walked toward him.

He looked at her as she approached. "What?"

"I wanted to thank you for getting me that mechanoid. It was very thoughtful."

"The Mother of Time told me to get it."

"Still, thank you. For everything." She offered her hand. "Welcome to the Elfreth."

Levin stared at her hand for a few moments before finally accepting it. "It still doesn't mean I approve of your being in this time. You're an anomaly and you set a poor precedent."

"You know I'm a person, too, right?" she said dryly.

"Oldest Elise!" Sammuia rushed up the stairs, breathless. "Raid on both eastern and western barricades. The western has already fallen. The Flat-irons are begging for help."

It must be serious for the Flatirons to have lost a barricade so quickly. The attacking tribe must have come in hard. She hoped it wasn't too late. If whoever was attacking managed to establish a foothold on the floor and secure one of the stairwells, then the entire building could be compromised.

"Where's Eriao and James?" she shouted, running down the stairs with Sammuia and Levin close behind. Already, several of the guardians were massing at defensive points along the stairwell entrances.

"Elder Eriao is rallying five teams in Lower Village and taking them down to the barricade."

"And James?"

"He is already fighting."

"Of course he is," she grumbled. James ran toward trouble. The stairwells were a mess as she fought the flow of elderly and children running up to the safety of the upper levels. She reminded herself to put a process in place for situations like this. The guardians and fights had to be able to move up and down quickly without being disrupted by civilians.

She reached the barricade level and saw Eriao directing teams of guardians to different sides of the floor. He was deep in a heated discussion with the Flatiron teacher and Maanx. The teacher's son offered her a slight nod as she approached. That was something, at least.

Crowe hurried to her. "Oldest, thank you for your people responding so quickly. "

"Of course," she said, putting a reassuring hand on the old Teacher's shoulder. "That's what alliances are for." She motioned to the teams of guardians nearby. "Let's get moving."

"No, Elise," Levin said. "You stay up here with Crowe."

She rolled her eyes. "I've had this talk with James and Franwil already. I don't need to have it with you. And Gaia help me if you say something about my being a woman . . ."

"It's not that," he said. "I'm not questioning your role or your ability. Or your gender, for that matter. I'm questioning the tribe risking you."

"I'm their leader. I need to lead them in battles."

He shook his head. "You can do that here. The old leader of your waste-land tribe was wrong to be in the midst of battle. He was needed for his decision-making, not his presence. It is the same for you. Besides, you're important for other reasons as well."

"I won't hide in safety while the rest of you risk yourselves." She took a step toward the western barricade.

Levin moved and blocked her path. "These guardians and I will fight because it is what we're here for. It is our role. Your role is to lead and to find a cure for Earth. We all risk our lives to protect you. If you throw everything away because of some misguided foolish and insecure need to show everyone what a great leader you think you are, you disrespect our sacrifices."

Elise opened her mouth and stopped. "Well, if you put it that way," she grumbled. Funny, James was never this hard to talk down. His argument was always about her well-being. Levin's, while completely detached, made so much more sense. "Staying in the middle of the floor up will do."

Levin looked at Eriao. "Two teams stay here with the Oldest at all times."

The war chief of the Elfreth agreed. The rest of the guardians divided into groups and went in separate directions. Elise got to work. She was becoming proficient at managing the Elfreth during battles. Over the next hour, she and Eriao took control of the situation, setting up communication channels to receive updates, organizing teams to where they were needed, and relieving those who had been in the fight too long.

The fight seemed to be more than just a skirmish. Whatever tribe, or tribes, were hitting them were pushing hard, coming in waves and from several directions. By now, other barricades had reported fighting, with a sneak attack on one of the south barricades almost succeeding. At one point, the enemy had managed to take control of the northwestern stairwell before finally being pushed back by a desperate surge led by James. There were moments when it seemed touch-and-go, and once, the enemy got so deep, the guardians had to move Elise's command center.

By late evening, it seemed the All Galaxy defenders had finally gotten the situation under control. James appeared a little while later, looking exhausted. His shirt was bloodied, and there was an ugly gash across his arm. One of his eyes was blackened and a fresh bruise filled his entire left cheek.

"What happened to you?" she asked, running to him in alarm.

"Levin's wearing our only set of bands so I'm only using this"—he held up a blaster rifle—"and this." He held up a bloodied metal pipe that looked like it belonged under a kitchen sink.

Levin arrived a few seconds later. He looked as if he had been dragged through hell and back as well. The two men appraised each other as if comparing who had come out of the conflict in worse shape. Levin's left arm was an ugly mass of bruises and scrapes, and he was holding it up as if it was dislocated. Elise shook her head. If she had really listened to his words earlier, she would have forbidden him from fighting on the front line as well. If he had perished in this fight, then the Elfreth would have lost their only salvager.

"I saw you hold up that entire east barricade by yourself for a while," James said. "You fought well."

"Prison doesn't dull your senses, that's for sure," Levin said. "I saw you lead the charge to me when my bands ran dry and I almost got overwhelmed."

"You two can keep score later," she bristled. She pointed at Levin. "You're done for the day. Get upstairs to Franwil and get that shoulder checked." Before he could protest, she jabbed him in the injured shoulder. "You're our only qualified time traveler right now. If it was your head busted instead of that shoulder, we'd have gone through a lot of trouble breaking you out of prison for nothing. Go."

He looked as if he was going to say something, and then smiled. It was the first time she had ever seen that look on his dry face. She actually hadn't been sure if he even could smile. However, there it was, and it was a little creepy. "Touché, Oldest Elise." He gave her a little bow. He turned to James. "You'll update her on what we saw?" James nodded.

"Update me on what?" she asked.

"I'll take it from here." James looked over at Eriao. "Bring every able body with us. There's something I have to show you."

He led the procession of sixty guardians to the east wall. They were met with another fifty or so Flatiron fights. To her surprise, he led them past the barricades and onto the bridge. The dead and injured were everywhere. Elise felt her stomach churn as they crossed to the other side. So many casualties.

James led her to the next building, where they turned the corner and entered a large central room. Elise gasped. There, caring for their wounded, were the people who had attacked them. Or, at least, their elderly and children tending the wounded fighting men and women who were dead or dying.

"They brought their entire tribe here?" she asked. "Why? That's insane."

"It's actually five tribes," James said. "And they didn't attack because they wanted to steal the Flatirons' supplies or floors. They attacked us because they were running from something and we were in the way. From what they told me, entire tribes are fleeing the north from something so bad that every man, woman, and child picked up their belongings, fled the only thing of value on the island, which in this case are the floors, and tried to punch through us toward safety."

"What could it be?" she asked. She already knew the answer. The Elfreth were probably one of the largest and most destructive groups to have arrived at the Mist Isle in some time. Even then, they were almost swallowed by the Isle and all its dangers. It wasn't a coincidence that something had followed them in here, something so terrible that it'd send all the other tribes running in a panic. This was all her doing.

Elise looked at the guardians behind her. "Put your weapons away. These people need food and water and medical supplies, not more fighting. Run upstairs and tell Franwil to bring all the healers down here. Now."

They looked at her hesitantly.

"Are you sure about this?" James asked. "We don't have enough supplies—"

"Now!" Elise snapped. "And find me the leader of this group."

TWENTY-SEVEN

Order of Things

It was the second day in a row James had nothing to do, no responsibilities weighing on his shoulders and nobody depending on him. It was glorious. He had not had a chance to rest when he first returned from space. The raids had been heavy, nearly around the clock, and he was needed to help defend the barricades. He was more than willing to take his place among the guardians. However, once Elise had decided to feed the raiders instead of fight them, the violence had dropped to almost nothing. Now, the Elfreth guardians and Flatiron fights were busier making sure their former attackers had a place to eat and sleep than anything else.

From his perspective, this was an unsustainable, losing situation and James wanted nothing to do with this foolish plan. Their stores weren't large to begin with. Blood corn and many of the other crops the Elfreth planted grew quickly, often maturing in a matter of days, but there was no way they could keep this up. Once word got out that Elise was giving out free food, the number of refugees flocking to the All Galaxy exploded. He understood what she was trying to do, but as much as he hated to say this, it was a much sounder strategy to eliminate the other tribes in battle than to be weighed down with caring for them.

The few times he had tried to broach it with Elise, she had stubbornly stood by her plan, continually citing some twenty-first-century saying that she'd rather use a carrot instead of a stick, and how these other tribes could prove valuable allies. When he told her that their supplies were far

more valuable than their goodwill, she flat-out scolded him for how little
he valued these wastelander people. In truth, she was right; he couldn't
deny his bias.

In any case, this little dip in violence gave him a few days of precious
rest and he was taking advantage of every minute. It was early evening,
and he was lounging in one of the corner suites high up in the All Galaxy
with Chawr and the rest of the flyguards as they passed around the remainder of a three-liter canister of shine, a home-brewed alcohol derived
from cany weed and a fungus common in this region. It was nasty stuff,
but there weren't many other options around.

Dox, the youngest and newest member of Chawr's crew, held up the
round metal container and tipped it to his lips, taking just a small sip before nearly dropping it. The young man, without a single hair on his chin
yet, made a face and hissed. For a second, he looked as if he wasn't going
to be able to hold it in. He hunched over, and a strange rumbling sound
emanated from him. The rest of the group looked at him attentively. A
second later, he raised his head and wiped the tears from his eyes. Bleary-
faced, he grinned. Aliette handed him a rag to wipe his chin and patted
him on the back. The rest of the group cheered and clapped their hands,
congratulating him on a job well done.

The boy—the man now—handed the jug over to James, who hefted
it in his hands. The liquid inside sloshed around more than he liked; it
was probably less than a quarter full. He held the canister to his lips and
took a long swig. He felt tinge of pain in his shoulder as he hefted the
canister up, but ignored it as the sweet burn of the shine poured into his
mouth. The pain, ever since that last jump, lingered, but the drink helped
make it bearable.

A part of him wondered and worried where his next drink would come
from after this container ran dry. After all, he was grounded. Grace and
Levin—now using his bands, flying his ship, and doing his job—were
back out in space. James wouldn't be able to fly out to acquire more shine.
He pushed that worry out of his mind. For now, he was content.

The canister was passed around a few more times. It was the last of
their stash, and the seven of them cherished every drop. By the time
they were done, half of the flyguards were giggling with each other,
acting like fools. James had always drunk by himself. He had always

associated alcohol with loneliness and isolation, so this jovial behavior felt foreign and strange.

His gaze kept wandering back to the discarded canister. Where could he get more? Now that he had free time on his hands, that worry dominated more and more of his waking hours.

"Chawr," he said, cutting through their boisterous chatter. "That brew equipment you had, it's still with the transports?"

The young leader of the flyguards grinned. "Yes, Elder. Oldest Franwil wanted me to ditch it but . . ." He patted his chest. "How could I do such a thing to my beautiful invention?"

"Maybe it's time we check up on the transports." Laurel grinned, smacking Chawr on the shoulder.

"Maybe." James rubbed his chin. The few remaining vehicles the tribe possessed were stowed with the rest of their large nonessential machinery behind a closed gate in a building parking garage near the Brooklyn Bridge. Elise had ordered the vehicles hidden there shortly after they crossed into the island. Several of the bulkier tools they needed to maintain the *Frankenstein* were stored there as well. They would be needed the next time the ship returned. He had a spare netherstore container. Going over there would be the prudent thing to do. Besides, it had been over a month since the Elfreth had locked up the garage. They really should check up on those valuable vehicles anyway. He'd run it by Elise in the morning.

That is, if she wasn't too important and busy for him now. Since he had returned, they'd hardly shared any time together other than sleep. Running the Elfreth and dealing with all the other tribes in the area took up all of her waking hours. Add that to the fact that she'd practically adopted Sasha, Elise had nothing left for James anymore. In a very short span of time, he had gone from the one person she loved and depended on to an afterthought. It was exactly what he had feared would happen.

"What is this?" a sharp voice snapped. The words lingered in the air.

The small group gave a start when Franwil stomped into the room, as much as an old bent-over woman could. She swung her walking stick in a wide arc, nearly taking Hory's head off. The lad was able to avoid the stick only by tipping backward on his stool and falling onto his ass.

"Oldest." Dox stood up. Too quickly, it seemed, as he had to lean against the wall for support.

"You, boy," she hissed. "Go help with the kowrus today. Sober up and make sure you smell like them before you return to your mother, or there will be trouble." She turned on the rest of the flyguards, waving her stick in the air. "As for the rest of you. You seem to have too much time on your hands. You were exempt from the barricades because of your work on the vehicles. Now that you do have some time on your hands, go tell Eriao you all wish to take shifts on the barricades."

She gave every one of the flyguards the stink-eye as they filed past, heads down and shoulders drooped. James made a casual motion to stand but a glare from her kept him in his seat. Most of the tribe had come to appreciate the valuable service he provided and had warmed to him because of that. The Oldest was one of the few who never had, despite everything he did to try to win her over.

When he and Elise first came to the Elfreth, Franwil saw him as dangerous outsider. For months afterward, when he used his salvage skills to repay their generosity with a steady supply of food and power, she saw only a dangerous chronman. When he fought and nearly died alongside them, she saw only a killer. Now she saw a drunk.

"And you!" she hissed after the flyguards had left the room. "You are supposed to be an elder, a leader among the Elfreth. Yet here you are, carousing and acting a fool. I expected better from you, chronman."

Expected better? James felt his hands shake, though he wasn't sure if it was more in anger or something else. Who did this old witch think she was to talk to him like this just because he wanted a drink? He had laid his life down for them time and time again. No, he deserved a drink.

He stood up and towered over her. "I just spent two months going through abyss and back. What's it to you how I choose to spend my downtime? Especially with my wards, who I trained to help the tribe."

Franwil was not intimidated by his size. She put her hands on her waist and looked up. "Duty is doing what is needed. Leadership is finding what is needed. That's why you cannot be trusted, chronman."

James choked. "Not be trusted? Are you kidding me? After everything I've done for you?"

"We were peaceful and happy for six generations before you arrived. Now, we have lost our home and many loved ones. Tell me what you've done for us so far."

Her words hit James in the gut. The anger faded, and, briefly, he saw himself through her eyes. He looked to his right, at his right hand raised high in the air. It had unconsciously formed a fist. He dropped his arms and shook his head. "I'm sorry, Oldest," he said finally, ashamed. "Elise and I owe a debt to the Elfreth."

"One she is repaying and you are not, chronman."

He nodded. "I will do better."

Behind Franwil's shoulder, Smitt's ghost walked into the room and stared at him with feigned surprise and interest. James wondered where the other ghosts were. Ever since Smitt had appeared, the others had faded into the background. He couldn't remember the last time he had seen the apparitions of the Nazi soldier and Grace. Even Sasha, whom he still saw once in a while, had pretty much faded from view ever since he returned to the Elfreth.

Franwil pointed at the door. "The kitchen staff needs help moving stores down to feed all the refugees. Make yourself useful. Go help them."

"Yes, Oldest."

As he walked out the door, the hallucination of his dead best friend fell in alongside him. "A year ago, you were a Tier-1 chronman running some of the most important salvages in the solar system. Now you are the kitchen help. How did you get yourself into this situation, James?"

"I'd rather be the kitchen help than do that shit job again."

Smitt grinned. "No, my friend. You only think that."

James tried to ignore the ghost as he walked down the stairs toward the storage area. However, Smitt's words bothered him. Inside, he knew his friend was right. It was one thing to hate what you did but know you were making a difference. It was another thing entirely to feel useless and unneeded. James's gut twisted into knots. He didn't know how he got to this place, but somehow, he had fallen into a deeper hole than he ever had back at the agency.

Black abyss, he needed a drink.

TWENTY-EIGHT

RIPPLES

I'm not sure I'm comfortable with this," Levin said for the sixth time. He knew his complaints were falling on deaf ears, but he felt an innate need to keep saying that until he got his way or it was too late. Since he was bringing up to Grace her carefully-devised plan, he knew exactly how futile his efforts were. After all, the *Frankenstein* was already at the jump point on the sun's side of the Main Belt.

Levin wouldn't have allowed a job like this during his auditor days, but it was no longer his call. Grace was his handler now, and even though he wasn't fully on board with the way she ran his jobs, he couldn't argue the results.

In the past week, he had run three smaller jobs. He had doubts about the planning of every single job, but all three had been executed perfectly. There had been some things she had to adjust on the fly, but overall, Grace Priestly was flawless, and he had learned not to question her decisions. Well, most of them.

"Which part aren't you comfortable with?" Grace quipped. "The part where you're jumping into the middle of an all-out brawl between the Core Planets and the Outer Rim colonies or the part where there's a ChronoCom outpost within spitting distance?"

"I'm actually more concerned about salvaging from a not-dead-end time line. The target survived the scenario. The outpost defenders fought off the Core Planets' boarding party."

Grace rolled her eyes. "You really are married to my Time Laws."

"And we're bending quite a few, if not outright breaking them. I'm just saying. There's a lot of questionable variables here. I'm jumping directly into a hot zone. What if someone sees me floating in space? What if someone in the station sees me using my bands and survives? What if—"

Grace raised a hand. "Hush." Then she ticked her fingers down one at a time. "Four, three, two, one . . ."

The room turned yellow, and Levin became temporarily disoriented. When he came to, he was treated to a bright and eerie light show in absolute silence. Blossoms of explosions erupted from all sides, leaving behind broken and twisted hulks of metal. Streaks of yellow fire and white-hot beams sliced through the backdrop of black space. A battle was at full pitch, with hundreds of ships on each side buzzing around in an angry and chaotic melee. There were ships of all sizes, small fighters in formation strafing and dogfighting large, older, Hades-class flagships belching choruses of rockets and lasers. There was so much happening that it threatened to overwhelm his senses, and Levin found himself just staring perplexedly at the hauntingly beautiful scene.

"Focus, Auditor. Look for the Bastion."

"I don't see it. Did we miscalculate the jump point?"

"I had to jump you just to the fringe of its location. Work your way in carefully. This job will require a bit more finesse, none of that bumbling you've given me so far."

The year was 2301, and this was one of the first of many massive battles waged between the Core Planets of Earth, Mars, and Venus against the newly rich and powerful Outer Rim colonies. Many historians considered this conflict the turning point of humanity's decline. Their species had stopped exploring and pushing the boundaries of space and turned inward against itself. Levin considered it the nail in the coffin. The Gas Wars of 2377 were just the victors of the Core Conflicts fighting over the spoils.

Levin snapped out of the hypnosis and scanned the area. The battle spanned hundreds of thousands of kilometers, but it seemed the fighting was most intense in an area just below him. Black Core Planets ships battled gray Outer Rim ships like furious hornets around a large circular structure that looked a little too unwieldy for a ship and a bit too small for a space station.

"That must be it," Levin said, launching himself toward it. He kept his body limp and relaxed, as if he were just another of the thousands of corpses jettisoned out into space. The odds of being seen amid this chaos were slim, but there was still a possibility. The last thing he needed to hear on the chatter was someone seeing a spaceman or an alien flying around without a ship. It took him thirty minutes to reach the station, which was longer than they had anticipated.

The OR Bastion forward outpost of the Kach Corporation was the Outer Rim fleet's primary objective. Their mission was to escort the Bastion to the sun side of the Main Asteroid Belt—the consensus border between the two factions—into an orbital point synchronous with Mars and provide a base of operations for Outer Rim incursions.

The fighting became thicker and more frantic as Levin closed on the Bastion. While the technology the Core Conflicts used here was more primitive than in the present, the weapons were not very far behind. A direct blast by any of these ships would decimate Levin's exo. He would need to be careful as he glided in. The antiship batteries of the Bastion were full-on painting the space around him as the Core Planets ships desperately tried to get close enough to land a boarding party. One of these ships would succeed in approximately fourteen minutes. He had to hurry.

Levin landed on the surface of the station. To his left, just a few meters away, a battery swiveled and spit angry beams out at the ships buzzing overhead. Levin had to get away. The gunner in the porthole might notice him, or even more problematic, the battery was probably a prime target for attacking ships. No sooner had he gotten two hundred meters away than an explosion erupted near the battery, shooting fire and debris out into space. It had missed the battery, which was still firing, but if Levin had been any closer, he could have been seriously injured.

He checked his levels: 46 percent. He had jumped farther from the Bastion than they had originally estimated. Space had a funny way with distances sometimes. Levin continued down the body of the station, using the map in his AI band, until he located the impact point that the boarding party would use a few minutes later. This was probably the safest insertion point. He found a portion nearby that was windowed, powered on his exo, and tore into it. As with most stations in this time, the windows were long and narrow. Breaking through the clear steel was easy enough, but it took extra levels to widen the opening enough for his body to fit. He was halfway in when the blast doors came down on top of him, which sucked out another 6 percent of his levels, keeping the doors from crushing him until he could squeeze inside. He rolled into the interior of the station and landed in a kneeling position next to a cabinet, hands and exo ready to engage. He was in a kitchen, which was perfect. No one was eating at a time like this.

Levin got to his feet and dusted himself off. "Grace, I'm in."

It was surprising how little kitchens had changed over the centuries. To his left were several large sinks. Two rows of ovens were behind them, and there was a large island to his right. He gave a start when a young man lying on the ground just a few meters away picked himself off the ground. He must have fallen down and clung to something when the room decompressed. The two stared at each other.

"Listen, son," Levin began. "I need you to stay in this room."

The young man, wearing what looked like a cook's uniform, looked barely more than eighteen. His eyes widened when he saw Levin and then he booked for the exit. He made it three steps before tripping over a coil. He scrambled back to his feet and ran to the other side of the room.

"You're wasting time," Grace's voice popped into Levin's head.

"I don't know if this kid is supposed to live or not," Levin thought back.

The young cook picked up a lasered butcher knife and held it up.

"Put that down," Levin warned.

The young man charged.

Resigned, Levin snapped the coil and flicked him against the far wall. The cook slammed into a set of shelves and collapsed to the ground. He didn't get up. Levin hoped he was fine, but then who knew what was supposed to happen? What if he was supposed to die and somehow now lived because of Levin's actions? That was the worst kind of ripple. He ground his teeth; he should have refused this job. It felt wrong in every sense.

Levin threw on the paint mod of an Outer Rim soldier and ran into the hallways. Fortunately, the armory was in the next wing over, not far at all. The hallways were packed with soldiers and repair crews. The Bastion kept taking fire. Explosions shook the outpost, knocking people off their feet.

The chaos was advantageous to Levin. He continued unimpeded toward the next section, following the steady stream of soldiers running to and from the armory. He found it ten minutes later, just as the lights of the Bastion dipped for a brief moment. A voice rang across the station warning of a boarding party and ordering security teams to intercept.

Levin was able to slip past a group of scared guards stationed at the armory entrance, most likely cadets, and proceeded to the end of the hall. The first several doors were opened and empty while the next six were closed and locked. He did a quick pass and moved to the far corner.

"I'm at the ammunition dump," he thought to Grace.

"Good, the priority is the clips and ammo, weapons secondary. Remember, only retrieve items from the back of the upsilon section. Anything outside of that will cause a ripple."

According to the chron database reports Grace had siphoned from the off-planet feeds for this job, the Core Planets' missile would strike the section directly on the opposite side of the wall sometime in the next ten minutes. The supplies in the rooms he was in would all be destroyed or blown out into space. This should make it safe for him to salvage.

Levin got to work, opening his netherstore container and tossing in anything within reach. He was able to clear six shelves of ammunition within minutes and had moved on to the next room, where rifles and other handheld weapons were racked against the walls. He activated his coils and began to pluck them from their mounts. The station shook again, and he heard shouting from the hallway.

"I need to hide."

"No time," said Grace. "Knock them unconscious and finish up. You need to be out of here in less than two minutes."

"Defensive positions, you slugs!" someone screamed. "Get those crates in place. Enemy incoming. We will hold this section from the Core Planets assholes at all costs. If one of those shit-breathing commie apes so much as steps foot into my beautiful armory, each of you sad sacks will be cleaning the floors with your tongues. Do you hear me, maggots?"

"Yes, sir!" a chorus of voices followed.

Levin hoped none of those grunts came to the back. He had cleared out three of the rooms and was almost done with the remaining room when he was knocked to all fours. His exo soaked up the majority of the hit, but his back still took some of the burn.

Levin rolled to his right, avoiding two more laser blasts. He shot out a coil and knocked the rifle out of a soldier's hand. Before the guy could shout out an alarm, Levin wrapped a coil around his neck and pulled, lifting the guy off his feet and crashing him into the ground. Levin squeezed the coil until the man's face turned red and he passed out.

"We're cutting it close, auditor," Grace said. "How much capacity do you have?"

A storm of footsteps was getting louder in the hallway.

Levin checked his readings. "Eighty-three percent."

"That's good enough. Pulling you out now."

The world turned yellow just as half a dozen faces appeared from the hallway. One person raised his rifle and fired. Everything turned black, and Levin found himself floating peacefully in the calm of space. In the distance, among the small blinking specks of stars, he saw the light of the collie approach.

"Not the smoothest operation," he said, "but I'd say it was our best work yet. I still think we're cutting it—"

"We have a problem," Grace barked into head. "I'm picking you up at high speed. Be ready."

A few minutes later, the *Frankenstein* streaked by him with the hatch open. Levin had to shoot his exo to try to match velocities with the collie. It was rough going for a few seconds. Eventually, Grace slowed the *Frankenstein* just enough for Levin to wrap a coil around the opening and climb in.

"What's going on?" he asked, as he closed the hatch.

Grace's face looked grim. "That ChronoCom outpost just went on high alert. I'm tapped into their emergency channels. Seems there is a giant ripple shooting through the chronostream right now."

Levin's worst fears were realized. A wave of concern and numbness washed over him. He should have listened to his instincts. "What happened? I thought we had the jump scenarios covered so there wouldn't be any."

Grace held up a hand as she listened in on the channel. She cursed and berated herself. "Stupid woman, Priestly. It seems the boarding party had taken over the armory. Originally, when the upsilon section was hit, the munitions exploded, taking out a significant number of the Core Planets soldiers boarding the station. When you salvaged all those munitions . . ."

". . . the explosion never happened," finished Levin grimly. "How bad?"

Grace shook her head. "Enough that there were enough Core Planets soldiers remaining to successfully capture the Bastion. It was repurposed for the Core Planets fleet and used as a launching point to attack the Outer Rim planets."

Levin was stunned. He sat down and held his head in his hands. In the true history, the OR Bastion was the launching point of every major offensive onto Mars for the first thirty years of the Core Conflicts. The station became synonymous with Outer Rim aggression, and there was no symbol more hated by the Martians. Over a thousand Martians had tried to suicide bomb the outpost over the years, none succeeding until one Esperanza Girard finally destroyed the outpost in 2331. By then, the outcome had become moot. Mars still celebrated Esperanza Day every year as a planetary holiday.

"What have I done?"

"The ripple may not fully reach the present," Grace said. "Luckily, the Core Conflicts will override the majority of the changes in the chrono-stream. ChronoCom is already enacting contingency jumps to tweak the time line and mitigate the damage."

"What have I done?" he moaned again. "I knew this jump was a problem."

"I will take full responsibility for this . . ."

"I don't care who is responsible. This is our fault! We just changed the time line!"

"I erred, and it happens," Grace snapped, standing her ground. "I'm only able to intercept read access from the chron database up-links to the outer colonies. I can analyze the scenarios, not run simulations. It's impossible to predict all contingencies, even for someone as brilliant as me. I'm still human, damn it."

Levin began to tear his bands off his wrists and slam them onto the table one by one. He hadn't felt so disgusted with himself since his early chronman days. "This is why the agency exists, so half-ass amateur bullshit like what we just did doesn't happen. Extrapolating one-way reads from the chron database without having it simulated is a surefire way of having more terrible screwups like this happen again."

"I'll be more conservative next time," Grace said coolly. "We'll keep it to smaller, easier jobs."

"Next time?" Levin opened his mouth and then realized nothing he said would matter. Grace was set on her course, as were James, Elise, Titus, and all the rest of the Elfreth. They were going to make these jumps with or without him. Somehow. He picked up the nearest object he could find—Grace's cup of tea—and threw it against the wall of the collie, shattering it.

Something Director Young over at ChronoCom once said echoed in his head. If a corporation was abyss-bent on jumping, they were going to find a way to do it. The only thing the agency could do was take ownership of it and try to mitigate the damage. In this case, Grace and James were going to make these jumps no matter what. The only thing he could do was try to minimize the harm.

"From now on," he growled, "I'm not jumping unless I decide it's safe. Understood?"

Without waiting for an answer, he stormed off to the back of the hold. He sat down on the bunk and clutched his head, feeling trapped and morally conflicted. For the first time in many years, the thought of poking a giant in the eye crossed his mind.

TWENTY-NINE

REPRIMANDED

James stayed busy the next week, helping the kitchen staff during the day and taking shifts on the barricade at night. The work was fine for the most part and both Franwil and Elise seem heartened that he had found something to do.

It bothered him that they somehow thought this was the best use of his time. He was a highly-trained operative skilled in many different fields. He had no peer as a scout or a soldier in the All Galaxy, with the possible exception of Levin, and few here outside of Grace, Titus, and Elise were better-educated. Hell, even with his weak technical background, by chronman standards, he was one of the most proficient engineers in the building. But here he was, moving boxes, breaking down crates, loading supplies, and then watching the barricades with a bunch of half-trained guardians.

These chores felt beneath him, as a former chronman and as an elder of the tribe. It was strange to him that he actually cared about his title. It bothered him more that neither Elise nor Franwil had more important jobs requiring his attention. Instead, both stopped by a couple of times during the day and seemed to approve of his working dutifully. Elise gave him a peck on the cheek and told him she was so happy he was back, and that was that. He was left to labor in the stockroom with the rest of the commoners while she went off to plan the future of the Elfreth.

At the very least, the hard labor helped keep his mind off alcohol, or the lack of it. As each day passed, though, his hands shook and his skin itched more and more. It was slowly driving him mad. By the end of the fourth day, he had made up his mind to take the flyguards to do a maintenance check on the vehicles once the crew had time. The crew and their work on the vehicles was the one responsibility that was still wholly under his control.

For now, James had to stand by and watch helplessly as Elise gave away their stores to more and more refugees fleeing from what everyone called terribly advanced alien invaders. The refugees who had made it this far south didn't know who these foreigners were, but James had a suspicion of the worst. He had pitched the idea to Elise to let him go north and scout, but it was a request she flatly denied.

James had just dropped off several crates of rations on the thirty-fourth floor and was returning to the storeroom to retrieve more. "Black abyss," he muttered, staring at the dwindling stacks of containers. When he had first returned from space, their reserves had threatened to overflow the room. Now, it was more empty than full.

The morning lines started before sunrise as crowds of Mist Isle tribes gathered, almost docilely, for their small share of food and medicine. Sometimes, they would offer something in return, but most of the time, it was complete charity. Elise just handed their food and medicine out as if the Elfreth had an endless supply.

He wasn't the only one unhappy. Eriao had thrown a fit when he found out what she was doing and had made such a ruckus, James had had to pull him aside to calm him down. Eventually, Eriao backed down, but he kept his displeasure on his face every time he watched the refugees.

The war chief of the Elfreth was a good man, but was in a little over his head. The previous chief had died during the attack at the Farming Towers, and Eriao was one of the few surviving senior guardians. A small part of James thought he should have been made the war chief, but he understood why Elise felt the need to promote from within.

Today, Eriao came to pay him a visit, imploring him to speak with her. "More and more of these stragglers come every day. What will we eat when the winter comes?"

"Oldest Elise and Franwil lead," James said, hefting one of the last containers of dried fruits the Elfreth had stored in preparation for the coming winter, the winter that hadn't even arrived yet. "They must have a plan."

"If their plan is to starve us, then they are doing a fantastic job," Eriao grumbled. "I knew it was a mistake once Oldest Qawol passed . . ."

"Watch your words carefully, Eriao." James scowled. This wasn't the first time he had had to stare the man down on Elise's behalf.

"I accept what has happened, Elder," the war chief said. "But you must see as I do. Please just try to talk some sense into her."

James looked around the room. The war chief wasn't wrong. They had to do something. Elise had a big heart, but this was tomfoolery. "I will tell her we need to limit how much we give away," he said finally.

"Thank you." Eriao leaned in close. "The Oldest is an intelligent and kind woman. You and I both know, Elder James, that the world is not so. We must protect her from all, even her kindness, if necessary." He patted James on the shoulder and walked out of the room.

James picked up a stack of boxes and left the storeroom. He proceeded down to the barricade floor, and continued outside the northern barricade, past the makeshift triage reserved only for the refugees, and finally to the food bank area the Elfreth had set up to accommodate the daily handouts. Elise hadn't left that area in two days.

He found her talking to a tall, thin man with a pale face and blond braided hair, typical of many of the tribes here. He wore heavy hardened-leather clothing with thick ropes bound around his forearms, and a long, ugly weapon on his back that had ax blades on both ends. A warrior, and by the way he was speaking with Elise, one used to being in control. Then something jogged his memory. He had fought this man the night when that tribe attempted to overwhelm the Flatirons. He was skilled with his double ax, and at one point almost lopped off James's arm.

James was definitely not comfortable with this guy standing so close to her. She barely stood taller than his chest. All the man had to do was reach out, and he could break her neck. She was the leader of the Elfreth. More importantly, she was the scientist who was supposed to cure Earth.

Elise saw him approach and brightened. "James, this is Murad, mayor of the Elmen tribe."

They nodded at each other as two men sizing each other up would. "We've met," James said. "Good to meet you without a blade in your hand."

"You, too, Elfreth. You fight well," Murad said. "Your Oldest tells me you are a chronman?"

"Former. They fired me."

"For what?"

"For her." He pointed at Elise, who blushed furiously.

Murad bowed. "Much respect to you then."

James found himself beginning to warm to the leader of the Elmen.

"Your Oldest and your people have offered us a soft hand even when we came at you with fists," Murad said. "We tried to take your floors by force and you opened your doors. For that, you have our eternal thanks." He bowed again.

"Thank Elise," James said. "I would have left you guys to rot in the cold."

Murad nodded. "I respect your honesty, chronman. I would have done the same. However, it is a good thing for my people that neither of us lead the Elfreth. Therefore, I wish to offer a gift in exchange for your generosity." He signaled to one of his people in the back. Eight of them carried over a large rectangular crate and placed it on the ground. James instantly recognized the markings on the outer shell.

"Oh, this isn't necessary . . ." Elise began.

"You don't need them anymore, do you?" James said.

A small smile appeared on Murad's face. "The chronman knows, and yes, in our haste to flee those invading my building, we took only the necessary and the valuable. After many days on the run, the necessary becomes more valuable than the valuable. We will never have need these again, even if they are worth more than all the rest."

"What is it?" Elise asked.

"A titan converter," James said. "The most advanced form of energy conversion ever created. It can change most forms of energy units to almost any other from. Very useful, and very expensive."

"Murad, we can't possibly accept this," Elise said.

"Speak for yourself," James cut in. "Of course we can."

Murad's people placed the crate at their feet. "It is yours," he said. "The Elmen no longer have machines that require energy to convert. It is also a heavy thing. My people have already carried this burden for too long. We have other burdens we must now address."

"It is a generous gift," Elise said. "We'll continue to provide you with the resources your tribe needs. If we all work together, we can accomplish so much more."

The Elmen chief nodded. "We would like that."

Elise saw Franwil and Crowe on the other side of the floor and excused herself. She had a knowing look on her face when she turned away from the Elmen chief and flashed James a smile. James and Murad watched as she hurried off.

"Your Oldest is small in stature, but she is mighty," the Elmen chief said. "She is not really from the wastelands, is she?"

"No, she isn't."

"From upside in space?"

"A little bit further, actually," said James. "Mayor Murad, you say the Elmen are from the north buildings? Were you there when these invaders attacked?"

He nodded. "They appeared out of the fog. Within a day, our neighbors, the Barrios Block, were subjugated. My people have been fleeing ever since."

"Can you describe to me what you saw? What these invaders were wearing?"

"Men and women who flew in the air, surrounded by white fields. They were joined by soldiers in white armor."

"Were there others in black? Wearing helms with single points?"

Murad shook his head. "I do not recall. I can lead you to them if you like. It is not too far, but it will be dangerous. Most of the tribes we passed are wary of strangers."

"No need." James pulled up a map. "Can you show me where they hit you?"

He spent the next hour extracting as much information as he could. He had originally hoped the attack was just tribal warfare, that the attackers were possibly an advanced tribe from farther north fleeing the Arctic zone, which was not an uncommon thing. However, the Elmen mayor confirmed his greatest fear.

They had been found.

It was the Co-op, and they were heading south, systematically taking over building after building. The good news was, they were being methodical. At this pace, they would reach All Galaxy within a month. The bad news was, they could afford to take their time. The Elfreth may have hidden in a maze shrouded by the EMP fog, but they were also trapped on an island. James had no doubt the Co-op had the entire Mist Isle fully blockaded. They were trapped. A single ship or person could slip through, but there was little chance all the Elfreth could escape undetected again. Perhaps, with so many places to hide, the tribe could hide deep underground and try to wait the enemy out. To do so, they would need to start hoarding supplies again.

First things first. James went down the food line and saw that it spanned the entire length of the bridge. He walked to the end and realized that it continued to snake around for as long as he could see. He returned to the front of the line and pulled the young man working it aside.

"Shut it down," he whispered. "Pass the message along."

"But the Oldest—"

"Just do it. That's an order. Spread the word."

The young man—James couldn't quite recall his name—took a hesitant step toward the girl serving the line next to him and looked back at James. Then, instead of doing as he was told, he ran off.

What the abyss? Where was that boy going? Irritated, James pulled the girl aside and told her the same thing he had told the young man. This time, she dutifully complied and passed the message. It earned him several scowls from the crowd. The mood in the room began to change.

"What in Gaia are you doing?" Elise barked, stomping toward him, flanked by both Franwil and Crowe. The boy trailed behind them, looking wide-eyed and terrified at James.

"We need to talk," he said, putting a hand on her back and leading her away from the curious onlookers.

"Don't touch me," she hissed softly. "I'm the Oldest. You not only countermanded my order, you're treating me like a little girl. Here's what's going to happen, James. I'm going to dress you down and then order you to continue the food lines, and then we're going to go to some place private and I'm really going to dress you down."

James knew Elise enough to know this wasn't the time, no matter how right he was. Appearing properly chastised, he ordered the food lines to start back up. Feeling a little humiliated, he watched as all the people who had waited for hours returned. He noticed the different way they looked at him, and then at her.

Afterward, Elise led him and Franwil to the back room, where she really let him have it. "Don't you dare do that ever again, James. We agreed that if we're in danger, then you do what needs to be done. Otherwise, talk to me first. Don't go over my head."

He put both hands on her shoulders. "The Co-op will be at our doorstep within a month. We had a nice short vacation here, but we need to hide. With the dense population and the structures, and now with someone salvaging again, waiting them out is an option. We need to consider it."

"You're not listening to me . . ."

"We need to start hoarding supplies, not handing them out."

Elise folded her arms. "I know they're coming, James. I'm expecting it."

He stopped. "What do you mean you know?"

"You don't think I didn't pump these people for information when I started feeding them?"

James reared back. "There's better ways to get information than giving away all our food."

"You're not listening, boy," Franwil interjected. "Oldest Elise knows what she's doing."

"I'm counting on them coming," Elise said. "We're not running this time."

"They'll kill us."

"They'll kill us no matter where we run. We can't run from these people. We can only hide or fight. In this city, we can do both."

"Elise," James was nearly begging, "we can't fight the Co-op. They're better armed, better trained, and have much more advanced technology. All we have are these . . ."

She leveled an eye at him. "Say it. I dare you."

"All we have are the Elfreth."

"No, that's where you're wrong. Why do you think I'm feeding everyone, James? As sweet and soft as you think I am, I'm not a fool. I'm done running from the Co-op, and so is everyone else on the island who lost their homes and loved ones. We can't beat them by ourselves, but we might have a chance if we fight them together. Are you with me?"

"You know I'll follow you through hell."

"Good." She reached up and gave him a kiss on the cheek. Then she gave him a not-quite-so-light slap on the same cheek. "Don't ever undermine me again. By the way, there's an all-hands meeting in two days. I'm calling all the knights of the Round Table together."

"What's a round table?"

"Never mind. Just make sure you're there."

THIRTY

A NATION

Elise had never thought in a million years that she would be forming a government. Her only leadership experience besides her ill-fated tenure as captain of the badminton team was as vice president of the scuba diving club in Berkeley. In fact, she detested politics and most forms of organized governments. Yet here she was, standing on the podium in front of forty-three leaders from all the tribes that had flocked to the All Galaxy. She felt her stomach do a few flips. Well, she had laid out the honey and the trap for all these good folks; now was the time to spring it.

The leaders attending led tribes of varying sizes. Some, like Abel of the Madison Greens, led a tribe that was a thousand strong, nearly equaling Elise's Elfreth. Others, like Jayul, of Spin-Spin, which lived on the mostly flooded ground-floor lobby of the All Galaxy, commanded only two dozen. Others were complete unknowns. Glads, the leader of a tribe of three hundred called the Carnegies, had just arrived a few hours earlier. Her people were still straggling to the tower in groups of tens and twenties.

In the end, Elise followed a rule her mom had always quoted from her time in the Peace Corps: "Hungry people are always too hungry to fight."

Instead of wasting manpower and resources waging wars, Elise had opted to feed the elderly and the children instead. Once all the fighting folks realized what was happening, they, too, had put down their weapons and got in line for soup and bread. Word had spread quickly that one of the tribes on the upper levels was not only powerful but rich. Why else would they give away free food?

Within a matter of days, the Elfreth had received twenty requests from smaller tribes to merge and representatives from dozens more to meet. It was then that Elise and Franwil hatched the plan to unify the tribes surrounding the All Galaxy and create a loose coalition. This meeting was the result. It was a larger success than she had dared hoped. Too large, in fact.

Elise had not bothered stipulating who qualified as a leader and a tribe. If someone had wanted to come, she let them. It wasn't like she was planning on setting up that old United States House of Representatives or anything, or was she? She really didn't have a plan for this. Maybe it was something she should have thought out a little better. It was too late now.

She spent a few minutes chatting with Crowe, making sure they were on the same page before the start of the meeting. The teacher was well-known and respected by all the other tribes in the area due to the Flatirons' control of the All Galaxy, easily the largest tower in the area, and his and the Flatirons' support was critical for the success of her plans.

Elise stepped to the podium and scanned the faces of the men and women as their chatter quieted. Many had come armed. She hadn't bothered to stipulate that they shouldn't, either. That had probably been an oversight. A few scuffles almost broke out between warring tribes when they had first gathered. Her hands shook. Her head barely rose above the lectern. She wished she was standing on something to make her appear taller. Elise looked to her left and saw Franwil, who waved and returned her attention to a bag of seeds she was munching on.

Standing next to her, leaning against a column, was James, looking uneasy and guarded. He seemed even more unsettled than normal, continually scanned the crowds, no doubt expecting an attack from someone in the audience at any moment. As if on cue, he looked her way, and their eyes met. His lips curved up into a small smile and he walked up to her and gave her a squeeze on the arm. "You can do this. Knock them out."

"You mean dead, right?"

He frowned. "Why would you want to kill them?"

Elise chuckled. "Never mind." James's encouragement did settle her a bit. He had that effect on her. She shooed him off the stage and then raised her hand. "Thank you all for coming." She waited for a response; none came. Of course they weren't going to respond. What in Gaia did she think they were going to do? Something told her the men and women of the Mist Isle were not the clapping type. The short awkward pause felt like hours. She coughed and continued, "You are all the leaders of your people . . ."

A man stood up. He was large, bald, and scarred all over his body. "Not all should be here," he said in a loud clear voice. He pointed at another large man next to him. "I, Durand, lead a group of three hundred. Polan only leads a group of fifteen. I have subchiefs with more tribe."

The one named Polan stood up, holding a machete in his hand. "Only because you Ziegfelds came in the night like the dark ones you are and murdered many of my tribe." The people between them scattered as metal blades hissed out of their sheaths, and less than two minutes into her meeting to peacefully unify all the tribes for a common cause, a fight broke out.

For a second, Elise considered letting the two assholes poke a couple of holes into each other before pulling them apart. James had moved in front of the podium and was waiting for her signal. She shook her head. If she was going to play leader, it was time she took such matters into her own hands.

She willed her wrist beams to a low setting and aimed it at the big-mouth who had started it all. She prayed she didn't miss. Her aim had improved since she had first gotten the bands, but it was still mediocre at best. She shot her beam and nailed Durand on the left shoulder, spinning him to the ground. Before Polan could take advantage of that, she plugged him in the chest as well. Both men lay groaning, stunned from the blast.

Elise tried to appear casual even as her hands shook uncontrollably. She resisted the temptation to pretend to blow smoke off her fists. "Anyone else?"

The room was quiet. Several of the leaders' eyes widened as the two men picked themselves up and got back into their chairs. Between her previous generosity with food and this display of power, Elise was pretty sure she had everyone's full attention. Her nerves were screaming, but she kept her face calm.

Once the room had settled, Elise took a moment to collect her thoughts. She thought about what they were trying to build today, and what she had to say to accomplish that. She saw in their eyes what they all desperately needed: hope, direction, and assurances for their people. Most of all, she could tell they were weary of the constant fighting. The looks of disdain they gave Durand and Polan spoke volumes.

That would be her opening.

"Those who wish to hold grudges and war with others in this room are not welcome here," she began. "You may leave now. If you stay, then you will all make vows that the past disagreements between all of you are buried." She paused for effect, waiting and daring any of these leaders to stand up and leave the room. When none did, she continued, "I am Elise Kim, Oldest of the Elfreth. Our line is long, stretching two hundred years in the wastelands. We hail from Philadelphia and Boston and now call the Mist Isle our home." She noticed a few of the leaders nod. Surviving two hundred years was no small feat out here in the wastelands. For the first time, Elise was thankful that Franwil insisted that, as the new Oldest, she learn about the Elfreth's history. The tribes put a lot of stock in stuff like this.

"There is an enemy on the island, killing and destroying our way of life. They enslave the tribes and take their buildings. Many of you have seen them firsthand and now flee for your lives. We know of this enemy. They are powerful, armed with technology and terrible weapons. The enemy are known as Valta and ChronoCom, and they are unrelenting. They came to Boston and we ran. They destroyed our friends and neighboring tribes, and we ran. Now, they are here on the Mist Isle and we know that there is no place to run. The Elfreth will stay and fight.

"As you can tell, we have technology of our own, and we have supplies. We are organized. However, we cannot do this alone. Help us. Join with us. Many tribes together can form a stronger nation than many tribes apart. If we work together, we can defend our floors and buildings. We can care for each other, share food and resources. Together, we can fight for the isle and push back the enemy."

"Would we all bow to you then, Elise Kim of the Elfreth?" one of the leaders stood up and asked. "Would we all become Elfreth?"

A chorus of no's rang across the room. Surprisingly, there were less than she thought there would be. It was a point of contention, though. These tribes were very independent and fiercely defended their identity. To ask them to join would be to tell them they were no longer the people they were. The grousing and arguments got louder, so much so that James moved protectively in front of the podium again. Eventually, the chatter died down, to her mild surprise, without her intervening. She waited patiently until all eyes focused back on her.

"Talk among us is good," she said. "It facilitates cooperation and ideas. As long as it does not lead to violence, we all should talk more. Well, except for my friend Teacher Crowe of the Flatirons." She gestured at him in the front row. "He talks far too much." She was met by a chorus of laughter. The old chief grinned good-naturedly.

"You will not be Elfreth," she continued. "You will still be your tribe. You can come and go as you please if it suits your people. However, we all will have an identity that binds us. The Mist Isle was once known as Manhattan. Why don't we honor that name once more?"

A new chorus of calls erupted, but this time, the tone had changed. Instead of trying to find reasons to say no or to quarrel, the leaders of the assorted tribes were now asking for details. How would the work and floors be shared? How would influence be divided? Would there be a council? Would every tribe have a vote? Who would be in charge?

The questions were endless. However, it had taken a herculean effort to get all of these people into one room, and she wasn't going to let this opportunity go to waste. Elise began to jot down the many questions thrown her way and then began to knock them down one by one. All the leaders had their own ideas of what Manhattan should be, and they all agreed to disagree on the same and opposite things. Everyone wanted everything, yet at the same time everyone wanted to give up nothing. The next few hours were some of the most frustrating in Elise's life.

In the end, though, well after night had settled over the isle, the Nation of the Unified Tribes of Manhattan was born—it was a dumb and tedious name, one that could only have been born from committee, where no one was happy with the end result, but they had wasted an hour debating it, and this was the best they could agree on. Damn bureaucracy. To her surprise, fewer than ten of the leaders had walked out during the entire process, and all but one eventually returned. All they had left to do was figure out the details, which, as her mom liked to say, was where the devil resided, but that could wait until tomorrow.

An exhausted but exuberant Elise walked up to a waiting James and leaned on him, wrapping her arms around his waist. "Straight to bed, mister, because I'm going to sleep until next month."

"You have to do this all over again first thing tomorrow," he said.

"I was being facetious. Just hold me and tell me I did a good job."

He squeezed her tightly. "Elise, that was spectacular. You accomplished something that no one in generations was able to do, and you did so without firing a shot. Or a third shot, anyway."

"Well, fear and a common enemy help just a little," she said.

James shook his head. "Doesn't matter. These people came to this meeting because they saw something in the decisions you made, and they came together tonight as a group. I am so proud of you."

He leaned forward and kissed her, and all the tension and stress she had carried fell away. She wrapped her arms around his neck and pulled him down for another kiss. When they finally came apart, she beamed. "Remember our first date back on Nutris? You finally figured out the right things to say to a girl. Come on, let's go to bed and you can tell me more about how well I did today."

THIRTY-ONE

Unsettled

James watched in the corner, out of the way, as Sasha worked in Elise's lab. Titus had confirmed his diagnosis that she was indeed suffering from Terravira mononucleosis, commonly caused by a combination of an unsuspecting immune system and the Earth Plague. Franwil was able to barter for some herbs, Levin salvaged some medical supplies from the past, and Grace built a single-punch tablet machine on the fly. It was a group effort, and for that, James was grateful. Sasha was doing better, though her cough lingered, and she tired quickly, but the pink had returned to her face, and she was more active now than in recent memory.

Right now, his sister was dousing a row of plants with a chemical formula Elise had created. Prior to her coming to the present, Sasha couldn't read or write. Now she was assisting scientists with experiments. James's chest swelled with pride. His hands quivered—he blamed it on his emotions—as she hummed to herself and went about her business. He watched as she carefully checked the samples for traces of the Earth Plague and jotted notes on a piece of cloth.

Black abyss, he berated himself. He was starting to think like a parent. "Can you take a break and go on a walk with your brother?"

Sasha, face full of concentration, shook her head. "Elise needs to spend more time talking to the other leaders of the tribes. She's depending on me to make sure all these samples are cared for. It's a big job."

"It is indeed," he said. "When will you finish?"

"When Sammuia and Rima come back. They're going to teach me how to make traps and Sammuia says I should learn how to cut a spear from a blood stalk."

James wasn't sure how he felt about that. It was a good skill for the Mist Isle, though. The floors on some of these buildings were as wild and dense as any jungle he'd visited. This may not have been the life he had envisioned for his sister, but the more time they spent with the Elfreth, the more he was confident that he was giving her a good life, no matter the challenges.

"I guess you don't have any time for your big brother anymore."

"Don't be silly, James," she replied. "We'll have all the time in the world. Just later."

He had to remind himself that they looked at things differently. For him, she had been gone for almost twenty years. Twenty dark, painful, guilt-ridden years. Sasha standing here was a miracle, one that had only existed in his dreams.

To his sister, he was still the same old James, her brother who took care of her, made sure she was safe, and told her what to do. Sure, he was different, bigger, more wrinkled, and not as funny, but he was still just James. Sasha hadn't had many good memories or friends as a child, so James wasn't going to fault her for making new ones. She was just a kid, and boring old James was just that. Boring. He reminded himself that this was just Sasha being a typical ten-year-old girl. This was normal.

Elise too had other priorities. The line out of her office— she actually had an office!—sometimes stretched all the way down the hall. People had to make appointments with her. She even had an assistant. Elise had changed from a frightened, temporally-displaced woman into the leader of the Elfreth, and now the new figurehead of a new nation, all in the span of a year. That woman was amazing.

Both had moved on. He wasn't the center of either of their lives anymore. Hell, he wasn't important to anyone. It had been weeks since anyone had come to him for help, with a request, or even questions. At first, it felt great not to have that responsibility, but now, now he felt useless and unwanted.

A shrill whistle snapped him back to reality. He had a sour taste in his mouth. Self-pity was a weak trait quickly weaned out of all initiates at the Academy. Those who wallowed too much usually washed out within the first year. He had to be better than this. Sasha and Elise deserved it. Still, the hurt in his chest was there.

"James," Sasha said, "can you take the kettle off and put a thermometer in there? Let me know when it's exactly twenty-seven degrees Celsius."

"Yes, Dr. Sasha." He hopped off the table and walked across the room to the electric grill.

"Don't be silly," she said. "I'm not a doctor yet, but Elise and Grace said I can be one day if I work hard and read the books they got me. Grace calls me a doctor-in-training."

James's heart almost leaped out of his chest, and tears welled in his eyes. "You sure can," he choked. "Explain what you're doing, doctor-in-training Sasha?"

Sasha was happy to chatter on about what she had learned. He could feel how much she loved and trusted him, and that meant the world still. James couldn't believe how much she had picked up in such a short time in the lab.

"Elder James," Wari, one of the guardians, called. "A voom approaches from the south."

"The *Frankenstein*?"

"Flyguard Chawr says no. He says the *Frankenstein* is not expected for seven days."

James grabbed his large gauss launcher from the counter. It was an older model Levin had scrounged from the Tech Wars. Its accuracy was awful, but the thing could take a beating, get wet and dirty, and still do its job. In a place such as this, reliability was an important attribute to have. It was also the only hand cannon in the tribe that had the kick of a tank. He jogged to the southern side of the building and leaned against the wall next to the window.

Ships rarely got this close to the All Galaxy. The density of buildings in this area made it hard for them to maneuver. Nonetheless, Co-op patrols had increased as of late. Three times this week, a scout ship had passed nearby, weaving slowly through the fog. All of the tribes in the area knew the importance of staying below the enemy's radar.

Any time one of their ships came close, a network of younger children would race through all the floors shouting warnings. The All Galaxy would change from a well-lit and bustling hive to just another dead husk in a sea of darkened buildings. Entire city blocks could go completely dark and quiet within minutes. This was critical, because if the Co-op ever found them, they could make a beeline right to their location.

At first, he heard nothing but the squawking of birds. The Mist Isle had a life of its own, with several species of predatory birds flying above the city, and thousands of other species living inside. Then he heard it, barely perceptible over the white noise, a soft grinding roar. He could tell that now-familiar sound from half a kilometer away.

"It's the *Frankenstein*," he said to Wari. "Stand down. Alert the others."

James trotted down to the landing deck on the seventy-third floor. Already, a dozen Elfreth had congregated on the balcony. The flyguards were there as well, ready to service the collie and prep it for its next flight. He wandered to the edge and looked down the skyscraper as the *Frankenstein* climbed up its side. One of these days, the Co-op was going to figure out that they were using the Battery Tunnel to sneak into Manhattan. Most of the underwater passages were blocked, but that particular one was wide enough for the collie to navigate slowly around the debris.

Combined with the collie's stealth technologies and the EMP fog on the island, it was all but impossible for surveillance to track the ship's movements. As long as the enemy continued to overlook the underwater passages, they could continue their operations.

The collie, still dripping wet, rose to the third roof, two-thirds up the building. James moved out of the way as it hovered over the platform and parked with a soft hiss. A few minutes later, Grace and Levin stepped out. The flyguards leaped into action and began to prep it right away for another flight. At the same time, a dozen of the younger Elfreth ran inside to unload the cargo. James walked to the edge of the roof and scanned the area: nothing but gray haze.

He looked back at Grace as she approached. "You're back early."

She jabbed a thumb behind her. "We had a little incident with a major ripple. The good auditor canceled the last jump."

James raised an eyebrow. "I told you he was awfully sensitive about stuff like that, and about the Time Laws specifically. Good job writing them. The rest of us have had to deal with those rules for centuries now."

She scowled and stomped away.

Levin appeared from inside the collie. "We need to talk."

"Can it wait until we finish unloading and get the collie covered up?"

"No, James, it can't."

James had known the man long enough to know he was serious. James was reminded of the many times he had been called into the auditor's office for a dressing-down. He noticed the Elfreth porters shooting glances their way. Every community gossiped, even wasteland tribes living in ruined decaying cities. Especially them, actually. The last thing the already-frazzled tribe needed was more gossip.

He motioned for Levin to follow him to the other end of the deck. He rounded on him once he was sure they were out of earshot. "First of all, don't voice your disagreement in front of the Elfreth. They are following us on loyalty and faith. The last thing we need is to give them doubt."

"The Elfreth will do as they're told," Levin said.

"They're not chronmen you can order around," James snapped. "They require a more delicate hand."

"Like yours, James?"

"Don't start with me, Levin. Now, what's got you all knotted up this time?"

Levin didn't bother lowering his voice. "We're doing this all wrong."

"That's a little broad," James replied dryly. "Which exact part of this are we not doing right, because I'm pretty sure there's a lot of things we're messing up."

Levin motioned at the group of Elfreth unloading the supplies. "I just almost caused a major time ripple getting a bunch of bullshit supplies."

"Those bullshit supplies are what's keeping you fed and the lights powered on."

"It's a bad use of resources and an even worse use of the chronostream."

None of this was news to James. He had had these exact same thoughts when he was the one doing jumps. He sat down at the edge of the roof and glanced over, seeing the writhing mist roll and bubble in the air. The drop was hundreds of meters, but the fog looked so thick it seemed like he could step onto it. If he squinted and angled his head, he could just make out a figure dancing in the mists. The figure stopped, and then walked directly toward him. James recoiled as Smitt appeared and leaped onto the edge of the balcony.

"You should try it sometime," his former handler said, balancing precariously on the ledge. "If I jump over the side, will you catch me, my friend? Oh, yeah, you're not wearing your bands anymore. You gave them to Levin. Now why would you do something so foolish? Remember what he did to Landon?"

"I'll never forget," he muttered.

"Did you say something?" Levin frowned. "You're acting strange."

"What's wrong with the Elfreth?" James asked, tearing his gaze away from his dead friend. He felt a sudden prick of anger at Levin's words. "The Elfreth took Elise and me in. They fed and sheltered us while you assholes tried to kill us. Not only that, they're the ones living off the land that the rest of us destroyed, and they're the ones trying to help us save it. Not the planetary governments, not ChronoCom, and as sure as abyss, not the megacorporations."

James never realized how protective he had become of the Elfreth until an outsider—James still considered Levin one—spoke ill of them. It was less than a year ago that he had been just as disdainful. Now, after everything they'd done for him, he was ready to defend them with his life. He didn't even realize how angry he was with Levin until he caught himself balling his hands into fists.

To his surprise, and for the first time that he could remember, Levin backed down. "You're right. Those were unkind words. The Elfreth have been supportive, and I had no right speaking like that. However, I stand by my point. We're doing it wrong."

"What do you mean?" James asked.

"We're trying to solve a global pandemic with local resources. We, the Elfreth, and Elise, won't be able to carry out the plan even if we did find a cure. These primitives are barely able to keep the lights on, let alone work on a problem this big. We're going into this alone and it's not getting us anywhere."

"Says the guy who's been with us for, what, a couple of weeks? Says the guy who was responsible for attacking the Elfreth in the first place."

"I was doing the right thing at the time." Levins voice grew louder. "You're in this situation because you got emotional. That's what got you into trouble in the first place."

"Seems doing the right thing got you into trouble as well, except you took a detour through prison."

"Only because I went after you."

The two stood toe to toe, scowling into each other's faces. James wasn't sure if he could take Levin in a fair fight, but he was wound up enough to try. They might be on the same side, but years of animosity and bitterness didn't just melt away because they had the same goals.

Fortunately, Grace got between them, waving her hand at her face. "You two are getting me all hot and bothered. This is less than useful, and neither of you is inspiring the masses."

Both of them glanced over at the two dozen Elfreth frozen in place, staring. James had broken his own rule. These people either looked up to or feared them. Either way, that made this little tiff look bad. The gossip was going to be rampant. Elise was going to hear of this.

"We're doing it wrong," Levin repeated in a quieter voice.

"Well, feel free to update us savages when you figure out a better plan."

Levin scowled and stomped away.

Grace's gaze followed the former auditor. She turned to James. "He's not wrong, you know. You and I have had this discussion before."

James shrugged. "Of course he's not wrong, but I'm not giving him the satisfaction of just being right. Unless he has a solution and an actionable plan, being right isn't enough. Besides, he still hasn't thanked me for breaking him out of prison."

She looked over at James and shook her head. "Sometimes, pet, you're a petty little shit, you know that?"

He shrugged and turned his attention back to unloading the collie. "I'd like to think I'm just standing up for all of us, the little people Levin's so quick to dismiss. This fight affects everyone. By the way, did you retrieve the medical analyzer machines and medicines for Sasha like Titus asked?"

THIRTY-TWO

SHOT ACROSS THE BOW

When Weck was a kid, he messed up a lot and ran with a bunch of tunnel rats. Finally, his pap had had enough and told him that he had better get his ass straight and pull his own weight in the colony. "Don't be a dreg," Pap had said, "because those that can't afford air don't get to breathe for free. They get shipped off to that shithole in space." He would point up into the domed sky and then reinforce his lecture with a metal rod to Weck's bent rear.

Eventually, Weck got the lesson beaten into him, and he followed his pap's advice. He stopped running with the tunnel rats, fulfilled his Luna citizenship hours, and began earning a respectable commission at one of the largest and most powerful megacorporations. By all indications, he had done what Pap had said. He wasn't a dreg. However, somehow, Weck ended up shipped off to that shithole in the sky anyway.

"I hate Earth," he said, chewing and spitting cany weed as his team of five hunkered down for the night on the seventy-third floor of a building identified on the map only as the Pierre. "I busted my ass so I wouldn't end up here."

Weck's hound pack was assigned the unfortunate task of surveying the block east of the Central Park jungle, south to Sixtieth and east to Madison Avenue. According to his pack leader, Co-op forces were coming through here next week, and she wanted every floor on the block fully surveyed.

Usually, that would be more than enough time for the job, but no one had accounted for how much trouble buildings next to Central Park were to survey. The dense jungle in the center of the Mist Isle had grown outward in every direction, getting its stinking tentacles into all the adjacent structures. Thousands of massive vines and branches—some as thick as a man was tall—jutted into the buildings through windows, cracks, and doors. Some of the larger plants had made their own entrances by smashing through walls.

To top things off, the wildlife here—Weck wasn't even counting the savages—was particularly dense. Already, in the first building, a relatively modest eighty-two-floor residence, his team had run into four different packs of large cats and a pit of humanoid snake creatures. His men had flamed out one of the cat lairs, but had decided to leave the rest to the main force.

Surprisingly, the tribes here were sparse. Nonexistent, almost. Weck and his men had thought the savages would congregate around the jungle, much like the wildlife did, but they had barely seen more than a few small groups here and there. They found evidence of habitation on several sites, some quite large, but they all seemed to have been abandoned. He guessed the Senior Securitate's new plan of spreading fear and terror among the primitives was working.

They did find a small savage tribe lingering in the area. Weck and his team of five had stumbled upon the twenty or so savages just as they were roasting dinner—some large deer-like creature. His boys had decided that they would rather have venison than their rations, and the twenty primitives weren't much of a threat, so they swooped in. The savages were taken by surprise and didn't put up much of a fight. Within minutes, Weck's pack had killed half the tribe and sent the rest scurrying away.

His men were clearing the floor when he saw a pair of eyes hiding under a blanket. He pulled the blanket off and discovered a young, scrawny boy, probably no older than eight. The little animal smelled like piss. Weck pulled him to his feet and pushed the savage against the wall.

"Not too smart, are you?" He grinned. He put his hand on the dirty urchin's neck and aimed the gun at his forehead. Before he could pull the trigger, the animal bit his hand and ran off. Smarting, Weck fired twice but missed both times. The little savage scurried under a broken table, and then fled the room.

Marl wanted to chase after him, saying it was more humane to put down the kid than to let him get eaten by the cats and dogs and snake-men, but the roasted venison smelled delicious, and it was getting dark. Whatever little light managed to shine through this accursed fog was fading, and no one felt like wading through the darkness looking for savages to euthanize.

Weck, shaking his smarting hand, sat down and threw his pack off. "Go after him yourself if you want. I'll be sure to eat your portion before you get back."

The rest of the guys laughed and settled around the fire. By all indications, the small tribe had been living here for years. They occupied half a floor of the building and even had crops on the balconies. Weck and his team ate their fill and stretched out around the fire.

"I can't wait until this project is over." Rindle yawned and stretched. "I thought when I got the commission, I'd be fighting the Radicati, not wading through this cesspool. I mean, every time I inhale, I feel like gagging."

Weck took out his pouch of cany weed and tossed it to Rindle. "You know, when I was a kid back on Luna, I once asked my pap why we lived there and pay for air if we can just move to Earth and get it for free. He smacked me on the back of the head and told me anything that's worth having is worth paying for. I didn't really get it until my first trip to Earth. He was an asshole, but Pap got it right."

"The frec air here is what the freeloaders deserve. Those of us willing to work and pay for it deserve the clean stuff," Rindle added. "Capitalism and corporations will save humanity." The men around them echoed in agreement.

"Listen up, boys," Weck said. "Turn in early. We got a whole block to survey and less than a week to do it. The pack leader's not going to chew me out for missing another project deadline. Rindle, first watch, then Zimm, Marl, and then Giggy. I'll take the morning."

"Why do you always get the last?" Giggy asked.

"You get to be the last when you're lead."

Weck's pack settled in just as night swept over the isle. Whatever dim light was shining through the haze was gone, and the only thing staving off the darkness was the small dying fire at their feet. The four not keeping watch were soon fast asleep.

It seemed no sooner had he closed his eyes than Weck heard a muf-
fled cry and then a shuffling of footsteps. Like any good soldier, he was
up in a blink with his blaster out. He must have slept a few hours at least.
The fire was only embers. The three men around him were still asleep
and he could hear a shuffling just outside in the hallway.

"Rindle?" Weck whispered, turning his head beam on. The line of light
painted the walls as he swiveled left and right. "Associate Hound Rindle.
Report." When he received no response, Weck kicked the man next to
him. "Zimm. Get up. Sweeps the floor—"

A thud in his chest knocked Weck onto his back. He had been in enough
battles to know when he had been shot. He groaned and looked down,
frowning when he realized that it was an ax sticking out of his chest. He
tried to call out an alarm but only hisses escaped his lips. Weck put his
left hand on the ax and tried to pull it loose. The pain almost made him
lose consciousness.

He slumped back down to the ground and watched as the night came
alive. Zimm sat up and stared mouth-open at the wooden handle growing out of Weck's chest. As soon as he tried to stand, a shadow flashed
from behind, and blood poured out of his opened throat. More shadows
flew into the room, several flying past Weck's head beam in a dark blur.

The other two men were able to get to their feet and fire off a few
shots. The room flashed as Marl's rifle strafed across it. He must have hit
several of the attackers, because a chorus of screams followed. Then his
rifle stopped firing and the blackness swallowed him whole. Marl fell at
Weck's feet, his eyes wide open.

Just as soon as the attack began, it ended, and the room was silent and
dark again except for Weck's head beam and the sound of his heavy breathing. Several bright white lights bathed the room, brightening it as if it
were day. Weck shielded his eyes as one of the sources shined directly
into his face. When he finally adjusted, he saw that he was surrounded
by savages. Weck's eyes widened as a small figure stepped in front of him.

It was the boy who had gotten away. The boy stared at Weck stone-
faced, then he looked up at the man next to him and nodded. The man,
draped in all black, unsheathed a knife from his belt. He offered it handle
facing out. The boy took it and looked at Weck. The words that came
out of his mouth sounded like gibberish.

"I don't speak savage." Weck coughed and spat blood. "I should have gutted you when I had the chance."

"He said he has avenged his parents by bringing us to their murderers. He claims all your deaths as his. We have given them to him."

The savage's Solar English was barely understandable, but it was natural; he wasn't using a comm band. "Where did you learn . . ." Weck never finished his sentence. The boy rammed the blade into Weck's chest opposite of where the ax was still lodged. He gasped and spat out blood, then he fell over to his side. Weck's last thought before dying was how much he hated Earth.

Elise walked with Eriao under heavy escort across the three kilometers from the All Galaxy Tower to the scene of the first battle between Manhattan and the Co-op. Both Eriao and Murad had counseled against her going, but she had insisted. This was the first volley of their war to drive the enemy off the island, and she wanted to witness it.

One of the lookouts stationed at an outpost in that area had heard gunfire. He had gone to investigate and found a boy running blindly through the building. The boy had told him what happened, and the lookout had sent the alert through to the All Galaxy. Elise had been awakened early in the evening and notified that a small Co-op squad had been detected. Eriao, now the de facto war chief of Manhattan, had made the call to stage an ambush and draw first blood. The two of them had decided to venture out to see the historical first battle together, though by all accounts, it wasn't much of a fight, ending within a matter of seconds.

They were escorted into the room, and Eriao immediately went off to the side to talk to Murad, who had led the battle. The first thing Elise noticed was the row of nearly twenty bodies arranged neatly at one end of the room. Murad had said they were the Taj, a tiny friendly tribe that never bothered anyone and only wanted to be left alone. Now most of them were dead by the hand of Co-op soldiers.

Elise looked to her left and saw the five other bodies. They wore a gray variation of the standard Valta uniforms and looked surprisingly ordinary in their corporate armor. Back in Boston, the Co-op had primarily used ChronoCom monitors to do all the hard lifting. She wondered why that was no longer the case. It didn't matter. The enemy was hunting them, and the Elfreth—no, the Manhattans—had finally hunted back.

She noticed one particular Valta guard off to the side. He had an ax and a dagger stuck into his chest. "What happened to him? He looks like he was executed."

The Elmen striker, standing next to a young boy, spoke. "The boy who survived, Foss, said this man was the leader. We gave the boy his justice."

Elise felt her body tighten at those words but kept her face calm. She knelt down in front of Foss. "You've had a long night. Would it be all right if we take you back with us to find you a warm bed?" He nodded and allowed the guardian to lead him away.

Elise spun on Murad. "No more executions. If we find a survivor, we take him back and interrogate him. We're not savages." She winced at that word. It had come out inadvertently.

"The invaders do not offer us the same quarter," Murad said. "We would have to share our food and bed with the enemy."

"Just because the enemy has no respect, it doesn't mean we won't. If they're alive," Elise emphasized each word, "bring them back. Understand?"

Murad nodded, though the expression on his face showed disagreement. "It will be your word, Oldest."

"Murad," Eriao said, walking up to them. "Strip the dead Valta troops of their armor and weapons.."

"Yes, War Chief."

Elise looked out the window at Central Park. "Does the Co-op avoid the park there?"

Murad nodded. "All do, Oldest. To walk into the Central is to walk into death."

"There's more of these small Co-op teams in other buildings?"

"We have had sightings of at least two more so far," said Eriao. "Scouts have reported other massacres like this over the past few days."

"Several small tribes are still scattered in the area. They are all at risk." Elise pulled up a map and ran her finger along the street until it reached the East River. She looked up at Eriao. "Can we defend everything south of this line?"

Eriao studied the map for a few seconds. "I'd prefer to move it further north, actually. That jungle on the western edge is a perfect defensive point. If our line is too far south and they break through, they can spill westward." He drew his finger a few blocks north of Sixty-third Street. "Make our stand here."

Elise took a piece of chalk and drew a line on that street from the edge of the park to the East River. She looked up at Murad. "Have all buildings south of that line checked for Co-op forces. That's our new border. I want all Manhattan forces moved up and ready to attack any of the enemy forces that cross it. It's time we start defending our people."

A small smile appeared on Murad's face. "Yes, Oldest." He tapped his hand twice over his heart. "We defend Manhattan."

THIRTY-THREE

PREY'S BITE

Kuo looked at the three-dimensional map of the island rising up from the table. She had just lost another veteran hound pack who last reported in on Seventy-fourth and Third. She noted the location on the map and checked the watch line.

All across the island, inside and outside Co-op-controlled space, her hound packs, trooper pods, and monitor squads had gone missing. It was as if the entire abyss-plagued island had risen up at the same time. In the past seventy-two hours, nine of sixteen units had failed to report, whereas she had lost only one in all of last month. Unfortunately, the damn fog made rapid responses impossible. Sometimes, it took over a day before she realized a team was missing. Could the tribes in the south half of the Mist Isle be this much more dangerous?

No, that was impossible. By all indications, these savages were relatively homogeneous in strength. There was no way any of the tribes could be so much more powerful than the others. If that was so, a dominant tribe would have taken over the entire island years ago. Something had changed. Either they had organized, or they were receiving outside help.

That last theory seemed most likely. Whoever had been hitting her people over the last few days had been smart enough to take all the bodies, but the evidence of battle on the walls and floors, the random ejected shells, clips, and shrapnel, told a different story. Everywhere her investigators looked, there were signs that these spear-chucking savages were teching up. Blaster fire, beam weapons, gauss projectiles. Someone, some corporation, possibly, was arming these primitives. The question was, who?

At first, Kuo thought it was the Radicati Corporation, Valta's leading competitor and enemy. However, it made little sense for them to get involved in this project, or to even know this project existed. The Radicati were busy waging a four-way war with Valta, Finlay, and the dominion colonies.

The fact that Kuo was so far away from that war made her grit her teeth. This project was important to the company's long-term strategy and was considered a promotion for Kuo, but this was still the backwater of the solar system and far away from the real action. The real climbers on the corporate ladder were the ones fighting on the front line.

The most recent development was certainly not going to help her cause. She had to send Sourn a status report by tomorrow. The last thing he wanted to hear was that she had lost sixty people to a bunch of rock-throwing takers living in squalor. To make matters worse, her most recent request to Young for more monitors had been rejected. Blast that nonprofit fool. The man was becoming a serious problem.

She was still no closer to locating the temporal anomaly. In the end, that was all that was important to Sourn and the board. She could waste hundreds of lives and thousands of units of energy and worth, but as long as she captured the scientist, this mission would be considered a success.

She still wasn't sure why the liaison was so adamant about capturing her, other than wanting to enforce the contract. It made little sense unless there was something critically important about this scientist. So far, Sourn had been tight-lipped about it, only saying something vague about how there was something this anomaly had that Valta needed.

"Senior," Ewa called, barging into the meeting room. "We just received word from the Sixty-third and York station. They're under attack by multiple groups of savages."

Multiple? Kuo checked the map. That was just six blocks away. How brazen could the enemy be?

"Did we send a response team yet?"

"Yes. A shocker pod has been deployed. According to the survivors, they were destroyed to a man. The last message from the trooper leader

at the station was that they were about to be overrun by an entire horde
of savages, and that it was a very coordinated attack."

Kuo was stunned. Shockers were her heaviest and most valuable units.
She had only been allocated a few of these pods. For her to lose one was
unimaginable. She checked her levels and hurried out of the room. "All
available personnel within a ten-block radius congregate at that intersection. I want a full sweep of the block. How many Valkyries do we have
available right now?"

"Two on patrol. Four standing by."

"I want all six in the air immediately."

Twenty minutes later, Kuo and a force of nearly two hundred swept
toward the building between York and the river. It was the largest group of
troopers and monitors she could muster at a moment's notice. Within
seconds, the six Valkyries had taken hover positions over the intersections
while the monitors took up defensive positions over all the bridges. Her
troopers began a floor-by-floor sweep of the eighty-five-story building.

Kuo flew through an opened window on the twenty-third floor, where
the Valta outpost was located. The station was the first of several built
alongside the major intersections of the bridges connecting the buildings
together. It was also especially important, because it gave her forces a van-
tage point on the Queensboro Bridge to the south.

According to the map, the lower levels of this building used to be an
old school. Over the years, additional buildings were stacked on top of
it, from medical facilities to long-term-care housing to a military training facility. During the Core Conflicts, it had been converted to a military resupply base, and then a refugee camp shortly before the civilized
world abandoned the entire island.

The battle played in her head. The enemy must have first come through
from the lower level from the north end. She found splatters of blood and
blaster fire at several locations. It had been a total surprise. However, none
of the signs pointed to consistent movement. Her people weren't pushed
back, and they hadn't taken defensive positions. The enemy must have surrounded them and hit them all at once. It had been a slaughter.

The outpost had seventeen monitors, six troopers, and two engineers
at the time of its attack. That singlehandedly made this the worst defeat
she had suffered since the beginning of her mission to capture the temporal anomaly.

"A coordinated attack with large numbers," she muttered. "Get an analytics team here," she said, pointing to a hole that seemed to have been burned by wrist beams. "Confirm the blast signatures. Scour the rest of this place. I want everything scanned and traced. I want to know every weapon used, every energy trace left over, every abyss-forsaken piece of DNA we can get our hands on."

Kuo stood aside and waited anxiously, half-enraged and half apprehensive as a group of her engineers collected samples and took readings. On the one hand, the aggression and brazenness of a daytime attack had shaken her confidence in her expected victory. On the other hand, there could be some evidence here that might explain what was going on. If that fugitive chronman was alive and still on the island, there was a good chance the anomaly was as well.

It took the better part of the day for her people to report back to her. In the meanwhile, Kuo ordered a push farther south. Her troops encountered four small tribes and a handful of wandering savages. They were going to be brought back to the main holding pen. However, instead of separating and putting them to work, she had a different plan. They must have some knowledge of the recent events. She intended to beat it out of them.

"Well?" she asked as her lead investigator came to report his findings.

"ChronoCom signatures, Senior," he said. "As well as wrist beams, twenty-second-century gauss rifles, twenty-third-century lasers, and what looks like . . ." He paused, and then looked up. "Bullets. The old-fashioned kind, some as old as the nineteenth century."

"Did the savages find an old cache of weapons?" she asked.

"I doubt it," the investigator said. "Some of these signatures come from weapons hundreds of years old. It's more likely that they were time salvaged."

So the chronman was illegally jumping again. Interesting. Why now? The jumps had seemed to stop shortly after Levin's attack on the Elfreth home in Boston. Why would he start back up? That would explain the increased fighting ability of these savages. However, if that was the case, then that would mean they were organized, and even more disturbingly, unified behind him. They now posed a danger to her forces.

The director needed to be notified at once. This was his jurisdiction and responsibility. He had pulled his surveillance off this fugitive after

Auditor Levin was incarcerated and the jumps had stopped. However, it was imperative now that ChronoCom perform its duty. At the very least, this was something she could hold over Young for a while. He had been increasingly disagreeable lately.

Even more importantly, this was necessary to her report to Sourn. The last few days had produced poor news, and she needed to show progress. Now she had proof the woman was still in the area. That would be enough. For now. Almost as importantly, she could attribute the recent uptick in her casualties and increasing enemy activity to these illegal jumps.

As the old business idiom went: there's always a reason to succeed and a hundred reasons to fail. The most important thing was always to cover your ass.

She turned to the nearest trooper. "Recall one of the Valkyries and have it ready to pick me up."

"Yes, Senior. Where to?"

"Chicago. I'm going to tear the good director in half."

THIRTY-FOUR

IDLE HANDS

The flyguards descended upon the pile of junk, systematically breaking down the debris and containers until they reached a large metal rolling door. James, standing next to a broken column in what used to be a parking garage, scanned the skies across the East River. There shouldn't be any Co-op patrols this far south, but the blockade over the river was constant, and they were close enough to the shoreline that carelessness or bad luck could get them spotted by a passing Valkyrie.

He looked down the ramp at where Chawr and his people struggled to push up the rusty rolling door with a manual crank. The door protested being forced open, its high-pitched shrieks slicing through the air, sending a shudder through James's body.

He hissed at Chawr to quiet it down and turned his attention back to the skies. They were out in the open on the edge of the downtown area near the harbor. The fog was light and the skies were clearer than he preferred this early in the morning, but they had a long day of work ahead of them.

He was the only one with anything resembling a modern weapon. The rest of the flyguards, not considered true guardians, wielded spears and ancient projectile weapons. Chawr had an electro shotgun, which at best could scratch the paint off a Valkyrie. Their little group could hold off wild animals and perhaps raiders, but without his bands, they were extremely vulnerable.

"We're in," Chawr said, as they lifted the door half a meter off the ground. The rest of the flyguards lay flat on their stomachs and rolled into the next room. James waited a few moments and closed his eyes, listening for the high-pitched whine of a Valkyrie or the low rumble of a collie. When he was satisfied, he jogged down the ramp, slid his rifle inside, and rolled in after them.

James stood up and looked around at what used to be a maintenance garage. Chawr barked out several orders and the crew got to work, making sure the vehicles were dry, checking energy levels, and starting ignitions. One by one, the vehicles rumbled to life.

"The starter is dead on this one," Aliette said, closing the hood on one of the trucks.

"Pull out the battery and take it with us," Chawr said.

The smile grew on James's face as he watched the young man lead his team. Just a few months earlier, Chawr had been a known troublemaker among the Elfreth. Now, he was a leader, a valued member of the tribe, someone the children looked up to. James's smile must have been obvious, because it caught Chawr's attention.

He looked over at James with a puzzled expression. "Yes, Elder? Something the matter?"

"Not at all, Chawr. You guys keep doing your thing."

His attention wandered to a large metal container tucked into the corner of the room. He tapped the hollow body. "Think you guys can mix up a batch?"

Chawr hesitated. "Oldest Franwil and Oldest Grace said—"

"Grace is off in space, and Franwil will never find out. Besides, who knows when we'll be back? Maybe never."

"Well, maybe we could brew up a little. We still have some blood yeast, kudzu growth, and catalyst soy left over. Would seem like a waste . . ."

"Have at it," James said, patting him on the back. "Aliette and I will finish with the transports."

Chawr nodded. "Bria, Laurel, Dox, help me brew some juice."

"But Oldest Elise and . . . ," Bria said hesitantly.

"Elder James said it was all right."

It didn't take much more effort to convince the rest of Chawr's friends to brew some shine. He watched as they built a fire. James felt his skin

tingle as he worked on the transports. He glanced to the side and saw
Smitt leaning against the wall, shaking his head. "What are you looking at?"

Smitt sighed. "Nothing I've ever said made you listen when it comes
to your drink, my friend. Why start now?"

"I'm glad we have an understanding."

"Can I say something, though?"

James knew what Smitt was going to say next. Irritated, he attacked
the valve he was twisting with renewed vigor. "No. I deserve a sip, so
don't try to make me feel guilty."

"Suit yourself."

"Did you say something, Elder?" Aliette asked, looking over from
where she was working.

"Just thinking out loud," James replied, purposely not looking Smitt's
way.

That evening, James and the flyguards huddled around the small fire
they had built and drank the first of a batch of raw shine. It tasted awful,
but the feeling of release it gave James, that loosening of tightly wound
nerves, was worth the burn and the pain.

The atmosphere in the group was light as they relaxed and joked around
the fire, giggling and chatting like children. James leaned back against the
wall with a content smile on his face. There was a sense of camaraderie,
something he hadn't felt since his Academy days, as Bria and Chawr narrated a story about the one time they added too much yeast and blew up
their old container, and how Hory and Gio tried to not to waste the
brewed booze by drinking it directly off the ground. Unfortunately, the
shine was still scalding, and the two burned their lips so badly they
couldn't talk right for weeks.

He howled with the rest as they ribbed Hory good-naturedly. He
clinked jars with them as they toasted Gio, their friend who had died
in the initial attack at the Farming Towers. For that evening, James felt
strangely at peace. Looking around the fire, he felt a kinship with these
kids, these flyguards. Elise might belong to the Elfreth, but these seven
were his.

By the end of the night, after five full jars of the bad liquor were gone
and the fire near the entrance was dying, they decided to turn in. James
found himself alone with half a jar of shine. He decided to clear some of

the smoke in the room from the fire. He rolled the door up another meter and left the garage. Jar in hand, he inhaled the cool night air in the
quiet streets.

The island was dead tonight, the sky black as space, the fog a translucent gray, and everything so ghost-quiet he could hear his heart
thumping in his chest. He raised the jar to his lips and let the smell burn
the hairs in his nostrils, and then he took a loving sip, savoring the
warmth coursing down his throat and through his body, keeping the
chill at bay.

He was terribly lonely right now, which felt strange. It had never bothered him before. Loneliness was an old friend. He had spent the better
part of two decades with only Smitt speaking into his ear. So why did it
bother him so much now? Then he realized: it was Elise's fault. She had
coaxed him out of his shell, his protective field, lured him with hope and
purpose, and then left him dangling in the wind once she had better things
to do. Now James didn't know what he was or where he belonged anymore.

For a while, he thought he was a chronman and the key to the Elfreth's survival. However, right now up there in space, Levin had usurped
his job and had taken the mantle of salvager. Having lost that, James
thought his place was by Elise's side. Now, she was too busy with her
Manhattan unification project. James was reduced to hanging out with
children fifteen years his junior. It seemed no matter what he did, he had
no place in the universe.

Smitt appeared next to him as he leaned over a concrete balcony.
"Aww, I didn't know you missed me that much. Your priorities are messed
up, though, my friend. First you hate being a chronman, and now you're
upset with Levin for taking your job?"

"Shut up," James said, taking a swig from the jar. It was nearly empty.
For a second, he thought about refilling it from the large jug. They were
supposed to be back at the All Galaxy at sunrise. Instead of thinking about
making the half-day trek back to the tower hungover, James thought about
the five hours he had left to drink before dawn.

"You should stop," said Smitt.

"You should shut up," James spat. "You don't get to tell me what to do
anymore. That's what you get for leaving me." He stomped away from
the parking garage.

"Come on," Smitt called after him. "You think I wanted to die? Let me tell you. Dying sucks."

"Yeah, well, so does living," James growled. He stumbled along the harbor edge, oblivious to his surroundings. If he laid down and died right now, would anyone miss him? Probably not. It had already been proven how easily replaceable he was. He might as well just jump into the dark brown waters.

James downed the last of the jar and hurled it as hard as he could into the harbor. He heard the cracking of glass somewhere out there in the darkness. He turned around and realized that he was lost. It was so dark out, he could barely see past his hands, let alone make it past mounds of debris and ruins back to the hidden garage. He shivered as the ocean air blew in from the harbor.

James tried to walk back in the direction he had come from. He made a few wrong turns and tripped on the uneven ground as he stumbled, hands outstretched, trying to feel his way back. After he nearly stepped off a collapsed staircase and plummeted to his death, he decided to just sit wherever he was and wait until light. The passageway was a wind tunnel, a shrill whistle laid over the otherwise quiet night. Shivering, James pulled his coat tightly around his body and tucked his knees in.

The hallucination of Sasha appeared next to him, huddled in a similar fashion. She leaned in, sniffed his breath, and then made a face. She looked away, her tiny body shivering in the cold. He could hear her light coughs being carried away in the wind.

"I'm sorry," he mumbled and reached for her. "I was supposed to take care of you."

She got up and climbed farther up the broken stairwell, moving to the corner to huddle with her back to him.

"Look, James, this is probably not a good idea," Smitt said, appearing next to her. He stood up and tried to pull James to his feet. "You're going to freeze to death, just like on Tethys. Come on, let's go." James pulled away and pawed his way up the cracked stairs to get Sasha, but when he got to the upper level, she was no longer there. He looked back down at Smitt, who shook his head. "Come on. Follow me."

James wasn't sure exactly where they went. He followed the voice of his friend, the darkened figure leading him deeper into the maze of buildings and ruins, through twists, turns, and small passageways until he was hopelessly lost. By now, he was so exhausted, staying on his feet was difficult. He collapsed again, sprawled on top of the jagged rocks, and closed his eyes.

A second later, he opened them, except this time, it was light outside, and Chawr was hovering over him with a worried expression on his face. The young flyguard was shaking him so hard he felt his head bouncing up and down against the hard rocks.

His eyes ached at the bright sky. He shielded them with his hands and sat up. "What happened? What time is it?"

"It is late morning." Chawr's voice was hushed, rushed. "Please, Elder. We must leave."

Late morning? They were supposed to have headed back toward the All Galaxy at first light. Moving the length of the downtown area during the day was dangerous. How could he have let this happen?

That was when James first heard it. Somewhere out there, the high-pitched whine of a Valkyrie attack ship whistled among the concrete ruins. He looked around and realized that he must have passed out not fifty meters from the garage entrance. "What am I doing here?"

"We woke up this morning to the sound of the enemy and then found you gone," Chawr said. "A few of us went out to search for you. I found you lying out here in the open. Thought perhaps it was a trap. I could not leave without making sure, though. Would not know what words to speak to Oldest Elise."

"Good kid," James said, scrambling to his feet. What happened last night? Did that walk through the city actually happen? Did he even make it out of the garage, or was it all in his head?

He and Chawr crept back into the garage. The rolling doors were halfway up; he remembered raising them last night. The rest of the flyguards were stacking the debris back in front of the entrance. They wouldn't be able to lower the door without alerting that ship overhead.

"Leave it," James said.

"But the gate is raised. Someone will steal—"

"That can't be helped. We'll come back and cover it later." He took a quick head count. "Where's Aliette?"

"She went north to search for you. I went south. If she does not return and we have to leave, we are to meet at the forest desk next door or the waterfall three down as the backup spot."

The rest of the flyguards gathered, and they moved single-file down to the lower level, through a crack in the wall, to the half-flooded basement of the adjacent building. They waded through waist-deep water up to a staircase through a lobby of a large building reclaimed by nature. They treaded carefully as large water snakes slithered through the waters, eying them with slitted, intelligent eyes before allowing them to pass.

Several black-barked trees had punched through a window and spread their branches, obstructing much of the ceiling. Enormous, twisted vines crawled up the walls and chest-high weeds wavered in the wind tunnel created by the the hallway.

The small group stayed low, moving deliberately through the brush until they got behind a counter covered by thorny flowers. They settled in and waited for Aliette, listening as the shrill whine of the Valkyrie overhead grew louder. It was soon followed by footsteps and voices, and then the sound of a blaster discharge and laughter.

The sounds of Co-op soldiers faded in and out, sometimes suggesting they had walked into the lobby, other times that they had moved on. James kept the group there for an hour, still hoping for Aliette to show up. Then, they moved two blocks down to the waterfall, where a river had diverted into a building and was now gushing out of the dozens of windows on its face. She wasn't there, either.

As night set, they decided to return to the garage. They found their transports reduced to burned husks, some of the metal still smoldering. Aliette's broken body, blaster burns on her back, lay just outside the entrance.

James and the rest of the flyguards stood around her, heads bowed. It was his fault; he knew that. No one looked his way, but he could feel their judging eyes even as they avoided him. If he had only not drank that accursed shine. If he had only stayed strong. He looked back up at the container they had used to brew the shit. It had been destroyed as well. It was a small solace.

"We bury her," he said. "Scavenge for anything that's still useful."

The flyguards spent the rest of the night burying their friend and recovering what was left of their small fleet of vehicles, their pride and joy. The mood was somber as they huddled in the darkness. This time, no one risked a fire.

The next morning, before dawn, as they prepared to leave, James made one more pass through the room to search for anything of value. He found a jar of shine tucked away behind one of the broken canisters. Anger flared and he stepped to kick the blasted thing as hard as he could.

He stopped. Something in him wouldn't allow him to be so wasteful. James glanced around at where the flyguards were prepping to leave and made sure no one was watching. He dipped down and tucked the jar into his sack, and then left to join the rest of the group as they began their long walk back to the All Galaxy Tower.

THIRTY-FIVE

RISKY BUSINESS

Levin sat in front of a small café just off the main street near Paseo de Moret in Madrid, Spain. He sipped what looked like a child-size cup of a coffee derivative known as the *café bonbon anís*. The thing looked so fragile and dainty in his hand he worried he'd crush it between his fingers. Not that it would matter in a few hours.

The drink had alcohol in it, something he wasn't aware of when he had placed the order. Levin didn't have a problem with alcohol; he had reigned himself in during his chronman days when he realized he was starting down the slippery slope toward the bottle, as many a chronman often did. Over the past few years, he tended to drink only on rare occasions. It wasn't that he feared the demon or temptation, but that it just wasn't a necessary part of his life anymore. The few drops of alcohol this tiny cup of coffee had were acceptable; it was actually quite tasty.

Down the street, Levin saw the cracked remnants of the Puerta de la Moncloa. Madrid's victory arch, damaged during the extensive bombings by the Libyans during World War III, had split in a dozen places. When the war had finally ended, the newly crowned Spanish Caliphate had decided to keep the arch standing, cracks and all, as a symbol of the struggle the country had endured in those dark years. Levin liked the way it looked, with the hundreds of pockmarks on its faces and the cracks like spider-webs down its edges.

A new, smaller monument was built at its base with large letters, stating:

THROUGH WAR AND EVIL AND SIN,
THE VICTORY ARCH STOOD—2131 CE

"Yes, it did," he muttered, raising his child-size cup of alcoholic coffee in a salute. He checked the bright cloudless sky. The sun was halfway down. "And it will for about another hour."

The year was 2170. At dusk, the city was going to get leveled by giant mountain walkers and then sunk underground by the AI hive mind's feared vanguard burrowers. Most of the district, about six square blocks of the city, would remain intact even as it fell a quarter of a kilometer underground and got buried under millions of tons of rubble.

Going down with it would be an emergency aid depot with forty tons of medical supplies slated for western Africa. Levin's job today would be to ride the fall of the district and retrieve the cache. He had come in two days ago to scout the area. Grace wanted him to hit a grain warehouse as a secondary objective if the situation permitted.

The job was already dicey enough. After all, the retrieval window was in the middle of the opening volleys of the AI War. He would have to work during a full-scale invasion, and then escape southeast to the coast and lay low until his return jump while a massive mechanical army on its way to Germany eviscerated Spain.

Then, after five days of hiding and hopefully not causing any ripples, he would have to move out to the sea and make a jump back to the present. It was an extreme hassle, but necessary. Madrid was a heavily time salvaged zone, and the region and this period were already littered with dozens of tears to the chronostream. Jumping from anywhere within thousands of kilometers was no longer an option in the time frame of the attack.

Fortunately, Grace, in her infinite intelligence, had found a narrow clean jump window. The odds of substantial ripples in a job like this were usually high, but the sheer destruction of the first few days of the AI War mitigated some of those risks.

"Levin, are you there?" Grace's voice popped into his head.

"Yes, Mother of Time." At this moment in the present, Grace was in the *Frankenstein* a hundred meters under the surface of the Alboran Sea. She would rendezvous with him once they coordinated their return jump. All this felt a little haphazard.

She had originally wanted him to go ahead and steal the supplies now. After all, she argued, it all gets destroyed anyway. However, Levin refused. Who knew what sort of mayhem he could inflict on the chronostream by attacking a warehouse in a heavily-populated area days before a dead-end time-line event?

Maybe the military would send in investigators and security that otherwise might not have gone there, and they would all perish during the attack. Maybe his early theft would somehow bring the city to high alert and warn them of the impending attack. Maybe the government would call in more of their military as a precaution and actually fight off the mountain hawks.

There were too many unpredictable scenarios, and Levin would not play a part in changing history like this, not even if it was Grace Priestly who asked it of him. One terrible mistake in his lifetime was enough. He'd rather die than cause another. For whatever reason, it was the Mother of Time who played loosest with the Time Laws she had created. Someone like her would have never made the tier as a chronman. That thought coaxed a grin out of him.

"Levin, I've detected a jump near you. Be careful."

He sat up a little straighter and lowered his head. That was the other fear of having a long-running job. ChronoCom may have detected his initial jump back here. The more time he spent in the past, the likelier it would be for the agency to send an auditor to investigate. If that was the case, he would be severely outgunned. Auditor bands were much more powerful than the chronman bands he had on, though strength of bands wasn't everything.

It could be coincidence as well. This was a heavily-salvaged area. It could be one of the hundreds of jobs ChronoCom had run here. Levin was pretty sure his luck these days wasn't that good. He considered dropping his paint job to save his levels for a possible fight. His paint job wouldn't do much good if he encountered an auditor. No doubt whoever was investigating would be armed with a band detector.

He decided against it. If the jump was just a mere coincidence and that chronman just happened to know him, he would have a difficult time talking his way out of it, especially if the chronman was from after he was tried and found guilty.

Levin got his answer a few seconds later. A woman in a beige lounge suit, fashionable in this time period, took a seat near his small table. She leaned forward, almost as if flirting with him. A waitress stopped by and asked if she wanted a drink, and the woman replied in perfect regional and period Spanish. Just like his comm band, it was too perfect.

When the waitress left, the woman leaned in. "No sudden movements, friend. You won't win a fight and you can't run. I'm Auditor Julia Gaenler-Phobos of ChronoCom, year 2512. You are under investigation for possible violation of Time Law Six for an unsanctioned jump from a nonauthorized governing body. You will immediately surrender, release your bands to me, and divulge the entities supporting your illegal activities. Are we clear?"

Levin cursed under his breath.

"What is it?" Grace asked.

"I'm sitting with an auditor right now. Twelfth of the chain."

"Can you beat her?"

"With auditor bands, possibly. With chronman ones, I'm not sure. More importantly, I don't know if I want to. I raised her to the chain myself. She's a good person."

"Did you used to sleep with her?"

"No, Grace. What does that have to do with it?"

"Because that woman is about to haul you back to prison or worse, and all you can think about is what a stand-up individual she is. Pull your head out of your ass and do your space-forsaken job."

The waitress returned with another of those tiny teacups and offered it to the auditor. She thanked the woman and took a sip. "So what will it be? Come easy and neat, or do I have to break you first?"

Levin chuckled. He remembered catching her practicing saying those words for the first time the night before her first retrieval of a wayward Tier-4 on Luna. "You missed a line."

She arched an eyebrow. "What?"

Levin put his cup down and leaned back in his chair. "You usually say something else after you give your first line. What is it? I forget. Something about how you could use the exercise."

Julia stood up and the soft orange hue of her exo surrounding her intensified. "Who are you?"

He dropped his paint job and studied the look of shock on her face.
"Hello, Julia. How did you find me?"

It took her only a second to recover. Julia sprouted four orange coils
from her exo and looked ready to attack. "The director told me the
wastelanders operating in the northeast were salvaging again. We've put
a heavier emphasis on tracking illegal jumps and their salvage movements. Of all people, I never thought you would be helping them. I heard
you escaped, but I didn't think you would ever betray the Time Laws so
brazenly."

"It's more complicated than that," he said. Was it? He didn't quite believe his words. "Julia, in all the years you knew me, did I ever betray the
agency or act without honor? Can you consider that there is more to all
this than you know?"

The auditor didn't waver, but she didn't attack him, either. Levin
sensed an opportunity. Julia crossed her arms and leaned back. "Very well
then, Levin. Now is your chance to defend yourself. Abyss knows you
didn't at your trial. There was a time when I would have scoffed at the
charges leveled against you. But, between the facts, witness accounts, and
your lack of defense, how could anyone think otherwise? Explain yourself now."

Levin kept his face neutral, though it pained him that she thought
of him this way. Her reasoning was sound. He would think the same if
he was in her position. However, the truth would only risk everything he
was trying to accomplish. "I cannot. Not right now, at least. I just have to
hope that our relationship still carries weight." It was a poor excuse. One
that said nothing and meant even less.

Julia pursed her lips and shook her head. "How the high and noble have
fallen. I shall choose to honor my old friend's memory by pretending this
wretch before me shares nothing more than his resemblance. The Levin
I knew would have never stooped to pulling on my heartstrings. The real
Levin always did the right thing. I will give you one last chance to do so.
Surrender and release your bands."

Levin stared at that small cup on the table, its brown milky contents
only half-drunk. He paused, tapping the table twice with his fingers. He

picked the cup up and threw its contents back. "Should we move to a more isolated place?"

The gesture wasn't lost on Julia. She pondered his suggestion for a few moments and then shook her head. "My handler says this area is as good as any. Once the war starts, this entire part of the city gets wiped out. Whatever ripples we cause here will heal within a day." In the distance, a siren began to wail.

Levin looked west at the setting sun. She was right. The first of the mountain hulks should be rising out of the ground at any moment. The radar would pick them up and a citywide panic would ensue. "Very well, then. If you agree, we wait until the attack begins before we conclude our affairs." He gestured to the waitress to order another *café bonbon anís*, this time asking for triple the alcohol.

He watched the waitress leave to fulfill his order. That was probably the last thing she was ever going to do. Part of him wanted to tell her to go home and hug her loved ones for the last time. Make her peace and say her goodbyes. Levin scowled. Julia was right; he had gone soft. He turned his attention back to the auditor, who was still standing in front of him, exo powered on.

"Put your coils away," he said. "Sit down before someone notices your exo."

"I find that ironic coming from someone who has so blatantly disregarded—"

He cut her off. "I've known you for eighteen years, Julia. That's worth something. Give me a few minutes and have a seat. Besides, it's starting to get dark. If someone looks closely, they'll notice your coils. You want to create unnecessary ripples?"

Julia reluctantly sat down and the two stared at each other, waging a contest of wills. She finally spoke. "I was actually happy to hear that you escaped. Most of the auditor chain didn't believe for a second the charges they leveled against you. I had thought you would be smart enough to hole up on some backwater shithole and never show your face again."

The waitress returned with his order. Levin picked up his cup and saluted Julia with it. "If I was going to hole up in a shithole, I would just stay on Nereid."

"Instead you're back on Earth running illegal jumps? What the abyss is wrong with you? Have you lost your last shred of decency, or is this some sick way of poking the giant in the eye?" Her eyes narrowed. "No, you were never motivated by wealth, nor by vice. What are you really doing here, Levin?"

He smiled. Julia didn't honestly believe he had gone rogue. She was just telling herself this because it would make their fight easier. He took a sip from his cup and placed it back on the table. "How's your aunt doing? The one you took leave for last year?"

"Nice try, Levin. You won't be able to work on my emotions. She passed away three months ago."

"I'm sorry to hear that. She was your last relative?"

Julia nodded. "I tried to move her to Luna the last few years, but she wouldn't hear of it. Born on Earth, die on Earth, she said. Stubborn old crone."

"I met her once. She visited you at the Academy when you were raised to the tier."

They continued their conversation, not missing a beat even when all the sirens nearby joined the chorus of wails. Minutes later, the news must have spread, because panic took over the streets. The denizens of the city, all thirteen million of them, would try to flee north all at the same time. By this time tomorrow, half of them would be dead. By the time the AI army reached Germany six days later, the attrition rate for Spain would be 97 percent.

The two of them stayed in their seats, even as crowds of people ran past them, screaming and looting. Fights broke out as mobs tried to board the last remaining transports that could fly. The sounds of explosions got closer. The ground rumbled. Large plumes of smoke began to rise from the ground, blackening the sky.

A few minutes later, the first of the gigantic mountain hulks appeared. Large, long metal black bodies with six legs, each as thick as buildings, stomped through the city, heavy coil-charged weapons shooting indiscriminately at anything that moved.

Several formations of defensive crafts buzzed by, shooting streams of light and trails of smoke at the walking fortresses. The first of the planes erupted into balls of fire directly over where they sat, raining debris and flames all around them.

Both Levin and Julia looked up as small specks of fire struck their exos, flickering their shields with each drop. Julia indicated something behind him and Levin turned to see the giant black metal foot of a mountain hulk no farther than a few hundred meters away.

"Is it time?" he asked.

She finished her drink and nodded. "Shall we?"

Her exo flared, and she shot six tightly intertwined coils at his shield, hoping to shatter it in one blast and end the fight quickly. She had a seventh coil that hovered above his head, no doubt anticipating that he'd dodge upward, so it would slow his movement enough the other six would hit their mark.

Levin was ready for this. He knew how Julia operated; he had trained her in exo combat himself. He pushed to the side, juking left. It would do him no good trying to outmuscle or outlast her levels. Auditor bands were superior to chronman bands in nearly every way except for power efficiency. The only thing he could do was outsmart her or catch her completely by surprise.

He launched himself into the air and flew directly at the first mountain hulk. Julia was above him in a second, easily keeping up as she tried to keep him pinned down. She launched coil after coil at him, attempting to lock a hold on him. If she did, she could utilize her superior levels to overwhelm him.

Levin chose to stay low, using his coils to push off the ground and the buildings to make himself more maneuverable. He sped around crumbling buildings and growing piles of rubble, diving into large fires and hiding among columns of smoke.

Their game of cat and mouse continued even as the fighting in Madrid intensified. Several times, her coils narrowly missed connecting with his exo. Several times, she seemed just about to lock him down. Every time, he was just able to squirm away, pushing off in an unexpected direction or jumping through a window.

At the same time, they had to dodge the attacks of the hundreds of guns the mountain hulks had shooting at them. Levin was hit with at least three, and even though they were technologically primitive by present standards, they were large and powerful. The blasts had drained his levels by over 40 percent. He couldn't take too many more direct hits.

He finally found his opening as he maneuvered directly under one of the mountain hulks. The two were flitting quickly back and forth, evading each other and the dozens of guns above.

She had lost him in the thick black smoke, and he had launched himself directly at her, hitting her like a battering ram in the side when she wasn't looking. His exo wasn't powerful enough to actually penetrate her shield, but he struck her at an angle that spun her around and disoriented her just enough for one of the mountain hulk's massive cannons to sight her. Half a dozen other guns exploded against her shield, bouncing her around in the air until her exo finally gave. Julia careened to the side like a wounded bird and leveled a small building as she crashed to the ground.

Levin watched from inside the adjacent building as the auditor picked herself up and staggered to her feet. Her shield had taken the brunt of the damage, but she was injured. Even auditor shields could take only so much before they cracked.

The two of them made eye contact, and then she looked up as a large shadow fell over her. Julia screamed and tried to run out of the way of the mountain hulks gigantic leg.

Levin didn't hesitate. He powered his exo and shot to her side within a second. Her shields shattered as he rammed into her and carried her to safety just as the leg came down once more, creating an eight-meter-wide indentation in the ground. Levin's momentum carried the two through the side of a concrete wall, and they crashed into the basement of a parking structure.

"Levin," Grace said in his head. "Get out of there. Your levels just hit twenty percent. Remember, you need to survive five more days."

The auditor struggled against him as he held her down. "Don't move," he said. He pointed upward and she stilled. A massive boom from the left shook dust and rocks down on them. A moment later, another boom, this time to their right, rained more debris.

After what seemed an eternity, he poked his head up from the crater they had made. It was pitch-black, except for a wide flat red beam scanning the walls. A few seconds later, a small floating ball hovered into view, making a metal clicking sound as it shined its beam around the room.

Levin motioned for Julia to stay still as he laid on top of her. The red beam passed over their crater. The bug was most likely searching for movement and heat signatures. It was a good thing their atmos blocked detection of this type. As the minutes passed, the clicking sounds faded.

After he was sure they were safe, he let go of her and helped her up. "Your levels are low," he said. "Do you have enough to jump back?"

Her eyes were looking out into the distance; she nodded. "I have a re-charge band. I can manage. My jump point is in eight days in Normandy. You?"

"Five days off the Alboran Sea. If you will excuse me, I have a salvage to complete."

"Why did you save me? I was going to take you in."

"You're a good auditor. You were just doing the right thing, as was I." He got up and climbed out of the crater.

"Wait, get back here," she called. "Levin, this isn't you. What are you doing?"

He stopped and bowed his head. "I honestly don't know anymore. I hope our paths never cross again, Julia Gaenler-Phobos." Without look-ing back, he walked to a crack in the concrete wall and hurried toward the medical supply depot.

THIRTY-SIX

MAD GENIUS

Titus 2.3 would never admit it to anyone in the All Galaxy Tower, but he was enjoying himself, at least a lot more than he thought he would when he first came to this little run-down future. He had an inkling things weren't heading in the right direction back in his time. However, no one could have predicted things could ever get this bad. They had and, frankly, Titus was having more fun right now because of it than he had had in over thirty years.

He had spent the tail end of his life on Venus attending stuffy Praetorian parties and working on theoretical science, spending most of his time bored out of his mind. Now, he was living on the edge, in a veritable Wild West. He chuckled at the irony of calling New York City a Wild West. With all the shit going wrong here, things were quite different in this crazy time, and he loved it. He had worked on more interesting things in the last few weeks than he had in the past twenty years.

Sure, there were downsides to things. He was living in Third-World-colony conditions where the electricity was intermittent, everything was filthy, and the food absolutely sucked, but this was the exact sort of situation that forced his genius to stretch and challenge itself. There were so many things demanding his attention and so few waking hours, literally, especially since there wasn't enough electricity to waste on something as mundane as keeping the lights on during the day.

On top of that, Crowe and Elise had given him nearly free reign to recommend any modifications he felt necessary for the All Galaxy building. In this case, Titus's list was easily over three hundred to-dos long, from implementing a new elevator design to a wired communication system to a new irrigation system. It would take him two lifetimes to fix up this old behemoth of a building to his highly-exacting Titus standards. He was going to be dead before he even got through a twentieth of the list, but he was flaming going to try.

Right now, he was working on a couple of things at once. The Nation had recently returned from the attack on a Co-op outpost and brought back a host of goodies, including a useful large-scale one-way shield that Titus was still taking apart and examining, and several large mounted guns that were meant for combat ships. Both items could be modified for their fight against the Co-op. This shield thing would work wonders along the northern barricades and these large cannons could be mounted on carts for a little heavy firepower. It just required a little tinkering on his part to adapt it to their needs. He whistled as he fiddled around with this amazing technology. Some of this stuff, the military tech especially, was hundreds of years more advanced than from his time. He felt like a dog chasing a thousand balls; he wanted to dabble in everything.

"Hi, Mr. Titus," Sasha piped, bounding into his workshop, flanked by James Griffin-Mars. The Elfreth had given him his own work space on the forty-first floor for his mad experiments. He preferred it because it was close to the dining hall.

"Hello, child." He beamed. "And how is my most important patient today?"

Titus had taken a shining to Sasha, not just because she was the main reason he had been given an extension on life, but because she reminded him of his favorite great-granddaughter, whom he missed terribly. Part of him wanted to look up his family tree and find out whatever had happened to his descendents. The wiser part of him knew it was probably best he didn't know. For now, he was content in transferring his affection to this precocious little girl.

"Better," she said. "I'm not as tired all the time, but my throat is still always itchy."

"How is she sleeping?" Titus asked.

"Still wakes up a few times in the night, but less than before," said James.

Titus studied the chronman and then averted his eyes. James looked tired. His eyes were red, his skin was unhealthily spotted, and his face looked bloated. Titus, standing next to him, sniffed. There was gossip among the tribesmen surrounding James lately. It seemed much of it was true, however faintly. Titus had a sharp nose. In any case, it really wasn't any of his business. He still felt like the outsider here and, frankly, he was more than a bit uncomfortable with the adoration some of these waste-lander people heaped on him.

Titus patted the stool next to his table. "Why don't you sit here, girl, and we'll take a look."

For the next twenty minutes, he checked Sasha over, pulling up her vitals and taking another sample of her blood. There was no easy cure for Terravira mononucleosis, especially given where they lived. The best he could do was give her antibiotics and nurture her immune system along until it could fight the constant bombardment of this environment. Fortunately, all signs pointed toward recovery. When he was done, Titus patted her head and gave her a piece of rock candy he had synthesized from one of his experiments. He smiled when she took a hesitant bite of it, and then her face lit up.

"She needs to be in cleaner quarters," Titus instructed James. "Also, limit her exposure to the animals for now. I know she loves them, but it should be temporary."

"What about her work in Elise's lab?" James asked. "Should she stop?"

"That should be fine. There's probably less Earth Plague in that lab than there is in the rest of the building, but make sure she takes the proper precautions and scrubs up just in case."

"Thank you, Doctor," James said, putting his arm around his sister's shoulder.

"Hey." Titus leaned in. "Did you, um, talk to Grace for me?"

James nodded. "I did. She says you're too old for her."

"We're practically the same age. At our years, does it matter?"

James shrugged. "She likes her men young."

"Flaming fuck." Titus scowled. He looked down at the girl. "Sorry."

"Hey, guys, sorry I'm late," Elise said, hurrying into his workshop. "I'm telling you. These chiefs are driving me crazy with their insane demands. For some reason, it's gotten into their heads that a camp's proximity to the All Galaxy is an indication of the tribe's importance. There's a large Co-op force moving in from the north down the west side of the island and all they can argue about is real estate."

"We just finished," James said.

Elise gave Sasha a hug and looked at Titus. "How is she doing?"

He nodded. "Much better."

Elise's smile grew from ear to ear. "Great, I'm so proud of you, girl. Ready for lunch?"

As the little family turned to leave, Titus tapped Elise on the arm. "Could I take a few moments of your time? I have some requests I'd like to show you for my workshop."

"Can you just relay your needs to Rima? She'll help address them." Elise noticed the look on his face and turned to James. "You two go on ahead to the mess hall. I'll meet you guys there shortly." She and Titus waited until James and Sasha had turned the corner and were out of sight. "What's up?" Elise asked.

Titus wasn't sure how to broach this, so he just decided to spit it out. "I think our chronman has a substance abuse problem. He needs help."

Elise's face melted a little at the news and she sighed. "I know." She sat down and buried her face in her hands. "You're not the only one who's talked to me about it. I don't know what to do. There's so much going on right now. I'm stretched so thin."

"It's getting worse," Titus said. "I've only been here a little while, and I see it. At one point, you're going to have to make the call for his own good. Put him into some sort of rehab program or something, even if it's against his will."

"How do you make James do anything against his will?" she asked.

"By making him realize what's more important," he said gently. "In his case, he's going to have to want to get better, but at some point, you might have to force his hand and make the hard choice. When that time comes, be ready and be strong."

"You ever have experience treating . . . problems like this?"

He shook his head. "Never, but I'm sure between Grace and me, we'll figure it out."

She nodded. "Thank you, Titus. The Elfreth appreciate all that you've done for us. I don't know how we can repay you."

He grinned. "Getting me more pillows is a good place to start."

"Done."

"And maybe convince Grace to go on a date with me?"

Elise made a face, and then without another word, left the room.

THIRTY-SEVEN

THE MANHATTAN WAR

The three kids didn't look anywhere over ten, but Elise couldn't be sure. They had just run into the Manhattan war council's forward operations center on the ninth floor of a former hospital on Fifty-seventh and Eleventh to report the latest updates from the main force. A sizable Co-op patrol had been noisily making their way south down Columbus Avenue over the past two days.

Reports from survivors fleeing the rampage were that they had already razed five small tribes and had enslaved a medium-size one. Elise and the six tribal leaders with her intended to meet them with three hundred Manhattan defenders, as the individual tribal fighters now collectively referred to themselves. Proudly, she might add. She thought that sounded much better than the originally proposed name: Manhattan mights.

All the defenders still held on to their individual tribal affiliations, be they Elfreth guardians, Flatiron fights, Lenox legionaries, or the Yorkville schnauzers. Elise was pretty sure the Yorkville tribe had no idea what a schnauzer actually was, and she didn't have the heart to tell them. Though perhaps it was all intentional, because their tribal chief's title was the Giant Schnauzer.

That was the way it was here in the wastelands. There were a thousand different tribes with a thousand different dialects, standards, and names. One of the advantages she wielded over the other chiefs was that

her comm band allowed her to understand and speak fluently every single dialect. This was probably the main reason she led the Manhattan Nation. Some of the chiefs had taken to calling her the Mist Queen, while
others wanted to give her the title of Main Hattan. She thought both
sounded ridiculous.

The children stood at the entrance to the war room as Elise and the
rest of the war chiefs surrounded a table holding a map of the nearby
blocks. She saw the orange and green markings on their cheeks, and Elise
tapped Giant Schnauzer Kamyke's shoulder. "Are they yours?"

Kamyke looked over his shoulder and nodded. "Report, Karol, Kris,
Knick. Don't just stand there. Come in."

That was also another thing about that particular tribe that Elise found
interesting. Everyone's name started with the letter *K,* for whatever odd
reason. She had asked Kamyke about that the first day they had met and
he had acted as if it was something that never crossed his mind. The
Yorkvilles were definitely one of the more eccentric tribes, that was for
sure.

Karol, the older girl, whispered into the ear of Knick, the younger
boy, and urged him forward. Looking nervous, Knick walked in and made
a shy bow. "All the schnauzers, fights, and big-ones are in place. Yiora
says the Co-op have set up camp on the thirty-second floor of the Upper
Kaufman Center."

"Thank you, brave Knick," Elise said. "And thank you both as well,
Karol and Kris." The young boy stood still, a silly grin on his face as he
blushed furiously. Kris had to walk into the room and, putting his arm
around his shoulder, lead him out. Elise looked disapprovingly at Kamyke.
"How old are they?"

"Karol and Kris are nine. Knick is seven and training under Karol.
They are doing their duty for the tribe," said Kamyke.

"Why are we using children as couriers and lookouts so close to the
front line?"

"All the couriers and lookouts are children. The older ones fight or
farm. The younger find a way to make themselves useful," said Kamyke,
"In the Mist Isle, every soul has a role to keep the tribe strong. For children
like Karol and Kris, being chosen is a great source of pride. They also
think it great fun."

"But is it safe?"

Kamyke shrugged. "It is safer than if the Co-op defeat and enslave us. Besides, I once saw little Karol kill a lai snake as large as you, Mist Queen, with nothing more than a rock the size of your fists."

Instinctively, Elise looked down at her fists; they were tiny. She had seen lai snakes in some of these buildings. They looked like boa constrictors on steroids with heads on both ends. Kamyke was probably right, though it still troubled her that she was putting children in harm's way. Nonetheless, one of the keys to the Manhattan Nation's early success was how quickly they could relay messages to their teams.

"The Co-op set up camp further away than anticipated," she said. "Will the couriers be all right traveling these distances?"

"It is better to be safe than sorry," Murad said. "It would be a heavy blow to the nation if you were injured."

Most of the tribes in the center of Manhattan had either allied with her or been captured by the Co-op. There were still pockets of wastelanders who insisted on taking their chances on their own. Most of them knew her alliance well enough to leave the couriers alone, but it still made her uneasy. There was still the matter of the wilderness in several of the buildings, especially so close to the overgrown jungle that used to be Central Park. Most of the couriers used well-traveled paths, but the risk was still there.

Over the next fifteen minutes, half a dozen more couriers, all children, reported in. A dozen more were sent out as the war council relayed instructions and the enemy's location to coordinate the attack. Elise watched the white pieces on the map—taken from an old chess board—close in on the enemy's location, the black king.

"That's the last to report in," Murad said. "On your command, Mist Queen." To the side, two girls stood at the door ready to deliver the order to attack.

"Stop calling me that," she said absentmindedly as she studied the map. Elise looked out the nearest window to check the light outside, and then nodded. She wasn't sure why they always looked to her for final confirmation, considering it was all of them who planned the attacks, but she took it in stride.

"Maanx's fights will hit them first from the north," Murad said. "They will buy a long enough distraction for the rest to strike a hundred heartbeats later from the other directions." That was another thing. Every tribe counted differently. It was maddening.

"All right," Elise said, summoning as much authority as she could. "Let's do this. Make sure the all the couriers are pulled back a safe distance first."

The messages were relayed and the couriers sent off, and then the waiting game began. This was the most unnerving part of the exchanges. What she wouldn't give to be able to send a message and have the recipient receive it instantaneously. That might be something she would add to Titus's already gigantic to-do list.

The way they waged war right now was the same way it had been done for thousands of years before the invention of instant communications, comm bands, radio, or heck, even Morse code. This weird EMP fog affected them almost as much as it did the Co-op, though she had to think it was much more disorienting to the enemy than to the native tribes.

The minutes ticked by as Elise and the rest of the war council sat on their collective asses. The others joked among themselves. She didn't know how they could be so relaxed. Half an hour passed, and Elise felt her heartbeat quicken. Had something gone wrong? Had she led her defenders wrong? What if it was a trap? Three hundred was a significant portion of Manhattan's forces. This early in the fight, she had utilized their superior numbers to their advantage. She wanted to fight every battle outnumbering the Co-op by a factor of five.

Elise began to pace up and down the room. It probably made her look frazzled, but she didn't care. The weight of responsibility was the heaviest when she knew she was sending people to die. This fidgeting was all she could do to fight back the tears every time she thought about that.

It was times like this she wished James were here. He would know how to handle these sorts of fights better than she ever could. He was dealing with his own demons at the moment. As hard as he tried, he couldn't hide the fact that he was drinking more than ever. It was hot gossip among the Elfreth. Many grumbled about James's potentially impaired judgment. It had already manifested itself a few times. The circumstances surrounding Aliette's death were particularly worrisome. The flyguards had unanimously defended James but many in the tribe secretly pointed fingers at him.

It was only out of respect for him and her that they did not openly talk about it. Elise didn't know how to help him. She already had so much on her plate. The best she could do now was to try to keep him safe where he couldn't hurt himself or anyone else. Part of her was angry at him for falling apart on her at a time like this. Another part of her was just worried sick about him. She wished she could be there for him right now, but people's lives were at stake.

Nearing the hour mark, three couriers finally reported in. They were out of breath and barely able to get a word out. One of them was bleeding from a cut on her forehead.

Elise, alarmed, rushed over to her. "What happened? Are you all right?"

The girl struggled to get the words out of her mouth. "The enemy saw the fights approaching from the north and were ready for them as they tried to cross the bridge. The fights were unable to close the distance. Instead, Teacher Maanx made much noise and played decoy. The Co-op left their positions and gave chase. Then the rest of our defenders came upon them from behind. The enemy were all captured or killed. However, our hurt was higher. Large Krisa of the schnauzers report that they suffered fifty-six injured but only nineteen deaths."

The relief on Elise's face was visible as a cheer escaped her lips. The other leaders in the room congratulated her on her victory, as they did after every battle. Elise thought that too was strange, since she wasn't the one fighting and dying. She honestly didn't do anything other than pace around in a room safely far away from battle.

There was a commotion at the door, and a new figure darted in. It took her a moment to realize that it was Knick. His shirt was wet with blood, and he seemed disoriented and terrified. He was panting heavily and ran to Kamyke.

"They have my brother and sister!" he sobbed.

Kamyke dropped to one knee and held the boy by the shoulders. "Who does? What happened? Are you injured?"

Knick was having a hard time getting the words out, but eventually, they were able to piece together the whole story. It seemed on their way back, the three children were captured by a Co-op hound pack.

"They shot Kris," Knick wailed, tears flowing down his face.

Kamyke swore. He saw Elise's furious gaze and bowed his head. "I am shamed, Mist Queen. Perhaps you are right about the children . . ."

She bristled. "Worry about that later. Knick, come here. Do you know how many? Can you show me on the map where they took your siblings?"

Knick nodded, and she led him to the table. He was so small, she had to ask Murad to hold him up so he could see the map. Elise pointed at the white queen chess piece. "This is where we are. Where did the Co-op soldiers find you?"

He pointed at a location on the map. "Floor sixteen, near sky bridge two. I saw four."

Elise looked at the others, alarmed. "That's only two blocks away. If we hurry, we can reach them."

The six tribal leaders exchanged worried glances.

Hans, the Grand of the Lenox tribe and oldest among them, shook his head. "With the guards, we are only eight. I am far too old and all of us far too valuable to risk on two children. I do not doubt the council's prowess, but against four Co-op, it is dangerous."

Elise gritted her teeth. "I'm not abandoning one of our own, especially a child. Besides, you forget I'm here as well."

"Please, Elise," Murad said. "You are many things to the Nation, but a defender you're not."

"Maybe not." Elise looked over to the corner where she had parked Aranea, the scout mechanoid she used to get around Manhattan. She had spent every spare second she had riding and practicing with it. It was not just like riding a bike again, but like riding a bike that was better in every way. Aranea was head and shoulders more advanced and easier to pilot than Charlotte. She had capabilities that Elise had never thought possible in a machine. She glanced at its shoulder-mounted cannon. She had yet to fire the laser gun, but was assured by Titus that the thing worked.

"I'm getting our kids back," she said. "You're all welcome to join me."

Elise pushed a hidden button on the side of the mechanoid's body and the torso split down the center and slid open. She got in, and a few seconds later was heading out the door, the mechanoid's eight legs clicking softly on the hard concrete floor. She had worried that she'd end up going alone, but was joined a few seconds later by Murad on one side and Kamyke on the other. Following close behind them were the remaining three leaders and two guards.

"I hope you know what you're doing, and risking, Oldest," Murad said. "The Nation falls apart without you."

"I don't know what this nation stands for if we don't protect our children," she replied.

The small group hurried east across six buildings, crossing the sky bridge over Tenth Avenue on the twelfth floor of a corner building. According to Aranea, she was moving at fifteen kilometers per hour. She was shocked to find that everyone was keeping up with her with little effort. They were hardy folks, these wastelanders.

It took them only a few minutes to reach the sixteenth floor of the building where the Co-op field team had nabbed the children. The group spread out and checked the area. One corridor had small amounts of still-damp blood and signs of struggle, blaster marks on the walls, but no sign of where the team had gone.

"They must have gone east," Kamyke said. "Probably to avoid our northern forces by circumventing the Central Park jungle."

"Which floor?" Murad said. "They could be anywhere. This is like searching for a grain of rice on a sandy beach."

Elise despaired. She knew the children were close, but they could be anywhere, on any floor. East might be the right direction, but this was a fool's errand. Just then, she saw a shadow moving in one of the side rooms. She motioned to her group and shot Aranea in. A second later, she towered over a terrified wastelander who was balled up in a fetal position covering his face.

"Please," he cried. "I have nothing."

Elise recognized the markings on his arm as belonging to the Ansonia Wigs, one of the larger tribes native to this neighborhood. She had personally tried to recruit them several times over the past few weeks, but had been rebuffed. Their leader, Tao Jan, had told her that the Co-op had not bothered her people yet and naively believed they wouldn't. Elise wondered if the Tao's mind had changed with the events over the past few days.

"We are from the Manhattan Nation," she said, backing away a few steps. "We are looking for some Co-op who stole our children. Have you seen them? Please help us."

The Ansonia Wig refused to speak with her, not that she blamed him. Aranea must be a terrible sight for some of these people. She waited outside as Kamyke, whose tribe had a relationship with the Ansonia Wigs, spoke with him. He returned a few minutes later.

"What happened to his people?" she asked.

Kamyke shook his head sadly. "Everywhere. Nowhere, he says. Attacked by the Co-op and now to the winds. They are no more."

"Did he see the children?"

He nodded. "He says they are moving east along the main passage on the fourteenth floor, parallel to Fifty-eighth Street. It's one of the more commonly used roads."

"Let's go," she said.

Her group took off in a full sprint, moving north a block, up several floors, and then east across a double-wide passage that cut through several other buildings. It took nearly thirty more minutes before they caught sight of a small group of people near the other end of a building. Elise, using Aranea's scoped vision, was the first to see them. They were dragging a smaller person by a rope and carrying what looked like another. Elise slowed the group down and glanced up at the ceiling.

"Close ground as quietly as you can," she said. "I'm going to come in from above."

She maneuvered Aranea up the nearest wall and began to climb it nearly as easily as if she were walking on the ground. This new functionality was the biggest upgrade over Charlotte. It took Elise several weeks before she was able to work up the courage to climb up a wall, and several more before she walked upside down on the ceiling, but now it was one of her favorite pastimes.

The passageway had a high vaulted circular ceiling, so she was able to climb up the very center and follow along the top undetected until she was nearly on top of the Valta field scouts. They didn't have much time left. The scouts were almost at the end of the building and about to enter a bridge. Once on the bridge, there was a lot less room for her to maneuver.

She looked behind her and saw that the rest of her people were still about two hundred meters behind. They weren't going to make it. In fact, the last portion of the passage had little cover. Half of her people would get cut down before they got close enough to engage the field scouts. All the field scouts had to do was look back to see them approach.

As if on cue, one did just that and signaled to the others. Another pulled out a monoscope while two raised their rifles. The last one dropped Kris and threw Karol to the ground. Elise cursed. This was an awful plan.

She had obviously not thought this through very well, and now people were going to die because of her stupidity. She decided to do the only thing she could think of. She struck first.

Hastily activating the laser cannon mounted on Aranea's shoulder—she hoped she was doing it right—she aimed the reticule, which popped up at one of the Co-op soldiers below. "Fire," she whispered.

Aranea complied and fired a green beam that missed her target by about three meters, blowing a small shower of marble into the air.

"Beam engaged," a man's deep voice said with a sexy British accent—it was one of the options during the setup. She had chosen this over the French woman. "Lock was not acquired."

"I didn't know you had to acquire one first," she grumbled, trying to match the reticule again to one of the Valta hounds. However, they had noticed her on the ceiling and had returned fire. Elise found out the hard way that trying to avoid blaster fire while aiming was really difficult. One of the blaster shots struck Aranea in the leg, and all her systems went fuzzy for a second. Elise nearly panicked as she moved the mechanoid out of the way. There was something about being shot at that really disagreed with her.

She skirted Aranea across the ceiling with more blasts from below exploding around her. Suddenly, the small explosions and orange beams stopped. She scanned the ground again and saw that her people had reached the enemy. She activated the reticule, but there was too much chaos below for her to get a clear lock. Instead, she dropped down from the ceiling and charged into the melee.

By the time she got there, however, the fight had ended. It was a brutal and short firefight. In the end, both Manhattan guards were seriously injured and Kamyke had suffered several broken ribs and a bad burn on his shoulder.

However, all four of the Valta soldiers were slain, and the children recovered. Elise jumped out of Aranea and checked on the boy. He was breathing but pale. The Valta troops had triaged his injuries and had probably been going to interrogate him once they got back to base.

She turned to the others. "I can carry two of the injured on Aranea. I'll meet you all back at the All Galaxy."

Murad nodded. "Get them home quickly. Well done, Elise. I was wrong about you not being a defender. My apologies."

"I didn't do anything," she said. "If anything, I messed up."

"You distracted the enemy long enough for us to engage them," he said, bowing slightly. "You saved many lives today. All hail the Mist Queen."

The rest of the room echoed the sentiment.

"Shut up, you guys," Elise said, blushing furiously. She climbed back into Aranea and picked up the boy Kris and the most seriously injured of the guards. "Get back to base, everyone. And good job."

Elise gave her people one last look before hurrying off to the All Galaxy Tower. Aranea moved at a fast clip, using the auto-navigation system to move across the three-dimensional maze of Manhattan at nearly forty kilometers an hour. They should be back at home in minutes.

She checked on Kris and the guard. Both were unconscious, but seemed stable. She made sure the mechanoid was holding them close to her body as she crossed through the last final buildings toward the All Galaxy. Within minutes, she had dropped the two patients off at the infirmary and was telling Titus to prepare for more injured.

"How many of ours dead from the main fight?" Titus asked as he ordered more cots to be brought in.

Elise smiled. "Nineteen."

He turned to her, surprised. "That's all? Well done, Mist Queen."

"Stop calling me that," she said, but she had to admit she liked it just a bit. For the first time since she'd become the Oldest of the Elfreth, she actually felt like a leader. Between the victory today and the successful rescue, things were finally starting to look up for her people. Now, if she could figure out what to do with James—

"Oldest," Rima said, running up to her. "Please come quickly!"

"What is it?"

"Just come! Hurry!" The girl took off before she could say another word. Elise ran after her as they went down a level to the barricade floor and headed toward the north end of the building. A crowd had formed near the main barricade. They parted ways before her until she saw the source of the commotion.

Elise gasped. "What in Gaia is going on!"

THIRTY-EIGHT

ROCK BOTTOM

James grimaced as he tilted his head back and held the flask upside down over his open mouth. It was the last of the shine from their excursion at the garage. No matter; he knew Chawr and the rest of his crew were rationing their portions. They wouldn't mind sharing with their mentor. Why should they? They looked up to him.

He stood up and hummed to himself, feeling the room sway under his feet. He closed his eyes and enjoyed this sensation of falling, of not being in control. The drink was hitting him a little harder than usual. He leaned against the wall as he stumbled his way down the stairwell toward the Elfreth mess hall. His AI band told him he was two hours past last meal, but he was an elder. They'd find something for him.

A few of the tribe passing by shot him awkward glances and then averted their eyes. It reminded him of the treatment he had received at the Tilted Orbit and Never Late during his chronman days. He scowled. He was no longer a chronman. Why did people keep treating him so poorly, as if he was some sort of outcast? No matter where he was, people were just so unkind. James's veins boiled and he began to get angry.

He thought he had left those judging eyes back in that supposedly more civilized previous life. However, here among the savages—no, he wasn't supposed to call them that anymore—they treated him with just as much distrust. James spent the trip down the stairwell working himself into a rage at the unfairness of his life. Would any place ever accept him?

James made a last-minute decision as he passed the fifty-sixth floor to detour inside and find his flyguards. He didn't need food right now, he needed another drink. He continued along to the smithy, where the flyguards bunked with a few of the other specialized groups. He really should have gotten food first, but he had other priorities right now.

Bria and Dox were in their shared quarters going over the construction schedule for the elevator bank Grace and Titus had designed for the building. The two of them stared as he stumbled in. They looked worried. Worried and mistrustful. That set James off even more. These flyguards were supposed to be his people, his crew. For them to look at and treat him the same way the rest of the Elfreth did was a betrayal. He was their mentor!

He was about to dress them down when he decided to get to the point. "Where's the rest of the shine we brewed back at the garage?"

Neither would meet his eye. Bria looked down at her hands in her lap while Dox stared hard at the ground. Neither said a word.

"Well?" he demanded.

"Elder . . ." Bria began.

"Oldest Franwil told us we weren't to give you more," said Dox.

The simmering anger that had been nipping at James since he left his quarters increased. However, he kept it in check and forced a smile. "Come on, guys, it's me. I've taught you everything you know. Help your elder out."

"But Oldest Franwil said—"

"Who cares what Franwil said?" James snapped. He stopped himself and struggled to remain calm. "Just give me a little of the shine. My back is acting up. That's all I'm asking." Indeed, his back had been hurting all morning. The little tweaks of pain sometimes became so debilitating it hurt to get out of bed. Only the booze helped him get through some of the worse moments. He took a step toward them. Bria and Dox, twenty and sixteen, respectively, looked frightened.

Finally, Bria pointed at the desk. "Bottom drawer, Elder."

James opened the two bottom drawers and rummaged through the contents until he found a dented flask. He hefted it in his hand and swished it around. Half-filled at best. It would have to do.

"Thanks, my flyguards." He grinned. "I'll see you guys tomorrow."

James waited until he left the room before taking a swig, feeling the warmth flow through his body and the edge in his nerves pulled back. He took another swig and stuffed the flask in his pocket. He had barricade duty now, whenever now was. He just knew that he was supposed to report down to the north barricade tonight, and looking out the window, it was dark outside. Barricade duty was just another job that he was way overqualified for; one more indignation on the long list stacked upon him.

Smitt appeared at the stairwell exit leading to the barricade floor and held up his hands. "Look, my friend. I'm dead, so listening to me might just mean you're crazy, but heading down there is a straight-up-awful idea."

"I'm fine," James said. "I'm needed at the barricade. Finally some people around here need me."

"Not like this they don't."

The Flatiron fight standing watch at the bottom turn of the barricade-floor stairwell looked at him and then averted his eyes.

"What the abyss are you staring at?" James snapped, his anger lighting up in an instant. Everyone was giving him attitude these days. What a bunch of ingrates. Sure, when he could salvage, at a huge cost to his health, they made him an elder and looked up to him. Now that he couldn't, they all turned on him as if he were a pariah.

"Look, James," Smitt said. "This isn't why they're all avoiding you."

"And you!" James turned on him, yelling. His voice carried up the tall narrow stairwell. "This is all your fault!"

James brushed past the fight and kicked the rusty metal door, his foot passing through Smitt's body, slamming the door open with a loud crack. Dozens of eyes followed him as he stomped his way through the hallway to the north barricade. At first, he tried to ignore them, but with each passing step, his anger reached new heights, and he began to throw those looks back in their faces. He stared them down until they looked away and pretended he didn't exist. That was the way he liked it.

The north barricade was silent when he got there. He walked up the stairs to the ramparts and nonchalantly nodded at the five others manning the parapet. No one acknowledged him, including the two Elfreth guardians. It was just another insult to gnaw away at James. This time, he chose to ignore the slight and do his duty. He looked over the side at the wide bridge connecting the All Galaxy to the adjacent building and overlooking the tri-section of Broadway and Twenty-second Street.

On the other side, seven tribes were camped on the bridge. They were spread out all the way across and occupied half of the floor of the River Ford building on the other side. Most of the allied tribes had moved to the lower floors or taken residence in the buildings surrounding the All Galaxy. The new ones—and they streamed in almost daily—were placed here until more permanent arrangements could be found. All in all, it was bound to be a quiet, slow night.

"You, Elfreth."

James heard footsteps approach as someone walked up the stairs. He turned and saw Maanx, the little snot. James had met the man a few times, and his disdain for all things Elfreth had been obvious from the beginning, worse now that Elise had become the center focus of this budding alliance. The self-important young man—he had to be in his early twenties—walked down the parapet, nodding to his three people and looking dismissively at the three Elfreth.

He turned to James. "You're late. That might be acceptable for your tribe, but the Flatirons do not tolerate such behavior. I especially will not tolerate this at the barricades."

Smitt appeared in front of James and leaned in. "Apologize and let it go. There is nothing to gain by arguing with a young hothead trying to make a point. You were late."

James sort of listened to his dead friend and tried to take a conciliatory tone. "I had something come up. It won't happen again."

"Perhaps we should have some of our commanders instruct your guardians how a good fight crew is run."

Was this kid purposely pushing his buttons? "Like I said," James said, in a slow controlled voice. "It won't happen again."

"It's no wonder your tribe lost your tower."

Smitt, shaking his head, stepped to the side and waved him forward with his hand. "Do what you have to do."

James froze and the blood rushed into his head. He looked Maanx up and down. He was tall and brawny, but his hands and face were smooth, partially from youth, but more likely from lack of experience. James knew guardians who were hardened veterans by the age of eighteen, and those who joined the ranks early had the scars, broken bones, and temperament to show for it. This boy had none of the three. "Who's going to teach my people? You?"

"You're the one they call chronman. Maybe I'll teach you right now." The young man, arrogant and perpetually angry, walked up to James and stared down at him as self-important bullies often did. James wasn't easily intimidated by large youths. He held his ground even as the taller man's face came so close to him that their noses almost touched.

"Leave the barricade. You are not worthy to stand among the fights."

"Worthy, eh?" James chuckled. "That's rich coming from a kid whose father is the teacher. Did he give you your command as a birthday present?"

The kid's face turned red. He grabbed the front of James's shirt. Left-handed. Kept a low guard. Favored his right foot. In one smooth motion, James trapped the boy's hand clutching his shirt, chopped down on Maanx's wrist with the forearm of his free hand, and spun, sending the young commander crashing headfirst into the wooden floor of the parapet.

He had to give the kid credit; Maanx recovered quickly. In an instant, the young commander was up. He lunged at James, throwing a wild hay-maker. Maybe the shine had dulled some of James's senses or the kid was quicker than James had given him credit for, but Maanx's attacks came close to their marks. Close, but not quite.

James stepped to the side, feeling his opponent slip and stumble. As he did, he shoulder-checked Maanx, sending him flying off the side of the barricade. The young commander fell four meters and landed on his side with a thud. He groaned, but got to his feet a second later. Resilient. Stupid, though. James jumped off the parapet and landed on his feet right in front of him.

Maanx pulled out a knife and lunged. James dodged a slash at his mid-section and popped the kid in the face. Maanx came again, this time trying to spear him awkwardly with the knife. James toyed with him, kicking the boy's ankle as he came in, sending him tumbling to the ground. The boy wasn't without talent; he was just raw. There was something familiar about the way he moved as well. He had some sort of training, though it was rudimentary.

"Is this the best the fights have, commander?"

Maanx roared and charged in again with two wild swings. James dodged the first and blocked the second with his arm, sliding in and throwing boy onto his back. James dropped a knee until it pressed down on the young commander's cheek. He caught Maanx's knife arm as the boy swung desperately, bent his wrist in awkwardly and plucked the knife out of his hand, then shifted his weight to the knee on the young commander's head and pressed down. A guttural cry escaped his lips.

"What in Gaia is going on!" Elise yelled so loudly her voice echoed around the cavernous room.

James saw her sprinting toward him with Rima at her side. He got off of Maanx and offered his hand. To his surprise, the boy accepted it. James pulled him to his feet and leaned in close. "Your footwork sucks. Next time, I'll show you how to properly hold a blade." He handed the knife back.

Elise got in between them and pushed James back. "What is wrong with you?"

He tried to brush it off. "I'm just showing Maanx a few tricks."

She turned to him. "Are you all right, commander?"

Maanx, still holding his wrist, nodded. He looked down at the knife in his hand. "The chronman and I were just running exercises."

Their eyes met and an understanding passed between them. James offered a small nod of thanks and then turned his attention to Elise, who jabbed a finger into his face. "We didn't mean to make a fuss," James said.

"Don't try to lie to me." Her eyes widened. "Oh, this is getting out of control."

"What's the problem?" he replied. "No one got hurt."

She turned to the guardians standing in a semicircle behind her. "Escort Elder James to his room. Place a guard there until further notice."

"Now hang on a minute," he growled. "You can't do that."

She rounded on him. "Don't you say a word."

"After all I've sacrificed for you and these savages," he yelled. "This is how you treat me?"

Elise slapped him. Hard. James's head swiveled to the side from the impact, and he saw stars. With a snarl, he stuck his face into hers and was about to tell her what sort of ingrate she was for mistreating and ignoring him when he saw the tears welling in her eyes. Something in him broke. It felt like a punch in the gut. The air in his chest abandoned him. His knees went weak and he fell on all fours.

Elise knelt down and ran her hands through his hair, pushing it off of his face. "Please go," she said softly. "We'll work this through. I promise."

James nodded numbly. She stood him up and gave him a soft squeeze on the arm, and then she took a step back and signaled to a group of guardians standing off to the side. Four pairs of hands grabbed him by the shoulders and arms, though gently. All of them looked unsure and frightened. He had trained them and led all of them into battle before. Instead of struggling, he allowed them to lead him away, only glancing back at Elise when he heard her sob.

The parade back up the floors to his residence was shameful. Word of his arrest had spread quickly and the people, Flatirons and Elfreth alike, came to watch the spectacle. The only thing that he could see was Elise's face at that one moment he broke her heart. That look of disappointment tore him apart. It was the same look many of the Elfreth wore as he passed by them. He was surprised that their opinions mattered to him. They did, and his attempt at a proud facade broke. He hung his head and stared at the ground.

They reached his residence, and one of the guardians held the door open for him. They stood around and tried to figure out what to do next. The Elfreth had never needed a jail before.

"I'm sorry, Elder," Poll, one of the guardians, stammered. "Oldest Elise . . ."

James pulled out his knife from his boot and handed it to him. "Next time, guys, check a prisoner for weapons and confiscate them. Sweep the holding pen and then put two guards at the door."

"Um, thanks, Elder," Poll said.

"And stop being so damn polite to a prisoner." James walked into the room and sat down in his desk chair. The door closed and he could hear the guardians chatting animatedly between them. He looked to the side and saw Smitt sitting in the chair on the other side of the desk. The two sat in silence for several minutes.

James finally decided to break the ice. "I've really messed up this time, haven't I, Smitt?"

Smitt nodded slowly. "You made a fool of the teacher's son for no reason other than the fact that he was a snot fluffing his feathers. He wasn't wrong to tell you to get off the barricade for drinking."

James stared at his friend, tears brimming in his eyes. "I never gave you enough credit for how much you took care of me. You weren't supposed to die. You were safe with your stupid desk job. Why did you help me?"

Smitt sighed. "Trust me. I'm the first to agree that I wasn't supposed to die. In fact, I should be enjoying the good life on Europa with a pleasure girl to warm me up at night."

"Why did you help me, damn you!"

"Because you're my friend, and that is what we've always done for each other."

"You should have just got pissed at me for knocking you out and then never talked to me again."

Smitt grinned. "And get stuck running Tier-5 runs with a bunch of fodders for the next five years? Nah, death is better."

James buried his head in his hands. "What do you think will happen now? Will the Elfreth exile me?"

Smitt shook his head. "More of the Elfreth look up to you than you think. They also all know you have a problem. They'll get behind you."

"What do I do?" James asked. "Tell me what to do next."

"Well, for starters," the ghost of his best friend said. "Let's finally address your drinking problem and apologizing to everyone. And I mean everyone. The list is going to be long."

THIRTY-NINE

ANOTHER WAY

There was bright yellow flash and Levin found himself floating in the depths of space in a small debris field where the old Lunar fuel depot used to orbit on the dark side of the moon. A few minutes earlier, he had witnessed the depot's destruction as a refueling accident cascaded a fire across the entire station. He had escaped with eight hundred liters of low-grade fuel and two tons of aluminum. Usually, this sort of jump wasn't worth a chronman's effort, but Grace and the Elfreth had a much lower bar than the agency.

Not for the first time, he felt a queasiness brewing in the pit of his stomach. This was the fourth jump in the past six days, the seventh jump since that disturbing encounter with Julia. Levin had had trouble sleeping ever since Madrid. He wasn't sure why, but the incident twisted him up inside, even though he knew he would have changed nothing if he had to do it all over again. For him, that was his benchmark for making the right decision: that with full hindsight, he would reach the exact same conclusion.

For some reason, thinking about Madrid angered him. His bitterness grew as he ran these inconsequential jobs. One after another, they sent him on errands to retrieve food, energy sources, clothing. What was the point? They were all stopgaps. What were they really accomplishing? All these jobs did was break more Time Laws and increase their risk of capture, either by ChronoCom during the jump or by the Co-op when they were sneaking under their blockade of the Mist Isle through that tunnel. The Co-op was bound to figure that out one of these days. Levin wasn't sure if Elise was actually getting anywhere with her supposed cure of Earth. It didn't seem like it, and if she wasn't, what was he doing out here? He reached the collie and signaled to Grace that he was coming in, making sure they had an atmos field up before entering. He passed the netherstore container link to her and, without saying another word, marched to the back room to lie down.

Grace appeared a few minutes later. She rapped the metal wall and took a seat next to him. "Clean job. Zero ripples."

He kept his eyes closed and rolled over. To be honest, he wasn't sure what had come over him. The past few weeks. The Bastion. Julia's face. All the jumps. He had forgotten how difficult it was to experience all those last moments. All that tragedy to parse, the faces of the dead dancing in his head. It was a lot to process, and he had so little time to do it, considering how condensed his jump schedule was. All he knew right now was that he wanted to be left alone to stew.

Grace was having none of that. "You're going to roll over and pout on me? Since when did you start acting like the chronman? I expected as much from our dour friend, but you, Auditor?"

Levin took a deep breath and sat up. "Apologies, Mother of Time. The effects of all these jumps are weighing me down. We need to locate miasma soon."

"James said he was working on it."

"He keeps saying that, but he seems more interested in the bottle."

"We've been trying to locate some for nearly a year. Your Chrono-Com keeps it tightly locked up. I have one more jump scheduled before we head back to Earth. After that, I promise we'll take a little break."

Levin sighed. "Let's hear it."

Four jumps on a six-day trip was insane. It was also an unfortunate reality, given the resources they possessed. Each of these jaunts out to space used up scarce resources. They had to maximize every trip. It was hard on the salvager, but he knew Grace had planned and scheduled everything as meticulously as possible.

"This should be easy," she said. "Year 2208. Juliano Bishop, a dear friend of mine from the Technology Isolationists. Fantastic logician and even better general. The man was always twenty steps ahead of our opposition. He actually died in 2210, but with the way my faction broke, I calculate the ripple will be quite minimal, especially since—"

Levin shook his head. "No. I won't do it."

"—the last few years were actually quite tragic for . . ." Grace stopped. "Beg pardon?"

He stood up. "We've gone over this. I won't go back and retrieve a person. I've already bent enough Time Laws for this supposed greater good, but I'm not retrieving someone."

"I don't make this decision lightly, Levin. We need him. The Elfreth need him."

"I don't care. I'm running the salvages and I draw the line at another human."

"If it's because it's two years before his death, I can work around that. There's an incident three months before the Battle of Charon that—"

"I won't do it!" he roared, slamming his fist on the wall. "In fact, I don't even want to jump at all anymore. What are we doing, Grace? I mean, really. What the abyss are we doing?"

Her eyes narrowed. "Most chronmen just resort to alcohol. But if you must know, we're fighting to give us a chance to cure the planet of the Earth Plague."

"Is that really what we've been up to?" Levin stormed off into the cargo hold in the back. He kicked the door open and gestured at the small stockpile he had obtained from his last two jumps. He jabbed a finger at the three pitiful piles of scraps that ChronoCom would never have spent the resources salvaging. "This is how we're doing it? You think this is going to solve anything?" He flipped the top off one of the crates and pulled out several stacks of empty plastic containers holding even smaller containers inside. He picked up a pile of these worthless things and scattered them to the ground. "You send me back to the twenty-second century to a doomed supply transport to get boxes of plastic boxes. What the abyss is going on!"

They stood in the cargo hold in silence for several minutes. Finally, Grace trotted over to one of the spilled containers and picked it up. She pushed a little button in its side and watched as a lid folded over the top with a small sucking sound and the sides of the containers frosted over.

She tossed it to Levin. "Invented during the early days of the Famine's March that wiped out entire cities. World War Three had just ended, and every country was scarred by the conflict. Food production was at fifteen percent of prewar days. Do you know what kept mankind alive? This thing!" She picked up another container and tossed it at him. "These worthless pieces of plastic are not only airtight, they freeze their contents for months, are antibacterial, and utilize so little energy I can almost power them with my body heat. What do you think the Elfreth need right now living in the dank and dark permanent fog of New York?"

He hadn't realized what the boxes were. He bent down and began picking up the scattered containers. One by one, he placed the smallest into the one sized larger, and again until they were all neatly compartmentalized. He held the final, largest box in his hand and stared. His hands were still trembling.

Levin suddenly felt deeply ashamed and very foolish. He hadn't lost his temper like this since his early days at the Academy. He had been raised in the harsh and unforgiving tunnels of Oberon. He had been an undisciplined youth, wild and always fighting for stupid and prideful reasons. Finally, unable to control him and tired of paying his many fines, his father had sent him off to the ChronoCom Academy, either to straighten him out or to see him dead.

Even then, it took several years of bad mishaps, a few nearly getting him tossed from the Academy his first two years, before he settled down and became a semblance of a productive member of society. It took the combined effort of all in the Academy—his teachers, mentors, and fellow initiates—for him to get his head straight.

In the end, he suffered an unknown amount of beatings, punishments, and solitary confinements before he became hardened and disciplined enough to achieve the tier and eventually the chain. Once he did, though, he learned to appreciate the agency and the institution that was able to forge who he was from who he used to be. It was a monumental task, once thought impossible by those close to him.

"I'm sorry," he said finally. "I'm just frustrated. I don't see what we're doing actually accomplishing anything."

Grace put a hand on his arm. "We make do with what we have, Auditor. We're three minds, you two barbarians, and a group of primitive aborigines in a bunch of hovels trying to cure the entire planet. The cards are stacked against us. I know our odds are low."

"What is the point?" he asked again, resigned, for the dozenth time.

"We're hunted by the authorities, disrupting the chronostream, and risking innocent lives. For what?"

Grace Priestly chuckled. "Because that's what dead people do. Titus, myself, Elise, even James, to an extent. We're all living on borrowed time, determined to make one last difference to justify our continuing existence, even if it seems impossible. You, on the other hand, had a life. You were part of an institution that gave you purpose and provided a vehicle for you to make a difference. Now you've lost that, and it pisses the hell out of you."

Damn woman could look right into his soul.

It takes an institution. Something about that word nagged at Levin. The words and images he couldn't quite focus on swirled in his head for several moments. Then it was as if all the pieces suddenly fit together neatly and crystalized into a clear image. It was so easy. Why hadn't he thought of this before?

"I understand now." Levin put the boxes back into their shipping crate and closed the lid. He walked with renewed purpose out of the hold toward the cockpit. "We've been approaching this all wrong. When do we head back to Earth? I need to speak with James."

Grace trailed close behind. "We still have that job retrieving Juliano."

"I told you I'm not doing that."

"Even after our little pep talk?"

He looked back at her with a rare smile. "Especially after our little pep talk. Come on, let's go."

FORTY

BEING A LEADER

"Teacher, words cannot begin to express my shame. I assure you this will never happen again." Elise sat in Crowe's office and kept a brave but humble front. Word of the incident had spread across the entire All Galaxy with few of the tall tales being anything close to the truth. The version Rima heard was that James was so drunk that he could barely stand, and that he had thrashed everyone at the barricade, Elfreth and Flatirons alike. And when noble Maanx tried to stop him, James nearly killed him, beating him to within inches of his life.

There were a hundred worse variations of the incident, each one more terrible than the previous. Some coming from the Flatirons were particularly far-fetched, claiming that Maanx had caught James in an act of espionage and that he was working for the Co-op. Others said James was on his way to assassinate the Teacher and was trying to take control of the All Galaxy for himself. No matter the stories, they got two facts correct: James was drinking, and he battered the son of the Flatiron teacher. Now she had a much larger problem to worry about. The trust and alliance they had so carefully nurtured over the past two months seemed overshadowed by this one incident. If an Elfreth elder could be so violent and unhinged, what did it say about the tribe that made him their champion? Elise didn't blame Flatirons for wondering.

However, she also knew that what she, the Elfreth, and the Manhattan

Nation had built here was too important, and they had gone too far for the Elfreth to be expelled. The Co-op danger was too close and all the tribes were too committed to this war. Not only was the All Galaxy the heart of the new government, it was also where all the tribes had centered their defenses. That meant expelling the Elfreth was not an option. If the Flatirons pressed that point, it would leave them with only one choice.

"There are many voices saying the chronman, or even all of your tribe, should be expelled," Crowe said, sitting at his desk. He remained calm, but she had spent enough time with him over the past few weeks to know he was furious. In many ways, he reminded her of Qawol. The old Elfreth Oldest was equally warm, wise, and hard at the same time.

"It is just one mishap, Teacher. We are taking steps right now to ensure this will never happen again." She tried to hide the worry in her voice. "We've built so much in such a short period. We can't throw it all away."

"I would not wish it so." Crowe nodded. "However, I will not allow today's incident to repeat, so how can you guarantee this will not happen again?"

Elise closed her eyes. What could she do? James's problem wasn't something they could cure. Things with him were bound to get much worse before they got better. Alcoholism during her time had decreased even though the amount of alcohol people drank had increased. Education and moderation were the key. There wasn't a magic pill to cure James's problem.

"I . . . I cannot promise that," she said.

"Then I cannot allow him to stay in the tower," said Crowe. "I'm sorry, child."

Elise's world shattered as the image of banishing James ran through her head. She knew she couldn't do it. It had been less than a year since they had first met, but James was everything to her. He was the rock she relied on in this crazy future world when everything else around her had gone to hell. Whenever she needed him, he was there, sometimes even when she didn't want him there. She knew he was devoted to her through and through. The very thought of turning her back on him and sending him away made her sick. She just couldn't do it.

"Give me a chance to help him," she pleaded. "He's a good person. I owe him, the Elfreth owe him that. Please."

There was a long silence, broken only by Crowe drumming his fingers on the desk. He looked off to the side and then finally back at Elise. "You will isolate him on his floor away from the rest. He is forbidden from the barricades or any Flatirons until he is no longer ill. If he relapses even once among my people, he is gone that day. Is that understood?"

Elise nodded several times. "Thank you, Teacher. James is a good man. He's suffered much in his life. He just needs my support and love. I need to be there for him. I am to blame."

"He is a chronman. It comes with their work."

"You wouldn't understand half the things he's gone through. The suffering and dreams. He's only told me some of it, whatever I could bear to hear, but the drinking is how he copes."

Crowe got up from his wingback chair and walked over to the cabinet in the corner of his office. He opened one of the doors and pulled out a small box. He stared at it for a brief moment before returning to her. He put the box in her hands.

"I know more than you could possibly imagine."

Elise's breath caught. Inside the box was a set of broken bands. She hesitantly picked up half a shattered exo and held it up. They were old, chipped and dulled, but nevertheless there could be no mistake about what they were. "You were a chronman?"

"A Tier-4." Crowe's voice was soft. "I cracked early, but held until I was near being raised a tier. The thought of continuing was too much, but I didn't have the courage to poke a giant in the eye. I salvaged often near the upper atmosphere of Jupiter. I'd seen the planet's force hundreds of times. Instead, I fled here and became a hermit until eventually, the Flatirons adopted me, very much as the Elfreth adopted you and your chronman."

"Does James know?" Elise asked.

Crowe shook his head. "He does not need to know, though it is not a secret. I'm sure I'm on some ChronoCom list somewhere. I doubt they care so much about me anymore, but it would please me if you did not make a point of it."

Elise nodded. "I promise, Teacher."

Crowe walked her to the door. "You need to isolate and put a guard on him at all times. He'll need support from you and his loved ones. That will be what sees him through."

"Have you had experience dealing with alcoholism?" she asked.

Crowe smiled. "That was how I got through it. It's practically part of the job description."

Elise thanked the Teacher several more times before hurrying up the stairs to James's residence. This was one of the few times she was grateful there wasn't a working elevator in this building, though rumors were rampant Grace and Titus were nearly ready with a prototype. She needed the thirty-two floors to tweak her demeanor from apologetic to enraged, and she spent the time walking up the stairwell working herself into a huff. By the time she reached the sixty-sixth floor, she was mad as Gaia and ready to confront him.

She eyed the two guards as she stomped toward his quarters. "Anything to report?"

"He's been quiet," Poll, the one on the right, said.

"Oldest, if he does try to come out, do you really want us to stop him?" the other guardian asked. "He's the chronman."

Elise looked at the clubs both of them had holstered at their sides. A crazed James would cut right through these two. Heck, even with guns he'd probably make short work of them. Still, it'd be better to give them a chance.

"Go see Eriao and ask for better weapons. Something that doesn't kill, like a stun gun or something." Did that even exist in this time? She wasn't sure, but she had a feeling they might need it over the next few days. "Unlock the door."

They did so, and Elise kicked it open as hard as she could. Unfortunately, it was a heavy door and the kick didn't quite have the result she intended. Still, hands balled into fists, she stormed into his residence. "You're in so much trouble, mister."

James, sitting in a chair looking out the window, lowered his head. "Is everything all right with the Flatirons?"

"For now, but kicking the Teacher's son's ass makes for awful public relations."

"I bet that punk is reveling in this right now."

"Actually, James, Maanx is the one guy who is making the smallest deal about this. He tried to excuse you entirely."

"But I'm not, am I?"

"No. The Flatirons and not a small number of Elfreth are scared of you."

"Have I been expelled from the All Galaxy?"

"Of course not, you fool," she said, walking up to him. She pulled a chair over and threw her arm around his shoulder. "I won't let that happen, but we have to do something about this."

He bowed his head. The sadness painted on his face broke her heart. "I'm sorry. I can't help myself."

She put his head in her hands and pulled him in to her chest. "You're just sick. We'll get through this together. Are you willing to let me help?"

"I'm sorry," he repeated.

"Stop saying that," she said. "Listen, I'm going to have to make some changes, and it's going to suck. I need you on board with me. Do you understand?"

"Whatever it takes."

Elise stood up. "Good. For the next few weeks, I'm your mother and boss, not your lover or friend. You got me?" He nodded. She made a circle around his room. "The first thing we need to do is to get you through detox. From this point on, you're officially grounded. You aren't allowed off this floor for a month."

"A month!" James looked horrified. "But what about the flyguards? The defense of the tower? The scouting and foraging trips?"

"Your only job right now is to get better," she said. "You're lucky I'm only restricting you to the floor, not just this room. I'm going to have some people come in a bit and turn everything upside down to make sure you don't have any weapons or booze lying about. Then I'm posting a guard"—she paused—"a couple of guards here around the clock with full permission to kick your ass if you get out of line. And if you start causing trouble, I'm going to have you restrained. You get me?"

James frowned. "I thought you were just going to inject me with an antidote or put me to work doing hard labor. That, I can deal with. I didn't think you were going to imprison me."

"You're not in jail, James. You're in rehab."

"Isn't that the same thing?"

"It's going to be worse, actually, but I'm going to be with you every step of the way. Sasha will, too, and so will Grace, Titus, and everyone else. You're part of the Elfreth whether they like it or not. Even Franwil will be here."

"Her I can do without," he grunted.

"Then I'll make sure she comes twice a day."

James stood up and walked over to her, putting both of her hands in his. "I said I'd do whatever it takes, so I'll do this. When do I start? I'd like to get some stuff taken care of before I get under house arrest."

Elise tsked. "Oh, darling. House arrest started the second we put you up here. Now sit, stay, and behave. I'll have someone bring you breakfast in the morning."

FORTY-ONE

SINGLE OPTION

The Valkyrie ship landed in a blue streak of light followed by an expanding ring of kicked-up dust. Senior Securitate Kuo stepped off the ship and strolled through the ruins of Manhattan. According to her AI module, she was standing at the intersection of Broadway and 110th Street.

This was one of the few areas on the island, still, where there was actually land. On both sides of the street, giant long-abandoned skyscrapers, with black windows like eyes, stared down at her. She ignored them, just as she did the mounds of rubble on the ground and the layers of gunk covering the building surfaces.

To her left, a slurpy brown river flowed at a leisurely place, making a sharp turn at the bend at the end of the block. The original bridge, connecting two buildings, had been long-destroyed and was replaced by a temporary metal crossing hastily erected by her troopers. The new bridge, just weeks old, already looked weathered and corroded. The elements on this planet were harsh.

This unified army was becoming a serious problem. While she was gone, the offensive had completely stalled, and the initial attacks from the savages had decimated her trooper and monitor counts. To add insult to injury, the director had cut her off from additional monitors, which was criminal, considering the critical stage of this current project. In the end, she got the supplies she needed to continue the project, if not the manpower.

A large shadow, followed by several smaller ones, swept by overhead, accompanied by the roar of engines coming to a hover above her as the supply convoy arrived. As well, a Hephaestus transport hovered over a landing zone with a restock of corporate weapons. Three Valkyries had just taken off, probably for perimeter patrol. The scope creep of this project had blown completely out of proportion. Sourn was throwing fits at every report. She knew he was getting heat from above, and that it was all rolling downhill to her. The longer this project dragged on, the worse her evaluation, and the longer she was forced to stay on this dirtball planet. She grimaced. She could visualize her career flushing down the drain.

Kuo continued past the heavy militarized zone and into an open field surrounded by a cluster of skyscrapers she had set as a forward operations to reinforce her project. One of the savages on watch at the corner saw her approach and shrank back into the shadows. By now, several thousand of these indentured served the project, and every single one of them knew who she was. They had every reason to fear her. After all, it was the only motivation these primitives understood.

The Co-op had become even stricter due to the increased fighting in the south. These indentured servants had been abandoning their posts at record numbers, most likely joining the enemy. Holding their families for ransom was no longer adequate motivation. Part of her wanted to just wipe them all out and be done with them entirely. However, without enough troops, it was far too easy for the Co-op to lose containment. It frustrated Kuo that she had to deal with such inefficiencies in her project.

Kuo entered a building on the ground level. She had chosen this building as her central base of operations because of its proximity to the front, as well as because it was one of the more intact in the area. According to her AI module, the building was originally a facility for higher learning called Columbia. Over the years, as the buildings grew taller and taller, it became the headquarters for a weapons manufacturer. As the war spread and business grew, the manufacturer had to reinforce it to survive bombardments, which explained its less decrepit condition.

The lobby of the tower was clean and organized, as was the rest of the floor. Kuo couldn't control everything, but she insisted on keeping her immediate environment within tolerable limits. Raised and educated in the pristine and desirable colony of Europa, she disdained the filth and unpredictable nature of this planet. Most of the more modern and affluent colonies were fully artificial, easily maintained, with every possible variable under direct control of the colony's administrators. The modular nature of all the colonies allowed for simple cleanup and repair as well. If a habitat zone failed, all a corporation had to do was clear out the residents, flush the entire module, and then repopulate.

Kuo took an elevator—installed by her engineers—to the sixty-seventh floor and walked down the newly-rebuilt hallways of her base of operations on Earth. She clicked her tongue in disapproval when she noticed Gav, her personal assistant, wasn't at his desk outside her office. The man should have known she was returning today and have been at his post. Not being ready was unforgivable. She would have to rescind his contract once it was up for review. She walked into her office and saw Gav standing in front of her desk addressing someone sitting in her chair.

"What is going on?" she began, and then stopped. "Liaison. An unexpected privilege." She shot Gav a furious glance as he bowed apologetically. He should have found a way to signal to her that one of the most powerful men in the solar system was waiting for her.

Sourn looked at her with open contempt as he swiveled her chair toward her. "Pour me a drink, Securitate. We need to have a talk." He looked over at Gav. "That will be all."

Gav bowed profusely before beating a hasty retreat out of the room. "My apologies, Senior," he said softly as he passed.

"We'll discuss this afterward," she replied.

"Don't be too hard on your assistant," Sourn said after Gav left. "He had little choice but to attend to me when I decided to drop by." He looked around. "Especially with this EMP fog hanging over the island. Fascinating piece of old-world technology."

"What drink do you prefer, Liaison?" she asked, displaying her assortment of liquor.

"Sparkling wine if you have any," he replied. "If not, I am content with beer. I have developed an enjoyment for ruck drinks in my time on this planet. If none is available, vodka neat will do."

She poured two glasses of vodka and brought one over to him. She made sure to drink from her glass first. Sourn took a disdainful sniff of it before taking a sip. She stayed standing and at attention as he leaned back and studied her. He placed the glass on the desk and spoke. "I take it Young didn't give what you asked for."

"We received a full supply requisition as needed to sustain the next two full cycles."

"But no more monitors."

"Afraid not, Liaison."

He tapped his fingers on her desk. "Are you wondering why I'm here?"

"I have a good idea."

Sourn leaned forward. "Your latest report. Trooper numbers have increased to 3,043 with another request for four hundred more to stand down two hundred twenty. One hundred ninety-three units of energy consumed, forty-six tons of consumables, and eighty-three deaths within the last seven days. Are these numbers accurate, Securitate?"

"If that's what I submitted, I stand by them."

Sourn stood up, raising his voice. "For what? You've made headway on three blocks to Sixty-sixth Street on the west end and actually lost a block on the east, getting pushed back to"—he paused as he sorted through his AI module—"Seventy-fifth Street. That means you've acquired a net gain of two blocks. Is this a good use of Valta resources? Explain to me what the abyss is going on here!"

Kuo gritted her teeth. "I make no excuses for the performance of those under me, Liaison. However, the situation has become more complex than originally estimated."

"Explain."

Kuo spent the next thirty minutes updating Sourn on the recent developments in Manhattan. She cited not only the enemy's vastly superior numbers, which was expected, but that they had recently unified under one banner to combat the Co-op. Not only that, she detailed to Sourn the savages' recent and substantial technological and tactical gains. They were now simply better armed and organized than they had been just a short month ago.

There was a pregnant pause after she finished. She could see the vice president of Earth operations' mind race as he considered the circumstances. "How are they arming themselves?" he asked finally. "I can see them working together. Even savages could have figured that out, but the leap in tactics and technology is puzzling. Who is helping them? Are they trading with the black market?"

Kuo shook her head. "Valkyries are blockading the entire island. From the different types of weapon use we've uncovered, we believe they have a salvager. It happened once with James Griffin-Mars. He could be jumping for them again, or perhaps the wastelander tribes have found another salvager to supply them. According to the latest report, agency auditors did locate an illegal salvage in Madrid that could be linked. Also, some of the markings on the weapons we've recovered have been linked to a major ripple near the Main Asteroid Belt two months back."

"Can your forces handle the situation without additional Valta reinforcements?" he asked.

"Not if enemy strength continues to grow, nor if ChronoCom continues to refuse additional monitors. The situation is becoming dire. My forces are already having trouble holding the blocks we do possess."

"I am not happy with this status, Kuo."

"Forgive me, Liaison. However, the situation has deteriorated to the point we may need to consider aborting the project. Capturing this temporal anomaly just might not be worth the expense anymore, regardless of contract morality."

Sourn sighed. "Normally, I would agree. However, that is no longer possible."

"Sir? Why not?"

"As you know, Valta recovered equipment from the Nutris Platform. It has come to our attention since then that the bacterial sequencer is DNA-locked to certain personnel. One of the sequencers in the past had caused a pandemic. Since then, the scientists locked use authorization of the bacterial sequencers to only a select few. All the scientists who had access to this particular sequencer in our possession perished with the Nutris Platform sinking, save one."

"This temporal anomaly has access?"

"We have identified her as Elise Kim, one of the head biologists. She is the only human alive who can access this machine."

"Couldn't we send another chronman back to grab and synthesize a sample of her DNA?"

"We've already tried that," Sourn replied. "The sequencer requires a full-body DNA scan to authorize. We need the temporal anomaly, and we need her alive. Therefore, aborting the project is no longer an option."

Kuo had a sinking feeling in her stomach. This information effectively locked her into completion or total failure. "I understand, sir. I could use another thousand Valta troopers."

"We are resource-constrained as it is, Kuo. The war with the Radicati goes poorly. Make do with what you have. It should be more than enough."

"Could you at least follow up with ChronoCom again? The situation is desperate."

"I will see what I can do." Sourn sighed. "I am disappointed in you, Senior Securitate. This will reflect on your review."

"My apologies, sir," she replied. "I will not let you down."

"You already have, Kuo. This was supposed to be an easy project. The cost overrun has become criminal. How could you have failed so utterly, Securitate?"

"The savages have proven resilient, Liaison."

"Enough excuses!" Sourn snapped.

Kuo felt her chest tighten. "I will see this project to fruition, sir."

"For your sake, you had better. Remember, the fate of humanity depends on your success. Stop fucking up." Sourn downed the last of the vodka and slammed the glass on the desk. He activated his environmental suit; the liaison had an aversion to Earth's environment. "Have my ship ready. I'm getting off this tainted planet as soon as possible. Don't even think you ever will until you finish this project."

Kuo's eyes lingered on the door as Sourn slammed it shut behind him. This project had become an unmitigated disaster. Sourn had made it perfectly clear that her career within Valta was now at risk. Frustration bubbled from deep inside. These savages were not going to be the end of her. Kuo was going to complete this project if she had to kill every single last wastelander savage on this island.

FORTY-TWO

WITHDRAWAL

It was five days into James's Elise-imposed rehab and lockdown, and he was in hell. No, "hell" wasn't an adequate word for it. James had been through hell before. He had survived the excruciating training at the Academy, fought his way through hundreds of jumps into terrible times in the past, and had seen many of the few friends he had in his life perish one by one. Each of those afflictions had torn a piece of his soul apart, scarring him terribly, but none of that pain and suffering came close to the misery he experienced right now.

For the first time in nearly two decades, he was denying his body alcohol. Or more accurately, Elise and the rest of the Elfreth were denying it, and he hated them all for it. His tremors began two days after his last drink. At first, it was a familiar sensation, the slight shakes and feelings of anxiousness. It wasn't something he couldn't handle. He had dealt with it to varying degrees for years.

It hit him hard right before dawn of the fifth day. He had woken in a cold sweat. His body ached all over, though he wasn't sure if it was from the withdrawal or from that constant pain that had plagued him ever since his last jump. He swung his legs over the side of the bed and stood up, then nearly fell over. It was uncommon for him to have gone this long without a drink. In most of those cases, he had been focused on other matters, either on a salvage or some mission. Busy hands and a working mind helped keep the edge at bay. If push came to shove, he had discovered a little trick early on: that just a few small sips while on jobs kept the shakes down.

This wasn't the case now as he lay trapped in his room completely dry. He had all the time in the world on his hands and he felt every single second as he lay in a cold sweat. James's body screamed all over as if he had been beaten and tortured. He tasted blood on his lips, having chewed them while he slept. He rolled out of bed and staggered to the mirror on the wall, courtesy of Elise, who had it brought up yesterday.

"Good way to self-reflect," she said.

James saw his gaunt reflection and the redness in his eyes. He touched his trembling hands to his cheeks and noticed how badly they shook. Ashamed of what he had become and terrified that these awful sensations were only going to get worse, he looked away.

He ran his hands along his chest and pressed them hard against his body, trying to will them to stay steady. His fingers itched, and no matter how much he rubbed them together, it was as if he couldn't quite satiate an itching sensation that was just out of reach. It was too much. James let out a snarl like a wild animal, giving into the pressure building inside him, begging for a release. He wanted to claw and scratch his fingernails along the walls to distract his nerves from the pain twisting inside his body.

James screamed at the top of his lungs, feeling the energy release. It felt good, briefly. A minute later, the sensation returned just as badly as before. James let loose in cries of misery until all the air had escaped his body and his head felt light. By now, his throat ached, and it hurt to breathe. He collapsed, weak, and the shakes returned. He sweated profusely, his body flashing hot, cold, and then hot again. He got back to bed and under his covers, shivering until his teeth rattling was the only noise he could hear.

Sometime in between all that—he was too busy suffering to notice when—some people came into his room. They were blurry figures, standing close by, observing but not making any moves to help. He wasn't sure if they were actually there. Could they be more hallucinations, figments of his diseased mind?

At one point, though, one of the figures approached him and laid a warm, damp rag on his forehead. "Elder," a young woman said. "Be at peace."

"Bria?" James asked, his voice barely a whisper. He recognized her only after several attempts, her wild mangy hair wrapped around her forehead coming into focus, a style of the Flatirons, something many of the Elfreth women had adopted. Beside her were Hory and Laurel, both looking worried and uneasy. They looked at him as if he were laying on his deathbed. "What are you three doing here?" he asked.

"We stand watch at the stairwell entrance, Elder," Laurel said.

A punishment. Another slight. These were his people, his wards, and now they were forced to be his wardens. He took a few deep breaths and sat up. He looked out the window and noticed that his sheets were soaked and realized it was still dark out. How could it not be morning yet? How could time be moving so abyss-damn slow? All those terrible moments he had just experienced, the tremors, pains, and sweats: Had time slowed to a crawl just to torture him, forcing him to experience every excruciating, painful second?

He tried to crack a joke. "Did the entire crew get shafted with having to watch over me? I'm sorry to have to put you through this."

They exchanged looks. "Elder," Hory said, "all of us, the flyguards, we demanded to watch over you. Oldest Elise had forbidden it, saying you wielded too much influence over us and that we were too close to you. She said that we would cave in to your demands."

"We told her it was because we were close to you that we would not," Bria said, dabbing him once more on the forehead. She wet the towel in a warm basin next to her. "Chawr would not accept their answer when they said no. We took our place at the door and forbid others from entering."

Laurel nodded. "As far as we're concerned, this is flyguard business."

For a second, the itching and shakes stopped as James looked back and forth among his three young wards. He honestly hadn't realized how much they cared. As far as he was concerned, they had just wanted to learn about ships and engineering, and he needed their labor. It was a fair trade, which was how things were at ChronoCom. "Thank you," he said simply.

"Don't thank us yet." Hory grinned. "We should get back to our posts. Is there anything we can get you?"

"Water." What James really wanted to ask for was whiskey. "Something to eat."

"I'll bring you breakfast once the kitchen rises," Laurel said. "We'll be right outside if you need us."

The flyguards left the room and closed the door behind them. He heard the click of the lock, and then he was alone. James forced himself to get out of bed and dragged himself to the balcony. The sweat on his body made the night feel even colder than it was. A blast of wind from below swirled the mist around him. It was strange to him that no matter how strong the air currents were, they never seemed to be able to push the fog away from the island. He inhaled and felt the coolness enter his lungs. It stung and shivered his body, but it momentarily calmed the craving eating away inside him. He took a few more deep breaths, bent over the banister of the balcony, and heaved. His insides seized and cramped as he suddenly felt like he was having a heart attack.

"Help," James moaned, turning toward the door. It seemed so far away. The booming in his chest felt like it was rocking the entire building as he got onto all fours and crawled his way to the exit. Leaning on the door for support, he pulled himself unsteadily to his feet. He banged on the door.

"I need help," he said, louder this time.

Immediately the door opened and he saw Bria and Laurel looking worried just outside. "Are you all right?" Bria asked.

"Listen carefully," he said. "This isn't working. I know you all mean well but I've been drinking for twenty years. Quitting like this isn't healthy. I'm going to die. Please, you're my wards. Get me just a little. Weaning my body off is the right thing to do. Just a little, a drop."

Laurel shook his head. "I'm sorry, Elder. Oldest Franwil and Elise said—"

"I know what they said!" James growled. He caught himself before his agitation got the best of him and reigned it in. He wasn't going to get what he wanted by being an asshole. "I'm just saying: I know my body. I just need a little to balance myself out. I feel like I'm having a heart attack right now."

Laurel began to close the door. "I'm sorry, Elder."

James blocked the door from shutting with his feet and grabbed Laurel's wrist. "I'm serious. I'm in a lot of pain here." The young man froze and tried to pull his arm back. James held on to it and stared intently at him. "I'm not fucking around. Just a little and I'll be fine."

Bria put one hand on James's shoulder and the other on his wrist. "Just a little," she said soothingly. She gently pulled his hand off of Laurel's arm.

"Laurel, get the flask. The one behind the shelf. Just make sure Chawr and the rest of the guys don't see you."

"Thank you," James said, never meaning it so much in his life. He relaxed and leaned against the door frame. Just the very thought of knowing a few drops were going to touch his lips physically helped his body calm down. His eyes didn't rest until he saw Laurel turn to go. He shifted his attention to Bria, trying as hard as he could to appear casual and collected. "I'm going to need you flyguards to keep me up to date on what's going on with the Elfreth and the fight. I know you're all looking out for me, but the sooner I get back to the fight, the better. You know that, right?"

"Of course, Elder." Bria told him of the past few days he had been holed up. The Manhattan forces had really taken it to the Co-op, hitting them hard and taking several of their scouts and outposts captive. The Co-op was unprepared for a coordinated and organized enemy and was, for the first time, retreating. The Manhattans were losing three to one, but that couldn't be helped. The monitors were so much better armed and trained than any of them, and the Valta troopers even more so. Regardless, they were finally chalking up victories, no matter how Pyrrhic they were.

"I'm proud of . . ." James's voice trailed off when Chawr and the rest of the flyguards walked into the room.

"I'm sorry," Bria said quietly and stepped away.

"Elder," Chawr said, hands raised. "We've sent for Dr. Titus. Go back into your residence."

"I trusted you . . ." James began to see red.

They were looking out for him. A small voice repeated it over and over again. Smitt appeared next to Chawr and shook his head. "Don't do it, my friend. Listen to that voice."

"You punks are trying to kill me," he snarled. "Get out of my way. I know where you ingrates stashed it."

Chawr shook his head. "We're dry, Elder. Oldest Elise spoke with us and we threw the rest away."

The thought of not having any within reach pushed James into a panic. He charged out the door, only to be surrounded by all six flyguards as they grabbed his arm and restrained him. They were children, though, all in their teens or early twenties. He threw them aside as if they were no more than nuisances, pushing them onto the floor, using his experience and skill to pull them off balance. That small voice in him was begging him not to hurt any of them, and he tried to listen, but he was slowly losing his sanity.

The flyguards continued to fight him, redoubling their efforts and throwing themselves at him every step of the way. Slowly, James tired. It had been two days since he'd eaten, and the shakes had taken a toll on him. He looked on in panic as they, step by step, pulled him farther from the door. A few moments later, he was back in his residence. And then pushed onto his bed. He thrashed as they piled on top of him, but it was futile.

"I'll . . ." James saw Chawr's puffy right eye. James must have struck him. It would be a beautiful black eye by tomorrow. He stopped struggling. ". . . I'm sorry."

They held on to him for several more minutes until Titus, huffing and puffing, walked into the room. The old man, face thunderous, scowled as he saw the pile of flyguards sitting on top of him.

"Do you know what flaming time it is right now, you junkie?" he said. "Couldn't you have an episode at a more godly hour, you inconsiderate ass?"

Smitt appeared over Titus's shoulder. "That *was* pretty inconsiderate, James."

The old man looked him over and felt his chest. "I'm surprised your heart hasn't burst out of your ribs and run laps around the room." He chuckled. "You, boy, run to the infirmary and tell them I want a beta blocker and benzodiazepine." He saw the blank look on Dox's face. "Oh, never mind. Fetch one of their healers." He looked at James. "Get some restraining straps, too. Just in case."

"You're not tying me . . ." James tried to scream.

Titus pulled out a rag and stuffed it into James's mouth. "You talk too much. It's still going to get worse, so here's the deal. You're my flaming patient now. I'll tie you down if you act up. I have terrible bedside manner, chronman, so don't piss me off. Are you going to behave?"

James nodded. He knew when he had lost. He tried to say something through the rag.

Titus pulled it out. "What's that?"

"I'm calm now. I'm sorry." He'd had to say that a lot recently.

"I'm sure you are, James." Titus grinned. "In fact, I'm going to move up here for a few days. You, girl, go to my room and pack some of my clothes and my bedsheets. And get a bunch of my pillows too. You two boys go move a bed to a nearby room. One that's heated and clean, damn it. I'm going to stay here with this junkie tonight, but it'll be a cold day on Venus if I'm going to let you interrupt my sleep. I'm an old man."

James sighed. Just when he thought it couldn't get any worse. "Can you at least tell them to get off of me?"

Titus shook his head. "Not until the boy gets back here with the restraints."

"But you said you'd only use them if I acted up."

"I changed my mind. When you become a Grand Juror, you're allowed to do stuff like that."

"Listen, you grouchy old bastard, there's no way in hell you're tying me up for the next few weeks!"

Titus stuffed the rag back into James's mouth.

FORTY-THREE

FAMILY

Levin was surprised James didn't meet him at the landing deck. The former chronman was usually waiting for them once they disembarked, either inquiring about the status of jumps or directing the flyguards on *Frankenstein*'s maintenance. It was as if the man couldn't fully let go of his previous life, no matter how much he wanted to. That, or he had too much time on his hands.

Both Bria and Chawr acted cagey when he asked them where James was. Chawr pretended not to hear and ignored Levin completely while Bria mumbled something about Elder James not feeling well. Stranger still, they refused to tell him exactly where he was. When he pressed them, they apologized and nearly tripped over themselves running away from him.

Levin wasn't particularly surprised with how most of the tribe treated him. As far as they were concerned, he was a complete outsider, a stranger who had just appeared one day and now dropped off caches of supplies every few weeks before disappearing again. Why would they answer his questions? The Elfreth, the flyguards especially, were James's people. Levin would have done the same thing if he were in their shoes.

His curiosity piqued, he set out trying to unravel this little mystery. He and James had important things to discuss, not only about Levin's role, but this entire mad operation. He first checked the three main Elfreth floors, and not finding him there, went down to the infirmary, and then to the barricade floor. When he asked about James, no one would give him a straight answer. Something had to be wrong with James Griffin-Mars. It wasn't until he ran into the boy who was friends with James's sister—Sammy or Sammuia or whatever—that he was able to coax, or scare, the news out.

"Elder James is very sick," the boy said. "No one is allowed to see him."

Levin grunted. "Sick" was code for only one thing. Due to the nature of their work, all chronmen were heavily immunized with every sort of vaccination imaginable. James couldn't catch a cold if he swam in a pool of the virus. No, the only real sickness he had was completely self-inflicted.

He proceeded up to the sixty-sixth floor, which was now completely quarantined for the chronman's rehabilitation. Two flyguards, Laurel and Hory, guarded the door. At first, they tried to tell him that James wasn't there. Then they tried to say that he couldn't see anyone "at this time."

"Get out of my way," Levin said.

They got out of his way.

Levin walked down the hall of the building to James's main living quarters and found him standing near a window looking out into the night fog with a heavy blanket wrapped around his body. Half of the blanket was soaked with sweat. He looked a shell of who he usually was. His face was deathly pale, and his cheeks were sunken in. Levin wondered when the guy had last been able to keep down food.

"You look like shit," said Levin.

"So I look a little better than I feel, then."

"At least you still have your sense of humor."

James turned and gave him a flat stare. "Do I look like I'm joking?"

Levin fought the urge to tell James about all the hundreds of times he had warned him about his bad habit. Instead, he got down to business. "How many days?"

James eyed the wall to the side. Four vertical marks with a diagonal line crossing through them and three more. Levin involuntarily made a face. The guy was in the worst of it right now. Not a good mental or physical state for anyone to be in, and even worse for someone with a job to do. As glad as he was to see James clean up his life, they had more pressing matters to attend to than his personal demons.

"Listen," he began. "Not the best time, but I need you functional. As much as I hate to say this, if it means you need to drink a little to balance your shit out, then do it. This is more important."

The look James gave him at that moment was a mix of incredulousness, eagerness, and straight-up murder. "Do you realize what you just fucking said to me?"

Levin pulled up two chairs and slid one over to James. He sat and motioned for James to join him. "Listen, remember the last time we spoke? I told you we were doing this all wrong and you told me to come up with a better plan?"

James nodded.

"Well, I came up with a better plan. Like I said, you're trying to cure the Earth Plague, and you're doing it with little to nothing. In your current state, you have a slim chance of surviving the winter, let alone curing the planet. You need allies."

James grunted. "Who the abyss is going to ally with us besides the Flatirons and maybe these Mist Isle tribes? Who, by the way, I'm sure are only doing this because we're the best-supplied tribe in the area. So who else, huh? The megacorporations? One of the moons?"

Levin paused before answering. "ChronoCom."

James choked when he heard that, and his body fell into a fit of coughs. His bloodshot eyes widened when he realized Levin was actually serious. "Are you lag sick already? The agency is in the pockets of the megacorporations. Earth Central is practically a subsidiary of Valta."

"The leadership is," Levin said. "Not the people. There's still good people there, and the best are on Earth. You're just too blind to see. If we convert them, the rest of the agency will follow."

"Did you tell Grace your insane plan?"

"Of course I did. Do you think I would have brought it up if the Mother of Time wasn't on board with it? We need help, and the agency is the best candidate to support us."

"I don't know how you're going to convince anyone," said James. "The monitors and handlers are just happy they weren't sent packing after failing the Academy, and the chronmen just want to earn out and retire. No one cares about the Earth Plague or the corruption."

"You'd be surprised." Levin leaned forward to James. "Come on, clean yourself up. We're going to Chicago. It's going to be dangerous, and I need someone to watch my back."

Levin stood up and went to leave the room. He stopped at the door and waited. James hadn't moved. The man just wrapped his arms around his shoulders and stared out the window. Levin had never seen him hurting so much. The two had been friends and enemies for twenty years and this was the first time he had ever seen the ex-chronman so vulnerable. He waited patiently for an answer.

After what felt like an hour, James looked up at him. "What you say makes sense. Curing the Earth Plague was never a serious plan anyway. At least it wasn't supposed to be. It was just a fanciful dream Elise had. I just went along with it because it made her happy and kept her spirits up. I never thought it would grow legs of its own and carry all these people with it. Now it's too late to turn back, and if we're actually going to make a go at this insane dream of hers, what you just proposed might be the best way to do it."

Levin nodded. "I'm glad you see it my way. Why play a game if there's no chance in winning, right? This plan gives us that chance."

"I can't, though," James said. "I'm sick right now and I can't be trusted. People got hurt because of me. I'm no use to anyone, especially to the people who love me."

"You can address this afterward," Levin said. "Time is of the essence. The Co-op is creeping closer every day. The sooner we get the agency on our side, the sooner we can all fight them together."

James shook his head miserably. "I promised Elise I would see this through. Besides, like you said, the Co-op is close. I can't bear to leave her and Sasha right now. I need to be here for them."

"And you staying here won't make a lick of difference," Levin snapped, stalking back up to him. "You can, though, if you come with me to Chicago. I can't do this alone."

James stood firm. "I understand what you're trying to do, but I belong here, protecting Elise, Sasha, and my people. I can accompany you after the threat is over. Not before."

"I believe the Elfreth's survival and convincing ChronoCom to join us go hand in hand. We need them, James."

"And I need to be here. I'm sorry; I've made up my mind. Why don't you ask Cole to help you? He's your flesh and blood. Put him to use."

A bubble of anger erupted inside Levin. He opened his mouth to retort, and then closed it. They both knew that Cole wasn't reliable. At least not yet, if ever. Asking Cole to come was a risk. His nephew had avoided him ever since they had arrived. Maybe it was time to bury the hatchet, though. Enough time had passed since Nereid that maybe they could try to start over. Cole was the only link to his family Levin had left. Perhaps this was their opportunity to work things out.

"Fine," Levin said finally. "I am leaving tomorrow. If you change your mind . . ."

James walked up to him. "I won't, but good luck." He stuck out his hand.

Levin stared at the extended hand and then turned away. "The world needs a better James Griffin-Mars. Give it to them."

Levin knew he shouldn't be angry with James. In truth, he wasn't, not really. The ex-chronman had different priorities and made the decision he thought was right for himself and his loved ones. Family trumped doing the right thing. Still, Levin couldn't help but feel disappointed. Then again, if put in James's shoes, he might have made the same call.

No, that was a lie: Levin wouldn't have. If family did trump the right thing, than he would have sent someone else to go after his fugitive nephew when Cole had tried to escape into the Ming Dynasty. Levin had known the consequences of his choices back then. He knew that bringing Cole back himself would ostracize him from Ilana, his sister, and the rest of his family back on Oberon. He also knew that if he had failed to capture Cole and bring him to justice, then there would have been gossip that he purposely let his nephew escape.

The smart thing to have done at the time would have been to assign someone else to do the work and let the chips fall where they would. Instead, he waded headfirst into a situation he could not win. Why? At the time, he had said it was the right thing to do. In truth, it was because of Levin's pride. It had forced him to personally bring in Cole to show the agency how dedicated he was to doing the "right thing."

Levin stopped at the intersection that would either lead to his residence or downstairs to Cole's. He hesitated. Just the thought of getting into another quarrel with his nephew drained him. Perhaps he should sleep on this for a night. Part of him wanted to head to bed and forget all about it. This plan was so brazen and outrageous that the odds of survival were low. It was better than the current doomed plan the Elfreth were following, though. Levin was not in the business of being a martyr. He'd rather follow a plan with low odds than one with no odds. He gave the door to his residence a longing glance before heading to the lower levels.

Cole had joined the guardian ranks shortly after they had arrived, and by all indications, was thriving with them. As a former chronman, he had quickly shown his value. He was quite popular, too, though that was never one of his problems. Cole didn't lack in charisma or skill; pulling a bunch of alpha-male assholes like the Apexes together showed that.

It took Levin nearly an hour to find his nephew. The Elfreth and many of their new allies had commandeered many of the lower floors for different uses. The entire tower was a hive of activity, a city within itself. Everything had changed so much over the past few months he barely recognized the place anymore. It wasn't like Levin had spent much time here. Usually, he and Grace would just return for long enough to charge the collie, rest a few days, and then speed off again.

Levin was finally directed to a hollowed-out apartment tucked away in the far corner of one of the less-used floors. Cole was lounging in the room with his team of guardians, smoking cany weed, a pungent herb commonly chewed to numb off-worlds against Earth's toxins, but also commonly smoked recreationally for its relaxing effect. The weed was banned in ChronoCom because of its addictive nature and its bad side effects when mixed with miasma regimens.

"Uncle." Cole didn't seem happy to see him, but didn't appear outright hostile. Perhaps it was the effect of the cany weed. "What brings us the honor?" There was only a small hint of sarcasm in his voice. He pushed one of the plastic chairs toward Levin. The four men and three women with him looked decidedly uncomfortable in Levin's presence. Who knew what stories Cole had fed them? One of the women was sitting on his lap.

"I'd like a moment alone with One Cole," Levin said, not taking his gaze off his nephew.

"My teammates are trustworthy, Uncle," Cole said. "Besides, we're all Elfreth now, aren't we?"

Levin swept his gaze across everyone. "Leave."

The battle of wills was waged and won within the blink of an eye. First, the woman sitting on Cole's lap shrank and got up. One by one, the rest of Cole's team followed suit. They didn't leave, though, which, to Cole's credit, was a sign of their loyalty to him.

Cole seemed as if he was going to contest Levin's order, and then finally nodded. "It's all right. This shouldn't take too long." The team filed out into the hallway. He picked up his half-smoked joint and took a puff. "What do you want?"

Levin sat down opposite him and looked around Cole's new quarters. They were larger and nicer than most; no doubt he had used his charm and rank to pull off these arrangements. It was a shame he had wanted to follow in Levin's footsteps and become a chronman. Cole had always been a talker. He'd had such a bright future ahead of him and could have been so much more. "You're fitting in well with the Elfreth, then?"

"Living in this hollowed-out shithole?" Cole sneered. "Not sure why we went through all this effort to bust out of Nereid only to come here. At least there's women here. How is reliving your chronman glory days, Uncle? Is it everything you remembered?"

The chasm between them was still there, though to be fair, Levin had not done much to bridge it. It wasn't surprising, really. Ilana, his sister, hadn't returned any of his messages, either. Sending your flesh and blood to prison could do that to a family.

"Listen, Cole," Levin said. "Mistakes were made, and now we're living with the consequences. Let's get past this. We're still family."

"Really?" said Cole. "Let's be honest. You don't think you made a mistake. You'd go back in time and capture me all over again. So what you're really saying is we're living with my mistake."

"I'm saying it's irrelevant," Levin retorted, his patience wearing thin. "We need to forgive and learn to trust each other again."

Cole finished the cany weed and tossed it out the window. He stood up and looked out into the dark fog. "You sent me to fucking prison, Levin, and you're my uncle. How do you expect me to ever trust you again?"

Levin found an opening here. "I'm heading to Chicago on an important mission. I need someone to watch my back. I want it to be you."

Cole looked surprised. "Even after everything that's happened, you're going to put your life in my hands? Are you that desperate?"

"One of us needs to start trusting the other first."

There was a long silence as Cole stared into the fog. Finally, he spoke. "I . . . I was angry for a long time, and to be honest, I still am. But, these past few weeks, as you're up there salvaging and James working with the flyguards and Elise leading these people, it's made me reevaluate my life. I've been dwelling on the past too much. Perhaps it's time I look to the future. When do we leave?"

"Dusk tomorrow," Levin said, offering his hand.

Cole accepted it and pulled him into a rough embrace. "You're not going to regret it, Uncle. Let me talk to Eriao and my team. I don't want them to think I'm shirking my duties."

That had been almost too easy. Levin watched as Cole went out to the hallway to tell his team, and wondered if he had made the right call. His gut told him no. There was a strong chance the boy just wanted to spend some time back in civilization, perhaps simply disappear once they got to the city.

Levin was willing to assume that risk. Like he had said, someone had to trust first. He knew in his heart he could heal this wound between them and rekindle their relationship. He had to. Perhaps it was just his pride talking. In either case, he was willing to take that chance.

FORTY-FOUR

THE ROAD TO RECOVERY

Titus and Grace's idea of recovery was stupid. The two of them had decided that they were both going to be intricately involved in James's rehabilitation and had come often to mentor and "life coach" him, and talk about his thoughts and feelings, whatever that meant. With Levin off to Chicago, Grace had much more time on her hands, and had chosen James for her new project. She also was trying to teach him to draw and practice a series of exercises called yoga, while Titus thought he'd enjoy learning to play a rock flute, a musical instrument indigenous to Venus. James was awful at everything.

Right now, he was sitting on his balcony trying to draw *Collie*, his old collie, from memory. It saddened him that even after twenty years of flying her, he had a hard time remembering her details. She had been a good ship, and James surprised himself with his nostalgia. He was going through a lot of that right now. It was one of the exercises Grace wanted him to work through: think about things in the past he enjoyed. The good moments, people and places and possessions, that had brought him joy.

It wasn't an easy assignment; good memories were few and far between. James found that he had little skill in drawing; faces were far too difficult, places were far too painful, so he resorted to trying to draw his beloved ship, which Levin had blasted out of the skies. That bastard; a new ship was another thing the guy owed James, especially after how he had commandeered the *Frankenstein*. If Levin lost that ship, too, the two of them were going to have words. James and the flyguards had put a lot of work into getting the *Frankenstein* space-worthy.

Smitt appeared and hovered over him as he hunched intently over the table. "What are you doing, my friend?"

"What does it look like?" James wasn't sure if he was supposed to talk to the ghost of his friend or not. Titus had told him that withdrawal would bring forth hallucinations, but he'd been seeing these apparitions since way before he quit the drink. The thought of alcohol—whiskey, specifically, though shine would do—made his body shudder. He was terrified that he couldn't drink anymore. Ever again. For the rest of his life.

The expression "rest of his life" had never meant much to him. He had always measured how long he'd live in months, if not weeks. The fact that he'd survived as a chronman for so long still surprised him to this day.

"I'd like to think I had more than a little to do with your making it so far," Smitt said.

James ignored him and continued to draw. He chose the hangar in Himalia Station as the backdrop and proceeded to populate the space around the ship with what he imagined would be there: a tech crew, power generators, module outputs. Then he focused on the details. His old ship was actually two different collies welded together, with one half of the ship nothing more than a patchwork of metal plates over holes. He couldn't quite remember the exact details, though; his memory of his chronman days had faded so much.

Smitt leaned over him. "Is that supposed to be me?"

James froze. He had inadvertently drawn two figures standing next to it. One of them looked like James, with short hair and a wiry body. The other, shorter and squatter, could only be Smitt. How had he put his friend in there without realizing it? He crumpled the blood-corn husk he was drawing on and threw it off the balcony.

"Hey, what did you do that for?" Smitt walked to the balcony and looked over the side.

James got up and paced the balcony. This boredom was driving him insane. Dox and Chawr were standing guard outside. The flyguards had wised up to all his attempts to let him out or sneak him a drink. No matter how many bribes or threats he threw their way, they were adamant. He was proud of them for standing up to him, though mostly he just wanted to beat them to a pulp. His throat was constantly parched, and he wanted nothing more than to purge this thirst inside him.

There was a knock on the door, and Chawr stuck his head in. "Elder, there's someone to see you."

"Is it Elise or Sasha?"

Chawr shook his head sympathetically. He was used to James asking him that by now. Every time someone came to visit, that was the first question out of James's mouth, and nearly every time, it was just Titus, Grace, or Franwil. It was getting to the point it pained James to even ask, but he couldn't help himself.

He should be used to the disappointment by now, but every time, James felt his heart drop into his stomach. How long were they going to keep punishing him? It had been over two weeks that he'd been locked up and they hadn't visited yet. It was starting to kill him. If anything, the urge to see them was becoming stronger than his urge to drink. The fact that almost everyone else had paid him a visit so far put him in a foul mood.

"Tell the Geriatric Brigade I don't feel like talking to them today."

"It's not any of the Oldests." Chawr hesitated. "It's Maanx."

"Abyss fuck me."

The young asshole couldn't wait until he got out, huh? Coming to gloat while James was in rehab was terrible form. He wondered if it'd set back his rehabilitation if he kicked the crap out of this kid again. It might just be worth a few extra weeks here in prison. Wait, no. The longer he was locked up here, the longer he wasn't going to see Sasha and Elise.

Smitt materialized again, on the couch, and stared intently as James walked toward the door. For some reason, the more he tried to ignore Smitt, the more that damn ghost kept appearing, offering unwanted advice and dropping his one-liners.

"Are you really going to keep pretending I'm not here, my friend?" Smitt asked. "Am I the thousand-kilo mutant in the room?"

"You're actually not, and you've always talked too much," James muttered under his breath. He nodded at Chawr to let the Flatiron commander in and readied himself to take a heap of abuse. Grace said he should apologize to the young commander when James got out of here. He might as well get it over with now, here in private, rather than having to do it publicly in front of his whole tribe. Chawr escorted Maanx in a few seconds later. James noted how strategically the flyguard placed himself between the two.

"Commander," he began. "Thank you for paying me a visit and saving me the effort of finding you. I want to apologize for the unfortunate—"

"You're a chronman," Maanx said.

"Um, is that a question?" James replied.

"My father trained me to fight. He fought like you do."

"Well, maybe not quite like me." James wasn't sure where Maanx was going with this.

"The Teacher was once a chronman."

Of course. He had noticed Maanx's moves were reminiscent of those used in Academy training, albeit a faint and sloppy impression of them, as if he had learned secondhand. In this case, he seemed to have learned from an ex-chronman who was thirty years out of practice. It also explained why out of all the tribes that the Flatirons fought off, they had agreed to let in the Elfreth. The story of how Elise and Crowe came to an agreement had always felt off, like some facts were missing. Now it all made sense.

"I did not know that. I would love to speak with the Teacher."

"My father was already old when I was born. He taught me what he knew of his chronman training, but I know he has already forgotten more than he remembers." Maanx walked past James to the middle of the room and turned around. "Teach me what he has forgotten."

That threw James. The last thing he thought the Flatiron commander would want was to learn from him. Could this hothead even be taught? Was he willing to listen and obey James's instructions? Did James even want to teach the kid? He wasn't sure.

"I'm not sure if this is a good idea. I'm in recovery, and there's a lot of people out there who think we just got into a brawl. The last thing I want them to see is us fighting more, even if it's practice. Besides, combat training is a teacher-student relationship. Are you sure you want to subject—"

"The Flatirons are at war. I need to be strong for my tribe." Maanx dropped to a knee and made a fist with his two hands. It was the same pose used by initiates at the Academy during training. "Master."

"Get up, man." James fidgeted as the Teacher's son remained kneeling in front of him. "Before someone sees this. Where did you learn that salute anyway?"

"Will you teach me, chronman?"

Chawr raised his hand. "I'd like to learn, too, Elder."

"I'm not opening an academy here."

The flyguard shrugged. "I'm just saying. If you're going to teach the Flatiron commander, I want in as well."

Just like that, in the middle of a rehabilitation stint, James acquired his first two initiates. He had never taught anyone before; the Academy disapproved of chronmen interacting with initiates. James thought it was because the directors and teachers feared the initiates would quit once they learned the truth about a chronman's life.

Starting that morning, James began training them the only way he knew how. He followed the strict discipline and structure that the Academy had instilled in him, half hoping that they would get disillusioned after the novelty wore off. Chawr and Maanx were attentive and enthusiastic students, though. The three of them spent the afternoon running through several basic exercises as he gauged their skills.

Right away, he noticed Maanx was a natural. The lad was not only physically talented, he was quick in his head as well as on his feet. He was also curious, often asking the right questions, which escaped Chawr's grasp. Now James realized that Maanx's position as a commander of the Flatirons wasn't just due to nepotism. The kid might have the personality of a troll, but he had abilities. If he had joined the Academy at an earlier age, he could have made a fine chronman.

They worked straight through dinner, and by the time they finished, all three were drenched in sweat. James felt wiped out as he toweled himself off. He nodded to his new students as they cooled down with the stretching exercises he showed them. He had been in so much pain from the withdrawal and so stationary in this room that he had forgotten how good it felt to move again. Moving around with the alcohol purged from his body felt strange, and all the sensations and reactions that had once been familiar now felt foreign. One would think his abilities would have sharpened, but if anything, they were much worse than before. James tried to tell himself that his diminishing reflexes were just the result of his acclimating to life without the drink constantly in his veins.

"Can we do this tomorrow morning?" Maanx asked eagerly.

"I have to help with the farm," Chawr said. "Can we start earlier?"

James made a face. "Let's see how you guys feel in the morning. There's no need to rush things."

He watched as the two bowed and walked into the next room, chatting pleasantly. He figured those two had never shared a word between them before. A smile appeared on his face as he made his way to bed. He hurt all over as he crawled his way into the sheets. Today had been a good day.

"Day's not over yet," Smitt said, appearing next to him on the chair.

"Go away," James said, lying on his back and closing his eyes. "I'm not talking to you."

"You can't ignore me forever," Smitt said. "In fact, I think it's time we figure this out."

"You're not real, just a hallucination from lag sickness and drink."

"You only think that, my friend. You've quit time traveling and drinking. Why am I still here?"

James turned over and drifted off to sleep with Smitt's words bouncing around in his head. Why was Smitt still there? The hallucinations of Grace, Sasha, and the Nazi soldier had all faded. He had seen them only in brief glimpses here and there, and usually as barely more than anything other than shadows in the background. This was his psyche telling him something, but what? Sleep draped over him quickly, and for a few beautiful seconds, everything was black and serene.

James opened his eyes and found himself sitting at the Tilted Orbit back at Himalia Station. Smitt was sitting next to him, pouring them both a shot of whiskey. He slid one over to James, and grinned. "See, I did warn you. You can't ignore me forever."

FORTY-FIVE

Closure

James stared down at the brown liquid sloshing around the glass cup. Half of it had spilled onto the counter when Smitt slid it over. He immediately felt the alcohol's pull on his body, as if it were a miniature black hole sucking him in. He caught himself staring even as he tried to look away.

"Why are you doing this? I'm trying to be clean."

Smitt acted surprised. "Oh, so now you're talking to me."

James's arms trembled and he willed them to stay flat on the counter. He couldn't pick up the glass. If he did, all his suffering and sacrifice would be for nothing. "Get that thing out of my sight. Please."

Smitt chuckled, took the glass, and gulped it down. "Too bad. That was a twenty-first-century double-barrel Luxe Empire special. Your favorite."

"What is Luxe whiskey doing in a dump like this?" James's breathing became labored and he squeezed his eyes shut.

"Why indeed, James."

This had to be a dream. A bottle of Luxe whiskey would cost more than this bar was worth. He turned from the counter and studied the rest of the Tilted Orbit. Now that he looked more closely, everything felt off about the whole place. Yet it wasn't like the vivid dreams he often suffered through where he couldn't tell reality from constructs in his head.

The bar, while loud, felt dead, flat. The patrons were darkened, as if shadows that had come to life. They all sat alone or in small groups with their heads down. He couldn't see anyone's eyes, nor could he hear voices speaking above the chatter. Where was the noise coming from?

"The real question is," Smitt said, pouring more of the precious Luxe-era whiskey into the glass, "if you know this is a dream, and now know this wondrous Luxe whiskey in front of you isn't real, would it hurt to have a sip? Is it cheating still?"

James looked down at the brown aromatic liquid calling to him. Beads of sweat dribbled down the side of his face. He gulped and stared. It didn't matter. His mind was as sick as his body. Just because this was a dream didn't make it any different, make him want the whiskey any less. He backhanded the glass, spilling its precious contents onto the counter. He jumped off the stool and stormed out of the bar. James kept walking until he was fifty meters outside the entrance. He hunched over and threw up.

Smitt materialized next to him, patting him on his back. "Well done."

"That was cruel," James choked, spitting out whatever was left in his mouth.

"You needed to realize what this is," Smitt said, pointing at their surroundings. "How what's happening here can affect you just as much as when you're awake."

"So that was a test?" James scowled. "Asshole."

"Oh, lighten up, James." Smitt shrugged. "Besides, I'm just a construct of your imagination, so technically, you're the asshole."

"No one ever argued against that."

"Come on," Smitt said cheerfully, pulling him up by the elbow and pointing straight at the wall.

He snapped his fingers, and suddenly they were standing in front of Earth Central. It had been nearly a year since James had seen the behemoth facility, and he was struck by how different it looked from what he remembered. Director Young had always prided himself on keeping ChronoCom's primary facility in relatively good shape. This was unlike him. Like everything else in this dream, Earth Central looked drab, dark, and dirty, as if they were in the future and Chicago, which wasn't very clean to begin with, had finally succumbed to Earth Plague.

"Why are we here?" he asked.

"I want to show you something."

The two continued down the once-familiar hallways. James had spent much of his Tier-2 and Tier-4 days at Earth Central. He recalled the first time he had stepped foot here, after his first transfer to Earth. Back then, he was still innocent and believed in the agency, believed in its noble goals. He remembered how he stood in awe of the facility, and how after spending most of his life on space stations and in underground colonies, he had reveled in Earth's openness. That was a long time ago. He was quite the idiot back then.

Now, as they walked through the main halls of the agency, past the Watcher's Board, which kept count of all agency personnel, through the ship hangar, and past his old quarters, the memories rushed back to him. Everything was a lie. This agency had long been corrupted, tainted by the influences of the megacorporations and their greed.

They entered the Hops, where the handlers babysat their chronmen. James saw another Smitt working furiously at one of the stations, sweat pouring down his face. His face was bloated and his clothing unkempt. Well, more unkempt and wrinkled than usual. He appeared skittish, continually looking over his shoulder. James looked to his left at the Smitt he had walked here with. They were definitely the same person, but not. The Smitt working at the console looked like he had gained fifteen kilos and hadn't slept in six months. James turned to the Smitt standing next to him. "Is this the future, because that you over there looks like shit."

Smitt rolled his eyes. "How can it be the future when I'm already dead?"

"Then what's wrong with that you over there?"

"This is the past after you defected from the agency."

James made a face. "Damn, Smitt, you gained a lot of weight while I was gone."

"No, dummy. That's your psyche imagining that I fell apart without you here."

"Well, did you?"

Smitt frowned and then shrugged good-naturedly. "I honestly don't know, because you don't know."

"I'm going to assume yes because he looks awful. Why are we here anyway?"

Smitt pointed at the door as a squad of monitors walked in. "Just watch."

The monitors made a beeline to the Smitt at the console and surrounded him. A second later, the unhealthy-looking Smitt made a move as if to flee the room and was roughly taken down to the floor. James averted his eyes as one of the monitors put a knee on Smitt's back and cuffed him. The two monitors pulled him to his feet, and one of them punched him in the stomach, doubling him over. Then they dragged him out of the room.

"Is that what happened?" James said softly. "I'm sorry. It's my fault."

"That's what you think happened," the Smitt standing next to him clarified. "But then, you think the worst about everything. Personally, I think I was arrested all dignified-like."

The two of them left the room and followed the monitors, though James already knew where they were heading. He knew what happened next.

"Do we need to see this?" he said softly.

"It's your dream," Smitt said. "You can stop it anytime. Maybe this is what you need right now."

James tried to change the scenario, change the story, or just teleport somewhere else. He concentrated and tried to will Elise here. To have Smitt and Elise meet would warm his heart. That could never happen in real life, but in his dreams, it would mean so much to him. Unfortunately, no matter how much he tried to control his dream and have that scene unfold, he stayed following twenty steps behind the two guards carrying a half-conscious Smitt to interrogation. Part of him wanted to jump those assholes and bust his friend out. However, the more pragmatic part of him knew that it would be a pointless exercise. It was more important for him to see what happened next.

They walked into a bare room with three metal walls and the fourth a reflective mirror. Only a table and chair served as its furnishings. This was the ChronoCom interrogation room. A huge ugly man, face crooked and scarred, wearing a Valta uniform, looked up cruelly at Smitt and licked his lips. "Tie him up."

"Who is that supposed to be?" Smitt asked.

"That Kuo asshole who killed you," said James.

"You know Kuo's a woman. Levin's told you several times."

"Oh, yeah." For some reason, James often forgot that fact. To be honest, he had heard this story a half-dozen times now from Levin, but he couldn't ever seem to remember any of the details. Now, however, he would have to live them. The giant ugly man morphed into a giant ugly woman, though not much else about her body changed.

Smitt gave James a sheepish look. "I guess accuracy isn't important."

James held up a hand and pointed at the imaginary Kuo. "I never met her before, so I guess she could look like that."

The Smitt tied to the chair whimpered as the imaginary Kuo cracked her knuckles. Immediately, James wished he knew how to change her so that she was small and harmless. He didn't, and winced as she raised an arm and struck his best friend in the face. Blood splattered against the wall.

"Where is James Griffin-Mars?" she asked in a low voice.

A white glow appeared around her body as she began to torture him, burning his hair and skin, even as she pummeled him. James felt his stomach knot up; he was torn between stopping this brutality and needing to know why he was witnessing this. He bit his lips and clenched his fists as Kuo picked up a scalpel and cut into Smitt. He felt sick as she burned Smitt's body with her exo, broke his fingers with a chisel, and electrocuted him until he went limp. Still, James couldn't move to stop her or look away.

He didn't know how long he witnessed this atrocity, and he wept as he stayed rooted in place, never having felt so helpless in his life. He turned to the Smitt next to him, but his guide was no longer there. Instead, he saw the Smitt he remembered walk up to the other Smitt and their two bodies merged.

Kuo cupped Smitt's chin in her hand. "This is your last chance, handler. Why are you protecting him?"

"James is my friend, that's why." Smitt looked straight at James. "He has more important things to do right now."

Everything turned red. For a second, James glanced in the mirror and saw Levin's face staring back at him, and then he charged Kuo. The glow of the exo burst around him until it filled the entire room. Everything became blindingly orange and then white.

James leaped out of bed. He willed his exo to expand to its fullest and tried to create a dozen coils. Nothing happened. It took a moment to realize that his chest was heaving, his face wet with exertion. It took him a few more seconds to get his bearings and realize that he was back in his room. James dropped to his knees and stared at the quiet emptiness. Somewhere, deep within the recess of his head, he could still hear Smitt's screams.

Behind him, someone spoke. "I think I was completely justified in losing my shit back there."

James looked behind him and saw Smitt sitting in the chair on the balcony, looking out into the heavy gray mist. One leg was propped up on the railing, and he held something in his hand. James wiped his face, now shiny with tears, and decided to join him.

He walked onto the balcony and leaned on the railing. He thought better of it when the rusted black metal shifted under his weight. He looked down and to his right as Smitt took another sip from what looked like a tin of beer.

"Is that what really happened?" he asked.

Smitt shrugged. "Does it matter?"

"No. I guess not." The two stayed silent for few minutes longer. James watched the roiling fog float on the wind as if it were alive. "For what it's worth, I'm sorry."

"That's the wrong takeaway, my friend."

James squeezed his eyes shut. "I know, but I am anyway. I'll get that monster if it's the last thing I do."

Smitt took a sip from his tin. "Again, wrong takeaway. While I appreciate the gesture, I couldn't care less about revenge."

James tried to recall the already-fading dream. He relived the rage that coursed through his body as he stood helplessly and watched the torture unfold. "I have something better to do."

His best friend nodded. "Worry about the big picture and the people you love who are still alive. Focus on them. The rest is irrelevant. Let me go."

James looked at the tin of beer in Smitt's hand. "Is that what I think it is?"

Smitt held it up. "The same discount sludge from the Fresh Fish back when we were initiates. Barely drinkable, but does the job. Here, you want some?"

James did. He would always want some. However, for the first time that he could remember, while awake, that is, he had more pressing desires. "No thanks."

Smitt grinned. "That's my boy."

There was a knock on the door. James looked back across his residence and then back down at Smitt. His best friend had disappeared. He looked up at the sky. "Be well, Smitt. I never got you to Europa, but I'll do you one better here on Earth."

James checked the time and then went to answer the door. His eyes widened. Maanx and Chawr were here for their early-morning training. What surprised him, though, were the twenty other guardians and fights standing behind them, including all the flyguards.

"You said I could invite others," said Maanx.

James buried the smile creeping up his face. His masters at the Academy rarely smiled. He walked into the middle of the waiting crowd. They all looked at him expectantly, hesitantly. Some of them bowed. Others saluted. More simply averted their gazes. No one knew what to expect. Neither did he, to be honest. James scanned the crowd and spoke in a clear voice. "From now on, you scrubs address me as Master, got it?" He was met with silence. "Do you understand?" he barked in a louder voice.

"Yes, Master!" the chorus replied.

James nodded. "Let's get started. I want four lines . . ."

FORTY-SIX

FROM WITHIN

Julia Gaenler-Phobos checked the levels of her bands, as she always did, as the two-hundred-year-old elevator raced up the floors of the Auditor Tower. She had to be careful in case the elevator malfunctioned or the cable snapped. It had broken once when she had first moved in. She wasn't wearing her bands at the time, so probably had been at risk of plummeting to her death. Fortunately, she was on the ground floor and the car dropped only a few meters. That would have been the ultimate insult, to work so hard to become an auditor at ChronoCom and then die in a freak elevator accident. No, Julia remembered to always have her exo powered on whenever she stepped foot in here.

The funny and slightly sad thing was, this potential death trap was newer than her personal collie, the one she took to space. Something about that didn't sit right with Julia, but it was what it was. Worrying about the present wasn't her job; making sure the past was pure was. It was a responsibility she was increasingly tiring of lately.

Julia had thought things would be different when she was raised from the tier to the chain, that once she went from the recovery side of the agency to standards, her perspective would broaden, and she would feel more fulfilled by her life's career. Instead, all it did was make her more aware that the ship flying her through space was older than some colonies, and that the universe was slowly falling apart.

The elevator jerked to a stop, and the doors opened, about a half meter below floor level. Julia sighed. This elevator car was waiting to kill an auditor in the most unglamorous way possible. Keeping her exo fully powered, she climbed up the ledge and pulled her bag of canned foods— her dinner for the night—out with her.

The Auditor Tower was one of the shorter buildings on the Chrono-Com campus, only thirty-eight floors tall with two residences per floor. There really wasn't need for more than the seventy-six units. With approximately two hundred or so auditors in the entire solar system, more than half of the Auditor Tower on Earth was uninhabited. It was one of the rare wastes of space the agency allowed.

They were auditors, after all. Auditors mattered; they were important.

That phrase was the first words the High Auditor—former High Auditor—of Earth said to her when she first reached the chain. She didn't know why, but more and more of his little bits of wisdom were filtering into her psyche lately. She shook her head. The encounter in Spain was still fresh in her head. Not only was it the only blemish on her record in three years, it'd left her with several sleepless nights.

The selection of the new and current High Auditor of Earth was something of a scandal. Julia was of the twelfth, which, while moderately high in the hierarchy, would have given her only outside consideration for the office. Julia didn't mind being overlooked. The high auditorship was a stressful and thankless job. All she had to do was look at what happened to the position's predecessor for assurance of that.

Imagine everyone's surprise when Miri, only sixteenth in the chain, somehow leapfrogged over everyone to become the High Auditor of Earth. It didn't take long to deduce what had happened. It was a badly-kept secret that Auditor Miri was Director Jerome's goddaughter, and was closely aligned with all the senior administrators. She would force Earth's auditors to walk in lockstep with the rest of the agency in the outer colonies instead of allowing them to be the independent and unbiased entities that they should be. To the abyss with the politics. To be honest, Julia was surprised it had taken Jerome so long to get Earth's auditorship under his thumb. It was because of Levin. He had prevented it.

Julia slung the pack of cans off her shoulder, listening to their dull thunk as they banged together, and opened the door to her residence. The first thing she did was undo her bands and put them on their charger. She flexed her fingers and stretched her arms, feeling how free they felt without the fourteen metal rings that almost never left her skin. Unlike most of the tier or the chain, she disliked wearing bands and took them off at every opportunity.

She placed the bag on top of her kitchen counter and pulled the cans out one by one, stacking them in a neat row. She had the option of eating at the Earth Central cafeteria, but much preferred to make her own meals instead of consuming the machine-processed standards. Cooking was becoming a lost art now that food had become all about efficiency. Some of the poorer colonies had reduced their daily consumption entirely to protein gel packs. Others provided just the bare-minimum options, rotated quarterly. In almost all cases, very few civilized colonies cooked anymore.

Julia looked at the books stacked neatly on shelves against the wall, a smile appearing on her face. She had broken the Time Laws only once, during a Tier-4 job in the late twentieth century. She had jumped into a public consumer facility that housed hundreds of small shops and had an hour to recover a long list of items before an electrical fire razed the place to ashes. That one time, she had stopped by a store that sold books and swiped three dozen on cooking.

She had by now attempted a third of those recipes. Many of the rest were impossible to cook due to some of their ingredients being extinct in the present. When her time with the agency was completed, she was going to spend the rest of her years trying to complete all the recipes she could. Her eyes followed the long line of books lovingly until she reached the end of the shelf. Her gaze continued across the room, hesitating for just a brief moment. Keeping her body relaxed, she walked over to where her auditor bands were charging and reached for her exo.

"Don't even think about it," a voice from the darkness said. "Take a step back."

That voice. Julia raised her hands and took the step back. "Lights," she said. The room illuminated, revealing a figure sitting on her couch. She cursed. "First you ruin my perfect record, now you're ruining my night."

"Hello, Julia," Levin said. "You look well."

She noted his bands. It'd be impossible to escape. Maybe there was something to keeping them on at all times. One never knew when a fugitive was going to break into your home.

"What do you want? If it's thanks for saving my life, forget it." She pointed at her charging bands. "If it's auditor bands, you know where they are."

He waved at the chair opposite him. "Have a seat."

She folded her arms and stood her ground. "I don't think so."

"You're not in a position to argue, Julia."

She shook her head. "I'm walking out of this room. Do what you must." He had already saved her life, so she knew he wasn't here to kill her. If he wanted the bands, he could have already had them.

"Please. Hear me out. That's all I ask."

"Fine. You have five minutes, and then I'm calling the monitors." What game was he playing? She noticed that he still hadn't powered on his exo. "What do you want to tell me?"

"ChronoCom is sick from the inside."

Automatic words defending the agency leaped to her lips, but she couldn't let them free. In her heart, she knew he spoke the truth. Everyone knew there were problems, cracks within the hierarchy. Questionable relationships and orders. Still . . .

"The agency has always needed to play politics with corporations and governments," she replied stiffly. "It is an unfortunate reality."

"We've done more than that," he said. "ChronoCom breaks the Time Laws for the highest bidder. The Nutris Platform explosion was staged. We were the ones to blow it up."

Julia's jaws dropped. "That's impossible. The ripples . . ."

"Wiped out by the Third World War," said Levin. "Carefully orchestrated and masked with the alerts disabled. That's the thing about ripples. The time line often self-heals. If someone prevents a ripple from alerting the auditors, no one is the wiser."

"That's preposterous," she said. "To allow something like that to happen, it would have to be a conspiracy of . . ."

". . . the highest ranks of the agency," said Levin. "Jerome personally undersigned the Valta job."

"And you're back because you intend to expose the agency?" she asked. "Frankly, Levin, I find that a worse crime than the charges you level at the directors. We are the only entity that is legally allowed to time travel. If you destroy confidence in the agency, then anyone who obtains jump bands can abuse the technology. Our ability to govern and protect the chronostream will be undermined."

"Even when you know the agency is corrupt?"

"It's the lesser of the evils."

"What about the good that ChronoCom is supposed to be doing?"

"We are doing good. We keep humanity from the void of extinction. You used to tell me that on a regular basis."

"But is it true?" He stood up, turned his back to her and walked to the window. "Look outside. Extinction is at our door. We've failed."

She followed him to the window and looked outside. "The agency is imperfect, but what else can we do but keep trying?"

He grunted. "I used to say that, too." He turned to her. "ChronoCom used to be about doing our best. It can be again. We can do better. Help me. Organize a meeting with the other auditors, senior monitors, and those who still believe in the agency's cause. Let's take back the original charter that ChronoCom was created for."

"They will need proof," she said. "Do you have any?"

He nodded. "I was building a case when I was indicted by the agency. It's heavily encrypted, so the administrators wouldn't find out. The agency never destroys anything. The evidence should still exist in the quarantined archives. You're an auditor. You should have access."

Julia studied him for a few moments and then shook her head. "No. I won't betray the agency until I have proof. Besides, even with my access, it may raise alerts. I won't risk it. If you want me to help you, bring me that proof."

"If I do, you will have this meeting?"

"If you can prove your claims, yes."

"Very well. Frequency Channel M0T11VES." He got up to leave, pausing as he passed by her. "It's good to see you again, Julia."

"Levin," she called after him as he was about to leave.

"Yes?"

"We're even now. Until you get me that proof, the next time we meet, I will take you down."

He nodded. "I expect nothing less. If it's any solace, I thought you would have made the logical candidate to be Earth's high auditor once I . . . was no longer able to serve."

"One more thing," she said. "How did you know I wouldn't take you down the second I saw you if I still had my bands on?"

He shrugged. "I didn't. Cole, let's go."

To her surprise, another figure emerged from her bedroom carrying a rifle in his hands. The figure glanced her way guardedly and retreated backward out the door after Levin. Of course, an auditor would never leave his security to something as thin as trust. In a small way, that reaffirmed Levin's judgment to her. At least the man hadn't totally lost his senses.

When they were gone, Julia went to her private stash of wine that she reserved for special occasions. She had only a few bottles left of the twenty-third-century vintage Triton she had been saving for the past decade. She took out one of the bottles and gave herself a generous pour.

She raised it into the air. "This is to you being wrong, Levin Javier-Oberon."

FORTY-SEVEN

PAST REVISITED

Levin's skin crawled as he shuffled along with the busy evening crowds on the southern side of ChronoCom Campus, where the Tier, Chain, and Admin towers were located. It felt like a lifetime ago that he had last walked on the streets between the low-rise buildings flanking the massive Earth Central structure, that dominated the soot-ridden landscape.

Prior to the outbreak of World War III, the Earth Central grounds were home to one of the most prestigious universities on the continent. After the old United States broke apart and a populist surge of counter-educational elitism swept through the country, the school fell into ill repute and then disuse. People became more concerned with surviving the famines and the nuclear winters than they were with getting an education. Eventually, ChronoCom took over the school grounds and its surrounding campus and built what became Earth Central.

He pulled his tattered coat around him as a large group of monitors and administrators passed. None of them paid him any attention. He felt strange as he stepped aside deferentially to let them by. An auditor, Marquez, High Auditor of Mars, walked out of a building and nearly bowled him over.

Levin stopped and bowed his head. "Apologies, Auditor."

Marquez gave Levin's paint job a dismissive glance and continued on his way. That surprised Levin to an extent. Marquez had always seemed one of the friendlier and more charming high auditors, at least whenever he was with Levin. It seemed the man's graciousness was limited to those he considered peers. Levin waited until Marquez was well down the street before he moved from the Chain Tower's walkway to a small café across the street. He sat down next to Cole in one of the outdoor areas. "Well?"

Cole, pretending to be watching the vid on the table, didn't look up. "Of the four you tagged, nothing. I did see Julia several times. She's stomping around in quite a hurry."

Levin signaled for a coffee. "Julia is an accomplished tactician and a magician in zero gravity, but if you tell her to put on a show, she falls apart a little."

"That doesn't sound like a great candidate for High Auditor of Earth."

"On the contrary, she would be perfect. It's the honest auditors with integrity that people follow."

"I thought it was the smartest and the strongest," said Cole.

The waitress came by and placed a cup on the table. Levin sniffed it and gave a satisfied sigh. He took a long sip. It felt like a lifetime since he had last tasted this bliss. He looked over at Cole. "That's why your Apexes were bound to lose to my People. You might have the biggest and baddest, but the instant anyone shows weakness, your gang eats its own. Just look at what happened to all your injured."

Cole snorted. "It's too bad we'll never find out now, isn't it?"

Levin let it slide. He had made his peace with his nephew, but the lingering resentment would take time. Cole would come around eventually.

They continued lounging outside, acting preoccupied and ordering just enough drinks to appear natural. For the next few hours, he watched hundreds of people walk by. It took some self-control not to show any sort of recognition at all. In this part of the campus, except for the rusks newly promoted to the tier, he had dealt with almost everyone in some capacity. A third here he knew on a first-name basis.

It was then he realized what had bothered him earlier. Levin didn't belong here anymore. He wasn't on their side. For the majority of his life, he was a key cog in this small world, and now he was on the outside looking in. He had been the High Auditor of Earth. The monitors loved him, most chronmen respected him, and the other auditors looked to him for leadership. However, that was all taken away from him in a flash. Now, there were few left here who would even dare say his name openly.

He was nothing, less than nothing. Levin had to admit he missed it terribly. Still, that was all in the past, and the past was dead.

Finally, as the rust-stained sun, seemingly shining behind a screen of oil, began to make its descent in the west, Levin found one of the marks he was searching for walk out of the Admin Tower. Vaneek was an auditor liaison, one of the many who helped coordinate communication between the auditor office and the many administrators at the agency. Like most, he was a failed initiate at the Academy, both of the tier and the monitor ranks. He had also tried his hand at becoming a handler, but was too slow in his critical analysis and planning.

Vaneek was slated to be shipped back to his home moon of Neso when Julia, who was one of the educators at the Academy, brought him to Levin's attention. He had initially taken one look at the boy's records and written him off. She said he was worth saving, though, so out of respect for her, Levin gave him a chance. Vaneek proved her right in every way. While the boy was weak in body and will, he was a born administrator: methodical, exact, and loyal.

Levin had first brought him in as an intern, and then as his assistant, in which capacity Vaneek had served faithfully until Levin was ousted from the chain and sent to prison. Levin had worried about what would happen to Vaneek, since they had worked so closely together. He was grateful to Director Young that they hadn't held their close relationship against him and allowed Vaneek to transfer to the Administrators.

Vaneek had just left the Admin Tower and was walking away from the café, down through the crowded streets to the permanent residences underground. Levin tapped Cole on the shoulder and the two followed, keeping a safe distance behind Vaneek in case he became suspicious. They continued down to the vast network of tunnels under the campus. The crowds thinned, forcing Levin to trail further back. Vaneek led them deeper to the sublairs, where many of the camp supporters, maintenance workers, and laborers resided.

Levin had never ventured to this area before. Those of the chain or tier or even ranks had little cause to ever come down here. Levin began to worry. He studied the narrow hallways and low ceilings. This was the perfect place for a trap. Was Vaneek leading them here? Did Vaneek see through their paint jobs and somehow realize who they were? They continued down to a basement-level residential area. Here, the rooms were small and close together, and the halls were so narrow, Levin's shoulders could almost rub against both sides. It was not a good place to try to speak with Vaneek. One shout, and he would alert dozens of people close by. Levin slowed to put even more distance between them.

Finally, Vaneek stopped in the middle of the hallway and knocked on a door. Levin and Cole waited and watched from around a corner. A few seconds later, the door opened and a figure leaped out at Vaneek. He put his arms around a young woman and lifted her off her feet. She pushed him into the opposite wall and they kissed.

This relationship did not seem like a professional one. The two looked like they were genuinely fond of each other. Levin had not expected this; Vaneek was an awkward and unsocial person. He hadn't had any friends—at least that Levin knew—when they had worked together. A tinge of guilt gnawed at him as the two young people went into what he assumed was her residence.

"Perhaps this is not the time," Levin said softly. "I want to catch him alone."

"What? This is the perfect time," Cole insisted. "Let's just get this over with."

He pushed past Levin and moved to one side of the door. He motioned for Levin to follow. Against his better instinct, Levin positioned himself on the opposite side. He raised a knuckle to the door. Cole grabbed his wrist and pulled him back before he had a chance.

"We're fugitives, remember?" Cole hissed. "I'm not taking any chances. If Vaneek decides to call us in, we're done. I'm not risking going back to Nereid on your relationship with the boy."

"How do you want to play this, then?" Levin said.

Metal glinted in Cole's hand. Before Levin could stop him, Cole took a step back, kicked the door down, and rushed in. He heard a startled cry and a scream and then the rustling of things being knocked over. "Hands up, both of you!" he yelled. "Don't you even think about touching that comm unit, you little bastard."

Levin gritted his teeth. This was not how he wanted to initiate contact with his former assistant. He hurried inside to defuse the situation. Cole had Vaneek pressed against one wall. The woman, half naked, was cringing on the opposite wall.

"Stand down," Levin barked, pulling his nephew back. "Damn it, Cole. This isn't necessary."

The woman tried to make a break for it. Clutching a blanket to her naked chest, she scampered toward the door. Cole, almost casually, caught her by the neck and flung her onto the bed.

"Leave her alone!" Vaneek cried and attacked Cole, clawing and scratching at his face. Cole head-butted him and knocked him to the ground. The woman began to sob loudly. Cole touched a scratch on his face and looked at the blood smeared on his fingers. "The little shit cut me." He raised his foot and was about to stomp down on Vaneek's head when Levin barreled into him, knocking him over. He pried the pistol out of Cole's hand and threw it to the side.

"Stand down, all of you!" Levin growled.

Cole scrambled to his feet and stuck his face close to Levin's. "Don't ever touch me again."

Levin pointed at the door. "Get out of here. Guard the damn hallway. Out! Now!" The two men stared each other down, and Levin didn't discount the possibility of coming to blows with his nephew. Finally, reluctantly, the lad held his hands to his sides and backed out the door. "Close it behind you." Shaking his head, Levin turned back to Vaneek and came face-to-face with the pistol. Vaneek must have picked it up while Levin wasn't looking. He raised his hands. "Hello, Vaneek. Please put that down."

"Aud . . . Auditor Levin? Is that you?" Vaneek whispered in a soft voice. "Are you with that brute?"

Levin had always considered Vaneek something of a ward, a little brother he had never had, and the stunned look on his face broke his heart. The pistol in his hand quivered, but he kept it leveled at Levin's face. The poor administrator never stood a chance. In one smooth motion, Levin clasped his hands together and wrested the pistol out of Vaneek's hands.

The boy didn't even acknowledge that he had just been disarmed. Tears streamed down Vaneek's face as he stared at Levin. "All those charges they leveled at you. I didn't believe any of it. When they brought me in to question, I didn't say a damn word. I called them liars and cheats, said you were framed." He shook his head.

Levin pulled out the pistol's energy source and placed each piece on opposite sides of the table. He looked at the girl who was huddled on the bed with her arms crossed over her chest. "Sit down. Please. I'll explain everything."

Vaneek dutifully complied, moving to the bed and putting his arm around the girl's shoulder. He checked a bruise on her cheek and then whispered something into her ear, pulling her protectively close. The anger in his eyes burned brighter than Levin had ever seen on young Vaneek's face.

Levin sat in front of both of them and took a deep breath. This was going to take a lot of explaining. Damn that boy Cole. "First of all, I am so sorry for what happened. This was never my intention. It was wrong and I assume full responsibility for Cole's actions."

Vaneek frowned. "That was Chronman Cole? I did not recognize him."

"A lot has changed."

"It's treason to even speak with you," Vaneek said. "You're putting my Katya and me in jeopardy just by being here."

Levin looked at the woman and smiled. She didn't return the favor. "You two are a lovely couple."

"What are you doing here, Auditor Levin?" Vaneek pressed.

"I want you to know I'm innocent."

"We all knew that already, Auditor. Are you trying to prove it now? If you are, you're wasting your time."

"I agree, son. However, there's more important things at stake." Levin took a deep breath. There was no easy way to explain this. "Vaneek, I need to ask a favor from you. I need your help retrieving an encrypted file from the quarantine archives."

Vaneek frowned. "It's possible, but why, if you're not trying to prove your innocence?"

Levin took a deep breath. "The agency has been compromised. I have the evidence in my personal stores, which should be archived. I need a direct access link to un-encrypt and retrieve my files. I intend to expose the corruption within the agency, and then I intend to put ChronoCom back to its original noble purpose."

"And you want me to help you do it?" Vaneek looked at his girlfriend and then at the mess within the room. "After what just happened?"

"This is important, son."

The young administrator shook his head. "You're asking me to commit treason without so much as an explanation. You have to tell me what's going on and then leave. I will contact you through a comm sub-channel within a day if I decide to help."

"Vaneek, I'm running out of—"

"That's my offer, Auditor. Think of the position you're putting me in. If you really are the man I admire, then you'll accept my terms. You owe me that much."

That was true. Levin was basically asking Vaneek to make himself a possible fugitive and betray all that he believed in. That idiot Cole hadn't made things any easier by coming in like that. Levin walked to the shelf and pulled down a bottle of synthetic wine. He picked out three tins, placed them on the table in front of them, and poured drinks. He raised the tin and took a sip. "Let me start from the beginning."

FORTY-EIGHT

A TRAITOR

Senior Securitate Kuo looked out the port window of the Valkyrie as it descended through the smog clouds hanging over Chicago. Her irritation grew as Earth Central came into sight. The director had the audacity to order her to personally oversee and "discuss" her latest reinforcement and supply acquisition. This must mean he was finally giving her the monitors she had repeatedly asked for. Why else would he summon her here, just to talk?

Her ship made a narrow circle around the building until it hovered fifty meters above the facility's landing pad. Kuo opened the doors and jumped out, plummeting fifty meters and landing on the hard concrete with a crash. Best to get this charade over with. Things were falling apart on the Mist Isle, and she had to get back as soon as possible.

She noticed the hundreds of eyes on her as all activity around the hangar stopped. This was the exact place she had fought Auditor Levin almost a year back. The taste of that defeat was still fresh in her mind. She looked around. Chances were, several of these lowly workers had been there then. Probably some of them had even shot at her. That memory burned. The fact that Levin had twisted the justice system so that they had all escaped still rankled her.

There was a Hephaestus transport in one of the docking bays being loaded with supplies. Lead Moyer was standing near the cargo bay overseeing the transfer. He saw Kuo approach and hurried to meet her.

Moyer bowed. "Greetings, Securitate, it's an honor and pleasure to see you, as always." She knew what the monitor ranks thought of her. The lead monitor must want a job at Valta.

"My supplies," she said briskly. "Any issues?"

He looked over his manifest. "Everything as requested, except for ration counts, of which we were only able to requisition ninety percent, rad shields at eighty-six percent, and blaster recharges at seventy-nine. Nothing we can't fulfill next week."

Kuo admit to being a little surprised. That was actually good, all things considered. "And the five hundred Valta troopers?"

"They arrived last night and are ready to depart with you."

"Excellent, Lead Moyer. What about my request for the five hundred additional monitors?"

Moyer hesitated. "Apologies, Securitate, but—"

"Cut to the chase, Lead. How many am I actually getting?"

"None. Again, director's orders."

"What?"

Moyer bowed. "I'm sorry, Securitate, but the director has put a hold on your request."

"We'll see about that," she spat. "Make sure everything is ready to depart when I am."

She left Moyer standing on the hangar deck while she went to find the old cripple. The nonprofits in the building scurried out of her way as she stormed through the administrator wing. The old man had been fighting her every step of the way. Now, at such a crucial moment, Young had summoned her just to hamstring her. How dare he!

Kuo reached the entrance to his office, created a large white kinetic trunk, and punched in the double doors. She split the trunk into two smaller ones—not an easy feat for space combat exos—and held the larger splintered fragments hovering in the air. She walked through the entrance, past the floating pieces, into Director Young's office.

Young was sitting at his desk reading a leather-bound book. He barely glanced up at her display of force. She had to give the old man credit; he wasn't easily intimidated. She stormed in front of his desk and waited. And then waited some more. She realized her tactical error when he licked his finger and turned the page.

"Did you recall me from the front just to deny—"

He held up a finger and shushed her. To her surprise, she stopped. Then, with a furious scowl, she placed her hand on his desk and powered her exo. The desk cracked down the middle and collapsed into two pieces.

Young lowered the book and stared at her handiwork. He closed the book with a slap and sighed. "That was wood. Real fucking wood. Do you know how hard it is to find an honest-to-abyss wooden desk these days? At least one that isn't moldy, full of termites, or covered in that fake plasti-wood shit they try to pass off as the real thing?"

"You call me back to Earth Central just to refuse my order for additional monitors," she growled. "Let me make myself clear, Director. My request is not a request."

"I denied it just like I denied your psychopathic request to grayon-gas all of the Mist Isle. There's a million people living there. Just because you're losing doesn't mean you get to kill everyone." Young rubbed his chin. "How are you losing to a bunch of wastelanders, anyway?"

Kuo balled her hands into fists. She shouldn't have to answer to him. However, he had what she needed. "The primitives got organized. They've risen up and are working together. My forces are outnumbered twenty to one. There are savages actually flocking to the Mist Isle in droves to volunteer to fight us. I need additional resources!"

"So it's true," Young mused. "The mining operations east of Neo-Pittsburgh have been reporting large migrations of wastelander tribes." He chuckled. "Congratulations, Securitate. You've managed to unite tribes that have been at war for two hundred years. Within the span of a few months. That's no small feat."

"All the more reason to get out of my way. A new organized nation of savages will be dangerous to ChronoCom's control of this planet."

Young put his book aside and got out of his chair. He made a slow circle around his broken desk and faced her, his mangled shoulder drooping badly as he stood in front of her. "What did you think was going to fucking happen when you begin wholesale murdering and enslaving them? Did you think just because you're in your goddamn white shiny suits that they were going to roll over and huddle in the mud while you blew up their homes?"

"How dare you? ChronoCom's contract with Valta—"

"—is being honored," he snapped. "That doesn't mean we'll allow you to misuse our resources, and it sure as hell doesn't mean I'm going to allow you to gas the damn island! Whatever happened to taking that scientist, anyway? I thought she was a desired asset. How are grayon gas and genocide going to get you any closer to acquiring her?"

"That is only as a last resort," she said stiffly. "If Valta is unable to acquire the resource, it sets a poor precedent for others."

"By killing the hundreds of thousands of people who live there," he mused. "You're setting some sort of precedent, all right. In either case, ChronoCom is denying your request for another five hundred monitors at this time and we sure as abyss deny you the use of weapons of mass destruction on Earth. Make do with what you have or get the fuck off the planet."

Kuo's exo flared and surrounded the old man. For a second, she considered ending the old short-sighted cripple's life. Life for the megacorporation employees near the gas giants was harsh. Survival and success were all about aggression and respect. An employee of Valta must wield both in order not only to climb the corporate ladder, but to survive, because there were always people beneath you who wanted your position. Sometimes, in interoffice politics, it was considered acceptable, even approved by leadership, to kill someone.

She could even argue that it was justified. Young was actively and purposely impeding a critical Valta project. There would be problems, however. Young wasn't without rank and stature not only within his agency but with all the major corporations. The director of Earth's time-salvaging operation carried weight and influence.

Interestingly, Young seemed undeterred. "Give it your best shot," he said, resigned. "I've bent over backward for you enough. I draw the line at mass murder."

"You fool," she spat. "Protecting those who do not contribute to humanity's survival is betraying your oath to your agency. I'll see you hanged for this."

There was a knock on the door.

"What!" both of them growled, turning to look at the terrified administrator standing at the door.

"Apologies, Director. Securitate." The administrator bowed several times. "Interrogation room three is ready, Director."

"Come with me, Kuo." Young said, limping out the door and not bothering to look if she was following.

Kuo was not used to following orders outside of headquarters and for a moment considered refusing. Valta was the superior partner in this relationship. To allow a ChronoCom entity the lead lowered her position. However, her curiosity was piqued.

For a moment, she thought they might have captured the one named James Griffin-Mars. Perhaps he had tired of living in the wastes among the savages and turned himself in. A life in Europa in exchange for the scientist was a worthy trade, though chances were, he would have to be taken out shortly after he reached the moon. Europa was a paradise, but like all stable colonies, it had to be tightly managed. An ex-chronman with a history of disorder couldn't be tolerated.

The two walked out of Young's office in the administrator wing and headed to the lower levels. The director walked painfully slowly, though he could hardly be blamed. In the gas giant colonies, unless he was incredibly wealthy or a person of importance, he would have long been put away or forced into a special needs center. Resources were low enough as it was without having to deal with cripples.

To her surprise, Liaison Sourn joined them on the way down. She hadn't even known he was here. The liaison had taken ill during his extended stay on Earth and now preferred to spend his time in off-world hostels, floating white ships that catered only to corporate citizens. Those giant vessels duplicated the comforts of the colonies, providing the clean air, sterile environments, and controlled atmospheres that the civilized world was used to up in space.

"What a pleasant surprise, Liaison," she exclaimed.

"Securitate," he replied with a cool look on his face.

Kuo knew he was angry with her. The past three reports she had filed with him had betrayed an increasingly grim scenario. He had every right to disapprove of her recent performance. He knew her declining status reflected poorly upon him, and unless she could make a proper turnaround soon, both their stocks within the company were bound to suffer. Coupled with her request for grayon gas, which was essentially her ceding project goals, there was little way either of them could report anything positive to the board of directors.

Sourn turned to Young. "I told you to only summon me if it was important. This had better be good." The relationship between the liaison and the director must have soured as well. Young didn't look like he cared, though. Of the three, he seemed to be the only one in a good mood.

They reached the interrogation rooms, and Kuo was brought back to the last time she had been here. She had been in that room on the far end getting the answers she needed from the sniveling handler. Then the High Auditor had stepped in and ruined everything. Her humiliating defeat at the hands of these nonprofits forced her to beg management to permit her to redeem herself by finding this scientist. Now, she was facing another defeat.

The three of them walked into the interrogation room where a metal chair, table, and a young man waited for them. She didn't recognize him; it was neither James Griffin-Mars nor Levin Javier-Oberon. Pity. That would have solved many of her problems. The young man eyed all three of them warily, but his posture was relaxed. He believed he had the upper hand, or at least something to offer or sell. There were no bruises or cuts on his body, and he seemed alert. Good. They hadn't started questioning yet. Kuo preferred to oversee these tasks personally.

"Who is he and why should I care?" Sourn said.

"Tell them what you told me earlier," said Young.

"There's a conspiracy to overthrow the agency, Director. I can get you the traitors," the man said. "Former high auditor Levin came to me—"

"That's internal ChronoCom matters," Young cut in. "Get to the other information."

The young man nodded and turned to Kuo. "I can tell you exactly where in the Mist Isle the temporal anomaly, the one who is also responsible for the wasteland tribes unifying, is located." He looked over at Young, who nodded. "In return I want Europa citizenship and a guaranteed position in the private sector."

Kuo was suddenly alert. If she had that information, the Co-op could stop slogging through the maze of buildings. She could end this blasted project within a day. "Agreed," she called up a map of the Mist Isle through her AI module and projected it onto the table through her eyes. "You'll be richly rewarded if your information is correct. Now, out with it."

The man pointed at an intersection near the central lower region of Manhattan. "This building right there. Right there is the heart of the savages."

Young leaned in to her. "Now you can have the extra monitors you requested. Do your job, Securitate."

FORTY-NINE

LOVE AND WAR

Elise had always been a power-to-the-people kind of girl when it came to government. In her university days, she had protested the rise of dolphin hunting and the dissolution of the Democratic Union's congress. At the time, suspending the people's voice was controversial, and might have even been necessary. The Confederate United States, a newly formed fundamentalist theocracy, had dug in its claws and corrupted the congress, gridlocking the entire country.

Still, the thought that her beloved country was no longer being ruled by the people drove her to march in the streets along with millions of others. The first few months of the Manhattan alliance, Elise had tried to instill this same democratic spirit into her young nation. Right now though, she wanted nothing more than to rule with an iron fist.

She had a stinging headache from the twenty largest tribal chiefs, mayors, teachers, kings, or whatever the Gaia they called themselves arguing over their next plan of action. The Manhattans had won a string of small victories over the past few weeks, having caught the Co-op completely by surprise. However, their enemy had readjusted its strategy and now the blocks between Forty-seventh and Seventy-fifth streets had become a neutral zone of sorts as the two sides fell into a stalemate. What her fledgling nation had to do right now was bring more tribes into the fold and push the enemy back. Instead, more often of late, these meet-

ings had dissolved into bickering about who got what buildings to live in and which tribe got how much of their shared resources.

Right now, six of the tribes were arguing over which of them were going to receive Levin's latest salvage of phase pistols from the twenty-fourth century. Elise had to carefully distribute the equipment among them. Every group had a convincing argument for why they needed the racks of forty weapons the most. The salvages were a large part of their recent success and an even larger part of why many of the tribes had orig-inally agreed to join the nation. Whether they remained if the salvages dried up was up to her. The Nation's unity was unraveling slowly, because their early success had quelled the desperation of many of the tribes. Now, they were forgetting why they had all agreed to work together in the first place.

Elise looked to either side, and it told her all she needed to know about how important this meeting was. To her left, Titus was busy jotting down a complex math equation. The old man had been obsessing over ways to build a new array of solar panels on the very tops of the tallest buildings and route them to the Manhattan Nation's grid. The current output, due to the constant heavy fog, was a fraction of what they needed. Elise's lab itself took up nearly 10 percent of what was available.

To her right, Grace was leaning into Teacher Crowe, chatting with her head close to his. The High Scion had taken a shine to Crowe and the two had been seen together more often than not. When Crowe found out who she actually was, he had nearly prostrated himself before her as if she were a religious figure. Typical ex-chronman. For a bunch of people who hated their previous jobs, they all seemed to think very highly of the woman who created the industry.

That was all fine by Elise. The two old lovebirds were cute together. The teacher was fifteen years younger than Grace, but that was how she liked her men. Better have her focus her affections on Crowe than James, anyway. However, if the two smartest people in the room were completely ignoring the conversation, it probably wasn't worth listening to.

Elise's personal life wasn't going much better than her leadership role. That was something she never thought she'd hear herself say. Elise had gone to visit James every day, though had stayed outside his residence. She passed the time sitting next to his door, eyes closed and listening.

She sometimes could hear him bumble around in his room, sometimes crying, sometimes snoring, usually just nothing. He probably didn't know she was there and was upset that she hadn't visited him yet. It made her feel better to know that she was close.

It was hard on Elise to stay away from him. Even harder when she could hear his agony. Titus had warned her that the first few days were the most difficult, and that James should be kept from his triggers for a while. He told her to keep their interactions to a minimum until the worst had passed. She hoped that happened soon. The Nation could really use someone like him right now. More important, his well-being was a constant weight on her. There was nothing she would rather do right now than drop this stupid meeting and sit at his bedside.

To make things worse, Sasha had become inconsolable. The ten-year-old had been clamoring to visit him as well, but so far, Elise had forbidden it. It wouldn't do the girl, who was still recovering from her own sickness, any good to see her brother like this. It was difficult to explain what they were treating her brother for and why she wasn't allowed to see him.

Elise sighed. She obviously made a lousy mother.

She leaned in to Titus. "Grand Juror, how is our patient coming along?"

Without missing a beat with his formula, he answered, "Considering it's only been three weeks, surprisingly well. The man is a flaming machine. I took him off his medications this morning. I believe the withdrawal phase is over."

Her hopes rose. "So he's almost cured?"

Titus faced her. "James will never be cured. It is something he will have to struggle with for the rest of his life. Now is the difficult part, where you and his loved ones come in."

"What do I need to do?" she asked.

"You need to be strong, and you need to show you're there for him."

"You mean I can visit him?"

A smile appeared on Titus's face. "As soon as this meeting is over."

Elise stood up and addressed the still-bickering leaders in a loud voice. "That's enough for today. Why don't we continue this conversation later? For now, Baron Kobi, pull your knickerbockers on the western blocks back until the good governor Mang and his marines can reinforce you. The rest of you, let's put the plan on that forward outpost at the Grand

Central Terminal for first thing on tomorrow's agenda." She rapped the table with small knuckles. "Meeting adjourned."

"Well, that's one way to end the meeting," Titus quipped.

She placed a hand on his shoulder and gave it a light squeeze as she hurried out. These high-level coordination meetings weren't that necessary anyway. All of these tribes knew how to fight in dense urban areas. All they really needed was someone to gather them all together, point them toward their common enemy, and sometimes babysit or referee their squabbling.

She made a detour up to the lab, where Sasha was going over the latest enzyme counts on the new batch of vaccines Grace and she had cooked up. Elise was trying to spend more time in the lab, though the responsibilities and demands of the Nation made that difficult. Mostly, she was able to sneak in some very early and late hours every day to oversee the progress and relay instructions. It wasn't enough. Fortunately, Grace and Sasha were here to back her up.

Now that the Mother of Time wasn't flitting all over the solar system, their research had picked up again. Sasha was learning quickly, as children often did. The girl definitely had a knack for science. She worked tirelessly and asked a lot of questions, which was a great temperament for this line of work. She was also fearless, which probably was not, but that was something that would be reigned in with age.

"Hey, Sasha," Elise said. "How do the new samples look?"

The girl handed her a tablet. "I recorded them all. I think they look good. Better than the last batch that killed everything."

Elise took the tablet and studied the numbers. "Better" was an understatement. Far better, in fact. The most recent vaccine had been able to hop over six different strands of Earth Plague. The only ones that it had issues with were in areas over thirty-five degrees Celsius, which unfortunately these days was more than half the planet. A few modifications to the formula would be necessary. She placed the tablet on the table.

"Go wash up. I have a surprise for you."

Sasha gave Elise one look and brightened. Elise's grin grew as the girl let out a high-pitched squeal and dashed off to rinse the gunk from her hands. There was only one surprise that Sasha wanted, and they both knew Elise wouldn't tease her with anything less. She waited until Sasha had scrubbed her hands thoroughly so she no longer smelled like ammonia and manure—they were dealing with Earth Plague samples—and then together, the two bounded to the sixty-sixth floor to what all the Elfreth now referred to as the chronman level.

She saw Hory and Chawr sitting in front of the door playing a game of finger blades. The two stopped as soon as they noticed her coming and stashed the knife. They knew how much she disapproved of that stupid game. "Oldest." Hory bowed.

"One day, when you two cut yourselves and go running to the infirmary to get fixed up, I'm just going to save the bandages and lop off the finger."

Chawr held up both hands and wiggled them. "Still all here, Oldest."

She rolled her eyes. "How's Elder James?"

"Quiet," Hory said. "We feared for today after Elder Titus took him off of his medicine. However, he is in good spirits. Earlier, he ran with us around the floor."

Elise had heard of that. Out of boredom or something, James had begun teaching a few of the guardians and fights how to fight. Within a week, word had spread throughout the entire Nation, and now, fighters from several tribes came to take classes. Supposedly, he had over a hundred students already. What a peculiar development. Elise considered this a fantastic turn of events. She couldn't imagine how boring it must be to be under house arrest for so long. Not only that, this was a fine way for him to rehabilitate his image among the tribes.

She put her arm around Sasha's shoulder. "We'd like to see him, please."

Chawr opened the door and let her through. Elise felt her heart beat faster as she approached his door. It felt like forever since the last time she had seen him. The two had certainly been apart for longer before. Some of his jobs, like the one when he went to retrieve Levin, had kept him away from her for over two months.

This time felt different though. Previously, they were involuntarily apart because of distance and work. He was gallivanting around Earth and the solar system while she worked on the cure. This time, the separation was voluntary. She had chosen, of her own volition and for his good, to extract herself until he was better. Did he understand why she had had to do this? Was he angry with her? A hundred worries ran through her mind as she walked to the door. She hesitated as she lifted her hand to knock.

Sasha didn't give her a chance to complete the motion. She pushed the door open wide and charged inside. "James!"

Elise heard a cry of surprise and then his voice calling Sasha's name. She leaned on the doorway, crossed her arms, and watched as Sasha leaped into James's arms. Her breath caught in her throat as he picked her up and twirled her around. What she saw was a stark contrast to the perpetual gray, brown, and rot that seemed to permeate through the isle. Maybe it was a little providence or a trick of the eye as a rare bit of the afternoon sun shined on him, but there was something alive and colorful, even magical, about that moment. It gave Elise hope that things in this miserable present could get better.

James hadn't noticed her, so she studied him, trying to see if she could tell a difference between the last time she had seen him, half drunk and sobbing, and now. The first thing that came to mind was that he looked rested, healthy, even. The second thing she noticed was that he looked thinner. His face was less bloated and splotchy, and his eyes weren't quite as dark, no longer sunken in like a raccoon's.

She gave the two Griffins some time, a brother and sister born six years apart who now had a quarter-century difference in age. James was more a father to Sasha now than brother, and it showed. After a few minutes, Elise finally spoke. "Have they been feeding you enough?"

James looked up and noticed her for the first time. His face twitched as their eyes met. Time slowed down, and she wondered how he was going to react. Was he angry at her for locking him up? James picked up Sasha and carried her over to Elise.

He leaned in close and kissed her on the mouth. "About time you came in to visit. I was tired of you waiting outside my door."

Her mouth dropped. "How . . . how did you know?"

He looked over at Chawr and Hory standing behind her. "See. You see those guards standing outside my door? That's where you made your mistake, Oldest. Those are my guys." Those two fools grinned from ear to ear until she shot them a glare. They managed to look sort of abashed until she smiled.

"Close the door," she ordered.

The three of them moved the family reunion to the couch. Elise sat on one side of him and Sasha snuggled up to him on the other. She studied his reactions as Sasha spilled out her life over the past few weeks to him, from Elise teaching her geometry to Franwil's continuing efforts to groom her as an herbalist to Rima showing her how to make a bow. The smile on his face fell once when Sasha told him about the new Flatiron boy who had been teasing her and always brought her flowers. In Elise's opinion, the girl should be a storyteller, because her tales were getting taller and taller.

James caught her staring. "What's so funny?" he asked.

"Nothing," she said, moving closer to him. "I think you'll make a great dad."

The three of them spent the rest of the afternoon together until Bria and Laurel came to relieve Chawr and Hory, and to bring up James's evening meal.

"I'll be back tomorrow," she said, throwing her arms around his neck and giving him a last kiss. "You keep on getting better."

"How much longer do I need to stay here?" he asked. "This floor is driving me crazy."

"Soon," she said. "Titus says in a few days." She paused. "You know I love you, right?"

He squeezed her tightly to him. "That's the only thing that kept me—"

The All Galaxy shook and the windows rattled. Everyone froze. The skyscraper rumbled again, this time followed by the sound of multiple explosions. A few seconds later, Chawr burst into the room. "Oldest, we are under attack by the Co-op."

"Where?" James asked.

"Everywhere!"

"Oh, no, they found us," Elise gasped. Both she and James stood up and headed for the door.

Elise pushed Sasha into Bria's arms. "Take her to the lab. There's a storeroom in the back that has a hidden cubbyhole. Sasha knows where it is. If you find Grace and Titus, take them with you." She grabbed James by the hand and dragged him out the door. "I guess you're getting out earlier than expected."

FIFTY

THE MEETING

Levin had every intention of honoring his agreement with Vaneek and waiting patiently for his former assistant to contact him, but he questioned his decision more and more with each passing day. Without a backup plan for how to obtain the encrypted files with his painstaking research of how far corporate influence went in Chron Com, he didn't have any other choice. Even so, he had nearly lost hope when he finally did hear from Vaneek a week later.

"Midnight. Cargo dock wing, D-Lio," was all Vaneek said before going silent.

Levin pulled up the blueprint of Earth Central on his AI band. D-Lio was a rarely-utilized underground hangar at the far end of the south wing of Earth Central, usually reserved for storing mothballed vessels: generation ships, sun beamers, and terraformers. Surprisingly, a large number of pleasure crafts, space yachts and the like, were housed there as well, their resource consumption too high for modern use. In any case, it was a strange rendezvous point. Not like Levin had much of a choice. With few other options, he had to trust Vaneek.

Levin looked over at Cole. "We're a go for tonight. Be ready."

Cole, sitting on a chair with his feet up on the railing, grunted. "So the skinny twerp got back to you after all."

His nephew had reverted to hostility after the situation at the underground residences. Whatever goodwill Levin thought he had built since pulling him out of Nereid was fleeting. Now, the sullen, angry Cole had returned. It was a shame. Levin thought they had made progress while in Chicago. They were bound to have ups and downs. Levin decided this was just a down period.

"Where is the rendezvous point?" Cole asked. He frowned when Levin told him. "That's out in the middle of nowhere. There's no way the quarantine archives are there."

"It doesn't matter. If Vaneek wants to meet there, we'll do it," Levin said. "He's our only chance to break into the archives. Let's not blow it."

He had considered telling Cole to stay behind. As much as he wanted a gun to watch his back, his nephew wasn't reliable. That violent outburst with Vaneek was so over-the-top it made Levin question Cole's mental state. Still, he was family. To tell him to stay behind at this crucial moment would likely shatter their relationship forever, and Cole wouldn't be here when he returned.

Cole had already disappeared for an entire day shortly after the incident with Vaneek. Levin had thought the last family he had was gone forever, but his nephew returned that night. Levin admitted he was surprised when Cole walked through the door. When asked, Cole just said he had needed to blow off some steam. He even reluctantly apologized for his behavior. It was better than nothing at this point. Levin forgave him immediately, because that's what family did. Or at least that's what family should do.

Right now, they were holed up in one of the beach slums along Lake Michigan two kilometers north of ChronoCom campus. The shanty houses here, frequently flooded by heavy rains, were home to vagrants, the drug-addled, and the poor. They were too violent and worth too little for the local authorities to bother patrolling. Their rickety one-room shack was tight and rancid, but after half a year in the Amazon Penal Colony and then half more in the Mist Isle, both of them were used to such miserable accommodations.

This area was also advantageous because Levin had parked the *Frankenstein* close by at the only place he considered safe from identification or theft: a hundred meters out into the lake and fifty meters underwater. The bottom of the lake was thick with wreckage, junk, and Earth Plague. In some places, the refuse was piled so high, it broke the water's surface. Levin had maneuvered the collie until it rested between two piles of garbage and then used the exo to carry him and Cole to land. It made for an easy escape if they were ever found.

Levin went over the blueprints and mapped out a route to the wing on a piece of paper. He and Cole spent the rest of the evening going over the plan, making sure they had memorized all the exit points, backup rendezvous points, and contingencies in case things went south. Being overprepared was ChronoCom's mantra. They were still Academy-trained former chronmen.

"Hey," Levin said, offering Cole a hand. "We get out of this alive. Together." Cole hesitated a beat before clasping hands. Levin pulled him close. "End of the day, we're family. We'll make it work."

"Yes, Uncle."

The two set off for ChronoCom campus shortly after ten in the evening. The entire city shut down after dark to preserve energy, so the streets were quiet and dark. They crept through the city's deserted beach until they found an entrance underground and then followed a series of blue tunnels down to a lower set of purple ones, past dimly lit heavily trafficked passages filled with vagrants and night market vendors sitting shoulder to shoulder on the sides.

Levin had powered down his atmos and exo to conserve levels, having been used to the uncleanliness within the ruins of Manhattan, but the stench in these poorly ventilated and heavily occupied underground tunnels was overpowering. He tolerated it for nearly an hour as they wandered through a veritable maze until finally reaching the blue tunnels again. He breathed a sigh of relief when they emerged on the surface just northwest of the ChronoCom campus.

The two cut back east and then south through a rundown residential area. The main groupings of the city's darkened skyscrapers could be seen to the north, jutting up to the sky like misshapen black teeth against the slightly lighter night. That meant visibility, unlike most days, was good. A bad night to be sneaking around.

They continued, moving through alleyways and broken streets until they finally reached ChronoCom campus. They slowed their pace and crept forward with more caution. The campus was patrolled by monitors, but they weren't difficult to avoid. Nighttime patrols were usually punishment, and no one took that job seriously. After all, who was stupid enough to commit a crime near the agency's base of power?

A breeze brought in the stench of sulfur and rot from the clusters of giant smokestacks to the west. Behind them, loud snaps and pops like gunfire echoed in the air. Levin motioned for Cole to pause inside the shadow of one of the buildings. Other than the sounds of cracking far in the distance, the only audible sound was the whistle of the visible gray wind that drew lines in the air. When he was sure their path was clear, Levin signaled for them to continue.

They dashed between the shadows of buildings and towers as the misshapen form of Earth Central loomed larger and larger. Several blocks and three patrols later, they reached the southernmost building connecting to the main building and continued around the perimeter until they found an entrance with a large, flaked-off D over the door.

Levin pressed his ear to it and listened. He heard nothing but the shrill whistle overhead. He looked at Cole and counted his fingers down from three. The door opened with a long creak and Cole, blaster rifle pressed against his shoulder, crept in. Levin waited a beat and followed.

The cavernous room had faint moonlight pouring through small slit windows where the walls met the roof. They could see the outline of a ship, a space yacht by the looks of it, covered by a tarp. The smell of oil and dust lingered in the air. Levin tapped Cole twice on the shoulder and pointed to the east side of the room. Levin walked the perimeter on the west.

Staying low to the ground, he went two-thirds the length of the building before a small light between the shadows of two ships caught his eye. He cut in to it and found Vaneek standing alone, nervously pacing back and forth.

The boy gave a start and looked his way. "Who's there?"

Holding his hands up, Levin walked into the light. "Thanks for agreeing to see me."

"Auditor Levin," Vaneek said, visibly relieved. "You're on time. Of course. Come with me."

"Where are we going? This can't be where the quarantine archives are located."

Vaneek looking nervous, chuckled. "This is just the easiest way to sneak you in. Come on, we're heading two more levels underground."

"Hang on," Levin said. "Let me recall Cole."

The young administrator fidgeted. "Does he have to come?"

"I'm in hearing range," Cole said inside Levin's head. "Your voices are echoing all over the room. Go ahead. I have sights on him and can keep an eye out on you from the shadows."

"Will do, Cole," Levin thought back. "Hey, thanks again for following through with this and watching my back. It means a lot."

"I'm just not going to let that little shit get the jump on Javier-Oberon. That's all."

Levin nodded to Vaneek and together, they headed further east, past the skeletons of several more ships, until they reached a staircase heading down to the sublevel of the building. There, more ships resided, most in worse condition than the ones above. This must be where the agency kept dead collies for parts. Hundreds of wrecks littered the room, some covered in so many layers of dust he couldn't make out what they were. Levin couldn't help but feel the many blackened portholes staring eerily at him as he passed by. They continued through the maze of ships until they reached a small clearing.

"What is going on?" Levin asked.

Vaneek held up the light. "He's here."

Dozens of lights shined brightly on him from every direction. It was a trap! Levin powered on his exo and prepared to punch through the ceiling. However, he noticed at least twenty other exos power on as well, all of them orange. He was surrounded by auditors.

Julia appeared out of the darkness. "Stand down, Levin."

Levin turned to Vaneek standing next to him, the betrayal painful, but not completely unexpected. He wanted to say something, either out of anger or regret. It didn't matter. This was how his life would end. In the middle of the night in an old warehouse. Without even a fight, for he had already decided that he wasn't going to fight Julia again. Not like it would make a lick of difference with all these exos here. He didn't stand a chance.

"I sought Auditor Julia's advice," Vaneek blubbered. "I didn't know what else to do."

Levin turned to her and held his arms up, exposing his bands. "As agreed, the next time you see me."

Julia rolled her eyes. "You're so damn histrionic, Levin." She walked up to him and pulled a metal device out of her netherstore container. He recognized it as a data reservoir when she placed it in front of him. "Your encryption key, Auditor Levin."

His confusion was followed by a small spark of hope as he punched in the 143-character code to decrypt his personal files. As soon as he did, Julia put her hands on the reservoir and spoke in a clear voice, "It's sent. Analyze and review."

He took a step toward her. "I have a master summary list you can access—"

The exo around her flared. "Don't move, Levin. Your life right now depends on what is in this reservoir. If it's not exactly what you told me, I'm hauling you straight to Young."

The next ten minutes stretched in the darkness. Someone behind him gasped. Another to his right cursed. Within minutes, the chatter in the room grew as the group surrounding him grumbled about his evidence. A silhouette stepped toward him, as did a few more until he could make out who they were. He recognized Hameel, head of Handler Operations; Moyer, the Lead Monitor; Rowe, High Auditor of the space sector; and Marn, High Auditor of Ganymede. A few moments later, as the conversation intensified and the crowd gathered around him, he realized that almost half of Earth's ChronoCom leadership was here.

"Cole," Levin thought as he waited. "How does it look from your position? I'm here with a group of seniors within the agency."

"Things are dead quiet," Cole replied. "Everything going all right down there?"

"So far. Stand by. This could take a while. Let me know if it gets hot topside."

"So you aren't full of shit." Julia sounded resigned. "You were never one to bluff, but I wasn't sure you weren't trying to con me, all things considered."

"This was a test?" he said. "You believe me? Why didn't you just retrieve what I asked when we met?"

"Don't be absurd," she said. "I'm not risking treason on your word alone. However, when Vaneek came and told me what you wanted him to do, I realized you might be telling the truth. I spoke with the trusted leadership within the agency"—she pointed at the others around them—"who are similarly disenchanted. We needed your encryption key to unlock the information, so we set up this meeting."

"The question I have," Moyer said, stepping forward, "is what are we going to do about it? I'm losing monitors every day fighting in the quagmire in New York. My people's lives shouldn't be wasted for the megacorporations' profits."

"Nearly sixty percent of all chronmen operations these days are commissioned by the corporations," Hameel added. "Fatality rates of the chronmen average sixteen percent higher on those jobs."

Rowe, likely the highest-ranking person there, asked Levin, "You wanted this information. You must have a plan. Let's hear it."

Levin looked at the group. It was small but influential. A good place to begin. "I want to start a coup, starting with Earth. We restore ChronoCom to its intended role of working for the greater good of mankind, without the taint of the megacorporations."

"The agency's main leadership all reside on Europa," Marn said. "Sleeping right next to the very corrupting influence we're trying to pry the agency from."

"We replace the entire leadership, then," Julia said.

"Earth has always been the key to salvaging anyway," Levin said. "We all know that. Whoever controls the planet's salvage controls the agency."

"Earth is still too large for us to handle, especially with this small group," said Hameel.

The conservation dissolved again into a free-for-all of opinions on the next best step. For the first time, it was clear that many in the senior hierarchy had a general dissatisfaction with the agency's direction. Everyone had thought that they were alone and been fearful of voicing their concerns. Levin's actions had broken the dam. At first, people shared their stories, and then, as often happens with a group of leaders and problem solvers, they all turned to solutions. The talk got louder and louder until arguments broke out.

"The chron database," Hameel said. "The chron database is key to all of ChronoCom's operations. If we take that over, as well as its backup on Luna, we control the agency."

"Two points of control," Moyer mused. "That we can manage. We might even be able to do this before the rest of the agency knows what is happening."

"Wait, you want to pull this off tonight?" Julia frowned. "We need to think this through. Carefully plan things out."

"We're a thousand meters from the chron database," Hameel replied. "If we leave Central, we'll never make it this close again. Otherwise, once Young sees that we've all disappeared, he'll know something is up and beef up security. Tonight is our best shot."

"Forget the database," Vaneek said, his voice drowned out by the chatter. "We need to take over the Hops instead."

"I'm with Julia on this," Rowe said. "We have thirty noncombatants with us. We can't put everyone in danger."

"We've all been through the Academy," Jan, the elderly lead statistician, said. "I still know how to use an abyss-damn gun. We'll fight." The guy actually looked like he was having fun.

"What do you think, Levin?" Rowe asked.

Levin looked at the group and considered their options. Moyer was right. Right now was probably their best chance to seize the chron database. Julia was right as well. They were in no shape for a frontal attack on the most heavily guarded data center in the solar system. However, they would be in even worse shape tomorrow once the agency learned of the insurrection and went on high alert. They would never be able to step foot into Earth Central again. Now was their chance. "Let's finish this tonight."

"We need to take over the Hops," Vaneek piped up again, louder, just loud enough for all to hear. The talk died down and everyone's attention turned to him. Looking nervous, he stepped next to Levin. "The only way we can pull this off is if the rest of the agency knows what's going on."

"What will taking over the Hops do?" Rowe asked.

"The people in this group," Vaneek gestured at them, "are some of the most respected people in the agency. You don't think that means something to the rank and file? We all look up to you. The problem right now is none of them knows what is happening. The Hops is the only place we can broadcast this information." He pointed at Levin. "Show them those files of yours. Let them decide."

"Hedging on their loyalty is a huge gamble," said Julia.

Moyer nodded. "No, the boy's right. The rest of the agency's loyalty is the only thing worth gambling on. If we can't convince them, we've lost anyway. Besides, let's be honest. What are you going to do even if you take the chron database? Holding the chron database hostage is a joke. Everyone knows none of us will risk damaging it. It would effectively destroy ChronoCom's only justification to be the managing body for time traveling. It would just give every corporation a free license to make their own jumps."

Moyer was probably right on that count. If it came down to it, Levin wouldn't follow through with his threat. If that was so clear to the lead monitor, it would be clear to Young as well. Levin scanned the group of people huddled around him. He hadn't expected things to move so quickly, but if it had to be, there was no finer group to fight with than the one around him. "We'll go now."

Rowe nodded. "Gather the loyal ranks and chains. The tiers probably won't get involved. However, with the element of surprise, we might not need them. That leaves just the administrators to take care of."

Levin put an arm around Vaneek's shoulder. "Good thinking, son."

Vaneek smiled. "Thanks, Auditor Levin. I'm just proud to be part of this—"

A red arc shot across the room and seemed to go right through the young administrator. The smile on his face wavered, and he looked down. Then his knees gave, and Levin had to catch him before he fell to the ground.

A figure walked from the source of the shot to the edge of the lit area. Cole, holding a blaster rifle, spat on the ground. "I've been waiting to do that. Good riddance to that little bastard."

"What did you just do?" Levin gasped, jaws dropping. "Why?"

Cole shrugged. "Because I don't like him. Never did, and besides, like you always tell me, Uncle, I'm earning my keep."

Levin's blood froze when a white glow burst from his body. Suddenly, dozens of exos, most yellow with a sprinkle of oranges, bloomed all around them. A small orb floated in the air above them and a three-dimensional representation of Director Young appeared.

The orb floated in the air and made a slow circle, carrying the image of Young with it. He appraised the entire group. "This is a bigger disaster than I thought. Rebels, at a critical time, when humanity's survival hangs in the balance. How could all of you possibly conceive of doing this? I am disappointed in so many of you. I'm sorry it had to come to this."

"It's at this very critical time that we must do this, Young," Levin replied. "We continue down this path and—"

Young cut him off. "Silence! You're a traitor and a criminal, Levin."

"How would you like us to deal with the traitors, Director?" Cole asked.

Young sighed. "This is going to be such a mess to clean up. The agency will be forced to replace a large portion of the leadership, but I guess it can't be helped. Cole, your new employer has already given you orders. See to it."

FIFTY-ONE

ASSAULT ON ONE GALAXY

The ten Hephaestus transports, twelve Valkyries, and forty collies swooped toward the cloud-shaped fog that shrouded the Mist Isle. From a distance, it looked like a giant misshapen dome filled with a living mist that writhed along the edges. Only the tops of the tallest buildings on the island protruded past the surface of the cloud.

The small armada came to a stop over the dome, hovering a few meters above its surface. The exhaust of the ships punched little dents into the fog but could never seem to disperse it. The fleet moved in a tight, flat, circular formation and adjusted its positioning until each ship was hovering at an exact assigned spot. As if on cue, they all moved together six hundred meters south. They readjusted again, rotating a few degrees clockwise. The circular formation was just large enough to cover a two-city-block radius around the All Galaxy Tower.

"Senior," a voice buzzed inside Kuo's head. "We're directly above the stated coordinates."

The rear bay doors of the Hephaestus opened, letting in a high-pitched shriek as a blast of cold air swept through the hull. Kuo walked to the edge of the ramp and looked down at the roiling mist just below her feet. She knelt down and ran her hands through the gray mist. Not wet, not cool, not anything. Just there. She looked up at the lighter clouds lazily floating through the air. This EMP fog was a fog in name only. How it came to be was a mystery, an ancient weapon and technology long since forgotten, but it had been such a constant thorn in her side. She would be happy when this project was over.

"All Co-op," she broadcast through her comm module. "No incendiaries or explosives. Watch your marks. The temporal anomaly is to be taken alive. Any harm done to her is an immediate forfeiture of contract. All others are expendable. Eliminate with extreme prejudice."

Kuo pulled up the schematics of the city overlaid by the location of her ships. The All Galaxy Tower was at the exact center of this circle. This time, the temporal anomaly would not escape. The traitor had provided detailed thought images of what the scientist looked like, as well as key intelligence for the attack. In her eyes, while the information was valuable, Kuo did not think it was worth what he demanded. However, that problem could be addressed at a later date.

"All ships, once you unload your cargo, pull outside the EMP fog to patrol the perimeter and await further instructions. Any savage trying to flee the island is to be cut down," she ordered. "Commence insertion on . . . mark."

The armada dropped into the dark fog simultaneously. Some ships fell just above the waterline while others stopped at strategic points: bridges, entrances, decks, and balconies. Every one of them unloaded their cargo in unison, pouring thousands of Valta troopers and ChronoCom monitors into the buildings against an unknown number of savages. Not that it mattered. Not this time. Previously, the savages were able to nullify the Co-op's superior firepower and skill with numbers and the ability to retreat into the haze and the Mist Isle's jungle. Now they had nowhere to run.

Her forces had the entire city block blanketed at every point of escape. Now all they had to do was methodically squeeze these savages until something materialized. It was just a matter of time before they found the scientist. The sooner Kuo finished with this unpleasant assignment, the sooner she could leave this hellscape and return home.

Kuo stepped out of the Hephaestus onto the main bridge connecting to the All Galaxy Tower on the north. Nine of her trooper pods were cleaning out the building behind her while three monitors squads held the connecting bridges. According to Cole, this floor, the thirty-fourth, was the linchpin of the operation. If the Co-op took this floor, then they had all the higher floors isolated and controlled the heart of this upstart wastelander nation.

She walked down the length of the bridge to the middle, where a group of her forces had stopped in their tracks. Kuo frowned. This heavily armed pod should have no issues cutting through the sticks, stones, and whatever the abyss these primitives were armed with. Yet, already, the shockers had activated their shells, a translucent hardened energy shield the length and width of a man that connected at the left forearm, and closed in ranks.

She approached the pod captain. "What is the problem?"

He pointed at the pile of trash at the end of the bridge. At first, it looked like nothing more than junk loosely stacked. Then she noticed the people standing near the top of it. In the center of the pile was a wide metal double door.

"You should be able to blow through that little problem," she said.

"If you look closely, Senior," he said.

Kuo did, and noticed the faint silvery glimmer in front of the barricade. She scowled. "That's our field cover, isn't it?"

The pod captain nodded. "Same signature. Probably stolen from the York outpost. The fact that we're on a bridge limits our options. It will be difficult to break through without explosives."

"No explosives. We cannot risk hurting the scientist," she said. "Have your men tested the edges?"

He nodded. "End to end. I sent two for close proximity readings. They were hit with blaster and beam fire for their efforts."

An interesting development. Not only had these savages managed to steal and repurpose a Valta one-way static shield, they were also now using the megacorporation's firearms. This made the task more difficult. She would just have to take matters into her own hands.

"Have your shockers ready to charge," she said.

Kuo shot straight up twenty meters through the glassless frame of the bridge into the haze, and veered straight at the skyscraper. The side of the building gave her minimal resistance as she punched through the wall, raining down rubble as she landed in the interior behind the barricade.

The hallways here were packed with savages racing around like mice. Waves of them charged at her even as dozens more opened fire with whatever weapons they had on hand. The initial volley that struck her shield caused her exo to light up the darkened hallway. She saw blaster fire, wrist beams, projectiles, even a primitive arrow burst into flames as it struck the white glowing surface of the shield. Each of the hits caused an expanding ring from the point of impact. The concentrated fire became so dense, she couldn't see outside the flashes of her exo.

Kuo checked her levels. They were already at 81 percent. The battle was actually taking a toll. She turned her attention to the barricade and was suddenly flung to the side. She crashed into the wall with extreme force. Her exo wavered for a second as she readjusted her levels. Down to 68 percent. What had just hit her?

She glanced down the hall and saw a large black cannon mounted on a wagon. If she didn't know better . . . No, that was a fusion cannon designed to be mounted on top of Valkyries. How did these savages get ahold of that? More importantly, how did they manage to find the energy to power the weapon?

She had far underestimated these savages' capabilities. Well, no matter. Kuo launched herself straight at the cannon, bowling over bodies as if they weren't there. She had to be careful. Chances were, the scientist she sought wasn't among the crowd, but she couldn't leave anything to chance. Kuo reached the cannon and created a white trunk. She wrapped it around the cannon and lifted it in the air, floating it with her as she made her way back to the barricade. Dozens of small sparks lit up the edges of her shield as small electrical bursts continued to chip away at her exo.

She hurtled straight at the barricade. She aimed for its center and released the long black cylinder-shaped weapon. The resulting explosion sent an expanding ring of pressure that bowled over the unfortunate savages in the vicinity. It was followed by a rolling cloud of fire and smoke that swept over her. For several seconds, she watched from inside the perfect sphere of the shield as smoke and flames curled around its edges. Outside it, the savages screamed in panic as fiery debris rained down all around them. A moment after that, her shocker pod was through, and then the real massacre began.

Kuo, still hovering five meters above, watched as her forces fanned out in their phalanxes in small lines. These particular shock pods specialized in riot control, and that was what these savages were. Nothing more than a rabble of barbarians charging against better-disciplined, better-trained, and better-armed professional soldiers. Within minutes, her forces had acquired a foothold in one of two main entrances. Within five, though outnumbered ten to one, they were pushing the savages back.

She stayed high above ground, overlooking the battle. It was dark up there and most of the savages had quickly forgotten her, especially with the massively armored white shockers bearing down on them.

Her levels were already lower than she had anticipated this early into the fight, but her involvement in this phase of the operation was no longer necessary. Ten minutes later, two monitor squads arrived from the north, followed by three from the west. She pulled the shocker pod back to rest and ordered the monitors to clean up the leftovers. The shockers would be needed elsewhere.

Within two hours, most of the heavy fighting on the thirty-fourth floor was over. Kuo walked down the hall, inspecting the results. The shockers were at 65 percent strength, which was surprising. She had lost forty-nine in the initial attack. The enemy, however, must have lost three hundred here, if not more. There were so many bodies lying about, it was hard to keep track.

She stood over the body of the captain and then looked over at the next man down the line. "You're pod captain now. When will your men be ready to move again?"

"Within the twenty, Senior." He saluted.

She nodded and dismissed him. One of the monitor squads canvassing the floor brought out an old man from one of the back rooms. They dropped him at her feet. One look at him told Kuo this man was more important than the usual rabble.

"Your name?" she asked.

"I am Teacher Crowe. You are standing in my home. Allow me to offer you a seat." He picked himself up and looked around, sadness painted on his face. "There will be many ghosts here tonight. Does this slaughter bring you the satisfaction you seek?"

Kuo ignored the question. "Where is the temporal anomaly? The scientist?"

"I do not know what you speak of. Please. Allow me to offer you a seat."

"The woman. Elise, the one from the past."

The old man shook his head again. "I do not know what you speak of. Allow me to offer you a—"

Kuo grabbed him by the front of the shirt and dragged him across the room to where the survivors of the battle—roughly two hundred of these primitives—were sitting on the floor. She threw him to the ground. She took a sidearm from the nearest trooper and pointed it at the nearest savage. "Tell me what I want to know or I start shooting these people one by one."

"I do not know what you speak of. Please. Allow me to offer you a seat."

Kuo pulled the trigger, striking a woman in the chest. "Let's try this again."

The old man struggled to keep his head high as tears fell down his face. Somehow, he managed to smile. "I do not know what you speak of. Allow me—"

She pulled the trigger again, this time shooting an injured young man. "His blood is on your hands, Teacher. In fact, if you tell me what I want, my army and I will be gone within the hour. We will leave you in peace. What do you say?"

Pain wracked the old man's face as he bowed his head. He squeezed his eyes shut, his body quivering. Kuo was getting impatient. Dozens of battles were still raging all around the block and she still had to locate the temporal anomaly.

She pulled the trigger five times, killing five more prisoners. Each time, the old man repeated the same phrase. Finally, Kuo turned the gun on him. "This is your last chance. The fate of more than you hangs in the balance today. I will rest easy regardless of what you say, so do not push me, old man. Tell me where this woman is."

Crowe wiped his face with a bloody sleeve. He turned his back to her and stared for a long time at his people, sitting on the floor. They all looked back at him. He smiled and nodded.

"I am Teacher Crowe of the Flatirons tribe. Allow me to offer you a seat."

Kuo pulled the trigger, and his body fell to the floor. Irritated, she looked over at the lead monitor. "Kill them all."

His mouth dropped and he took a step back. "Securitate, they've all been disarmed. They're prisoners. We don't—"

She created a trunk and picked up the monitor by the neck, lifting him off the ground. "I don't know how your nonprofit agency runs your operations," she spat, "but Valta military does not tolerate insubordination. Do you understand me, Lead Monitor, or do I have to publicly execute you to set an example of how a real military behaves?"

"Yes, Securitate," he managed.

"Senior," Ewa said, trotting up to her. "Most of this floor has been secured, save for the four primary stairwells and small pockets of resistance. Scouts are reporting from the adjacent buildings. Fighting is heavier than anticipated, but we should have them all secured by nightfall."

"Any signs of the temporal anomaly?"

"Not yet."

Kuo pulled up the blueprint of the building on her AI module. "Take a team up to the seventy-ninth floor. The traitor says the temporal anomaly has a high probability of being there."

"Your will, Senior."

Kuo watched as Ewa left with her pod. Then she looked at the lead monitor, still dangling from her trunk. His arm flailed at the translucent white bonds wrapped around his neck. His face was turning a deep crimson. She dropped him and watched as he gasped for breath.

"See to my orders, Lead Monitor, or I will find someone who can."

Kuo turned around and motioned for the shock pod to follow as she headed to the opposite end of the massive floor. Pockets of savages were still fighting in small groups and had to be cleaned up. She was about to leave this section of the floor when she paused, and waited.

Then she heard it, the lead monitor's voice. "All right, boys. Let's get this bullshit over with. Squad one, line the prisoners up in a row." His voice cracked. "On my mark."

Following orders was important. If you allowed disobedience once, you invited disobedience again. Kuo powered on her exo and shot toward the sound of the nearest battle.

FIFTY-TWO

THE FREE NATION

Elise watched as Bria picked up Sasha and scurried to the higher levels. She could tell that James was fighting the urge to follow them. There was another explosion. The building groaned and swayed as dust drizzled from the ceiling. People screamed. Somewhere below, a baby wailed. So much pain and suffering in the air. Elise couldn't help but feel responsible for all of it. She had to do something, but what?

James grabbed her by the shoulder. "You should go, too. Hide in the blood corn fields. I'll find you when this is over."

"No, she replied. "You go. She's your sister, James. I can't hide while everyone else fights and dies for this thing I started." She didn't give him a chance to reply as she bounded down the stairs.

He caught up with her and spun her around. "Elise, please. They're looking for you. Look at the big picture. You're the key to everything. You'll be no use in the fight, and you're definitely no use to anyone dead. Stay alive and find a way to cure the Earth Plague."

She knocked his hand away. "Don't start with me, James. Help me or get out of my way."

She reached the fifty-sixth floor, where a large crowd of the Elfreth had gathered. It was chaotic. Most of the guardians were on one side of the floor near their headquarters, equipping weapons and waiting and organizing into groups. The war chief was barking orders, but looked frazzled.

She pulled him to the side. "Eriao, are you all right?"

He nodded, but she could tell he was flustered, sucking in deep breaths as he spoke. "The Co-ops have found us. Couriers report fighting in every building. The Flatirons are trying to hold the barricade floor as we speak. Several floors in between also report enemy units. Many of the team aren't here yet and," he pointed at the other end of the room, "we have to move the rest of the tribe to safety."

"Take a deep breath," she said. "One thing at a time."

"You should be taken to safety," he said. "I'll have a team of guardians escort you to the higher floors."

"Don't you start, too," she snapped. "And no escorts for me. I want all the guardians fighting and saving lives."

Eriao looked grim. "Without backup, it's only a matter of time before we fall. Since the initial attack, we've been cut off from the other buildings."

She swore. The situation was worse than she expected. "We need to hold the stairwells," she instructed. "Organize the guardians. I'll handle the civilians."

"They will be ready soon, Oldest."

Elise looked back as Eriao walked to the mass of guardians milling around the floor. She had doubts he could get everyone under control. Well, he was her war chief, so she had to trust him to do his job. For now, she had her own job to do. She ran to the other side, where the civilians huddled together. Many seemed in shock from the rumbling and shaking of the building. Others were only half dressed, some still blinking the sleep from their eyes.

Elise climbed on a chair and shouted instructions at the top of her lungs. Fortunately, everyone on this side of the floor followed directions a lot better than the guardians. Within a few minutes, she had split them into groups and assigned each to a separate, higher floor to hide in the farming fields. She didn't know where the enemy was, so wanted to spread the groups out as much as possible.

She looked back at the other side of the room and winced. Eriao was not getting the guardians under control. She hopped off the chair and went to help him. The poor man looked utterly lost as he tried to merge partial teams with other partial teams, and pairing the teams without leaders to others without a team.

She tapped him on the shoulder. "Elder Eriao——"

An explosion rocked the building, and then all the windows on the east side of the floor shattered. Eriao pulled her down as glass shards blew inward. A Valkyrie hovered just outside, strafing the side of the building indiscriminately, mowing down anyone who was unfortunate enough to get in its crosshairs. A few brave guardians crept up to the window and returned fire. Their bullets bounced harmlessly off its hull.

She watched in horror as the attack ship finished pivoting and came back, spraying more red-lit death across the floor. Pieces of hot metal, plaster, and concrete exploded and melted all around them. A testament to their courage, the badly outgunned guardians tried to attack the ship. One of them charged forward, only to be cut clean through the waist, spraying blood across the floor. Several more who made it to the windows shot at the ship ineffectually with their rifles.

A large blast to the flank of the hovering ship suddenly tilted it sharply to the side. Another followed, spinning it around. The ship tried to pull up, but a third blast knocked it into the side of the building. It bounced off the wall, taking out another set of windows, and then careened down into the fog. She looked off to the side as James, holding a big, wicked-looking gun almost as long as she was tall, leaned over the edge of the building and studied his handiwork.

Satisfied, he turned and addressed the room. "Valkyries are heavily armored in the front and rear. Their sides, though, are easy to crack open." He hefted the big gun in his hands. "Next time, don't even bother unless you have one of these babies. All right, gather up. The troopers and monitors, you all know how to deal with. I give all of you fair odds against them any day. The real pain in the ass will be the exo-powered and shock troopers."

He must have realized he was overstepping his bounds, since he glanced over at Eriao, who just motioned for him to continue. James planted the big gun vertically on the ground and leaned on it. He scanned the room and continued in a loud voice, "For shockers, you need to make sustained blows to their armor. For those wielding exos, you need to either drain their levels or temporarily overwhelm their shields. This is how you do it. When fighting, it's important you spread out as much as possible. The reasons are twofold. One, depending on their skill, exo-wielders have limited control over their coils. Securitates usually only create a large one, called a trunk. You split up so the asshole can't take out more than one of you at once. Two, shielding is based on focal density, meaning it directs its energy toward points of impact. You can overwhelm an exo with concentrated hits on opposite sides."

He had the complete attention of the room as he launched into a demonstration. The guardians were completely silent as they processed his instructions, many nodding as they gripped their weapons. Others began to whisper to each other and compare notes. A few minutes later, James took charge of all of them and organized them into teams.

Along with everyone else, Elise couldn't take her eyes off of him. For a split second, the James she knew, the person she had sorely missed the past few months, was back. The confidence, strength, and control had returned. He seemed lighter, as if a large burden had lifted off him. She would almost say he glowed, but to be honest, that was going too far. James never glowed. Still, she wasn't going to lie; she wanted to jump him right there.

The war chief of the Elfreth had his arms around his chest and an unreadable expression on his face. Elise whispered to Eriao, "I hope you're not upset he just took over like this. I'll talk to him."

Eriao, whose eyes were still locked on James, grunted and replied, "Do you know what I used to do before you made me war chief, Oldest?"

"What?"

"I was the mapmaker." He cracked a smile. "I liked to draw as a boy. I learned to fight from many years of exploring the land so I could draw good maps. I would gladly offer the honor of war chief to the chronman and return to my drawings."

She put an arm on his. "Maybe after today, not before. We need you more than ever today."

Soon, the hundreds of guardians had organized into teams and were being assigned responsibilities, some escorting the civilians up into hiding, others holding stairwells and sweeping the floors, and the rest heading down to the barricades to assist the Flatirons.

Elise headed to her private room and threw on her control suit. A few minutes later, Aranea was powered up and ready to go. She moved the mechanoid out of her stable and toward where James had set up an impromptu command center.

He looked up from his work and stomped toward her, his face hard.

This was getting old. She knew his overprotectiveness came from a place of fear and guilt, but she still wished he'd get over himself. Elise braced herself for a dressing-down and readied her retort.

He looked the mechanoid up and down. "It's seen battle. First you lock me up, then you take over my job."

"Someone had to man the fort while you got better."

James pursed his lips and pointed at a team of guardians waiting at the stairwell's exit. "Take that group over there," he leaned in and whispered. "I don't know anyone's names."

"Kat, Sutt, Comi, Idivi, the short guy—name starts with a 'Yosh'-something—the grumpy guy who mumbles a lot, and the rest I don't remember," she said.

"Not helpful. Go to the lab and check on Sasha and the Geriatric Brigade. Make sure they're all right. Listen, if things go poorly, grab Sasha and make a break for it. Use Aranea and clear to the south building. It's close enough for the mechanoid to make the jump, got it?"

"I promise I'll keep Sasha safe." Elise actually didn't want to make that promise, since that sounded an awful lot like running away. Still, if things got really bad and she could save Sasha, she knew she would. Before James could step away, Elise opened Aranea and threw her arms around his neck. She planted a big kiss on his mouth and squeezed his body close to hers. "Don't do anything that doesn't bring you back to me, you hear?"

"Not death, not time, and not a bunch of megacorp assholes will keep me away from you," he replied, squeezing her back.

"That wasn't exactly romantic but I'll take it." It was what she had come to expect from James. Words of affirmation and love had never been his strong suit, but his love for her was without question.

"I love you, Elise." He raised his voice and looked at those assembled nearby. "Guardians, let's move! The enemy shall not step one level higher toward our homes, you hear me?"

"Yes, Elder!" they shouted in unison.

FIFTY-THREE

THE COUNTER

James watched as Elise took one of several smaller groups of guardians up to the higher levels. He didn't like having to send her into possible danger, but sending her toward the sky was much safer than down to the hell below. The reports from the survivors of the barricade floor were that the battle had been a massacre.

He waited until he could no longer see the mechanoid before turning his attention back to leading the counterattack. The small army of guardians and volunteers with him now filled the floor to capacity, with several of the volunteers waiting for orders in the stairwells. James consulted with Eriao before they agreed on a strategy. It would be impossible to protect every floor, but they had to do their best to keep a single front in order to minimize the enemy's chances of hitting their people from the rear. To do so, they would have to maintain control of all the stairwells.

James was finishing sorting the groups when he came across Maanx. He pulled the young commander aside. "Shouldn't you be with your fights?"

The young commander looked anguished. "I was with Chawr practicing your teachings when the enemy attacked. I was unable to reach my people in the chaos. It would be too easy and small a death to try to reach the barricade floor on my own."

James nodded. "We can use another commander to lead the guardians."

"Put me where I'm needed, Elder," said Maanx.

James and Eriao divided the guardians into four groups led by Eriao,

James, Maanx, and a guardian named Tidhar. Each group was composed of approximately equal parts guardians and volunteers who wanted to fight rather than hide in the fields. James turned nobody away.

It warmed him to see several familiar faces flock to his group, including all the flyguards. He nodded to Chawr and Hory, and patted young Dox on the shoulder. Laurel snuck in a few minutes later. When they were as ready as they were ever going to be, he signaled for everyone's attention.

James felt awkward standing before these people, these supposed savages whom a year ago he had disdained. He received a few uncomfortable glances, but that wasn't unusual. He had gotten those ever since he joined them. It was different now. Before, he didn't care what any of them thought of him. Now, he wanted to earn their respect, especially after his recent weakness.

"Today, you are all guardians," he said in a loud voice. "You are all that stands between the Elfreth and those who wish to harm us. Each floor that the Co-op climb is one floor closer to your mothers, fathers, and loved ones. We will not allow them a chance to climb. We will not allow them any floors. We will push them down to the waters. We will drive them out of the All Galaxy. We will chase them until they leave the Mist Isle, until they no longer stand on Manhattan lands. Do you understand, guardians?"

"Yes, Elder!" they roared in unison.

James nodded. "Good. We meet at the barricade floor or not at all."

The mass of guardians and volunteers cheered and then separated into their groups, each moving toward their assigned stairwells. James led the ones in the north, Maanx the south, Tidhar the west, and Eriao the east. Every stairwell group's orders were to go down a level and send teams of five out to scour the floor. Once that team reached the opposite stairwell, each would send a courier to the adjacent stairwells. Once everyone received two couriers, they would continue down another level.

The groups went down one at a time. Surprisingly, they found minimal resistance until they reached the infirmary floor just above the barricade floor. Thick Co-op presence stalled their progress. Because they controlled all four main stairwells, the Elfreth were able to surround the enemy who had taken over the medical rooms and rush them from all sides. After twenty minutes of heavy fighting, to his surprise, the remaining Co-op forces surrendered.

James walked through the floor as the dozen or so Valta and Chrono-

Com personnel were rounded up. There were also three dozen injured Co-op troopers, a near equal number of monitors here, and twice that number from the Nation. He was encouraged by the relatively light casualties among his people until he realized the majority of the Co-op were doctors and medical personnel.

He walked over to one of the injured Elfreth. "Did they mistreat any of our injured in any way?"

The elderly man shook his head. "They moved some of us away to the sides but otherwise left us alone. When Baala over there needed her medicine, one of them administered it."

"Thank you," James said, patting the man on the shoulder.

The enemy were lucky they had treated the Manhattans with care. Otherwise, James would have no other choice in how they were handled. He walked over to the small group huddled in the corner. He recognized one of the prisoners, Cail, an agency doctor who commonly administered the miasma regimens to the chronmen. They acknowledged each other, but remained silent.

"Listen here," he said to the group. "You're no longer involved in this fight. Stay that way, and no harm will come to you. If you wish to care for the wounded, we'll allow it, but only if you care for everyone, your and my people both. Agreed?"

The prisoners exchanged hesitant looks before the ChronoCom doctor he recognized stood up. A few seconds later, the rest of the agency medical staff followed suit. Only the Valta personnel stayed sitting on the floor. James nodded to Cail and watched as they got back to work.

He signaled to the nearest guard watching over them. "None of them are to leave the floor."

He met with Eriao, Maanx, and Tidhar in a corner room as they planned their assault on the main barricade floor. They didn't know the enemy's strength and had to assume the Flatirons were completely wiped out if the Co-op controlled all four of the stairwell entrances.

"What about the rest of the Manhattan forces?" he asked.

"Unknown," Eriao said. "We lost contact once the barricade floor fell. That floor is our only way out. However, the sounds of battle echo all around the block."

"We can hold the stairwells forever," Tidhar said. "Why don't we make them come to us? We still own the farming floors. We won't starve."

Eriao shook his head. "The barricade floor is the only way out of this tower. The enemy could just wait us out. Besides, they have already proven that they can reach any of the higher floors if they choose."

"Then we have to take it no matter what," Maanx said. "Four entryways. We hit them all at once. Hard. Connect our lines, and push them out of my home."

"They'll bottleneck us where we can't use our numbers. It'll be a slaughter," said James.

"What can we do, then?" Tidhar asked.

James stood up and paced. There was so little room for his people to maneuver. The damn Co-op could effectively trap his people up here forever. Hell, the bodies of his dead would clog up the stairwell if the Elfreth launched a frontal attack. He walked up to the blown-out window and looked out at the fog.

It was at least a thirty-meter drop straight down, and the bridges below were barely visible through the haze. He stuck his head out and looked around. The window openings above were just a few rooms over. He checked the bridges on the west end. The nearer one was far enough away he couldn't even see the bridge.

He turned to Eriao. "How much rope do we have?"

The war chief shrugged. "We use rope for many things. The farmers harvest vine from the bean husks and use them for binding shelter. The elderly use the same to weave clothing and blankets. It shouldn't be too difficult to gather up."

"Grab some. As much as we can," James said. "I have an idea."

It took longer than he liked for them to gather all the rope from the upper levels, but in the end, they had enough to send a third of the guardians over the side. James himself would drop with the group at the northeast bridge. Five guardians to a vine. Seven vines to a bridge. James would have preferred to send more, but it would have to do.

Eriao patted him on the shoulder as he got ready to go over. "Five person beats, my friend. Be ready." The Elfreth didn't have a solid understanding of time, and their math was based on persons, feet, hands, and individual toes and fingers. One person was twenty beats. In a way, it made perfect sense. It just took James a while to get used to it. My friend. As always, that phrase triggered thoughts of Smitt, and he glanced around. This time, the hallucination was nowhere in sight. Not seeing him made

James sad, in a way. He knew it wasn't real, just a product of his alcoholism and lag sickness, but every time that apparition spoke to him, it felt real. He wondered if he would ever see Smitt's face again.

"Are you all right, Elder?" Eriao asked.

James snapped out of it and realized he was still straddling the window on his way over the edge of a skyscraper. He nodded. "I'll see you downstairs."

"Or dead."

James grinned. "Downstairs then, either way."

He took a handful of the stiff vine and wrapped it around his hands. Slowly, he rappelled down the side of the building, trying to make as little noise as possible. When he was a meter down, a guardian joined him. A few meters after she climbed down, another guardian followed.

They continued down until he reached the end of the rope, which was just above the bridge's opening. It was still a four-meter drop to the bridge and the scattered debris from the barricade littering the floor below made the fall tricky. A bad slip or landing could easily alert the Co-op or cause a broken ankle. He looked to his right and left and waited until all his people were in place. The beats ticked by as they all waited, dangling from the vine.

His thoughts wandered to Elise, and he wondered if he had made the right decision leaving her to fend for herself. Sending her upstairs was the safest choice, even though it meant he couldn't watch over her. He hated that this was what he had had to do with both her and Sasha.

He closed his eyes and listened. Below, he could hear the sounds of movement, shouting, and general chatter. Nothing that would signal an attack. Three Valta troopers appeared, patrolling out of the All Galaxy and marching down the length of the bridge. They would have to be taken out silently and quickly.

He let go of the vine and dropped right behind the group. He swept the feet of the nearest trooper with a low kick and then lunged for the second, throwing his arm around the man's neck and dragging him down. A quick snap of his head and the body went limp.

As he turned to engage the third trooper, a sharp crack across the side of his face blurred his vision, and he fell to the ground. He rolled to the side just as blaster fire kicked up fragments of the concrete next to him. He rolled to his feet and took another blow to his midsection, doubling him over in pain. He glanced up at the black muzzle of a blaster rifle.

Before the trooper could pull the trigger, a dark shadow fell over him, knocking the trooper to the ground. Several more shadows followed as his guardians came to his rescue.

Hory plunged a knife into the man's neck and then looked at the others. "This blaster is mine." Others called out their spoils.

Chawr appeared beside him and offered a hand. "Are you all right, Elder?"

"I'm fine," he said gruffly, accepting the flyguard's extended hand. His pride hurt more than anything. These jokers shouldn't have posed as much of a problem as they had. He was losing his edge.

"Is everyone all right?" he asked.

"I think I sprained my ankle, Elder." Dox winced, limping up to him.

"Well, suck it up," James replied.

The sound of shouting inside the building suddenly swelled, followed by the whine of blaster fire. James motioned for the guardians to follow as he crept up to the remains of the northern barricade. He huddled behind the broken pieces of metal double doors and peered inside. Most of the Co-op nearby were surrounding the stairwell entrance off to the side. The Elfreth's attack must have been less effective than they had hoped. It looked like the Co-op were pushing upward.

"All right, bridge crew," he ordered. "Ignore the big armored ones. They'll take too much work to bring down. Aim for just the smaller troopers." He signaled for the guardians to spread out along the entranceway, grabbing cover when they could or staying farther back so they could hide within the fog. He held up a hand and waited until everyone was in place.

In unison, they all opened fire at the same time, taking out several rows of troopers with the initial volley. His guardians were able to sow chaos among the Valta ranks, but the well-trained enemy recovered and reorganized. A shocker pod appeared a few seconds later and laid suppression fire long enough for the Valta troopers to mount a firing line.

Blaster fire barraged their position, taking out many of his people who hadn't taken cover. The rest of his crew returned fire as they could. It was chaotic, and most of their fire went wide. The heavy shocker's concentrated blaster fire, however, was shredding their cover, and pretty soon, several more of his guardians fell.

James had hoped that his team could cause enough confusion to make some inroads into the barricade floor, but as the fight continued, they lost ground. He had far underestimated the enemy's strength. If his group was having this much trouble, then the ones at the other bridges must be faring equally poorly, if not worse. After a few minutes, he had no choice but to order his guardians to retreat farther back into the fog.

As his people retreated, the shockers strafed several stragglers. James and four others ran forward to drag them back. He picked up a young woman while the others grabbed two men. He had underestimated how close the shockers were. The next time he looked back, half a dozen of them were boring down on him.

A blaster shot near his feet knocked him off balance and he tumbled to the ground. He scrambled for his rifle, but it was too late. The shocker could cut him down at close range or just step on him. He rolled on his side as a large metal foot came crashing down on where he had been moments earlier. He cursed, realizing he had just rolled away from his dropped rifle.

The shocker leveled its massive forearm cannon squarely at his chest. James waited for the end to come, still hoping to dodge the blast at the very last second and scramble to safety. A roar suddenly erupted from somewhere inside the building, and then the white glow of an exo-wielder appeared at the end of the bridge.

"Shocker Pod Six. Recall. Command delta imminent! Now!"

As if on cue, all the shockers stopped in their tracks and retreated into the building. James couldn't believe his luck. About time something went his way in all of this. Still, it had been too close. He was alive right now only by sheer luck. The chronman he used to be would have scoffed at the many mistakes he had just made.

"Elder, look!" Chawr pointed at a plume of flames rising at the far end of the floor.

More sounds of fighting erupted from inside the All Galaxy, and the ranks of the Co-op seemed to have fallen into chaos. What in the abyss was going on?

The remaining guardians scrambled to his side. "Orders, Elder?" Hory asked.

"I don't . . ." James reminded himself that he was never to say that in front of the troops. However, in this case, it was the absolute truth. "Well," he shrugged, "I guess we do the only thing left to do. Let's go. Charge!"

His guardians followed him into the building, where all hell had broken loose.

FIFTY-FOUR

THE UPPER FLOORS

Elise and her team entered the south stairwell and made their way up the stairs, joining the flow of civilians fleeing to hide in the fields near the top of the building. It seemed the enemy was hitting them everywhere. Guilt nagged at her as they passed sporadic fighting on several of the floors, even more so as a steady stream of guardians—many with injuries—made their way down as she went up. Elise knew she had to trust the rest of the tribe to do their jobs. Still, the higher she climbed, the more difficult it was to ignore her people. Finally, she caved and began to ask the injured if they needed help.

"Is everything all right? Do you need assistance?" she asked a guardian leaning on a wall next to the stairwell door at the sixty-fifth floor.

The young woman, face bloodied and holding her left arm, shook her head. "They came in through the east window. My team and Gill's have it under control, Oldest. We took 'em. Gill's arming his guardians with Co-op guns right now. We're heading down to the barricades next."

Elise wasn't sure if she believed the woman, but nodded and continued up the stairs. Five other times she stopped to ask small groups of guardians about their status. Four of the guardians claimed to have maintained control of their floor, which was surprising. The Manhattan forces must be doing better than she thought. Maybe they had a chance to win this after all.

Her optimism was short-lived, however. She reached the landing balcony on the seventy-third floor. There were a dozen guardians lying in the stairwell leading up to the door and easily another half dozen farther up. The doorway had been blown out. Bodies, scorch marks, and debris littered the area just inside. She found the nearest conscious guardian and asked if someone was in charge. He directed her to a small group huddled in a circle around a table. She signaled for her team to guard the perimeter as she moved in to see what was going on.

There were nine full teams waging a pitched battle with a group of the Co-op. The enemy had taken over the landing pad and one of the stair-wells. The guardians so far had sandwiched the Co-op from moving up or down the stairwell at the seventy-second floor, but they were slowly losing ground here in the interior. The Elfreth outnumbered the enemy five to one, but they were getting slaughtered by Co-Op shockers.

"Can you hold?" she asked a man named Safa who was directing teams near the rear.

He bit his lip and bowed his head. "Apologies, Oldest. We will die holding it as long as we can."

The sounds of the fighting grew closer. Most of these guardians were exhausted. Some seemed more dead than alive. With most of their forces heading to the lower floors, these teams weren't getting any reinforcements either. Elise did the only thing she thought made sense.

"Give them the floor, then. Order everyone back to the stairwells. Just bottleneck the hell out of it for as long as you can," she ordered.

"We cannot do that," Safa said. "Mata has five teams trapped in the main supply room. If we leave them, they will be butchered."

"Do we know if they're alive?" she asked.

"Yes, Oldest," Safa said. He pointed at one of the bodies lying nearby. "Moor was their courier. They are well entrenched in a defensive position but unable to move. He was able to deliver the message before death. If we retreat, I fear all fifty will be lost."

Elise considered her options. That was a lot of guardians to sacrifice. There were few options available to her, and even fewer good ones. The supply room was a warehouse in the center of this floor. It was a veritable maze, with dozens of shelves and crates. Moving in there would be very dangerous. However, leaving five teams to die wasn't an acceptable alternative. Part of Elise wished she hadn't asked for a status. Now that she had, the burden of making a decision was on her. If she decided to leave those guardians there, their blood would be on her hands. She wouldn't be able to live with herself then.

"Hell to Gaia," she said. "Let's get them out, then. I'm not leaving anyone behind. Can you signal our people at the other stairwells? We hit them all at once."

"Yes, Oldest." He motioned for two of the younger guardians to approach.

Elise checked the internal clock in Aranea. She counted a measured pace to five. "That's the beat. Two persons," she instructed. "Now go."

Elise was still pretty new to fighting, and the anticipation was killing her. She was so nervous and sweating so badly in Aranea that she lost count somewhere between ten and fifteen. However, there was no need for her to keep track. All the guardians around her were stomping their feet in unison. As if on cue, they charged forward. To the side, a surge of guardians from the west joined them.

They encountered a group of twenty Co-op as they poured into the supply room. Half the enemy wore standard Valta white uniforms while the other half looked like walking tanks. They stood three meters tall and had armor that looked like metal plating. Luckily, the guardians' sudden onslaught took them by surprise.

Unluckily, it didn't seem to make much of a difference. The two sides exchanged fire and many more of her people were cut down by the enemy than vice versa. In fact, it seemed nothing fazed those big armored Valta brutes at all. All the guns and beam weapons her guardians used seemed to bounce off of those things. No wonder they were having trouble.

It seemed, however, that the big gun on Aranea was another story. The armored tank guys had ignored her until she fired a shot from her shoulder cannon and hit one square in the chest. The big robot thing's armor literally exploded. This got their attention. The rest of the heavy tank guys began focusing on her. The only thing Elise could do was run and dodge their constant fire. Unfortunately, Aranea was half again as tall as the nearest guardian and stuck out like a sore thumb with her smooth metallic blue skin and eight long spider legs. One of the guardians standing in front of her got caught in the crossfire and fell. She had to get away from the group.

Fortunately, running away with Aranea was one thing she had gotten quite good at. She bounded up to the ceiling to draw fire away from her people and scurried across the room, zigzagging in all directions as the tank guys continued to shoot at her. It was almost a miracle that none of the blasts hit the mechanoid's critical components. It wasn't for lack of trying. The blasts from the tank guys kept blowing out fragments of the ceiling around her, raining debris onto the ground. The mechanoid was fast, though, and Elise had gotten quite skilled at maneuvering her, so most of the enemy fire missed, and what did hit was absorbed by her armor plating.

Elise couldn't be sure her plan to draw fire away from the guardians had worked. She was too busy running for her life to see what was going on, but she preferred to think that she'd bought enough of a distraction for her people to close in on the Co-op. It took her a while before she realized that the heavy enemy fire following her had stopped. She pivoted Aranea to see what was going on, and her mouth fell open.

She must have bought enough time for all the guardians—joined by Mata's team and numbering over 150—to close the distance, and now they were mobbing the twenty Co-op troopers like an army of ants over wasps. The outnumbered Valta troopers stood no chance as her people tackled and wrestled them to the ground. The larger, armored tank guys, however, required more effort. Half a dozen guardians piled on top of each, yanking at their armored pieces and shooting point-blank into their exposed joints. The armored troopers fought back. Their suits must give them superhuman strength, and they were smashing guardians and tossing them left and right.

There was too much chaos for Elise to get a clean shot, so she watched and worried. More guardians poured in from the stairwells until finally, all that remained standing were the Elfreth. "Winning" probably wasn't the right word. Her casualties were high, easily more than a hundred compared to the twenty Valta. Had she made the wrong choice? Still, a victory was a victory. All of the Co-op had been killed or captured, and the remaining guardians were dividing the enemy's weapons among themselves.

"Oldest," Safa said, limping toward her. His entire left side was bleeding, and his face was pale. "Victory is yours."

"We lost twice the number we were trying to save," she said. "I failed us."

"Not so, Oldest," he replied. "To die fighting for the tribe is worthy.

We lost many good guardians, but we also defeated the enemy and held the floor. This will save many more lives, and it is all because of you."

Elise wasn't convinced, but she had more important things to worry about. The fight on the landing pad floor had taken longer than she had expected. She let Safa take over the cleanup, found the survivors of her team—all except for Sutt—and hurried up to the lab. She hoped Grace, Titus, and Sasha were all right. They should be, if they were hiding in the secret crawl space. Still, Elise wouldn't be able to live with herself if something happened to James's sister, especially after she had promised him she would make sure Sasha was safe.

They reached the seventy-ninth floor and spread out around the lab. It was quiet here, a far cry from the chaos below. The lab took up the entire floor and was divided into several sections for her to run tests and samples.

"Grace, Titus?" Elise called, moving Aranea carefully around tables holding sensitive and fragile instruments.

She passed the main work area and proceeded to the first incubator room. As the mechanoid skirted the rows of her samples, one of the shelves filled with stacks of glass aquariums tipped over on top of her. A giant robotic metal hand swatted at Aranea, clipping her on the shoulder. The mechanoid spun around and came face-to-face with one of the giant armored tank guys. The big shocker drew his arm back and swung at her.

Elise managed to skip Aranea backward, and then opened fire, hitting the tank guy point-blank in the chest. Where had he come from? She looked around and suddenly saw several more Valta troopers swarm into the room.

One of the regular troopers blindsided her. The trooper jumped on top of Aranea's base next to her body. Before Elise could swat him away, he aimed down and fired at one of the mechanoid's legs. Elise used both arms to bat at him, sending him flying across the room. The screen in front her face blinked red as the damage reports scrolled across her line of sight. One of poor Aranea's legs had been completely severed.

Why did he shoot Aranea's leg instead of Elise's head? At that range, he could have killed her easily. She didn't have time to ponder that as two more troopers attacked from both sides. She was able to shoot one as he came in, but the other was able to get several shots off. This time, one of the legs on her other side was crippled.

They must be doing this on purpose. Then she realized why. They knew she was inside. They were trying to capture her alive. That was probably why those troopers and tank guys on the landing pad floor kept missing her. They probably knew as well and were trying to disable Aranea without injuring her.

"Damn it, Elise," she growled. "Get out of here."

In the other room, she saw her entire team get cut down as more of the Co-op moved in. Her thoughts immediately turned to Sasha, Grace, and Titus. Were they all right? Captured? Already dead? And then she realized she had to worry about herself first.

Elise tried to fall back to the nearest window, but Aranea was badly crippled and could only limp toward the exit. Two troopers and a tank guy came at her. She was able to fight them off, if barely, having to skirt to the side and shoot a trooper and the tank guy while wrestling with the second trooper.

Elise reached the window opening and tried to launch Aranea to the nearest adjacent building, but the mechanoid was too damaged to make the jump. The last two surviving guardians of her team tried to fight their way to her, but were also shot down. She changed plans and tried to make her way to the nearest stairwell, not ten meters away, when suddenly she stopped crawling forward and started moving backward.

Panicked, Elise punched all the commands on the mechanoid but nothing was responding. In fact, all systems said she was still moving forward. It was as if she were . . . floating. Then she noticed the faint white glimmer surrounding the mechanoid. Something rotated her until she saw a woman in a white uniform bathed in a white glowing light.

"You must be the Nutris scientist," the woman said. "I am Securitate Ewa. We've been looking everywhere for you."

Elise did the only thing she could think of. She pulled the trigger on Aranea's cannon and tried to blast whoever this was to bits. The cannon discharged, and for a second, both of them were blinded as the woman's shield lit up. And then Elise heard the sound of metal tearing as Aranea's gun was ripped from the mechanoid's shoulder and flung to the side.

"Now," Ewa smirked, "let's get you out of this contraption, shall we?"

The center of Aranea split in two as an unseen force pried it apart. Elise felt a static heat and shock, and she heard screaming. It wasn't until later that she realized that the screaming was coming from her.

FIFTY-FIVE

FAMILY AFFAIR

The darkness around them lit up as the first barrage of enemy fire and exo coils blanketed the rebels. Levin and many of the auditors had expanded their own shields at the last moment to protect those without exos, but they weren't able to envelop everyone. Buchanan, the medical quartermaster, an avowed pacifist and one of the kindest men Levin knew, was thrown against a wall like a rag doll by a chronman's coil. Several others, senior and head administrators, doctors, handlers, and engineers, suffered similar fates as more coils and wrist beams cut them apart.

"Phalanx cover. Pull back to secondary position," Rowe barked. "Julia, get the noncombatants to safety. The rest provide cover."

The auditors moved closer together and meshed their shields, forming a spherical barrier around the entire group. Moving in unison, they retreated to the back of the room into a space between the wall and the large wreckage of a Hephaestus transport. Any of the monitors and chronmen who charged their position were cut down. They were safe for now, but they were trapped.

"The closest exit point out of Central is the sewage ducts to the south," Julia said. "We should escape while we have the chance. Build a resistance."

"No," Hameel said. "Nothing's changed. We should take the Hops now, especially with the bulk of our monitors occupied. If we escape now, we'll never make it back in here."

Levin kept his eyes glued to the rear of the wreck shielding them. Two monitors tried to charge around the corner, only to be stopped and flung backward by one of his coils. He looked around the corner of the transport. Young's forces were spreading out around the room, preparing to attack their position. They were almost all chronmen and monitors with a few auditors among them. Several of the monitors were carrying exochains as well. He glanced back at the group around him. He had some of the best within the agency here. They were at a disadvantage, but it wasn't overwhelming.

He turned to the group. "We have a chance if we fight."

"And none if we flee," Moyer added.

Rowe looked at Julia, who reluctantly nodded, and then at Marn. An unspoken understanding passed between them. "That settles it," he said. "We fight our way to the Hops."

"The corridors are too narrow and the entire building is probably on high alert," Julia said. "They'll box us in. It's better if the main party keeps these jokers occupied, and a small group slips out."

"I'll go with Hameel and Levin," Moyer said. "Hameel has the respect of those in the Hops, and I have access to the entire building."

Julia gave Levin a hug and held her hands out. Her bands unsnapped and she offered them to him. "You're going to need these, Auditor Levin."

He nodded and gave her his chronman bands. "I'll see you later, or on the other side."

Rowe pointed at the door farther down the room. "There's your exit, Levin. We'll cover you. Get moving."

Levin, Hameel, and Moyer waited as Rowe led the charge out, surprising the agency's forces on the other side. His heart ached when he saw a few of his friends fall, including Marn, someone he had known since his Academy days, and Pendlol, a chronman he had mentored. The room became a battlefield as the small group of auditors, chronmen, and administrators fought the agency force three times their size.

Levin waited until the forces were fully committed before signaling to the other two to follow. They ran down the length of the wall, taking wrist beam blasts until they reached the double doors. Levin held the shield up for Moyer and Hameel to pass through. He looked back at the desperate battle raging throughout the room.

Rowe was battling three chronmen and half a dozen monitors at the same time. One of the monitors had an exo-chain attached to him. Julia was locked in combat with another auditor. Even Jan, who looked like he hadn't held a rifle in years, was exchanging fire with two monitors. One thing that stuck out to him was that some of the monitors had changed sides, or at least it seemed that way.

Levin couldn't help but feel as if he was abandoning his friends and comrades. He gave the room one last look, and with a snarl, created a dozen coils and latched them to the nearest ship, then pulled it violently toward him as he went through the door, blocking the exit. "Let's make their sacrifice worth it," he said to Moyer and Hameel as they raced down the corridor. They avoided the main halls as much as possible, only crossing them when absolutely necessary, and using Moyer's access to use the maintenance passageways. It was still the middle of the night, so traffic at Earth Central was light, save for the squads of monitors converging on the battle in the south wing.

Levin, taking point, walked out of a stairwell into the Hops Wing and was immediately hit with an exo-chain. A wrist beam struck the shield near his face, knocking him down. Out of pure reflex, he kicked out with his leg and swept his attacker. Both of them picked themselves off the ground and squared up. Levin was a beat faster. Unable to create new coils, he launched himself at the man before he could stand and hit him in the face, knocking him down again. A second later, he was surrounded by six monitors.

"That's Auditor Levin!" one of them gasped.

"Be careful. The director wants him alive," another said.

"I called for backup," a third replied. "A chronman should be here any minute."

Levin prepared to engage them with his fists and feet. Six on one wasn't the world's worst odds for an auditor, but he doubted he would come out of this unscathed. He motioned with his fingers for the monitors to approach. "Let's see if you remembered some of the lessons I taught you, Meara. Doogs, you'd better keep that left guard up, because I know you like to drop it. Palh, you might want to sit this one out. You're, what, a couple months from retirement?"

The group of monitors suddenly looked very uncomfortable. They exchanged glances and all but one lowered their wrist beams.

"What are you guys waiting for?" the youngest-looking auditor—one that Levin did not recognize—said. "Get him!"

"Look, Auditor," the one named Doogs said. "This isn't personal, just duty."

"Screw this," Meara spat and took a step back. "The High Auditor saved my life against that Valta bitch. I'm not taking him down in their name."

The others murmured their agreement. All except for the youngest. He wavered, his head swiveling back and forth between Levin and his more experienced peers. Levin almost felt bad for the kid, except he was pointing a beam weapon at him. He was probably a few months out of the Academy. It was an impossible choice, really, for someone with so little experience. He prepared to do the merciful thing and take the decision out of the kid's hands without killing him.

"Release the auditor now, monitors," Moyer commanded as he walked out of the stairwell directly into the center of the standoff. He looked them all over as if he were dressing them down in his office. To Levin's surprise, the exo-chain slid off. Moyer stared down the youngest monitor, who was still aiming his wrist beam. "Monitor Seth."

"Lead Moyer!" The one named Seth gave a start at the mention of his name. For a second, he nearly saluted the lead monitor, remembering at the last second that he had been ordered to capture him. He shifted his wrist beam to Moyer.

Moyer stepped up to Seth and wrapped a hand around his wrist. "Are you prepared to shoot me with that, son?" Seth's arms trembled so badly his teeth nearly rattled. Moyer swatted the arm away. "Then don't point it at me." He turned to the other monitors. "You all know the High Auditor. You sure as abyss know me. Who do you follow?"

"What the hell is going on?" a new voice shouted. A Tier-3 named Shvet hurried into the room. "Why are you all standing around? Apprehend those traitors!"

Before he could say another word, an exo-chain struck Shvet in the side and wrapped him up, causing him to fall to the ground. Two of the monitors were on him in an instant, incapacitating him.

Moyer smirked at Levin. "What did I say? These are my people." He turned to the monitors. "Can you escort us to the Hops?"

"Yes, Lead Monitor," Meara said.

"Good," Moyer said. "Let's see who else we can round up."

Moyer and Hameel, now guarded by Levin and six monitors, walked confidently through the main hallways. Several other monitor squads ran up to meet them, but none dared to fire. Moyer would hold his hands up and ask them the same questions he asked the ones now protecting him. What did they believe? Who did they follow? Why were they following these orders? The older man had taught Levin at one point in their training. Levin might have been respected by everyone within the agency on Earth, but Moyer was beloved. He was the leader of the monitors and had taught every living chronman and auditor at some point in their career.

More often than not, the monitors they encountered ended up joining the group. Their numbers swelled to twenty. Then over forty. However, for every monitor that joined them, two refused and fled. By the time they neared the Hops, there was little doubt that Young knew where they were heading. As they rounded the hallway to the Hops's entrance, they were blocked by a larger group of monitors.

Cole stood at their front.

Levin growled. This final betrayal had burned him deeply. During their walk up to the Hops from the supply hangar, a hundred scenarios had run through his mind for why his nephew would do this. Maybe he had been captured by Young and forced to betray him. Maybe they had threatened his mother. Maybe there was more to this than Levin knew.

In the end, Levin came to the conclusion that Cole had just received a better offer. He most likely played Levin in order to get to Chicago and was just waiting for the right time. Used the information he had about what Levin was doing to trade for a pardon. What could he have offered them? Of course. Cole betrayed everyone. That boy had run out of chances. Levin had already decided that the next time they met would be the last for one of them. As Levin looked across the room at Cole, he realized that the next time had come sooner than he had thought.

"What did they offer you, Cole?" he asked. "A pardon? A job? Passport to Europa?"

Cole laughed. "All of the above, Uncle." The white of a Valta exo bloomed around him. "It's Securitate Cole to you, fugitive."

"All right, boys," Moyer said. "Make me proud. Get us into the Hops."

Both sides lined up to attack, but Levin knew the real fight would come down to Cole and him. His nephew had more powerful bands; Levin's experience with Kuo had already taught him that lesson. However, bands were complex tools that required skill. One couldn't slap on new bands without experience and wield them effectively.

The two sides charged, coils extended and wrist beams flashing, as if they were in a medieval battle of old. Monitor armor was particularly ineffective against beam weaponry, so the contest would have to be decided up close. Levin and Cole were on opposite ends of the battle and would have to wade through opposing monitors to reach each other.

Cole took to the air and created a large white coil, half again as tall as he was. He swung it like a staff in wide sweeping motions, bludgeoning Levin's people in threes and fours. Levin, on the other hand, created a dozen coils at once, using them to move over the battle like a giant kraken, plucking enemy monitors up into the air and tossing them across the room.

They met in the center, Cole wielding the trunk awkwardly, Levin dancing agilely in his auditor exo. It had been too long since he had used one of these. He missed the smooth responsiveness and extended reach. He juked to the left as Cole brought the trunk down, smashing the ground and taking out three monitors at the same time, one of them Cole's. Not that Cole cared about that.

Levin, however, did care, and was hampered. There wasn't a lot of room for an exo built for maneuverability in a hallway only six meters tall and ten meters wide. He jabbed Cole several times with his coils, only to have Cole's more powerful shield rebuff them.

Levin could see the strain on Cole's face as he concentrated on the trunk. The boy was out of practice after his stint in prison, and wielding an unfamiliar exo so unlike a chronman's was taxing. Wearing Cole down was going to be Levin's best tactic. He continued to pepper Cole with longer coils, staying just out of range of the Valta exo's lumbering trunk.

In frustration, Cole launched into the air after him, which was a mistake. Space exos needed anchors in gravity to ground the band wearer. When he swung his trunk, the centrifugal force caused him to crash into a side wall, taking out another five of his own men. Levin moved in for the kill and stung him half a dozen times with his coils, cracking and draining Cole's exo of its levels, then pulled back just as Cole got to his feet.

"You're going to hurt someone with that if you're not careful," Levin said.

Cole roared and lashed out, regenerating his trunk and punching Levin. It hit Levin flush and sent him careening into the wall, knocking him right through it. Disoriented, Levin checked his levels. They were already down to 28 percent. The bands were only at half when Julia had handed them to him. That meant he might be able to sustain one or two more hits.

Levin surveyed the battlefield. Outside of his fight with Cole, Moyer had made little progress toward the Hops entrance. Levin saw why a moment later. Reinforcements had been filtering into the hallway the entire time. Levin's people were getting overwhelmed.

He focused his attention just in time as Cole barreled toward him, Levin was just able to dive underneath as the Valta exo sailed overhead and smashed into the opposite wall, taking out two more enemy monitors in the process. This gave Levin an idea.

Much to the annoyance of the monitors trying to protect his flank, Levin shot himself into the thick of the enemy, using his dozen coils to sow terror. It required all of his concentration to control his extensions as if they were a part of his body. He was focusing so hard that he nearly missed Cole charging at him again like the untamed bull that he was.

This time, Levin almost got out of the way. Cole clipped him on the way in and Levin crashed into a group of enemy monitors. His levels were precariously low now; the fight had already lasted too long.

"I told you to be careful," Levin said. "You're hurting your own people more than I am."

That fact wasn't lost on Cole's monitors, as those around him seemed more concerned about him than they were about Levin and his forces. Cole ignored them, though, as he re-created the trunk and tried to batter Levin once more. Again and again he missed, each of his swings getting slower and slower, but still hurting those standing nearby.

Finally, it seemed Cole's men had had enough. His latest clumsy attack took out an entire squad of Young's loyalists. One of the lead monitors turned on Cole, latching an exo-chain onto him and ordering him pulled back. Cole screamed and threatened the squad leader, demanding how the man dared touch a Valta securitate. He then attacked the lead monitor, which only exacerbated the situation.

Levin had returned to safety behind his monitor line. His bands had depleted, so he armed himself with a baton he found on the ground. By now, it seemed both sides had had their fill of fighting. Levin caught sight of Moyer speaking with that same squad leader, and then a few moments later, both sides ordered their people to stand down.

Moyer walked up to Levin and leaned in. "Drop that baton. Monitor Lo only agreed to the cease-fire because he thinks your exo still has juice." Levin dropped the baton and settled into a pose as if he were about to launch into the air with his bands. Moyer grinned. "I told him what I intended to do, and that if he disagreed with the results, we would all surrender after I broadcast the message and the information."

"Surrender?" Levin frowned.

Moyer shrugged. "There's another hundred monitors next door. The only reason we didn't get our asses kicked earlier was because there's not enough room in this hallway and that crazy shithead nephew of yours was causing too much damage to his own side."

"All right then," Levin said. "Get the message out. I hope you're convincing, because frankly, Nereid sucks."

Moyer smiled. "Come on. Let's see if we're both as popular as we think we are." He signaled for Hameel to come up from the rear. The head handler looked nervous as they approached the Hops entrance.

"You can handle the handlers?" Levin asked.

Hameel shrugged. "A little less than half of them hate my guts. Fortunately, that means more than half of them like me."

"I guess that'll have to do." Levin grinned.

The three, along with their escort of monitors, stormed into the Hops. Spooked handlers froze, some standing and putting their hands up.

"Back to your positions, handlers," Hameel said. "You all know who I am, and who these two men are. Trust me when I say this is for the good of the agency. Prepare a system-wide broadcast to all units, tiers, chains, and ranks."

One of the handlers raised his hand. "Including the comm silent operation out east?"

"What operation is that?" Levin asked.

"The joint one with Valta," the handler replied. "They're about to destroy that new wastelander nation."

FIFTY-SIX

PROJECT CLOSE

Senior Securitate Kuo watched the battle unfold as the savages made yet another pitiful counterattack to take back the floor. The enemy had repeatedly tried to establish a foothold at all four stairwells and were rebuffed every time. In fact, her forces had not only kept the savages bottled up in the stairwells, they were outright pushing them back to the higher levels. The most recent report from Pod Captain Howser was that the eastern stairwell had been routed. Kuo expected to regain control of the infirmary shortly.

The savages were somehow able to coordinate a simultaneous attack from the surrounding bridges. She wasn't sure how they managed to accomplish this, but those weak attacks had been easily handled as well. The best the wastelander tribes could do was cause a minor distraction before her shockers pushed them back into the fog.

Yet victory wasn't within her grasp; she had thought she'd already firmly clenched it in her hand, but was uneasy. The reports from the other buildings had been late, delinquently so. What little information she had received so far had been scattered and unactionable. Mostly, the updates were that the enemy was more entrenched than expected, "still securing zone," "need to recalibrate critical path," and other bullshit excuses for not hitting mission milestones. And it wasn't just a few of the pods; it was the majority of them.

She watched as more of her troopers entered the stairwell. It was only

a matter of time before this fight was over. A collie flew through a hole
in the wall and landed next to a row of other collies on the south side of
the building where the monitors had set up a base of operations. For the
past hour, Co-op ships had been flying in and out, unloading supplies,
generators, and tents. This floor was her command center until the mission was over. Optimally, that would be within a few days, but Kuo wasn't
going to leave anything to chance this time. After months of constant ha-
rassment, she had finally found the savages' home and intended to grind
the source of her annoyance into the ground.

Ewa appeared a few minutes later. "The mark has been acquired and
is currently loaded onto a waiting collie. She is unharmed and incapaci-
tated via a cryo module. Once the collie is finished with unloading, it
has orders to return directly to Earth Central."

"Get a security shocker pod guarding that ship and a squadron to escort it back to Chicago," Kuo instructed. "I want to leave nothing to
chance."

A Valkyrie flew in through the opening and came to a hover just
inside the building. The cockpit opened and the pilot dropped to the
ground. Kuo frowned. What was the problem? She recognized the pilot;
Blackmoore headed the squadron of Valkyries supporting her project.

"Why is your ship blocking the entryway, Wing Captain?" she asked
as he approached.

"There's something going on with the collie fleet, Senior," he said.

"What do you mean?" she asked.

"All of their communications went dead and they dropped out of position into the Mist Isle. I pinged Wolfe, my ChronoCom counterpart,
for an explanation, and he went comm dark, so I followed him. When he
came in here, I decided to block the opening until we get an answer."

Kuo looked over at the collie pilot speaking with the lead monitor.
"Let's see what the problem is." She strolled to where Wolfe and the lead
monitor were huddled in an intense discussion. The two of them saw her
approach and seemed to come to an agreement. The lead monitor walked
away before she reached them and began issuing orders to his people.

"Is there a problem, Captain?" she asked.

He bowed. "None, Securitate. I do not know what you speak of."

"I'm told all the collies have abandoned their assignments. Explain
yourself."

"We've received new orders from Earth Central," he replied. "All agency personnel are to abort this mission immediately."

"What is the meaning of this? Who authorized the recall?"

"I am not authorized to relay my orders to a foreign entity."

"We'll see about . . ." She glanced over at the group of monitors whose area had suddenly become a hive of activity. She scowled. They were breaking camp before they had even finished setting it up. "Stand down, monitors. You will all remain at your posts."

To her dismay, the nonprofits ignored her. The lead monitor, the one she had strung up by a trunk earlier, said a few words to his men and then approached. His face was stern and neutral, but there was something else behind it that hadn't been there before. Something in his eyes or possibly a slight twitch to the curve of his lips. That's what it was. He was smug.

"Apologies, Securitate," he said, not sounding apologetic at all. "Your command over ChronoCom personnel has been rescinded. All our collies at this moment are communicating those orders to our forces on the ground."

Kuo felt that assured victory slipping from her grasp. "Director Young will have—"

"Pardon, Securitate," Captain Wolfe interrupted. "Young is no longer in command of Earth Central. In fact, I have been sent here to inform you that all Valta presence has been expelled from the planet. You are to cease operations and withdraw immediately."

Kuo studied the two ChronoCom lackeys trying to stand up to her. It wasn't a coincidence that Wolfe had his hand on the handle of his holstered pistol and the lead monitor had his wrist beam at the ready. What had just happened at Earth Central became very clear. Well, the timing wasn't perfect, but Valta had already accomplished its core objective on Earth. Destroying these savages would have been a nice bonus, but hardly necessary. If anything, she'd have been doing these nonprofits a favor.

"Once word of your little coup reaches Europa," she smirked, "Director Jerome will have all your heads."

"That is a ChronoCom matter and no concern of yours," the lead monitor replied. This time, he had the audacity to raise his wrist beam and point it at her.

"Very well," she replied. "Securitate Ewa, remove the temporal anomaly from the collie and load her onto the Valkyrie. Wing Captain, take her to orbit and rendezvous with the *Proliferent*. Tell the admiral the project is concluding and to expect a full retrieval of resources."

"Actually," Wolfe said, "I have orders to return Elise Kim back to Earth Central. Her status, displaced out of time, is a ChronoCom matter."

Before he could say another word, Kuo created a trunk and punched his body, the blow most likely crushing several of his bones. She sidestepped the lead monitor's wrist beam shot and hit him with an open hand on the front of the throat. He rolled, clutching his neck, gasping for air. Kuo put the heel of her boot on it and pressed down. The lead monitor pawed at her ankle, trying desperately to push her off. Kuo put more weight on her leg until his twitching stopped.

She signaled to the wing captain. "Take the mark now."

Her actions, however, had not gone unnoticed. Before Blackmoore could take three steps, a dozen monitors blocked his path. More monitors appeared and took position next to them, forming a defensive line around their camp.

"Securitate Ewa," Kuo said, staring the rabble down. "Recall shocker pods six, nine, and twelve. Command delta imminent." She took a step toward the line of monitors, daring any of them to fire the first shot. "Regrettably, ChronoCom has broken their contract with Valta. We will take this grievance to the true command of your nonprofit agency. You do not need to be involved. This is far above all your pay grades. Stand down or face the consequences."

One of the older monitors at the front had his eyes fixed on the lead monitor's body at her feet. He looked up and snarled, "Fuck you, bitch! I was at the hangar that day you killed nine monitors. Today's payback."

He raised his right arm to fire at her and was dropped by blaster fire square in the chest. Kuo heard the powered footsteps of a shocker approach from behind. It was soon followed by Ewa and more shockers until there were a dozen of the giant armored troopers on either side of her. She smirked and scanned the rest of the monitors. "Any more of you foolish nonprofits wish to question corporate authority? You should know that—"

Half a dozen beams struck her shield as the monitors opened up on her and the shockers. The rear of the floor, which was supposed to be the safest defensive point of her operations, suddenly became a new battlefront. Kuo leaped behind cover while her forces engaged these traitors.

She checked her levels: 30 percent. She hadn't had time to recharge her exo modules since the fighting had begun. It would have to wait; she should have enough to take care of this distraction.

Wing Captain Blackmoore took several beams to the body as he scrambled for cover. He fell onto all fours and tried to crawl behind the shocker line. One of the shockers left the firing line to cover him, but that only brought more attention to them. Both fell to the enemy's concentrated fire.

Securitate Ewa did not fare better. She was caught off guard by the initial exchange, and was in similar trouble as she tried to leap over the monitor lines and reach the parked collies. A concentrated barrage knocked Ewa out of the air, and she crashed right into the monitors' midst. A moment later, Kuo saw the red of an exo-chain and then lost sight of Ewa in a swarm of monitors.

Fortunately, several other pods of her forces noticed the fracas and soon reinforced her ranks. They did, however, have to abandon their positions at the stairwells and bridges where some were still fighting. It couldn't be helped; this new front against the monitors, with the temporal anomaly in their possession, was the priority. The rest of this operation was irrelevant. She eyed the row of collies in the back. This fight was just a distraction, one she should take advantage of. The monitors currently had superior cover behind their supplies brought in for the base, but her forces had them pinned in the southeast corner of the building.

Kuo moved away from the front line and hugged the east wall as more of her troops joined the fight. There was a narrow gap here between the wall and a row of tents. With a little luck, as long as her forces kept the monitors busy, she could move in and acquire the asset before they were the wiser. The sounds of fighting intensified, which made her job a little easier. She began to make her way down the narrow path.

She wasn't the only one with this idea. She was halfway to the collies when a group of monitors came down from the opposite side, no doubt with the intention of flanking her forces. The two sides saw each other at the same time. The monitors raised their wrist beams. By then, it was too late; Kuo powered her exo and was on them in an instant.

There were four of them. The first took the brunt of Kuo's charge as Kuo ran her over with her shield. The second, she grabbed with her trunk and shot straight into the air. The monitor screamed as she flew up in a lazy arc and fell halfway across the floor. The third managed to get a shot off that went wide left. Kuo palmed her face with her left hand and slammed her into the wall. The last tried to flee. He got four steps away from her before she wrapped a trunk around him and held him suspended in midair.

Kuo detested people like him. She *tsked* as she walked by. "For your cowardice, you receive the slowest and most painful punishment." She took in the fear plastered on his face and squeezed the trunk slowly, tightening its grip on him bit by bit. His body sizzled as the surface of the trunk cooked his skin. The man tried to scream, but there wasn't enough air left in his body for much sound to escape. All he could muster were soft moans. At some point, not far into her work, he passed out. That didn't surprise her.

Kuo squeezed the trunk harder until his body exploded. She dissolved the trunk. What was left of the monitor, crushed bones, skin, and blood, fell to the floor in a messy heap. A cruel smile appeared on her lips. This man deserved every second. If a person was to don the garb of a soldier, he had best honor the resources spent to train and arm him. Otherwise, he was a waste.

She continued until she reached the first of the parked collies. A warning appeared on her AI module. Her levels had just reached 15 percent. They were low, but she was nearly finished. Once she recovered the temporal anomaly, she could just fly the still-hovering Valkyrie and leave the planet. Her forces would have to fight their way out, but they were of secondary concern.

The first collie's hatch was already open, the pilot frantically working at the console. His mouth fell open as she walked in. "What is . . . ?"

She lashed him with the trunk, killing him and destroying half the cockpit in the process. As Kuo searched the ship, a monitor ran in; either he had seen her enter or he had been hiding from the battle. In either case, he was able to get a shot off that was harmlessly absorbed by Kuo's shield before she picked up one of the supply containers with a trunk and bludgeoned him with it.

Kuo finished searching the ship and continued to the next one. She launched herself to the roof of the adjacent collie and took a moment to appraise the current state of the battle. The monitors were attempting to push her forces back with varying degrees of success. Her shocker line was holding, but there were noticeably fewer of the tall armored troopers than just a few minutes ago. The lack of explosives in their arsenal was really hampering her forces, especially in this situation. Several of the stairwell lines had splintered as well, and one of the northern bridge lines had completely shattered. She had to hurry; things were falling apart.

The next collie was still loaded with cargo, and it took Kuo several minutes to pull out all the containers before she quickly made her way to the next collie, and then to the one after that. She continued around the side of the ship and noticed a young monitor off to the side staring at her. He was frozen in place, shaking badly. She took a step toward him and he jumped, falling onto his back. He scrambled a few paces away from her on all fours before getting back to his feet and fleeing. Kuo let him go. She didn't have time to chase cowardly nonprofits.

Kuo continued searching the row of collies for the temporal anomaly, killing monitors who got in her way. There were nearly twenty collies. Still, as long as none of them took off, that temporal anomaly was here somewhere. She found two monitors guarding the hatch of one collie near the back. They both saw her as she rounded the ship and fired. She dodged one beam and her shield blocked the other, and then she attacked, not bothering to create a trunk, to conserve levels. The closer monitor fired again, but she was able knock his arm upward. She rammed a fist into his gut, turned and threw a spin kick across the other's face. Both of them fell at the exact same time. Kuo looked down at her handiwork. No wonder these worthless creatures worked at a nonprofit agency.

She opened the hatch and found a woman snoring softly on a metal bench in the center of the collie. A cryo band latched onto her wrist was connected to the collie's source panel. Kuo tilted her head and studied the temporal anomaly. This slight person was the Nutris scientist who had kept her on this mud ball planet for the past year? She was the source of all her recent frustrations? This girl had better be worth it.

She took a step into the collie and suddenly felt the pull of an exo-chain around her shield. Before Kuo could react, she was pulled roughly to the ground. She tumbled and was instantly on her feet. Immediately, she took a full round of blaster shots, depleting her shield to critical levels. It still held, but the exo-chain prevented her from creating a trunk.

Kuo lashed out blindly. The holder of the exo-chain couldn't be too far away. She was rewarded with a grunt and then another pull as both of them tumbled to the ground. Again, she was back on her feet in a second. She faced her assailant. He was a gaunt man, thin and pale, unclean. Definitely not one of the monitors. A savage, perhaps?

He glared at her with hate in his eyes. "I've been looking forward to running into you, Securitate Kuo. I have a debt to repay that is long overdue."

FIFTY-SEVEN

CORPORATE CONFLICT

Within a very short span of time, James and his small force of guardians became inconsequential in the battle for the All Galaxy Tower. Something near the back of the floor had attracted all of the Co-op's attention away from the bridges. Not that James was complaining; they were getting their butts kicked. Even now, scores of the Co-op were rushing toward the south end of the building. Had Murad's Elmen or Kut's Wallstreeters, the two tribes who occupied the building south of the All Galaxy, broken through and sent reinforcements?

James ordered his guardians to take a position at the shadow of the entranceway. Staying low, he moved forward on his own and snuck into Crowe's office off to the side. He hoped the old man was safe, but anyone who'd been on this floor when the Co-op attacked was probably dead or captured. Since the enemy had first attacked, he had not seen any of the Flatiron fights, and that saddened him. That meant their entire tribe's blood was on his hands. Just like Oldest Qawol's. Just like Smitt's.

He entered the room and silently crept along the near wall, hiding behind one of Crowe's wingback chairs. The Co-op had turned this room into a makeshift guard tower. A rack of blasters was laid neatly next to the door, and there were stacks of energy magazines next to it. Next to the fireplace, if James didn't know better, he would have sworn was a coffee machine. For a second he wanted coffee badly. It had been months since he last drank a cup, and going clean only made his body want another vice to latch on to.

Someone at that far end of the room coughed. James froze and peered over the side. A figure stood in the shadows with his back to him. How James hadn't notice the man in the white uniform was beyond him. His senses were failing him, forcing him lately into several mistakes, careless ones that could get people killed. That had already gotten people killed. He counted a few beats as the trooper whistled and continued loading energy magazines into blaster rifles and then racking them against the wall.

James waited. A window of opportunity came when the trooper knocked over a small stack of the magazines and got distracted. James leaped out from behind the chair and closed the distance. One hurdle over Crowe's desk, and he was on the trooper, swinging once with his rifle to knock him down and then raising the butt of it high into the air to bring it down on the man's face.

James slammed the rifle down to crush the trooper's skull and stopped centimeters before it would connect. The initial blow had knocked the trooper's white helmet off. He was a teenager, a young one at that, probably the lowest ranked of the Valta forces relegated to this guardhouse. It brought him back to the Nazi soldier he had killed at Königsberg Castle, the unknown young man who was just about this kid's age. He wondered only one thing at this very moment.

"What's your name, kid?"

The young trooper, terrified, eyes squeezed shut with one hand trying to protect his face, pried one eye open. "Wh . . . what?"

"Your name. What is it?"

"Es . . . Estan."

James took a step back. "Get up, Estan. Are you armed?"

The young trooper shook his head and scrambled to his feet. "I . . . my . . . ," he stammered.

James pulled the boy to his feet and motioned to the door. "I'm going to let you live. Dying here is shit for someone so young. Stay out of this fight. If I see you again, I'll kill you, so just go."

"But I'm contract bound to——"

"Get out!" James pushed the boy hard until he tumbled into the hall. The young trooper fled, whatever else he was screaming lost in the chaos

of the battle outside. James looked over to the bridge entrance and signaled for his guardians to join him. His twenty survivors, staying low,
scrambled into the room a moment later. James handed each one a blaster
rifle as they walked in.

"Why did you let that Valta go, Elder?" one of the guardians asked.

James shrugged. "Just paying a ghost back." He gave them all a quick
crash course on how to handle the Valta rifles. "Better versions of the
crap you've all been using. It's a little heavier, but there's no recoil like
the projectile weapons. You also shouldn't have to worry about reload-
ing as often." He gave the group about a minute of practice before urging
them out of the room. Chances were, that young trooper had not heeded
his advice and had gone to find help. James would hate to have to kill him
so soon after letting him live.

It seemed he didn't have to worry about that, though. Whatever chaos
was unfolding on the other end of the cavernous room was spreading.
Eriao led a large group of guardians out of the eastern stairwell and
punched through the Valta lines. The northern stairwell was experiencing a similar surge, though the enemy line there held for the moment.

James climbed onto a stack of containers hugging the east wall and
looked to the south. His mouth dropped. How could this be possible? The
Valta soldiers were fighting ChronoCom monitors! He looked over to his
left, where the guardians at the north stairwell struggled to make headway. He should be there with them right now. However, something bigger was happening.

"Elder James," Eriao said, running up to him. "It is good to see you
still breathe." A crowd of his guardians from the eastern barricade rushed
past him toward a group of troopers holding back the northern stairwell
guardians. "Shall we join them? If we can merge your group with mine,
we might stand a chance of pushing the enemy back."

James couldn't take his eyes off the south end of the building. The
fighting there was the heaviest, and the monitors were slowly losing. The
only reason the Elfreth had any chance right now was because the Valta
forces were so focused on the monitors. Once defeated, the megacorporation could just turn around and wipe out the Elfreth.

He grabbed Eriao by the sleeve. "Listen, we need to help those people
over there."

The war chief frowned. "The monitors? Why? Let them kill each other."

James shook his head. "The only reason we've made any headway here is because they're fighting. Once Valta wipes the agency forces out, they'll crush the Elfreth."

"What's to say if the monitors win, they won't crush us as well? Let them weaken each other, and then we take our chance with the survivor."

It was a tempting plan, but James's gut told him otherwise. Eriao was rightfully biased. The agency was responsible for the attack on the Farming Towers that killed many of the tribe, but things had changed. The man who had led the attack on the Farming Towers now actively salvaged for the Elfreth. The woman they had taken in as a refugee now led them. Something Levin had told him before he left for Earth Central rang in his head: they couldn't do this alone. Elise, Grace, Levin, the Elfreth, all of them, needed help if they were going to survive and make any of this work.

"ChronoCom isn't the real enemy," he said. "They're the lesser of the evils."

Eriao was not convinced. "These same people were killing us only hours ago."

"Take control of the guardians at the north stairwell."

"What are you going to do?"

"I need to find a way to get in touch with the monitors. We need to work together. That's the only way we can we beat Valta."

"Are you sure, Elder? Is this really the right choice?"

"I don't know," James admitted. "But I believe so."

Eriao grimaced and then finally shrugged. "How do you intend to reach them?"

"I'm not sure," James replied. "Sneak or fight my way."

"You'll never make it alone. Valta controls the entire center and has those monitors completely surrounded." Eriao put a hand on his shoulder and pointed to the east side of the cavernous room. "There is where their lines are thinnest." A dozen pods of Valta troopers were positioned from near the center of the floor all the way to the wall. There were still fifty meters of troopers he needed to get through to reach the monitors, but that was far fewer than the hundreds of troopers and shockers battling the monitors and Elfreth on the other parts of the floor.

"I guess that's where I'll try," said James.

"I will send guardians to help you clear a path," Eriao said.

James shook his head. "A few won't make a difference. It'll just attract more attention."

"Then I will send all of them."

"Wait, no," James protested. "You need them to relieve the guardians at the north stairwell."

"If you truly believe what you say is critical to our survival, then they will have to hold a little longer."

Throughout most of his life, James had always been ready to die: when he was a teenager trying to survive at Mnemosyne Station, when he was just an initiate at the ChronoCom Academy, and when he was a chronman for twenty years. He was ready to lay his life down for Elise and even the Elfreth. For them to do the same gave him pause.

"It'll be a massacre," he said quietly.

Eriao looked around the room. "Look around, Elder. It already is. Let us find a way to end it."

Within a few moments, the war chief had rallied all of his guardians and ordered them to strike at a single point in the Valta line and drive a wedge between the troopers on that line to the monitors on the other side. James watched as the guardians lined up and prepared to charge the Valta defensive positions, humbled at their faith and bravery. The crew that was with him at the bridge lined up at the front. The surviving fly-guards pushed their way through the crowd until they were at his side, his honor guard. Chawr stood to his left, Hory to his right, and Dox right in front.

James leaned in to Chawr. "You know, you can't die. Who's going to maintain the *Frankenstein*?"

Chawr grinned. "Why, you, Elder."

Eriao screamed at the top of his lungs, and then the large mass of guardians charged at a full sprint, shooting as they covered the distance between the two forces. The troopers opened up on them, and the first line of guardians fell. A few seconds later, the guardians crashed into the make-shift line of crates the Valta forces hid behind, and then the two sides meshed into a general melee.

James, keeping his blaster rifle working, taking out troopers as he moved, sidestepped, fired, and moved again. Dox fell first, taking a shot to the chest meant for James. Hory disappeared a second later, pulling a trooper to the ground. James wanted to stop and help him, but Chawr pulled him forward by his shirt.

Something struck James from his blind side, and two troopers towered over him, whaling on his arms and chest. He dodged a blaster shot and took out a trooper's knee with the end of his rifle. He rolled to his side to avoid a stomp and then tripped the other. He got to his feet and finished off both with two quick shots.

He turned to his left and came face-to-face with a new attacker. It was the same young trooper he had spared at the guardhouse. He still wasn't wearing a helmet, but he had somehow managed to find a blaster. The two stared at each other, both waiting for the other to make the first move. Something in James hoped desperately that the boy would retreat. Instead, the boy raised his rifle.

James got his shot off first, instantly killing him. He stood over the young man and shook his head. Even when he tried his best to spare a life, death somehow claimed what was due. He looked around for Chawr and found his flyguard's bloodied body lying on the ground. Blood dripped from his mouth and from a gaping wound to his stomach.

James felt his knees buckle. He had lost many men under his command, both as a chronman and as an elder, but this one hit him the hardest. He remembered the first time they had met. Chawr had offered him booze in return for bringing the Elfreth supplies. He had also been the first to volunteer to learn to work on the collies. He was also the one who had protected Elise when ChronoCom had attacked the Farming Towers and James hadn't been there. And now he had died protecting James.

James wanted to sit there with the boy, but didn't have the luxury of mourning properly. The best thing he could do to honor Chawr was to make his sacrifice count for something. He took a deep breath and continued on. The Elfreth charge had stalled, and they were slowly moving the wrong way. However, they had thinned the Valta ranks enough that James, staying low, was able to sneak through a maze of tents and containers until he reached the monitors' ranks. He was immediately apprehended by a squad of monitors.

A wrist beam blast narrowly missed him. James raised his hands. "Don't shoot. I need to speak with the lead monitor."

The man approached, arm held up. "A savage that speaks Solar English? What do you want?"

The monitor next to him did a double take. "That's James Griffin-Mars."

"Black abyss," a third monitor said. "I can't believe you're still alive."

"Take me to the lead monitor now!" James exclaimed. "If you want to beat these Valta assholes, you're going to need to work together with the wastelander tribes."

"Isn't he a traitor?" the first monitor asked.

"Get your priorities straight, monitor," James snapped. "There's no time. People are dying, and you're losing right now."

The second monitor nodded and signaled for James to follow. They escorted him to a tent where several lead monitors gathered around a crate they used as table. James recognized the one in charge. Pollock was several years younger and had failed to reach the tier. Since then, however, he had made a name for himself within the monitor ranks and was seen as a potential successor to Moyer one day.

He frowned. "Chronman James Griffin-Mars. This is unexpected. What are you doing here?"

"What happened between the agency and Valta?" James demanded. "Why are you fighting?"

"There's been a coup at Earth Central," Pollock said. "We're taking back the agency from the megacorporations."

"Auditor Levin involved?"

Pollock looked surprised. "How did you know?"

"No time," James said. "The wastelander tribes out there want to ally with you against Valta."

Pollock frowned. "Have you spoken with their leaders?"

"I'm leading them. Right now, they're desperately trying to break Valta on the east side. We can help each other."

"How can we trust you?" Pollock asked. "You betrayed the agency."

"Did I?" James replied. "Perhaps we're both finally on the right side. There's no time to debate this. We need to work together, or none of us will make it out alive. If we coordinate, we can pincer them between us."

Pollock exchanged a few words with the other lead monitors in the tent. They came to an agreement, and then he slid the map toward James. "Show us the positions."

James pointed to the area the guardians had wedged off to get him close to the monitors. "The tribes here will know not to fight with monitors unless attacked first. If you connect with them here, we can open a united front. Then as word spreads, we can cut them off here, here, and here."

Pollock signaled to one of the leads to check out that flank. A few minutes later, the lead monitor returned and confirmed what James had said. The group of lead monitors began to form a new strategy, sliding their concentrations slowly to the right. Over the next few minutes, the monitors linked up with Eriao's forces at the east stairwell. A little while later, they did the same with Maanx's at the south stairwell.

Once communication between all three forces was opened, they were able to coordinate their attacks, sometimes entrapping Valta from two sides at the same time. James stayed at the monitor command tent to act as a go-between for the tribes and the monitors. The trust between the two sides was still thin, and a few misunderstandings between monitors and tribes ended with battles. Slowly, however, they started to make a difference against their common enemy. The combined ChronoCom and Manhattan force reversed Valta's advances and was even able to push them farther back to the center of the building.

A monitor ran into the tent. "Lead Monitor," he gasped. "I just saw Securitate Kuo at the collies."

Pollock swore. "What the abyss is she doing there? Probably trying to hijack a collie to save her own hide. Well, I can't worry about one Valta commander right now."

James's blood froze and he clenched his fist. "Where are the collies?"

Pollock frowned. "You can't take on a securitate without bands, James, and I can't spare the manpower to help you take her down. The best thing to do is let her escape."

"I won't let that happen," James replied, the dream of Smitt's death fresh in his mind. "You have the situation handled here. I'm going after Kuo."

Pollock was about to say something, and then stopped. He went to the far side of the tent and pulled an exo-chain out of the container. He offered it to James. "Take this. It's the best I can do."

James nodded. "Thank you, Lead Pollock."

Pollock waved him off. "I'll send monitors as soon as I can spare any. Until then, stay alive. And if she's trying to escape, for abyss sake, just let her go."

"Not going to happen." James picked up the chain and sprinted toward the back row of collies. The only thing he could think of right now was Smitt and his promise to bring his murderer to justice. This could be his only chance to make things right.

He found her just as she killed two monitors outside one of the collies. He charged forward and latched the exo-chain on her. He yanked, pulling her off balance, and then unloaded his blaster at her shields. Unfortunately, it still held. He had to give it to Kuo: she was faster than he had anticipated. She kicked out and tripped him, and they tumbled to the ground. Both of them were up and circling each other in an instant.

"I've been looking forward to running into you, Securitate Kuo," he growled. "I have a debt to repay that is long overdue."

She gave him a look of disdain. "How would a savage know my name?"

"You murdered my friend. I'm here to repay the favor."

Kuo did a double take and laughed. "James Griffin-Mars. At last we meet. I assume you're referring to your handler. I forget his name."

"His name is Smitt David-Proteus, you psychopath," he snarled, unloading his blaster at her.

Kuo tried to dodge the blast, but the exo-chain prevented her from moving too far away, and her shield took the full brunt of the blast, causing it to light up and flicker. James realized it must be low if it was struggling to absorb a single blaster barrage. Kuo charged even as he continued depleting her exo's levels. She slipped to the side and lunged at him, only to be sent crashing to the floor as he swung the exo-chain in the opposite direction, tripping her up.

James gripped the handle of the exo-chain warily as she got up. The chain was like a leash on her. As long as he had control of it, he could keep yanking her off balance and prevent her from escaping. Kuo tried to feint to the left, but James pulled in the opposite direction. She stumbled and he hit her with another blaster shot. This time, it penetrated the shield and he grazed her shoulder. She shrugged it off.

She tried to attack him a few more times, but each time, he was able to use the exo-chain to throw her just off balance enough to pepper her with more blaster fire as she came in. It would only be a matter of time before the shield fell, and he could kill her.

"Give it up. You're not escaping justice again," he growled, spitting out blood. He had yanked her to the side when she surprised him by lunging toward him and managed to get a clean punch flush on his jaw, knocking a tooth loose. They had both crashed to the ground.

Kuo picked herself up and smirked. "Why would I do that if I'm winning?"

"You're not—" He jumped to the right as she dashed toward him, using the exo-chain to veer her farther to the left than she intended. Kuo changed direction and came at him again. This time, she did something that surprised him.

She deactivated her exo.

Without the active shield to latch on to, the exo-chain became useless. He yanked the chain to the right but succeeded only in throwing himself off balance. The result left him vulnerable, and he paid dearly for that mistake as she charged. She kicked the rifle out of his hand and hit him in the jaw, causing his legs to buckle as he fell to the ground.

James was up in a second and attacked, focusing on hitting her injured shoulder. Somehow, she was able to dodge or roll with his blows to avoid taking damage. He had to admit, she was quick. Even though he had had the advantage all throughout, she still managed to land several blows.

He ate a punch to the gut and then an uppercut that snapped his head back. He staggered and tried to protect his face, but she felled him with a long sweeping kick to the side of the head. Dazed, he spun to the ground and found himself facedown, wide-eyed and stunned. He rolled to his right and kicked out.

Kuo avoided him with ease as she took a step back and circled. She studied him the same way a predator would study lunch. "You're disappointing, chronman. I would have thought a Tier-1 would be more impressive, especially after the hassle you've put everyone through."

He picked himself up and went at her once more. She sidestepped his lunge, blocking a punch and stepping down on the side of his knee as she skipped away. James's leg gave out and he crashed to the ground once more.

Breathing heavily, he picked himself up. His body ached all over, and he was unsteady on his feet. He didn't want to admit it, but he was a shell of what he had been during his salvaging days. He feinted left and went low, sweeping at her feet. Kuo wasn't fooled and stepped backward, tapping him once on the side of the face with her fist as she danced away.

James knew he was slowing down, though to be honest, he hadn't been that fast to begin with. The decline had been small at first, and then after that last jump with Titus, it was as if his body had betrayed him. He had just refused to admit it. It was probably a lucky thing Levin had taken over salvaging duties. If not for the lag sickness, his increasing number of mistakes probably would have gotten him killed. At this very moment, part of him wished the ghost of Smitt would appear to stoke his fire a little, but he knew that wasn't the problem. He just didn't have it in him anymore.

"That temporal anomaly." Kuo spoke as matter-of-factly, as if she were just talking about her day. "Is she your woman? Is this why you did what you did, chronman?"

Thoughts of Elise being harmed enraged James. Elise depended on him, and this woman was hunting her. He wasn't going to fail Elise, not like he had Smitt or Sasha or the Elfreth so far. He had brought nothing but death and pain to all those who loved and cared for him. He had to make things right. He owed it to them.

James clenched his fist and circled close, biding his time. All he needed was one crack at her. If he could get his hands on her, he could drag her to the ground, where she couldn't use speed against him. He had to get closer. "I did what I did for a lot of reasons. For love, humanity, my soul. Not profit and power, which probably is a foreign concept to a corporate slave like you."

"Is that what you think we're doing?" She laughed, again that casual, carefree attitude. "Oh, you misguided nonprofit, if you only—"

They were less than a meter apart. James took the opening and shot in, trying to wrap his arms around her smaller body and muscle her down. Instead, he grabbed a fistful of air as she slipped out of his grasp and kneed him in the face. James blacked out, or at least he thought he did. When he came to, his head pounded and everything was so loud. Sounds of explosions and shouting everywhere just made things worse. His mind couldn't seem to process all the external stimuli. It took several moments for his eyes to focus and make out the face hovering over his.

Kuo was kneeling over him, looking off to the side. He reached for her and she casually swatted his hand away. She looked down. "I do commend you for trying. The solar system could use more men of conviction like you, if it wasn't for your poor judgment. In any case, I believe the situation here has deteriorated. Fortunately I have what I came for. I could kill you, but that would be a shame. You see, you have done more for Valta than you could possibly imagine. For that, we are in your debt."

Securitate Kuo stood up and raised her foot. "Goodbye, Chronman James Griffin-Mars. You'd better hope we never meet again." Then she brought the heel of her boot down on his head.

EPILOGUE

In the end, the data did all of the damage, even though there wasn't a smoking gun. There didn't need to be one. Levin had spent the weeks leading to his arrest and trial compiling what was mostly common knowledge within the senior ranks of the agency. It was the combination of the data that painted the larger and clearer picture of the corruption. Add that to the already simmering anger throughout the agency, and the rebellion was started.

Levin and the small coup on Earth Central were simply the match that lit the fuse, and it spread through all of ChronoCom, first consuming Earth and then their outposts and stations on Venus, Luna, and Mars. By the time the rest of the agency blocked all traffic to the Outer Rim colonies, it was too late, and the damage was done.

In the end, the majority of operatives on Earth Central sided with the rebels. Moyer controlled the loyalty of the monitors, and Levin, that of the auditors. The rest of the personnel, the engineers, support crews, and medical teams, had little choice but to go along. Levin liked to think that they would have supported him anyway. They, too, were directly affected by ChronoCom's continuing corruption.

The only unknown was the chronmen, but that came as a surprise to no one. The tiers were always an unreliable and unpredictable group. Most of them were indifferent to who they served as long as they were taken care of. That's how chronmen were. In the end, they split. Roughly a third of the chronmen on Earth pledged their loyalty to the rebels while another third fled toward the outer planets. Levin could have prevented them from fleeing at the hangar, but he decided that giving them the choice and showing the rest of the solar system that those who remained stayed of their own volition was worth the collies and bands and resources lost.

The last third was still undecided and had asked for an audience with the new leadership of the rebel agency. Led by a Tier-1 named Brock, they were most likely going to ask for more say in how jobs were run and for better contract percentages to earning out on salvages. Both were terms Levin was keen to accept. The chronmen had been used as tools for far too long. It was time their voices were heard. Regardless, he would deal with that headache tomorrow. Today, he had something else on his mind.

Wearing auditor bands once more, he walked up the stairs to the Administrator Wing of Earth Central. His thoughts were all over the place as he stepped in front of the Watcher's Board just outside Director Young's office. Julia and Rowe had offered to accompany him to see the director, but Levin, as the catalyst for all this, thought he at the very least owed Young a one-on-one sit-down.

The Watcher's Board hadn't updated yet. He wondered how the numbers would reflect the events from last night. The coup had effectively fractured ChronoCom into two separate entities: Earth and the inner planets against the rest of the solar system. Some were already calling it the Second Core Conflicts. Levin hoped to the abyss it didn't end up like the original.

A little less than half of the group that met with him at the hangar had survived the battle last night. Those were better numbers than Levin could have hoped. He would need every single one of those leaders to help hold things together and to guide the agency back on course. By his estimation, his new ChronoCom—and it was his responsibility now—had only a quarter of the agency's previous holdings and personnel, but with Earth it controlled approximately 70 percent of all salvageable time lines. Earth was by far the most resource-rich and least expensive repository to salvage. That put them in a very strong and delicate position with the rest of the solar system.

On the one hand, humanity couldn't survive without dealing with the rebel ChronoCom. On the other hand, if the rest of the solar system decided that the old regime was the right one, and supported destroying this rebel group, could he do anything about it? Could any of them?

Levin looked to the right at the double doors leading to Young's office. It had been almost a year since Levin had last stepped in there. Young had barricaded himself in the office when it became clear that he had lost control of Earth Central. Levin decided to leave the old man in peace and deal with him last. The director deserved that much. He walked up to the large doors leading to the office and knocked. The metal clanged with a dull hollow thud.

"Come in," the director said from the other side of the room. At least he was still alive. Levin had considered the outside possibility that Young had committed suicide, but the director was too tough to do something like that. It just wasn't the old bastard's style.

The double doors creaked as he walked in. Levin closed them behind him. Young was sitting at his desk reading a book and drinking a dram of whiskey. There were half a dozen other bottles lying about his desk. He must have spent most of the night trying to drain his entire collection. Levin went to the other side of the desk and stood patiently.

Young, as he often did, took his time, licking his fingers as he flipped the pages. The two continued for another fifteen minutes until it seemed the director found a good stopping point. He closed the book and set it aside. He picked up the glass of whiskey and took a sip.

"Still a stick up your ass, I see. You can sit."

"Thank you, Director." Levin sat down in the chair opposite the director.

"It's been a while since the last time I hauled you in here."

"I haven't had much opportunity as of late. I see you redecorated. New doors and a new desk?"

Young scowled. "Courtesy of that Valta bitch. No respect for real wood."

Levin pointed at the wide assortment of bottles on the desk. "I also see you're trying to drink it all before we take you away."

The director snorted. "Damn straight. I spent half a century collecting this shit. Do you actually think I'm going to let it all go to waste on you hooligans?" He leaned back in his chair. "So what will it be? Firing squad? Are you going to hang me?"

"Not even going to try to ask for a pardon or some sort of forced re-tirement?"

"I did try to have you shot on the spot."

"That does put a damper on our relationship, though not much. I've known you long enough to expect certain things."

"What are you going to do to me, then?"

Levin considered his options. Most of the others in charge wanted to execute or at the very least imprison Young. As the High Director of Earth, he was integrally linked to the corruption within the agency. Levin recalled something the director once told him here in these very chairs. There was more to this office and position than just being a good admin-istrator.

The rebels' survival over the next several months would depend on how they fared negotiating new terms with the megacorporations and gov-ernments that depended on their salvage to survive. He hated to say it, but with two ChronoComs to deal with, all those entities could demand better rates and terms from both. Now with competition, it would be capitalism at its finest. There was some heavy irony here. These were skills Levin simply did not have. There was a man sitting opposite him, how-ever, who had the right experience.

"How about a job?"

Young frowned. "Doing what?"

"Similar to what you're doing now. We need someone skilled in negotiating terms with the corporations and colonies."

Young took a sip of his whiskey and pondered. He poured some into another glass and pushed it toward Levin. "Let me get this straight. You lead a rebellion against the agency and throw the entire solar system into complete chaos just so you can put the same people who you be-lieve are the source of this so-called corruption back in power? I don't get it."

Levin took the glass and toasted Young with it. He took a sip. What-ever whiskey was in here was amazing. He found himself distracted by it. "What is this?"

"Luxe Empire. You'll find none better."

Levin took a few moments to savor the drink before continuing, "You'll be operating in the same capacity, but following new rules. If you accept the position, you follow the Time Laws to the letter. We protect the chronostream and the integrity of the agency. This ChronoCom cannot be bought."

Young laughed. "You don't even realize what you've done. Negotiating new salvage terms for your rebel agency won't be a problem. You have much bigger issues to deal with."

"Like what?"

The director shook his head. "I assume you've cut off the master chron database access to the rest of the agency. That means they won't be able to maintain integrity with the chronostream. You think they're just going to stop salvaging because they don't have access? What about the megacorporations and governments? If they see that the other Chrono-Com isn't following the rules, why should they? You're going to have every jackass with jump bands trying to do their own salvages. The chronostream is going to be devastated. Are you going to be the one policing it all?"

The ramifications of what the director said hit Levin like a bucket of cold water. He felt his nerves go numb as he considered those words. It wasn't just possible, it was probable. Had his actions just destroyed the one thing he was trying to protect? At the very least, he would have to give the chron database access to the other ChronoCom just to help maintain the chronostream, which eliminated any advantage he had over the other faction.

"I didn't think of that," he admitted.

"That's always been your problem, Levin," Young snapped. "You only think two steps ahead when someone in your position and in my position needs to think ten steps ahead. You don't think about the long-term effects of your actions. Anyway, I accept your job offer. I assume I'm being stripped of my directorship. Am I reporting to you now?"

"Actually, I have someone else in mind. You'll be reporting to the Mother of Time."

For a second, Young looked confused, and then his eyes widened and his face turned pale.

James woke up under a bright light, freezing and in a lot of pain. Maybe he was dead. He recalled stories about a centuries-old religion that spoke of dying and moving toward a white beam at the end of some tunnel. He guessed it was fitting that death would suck as much as living. So much for finally being at peace once a person crossed the threshold. He tried to look at the bright light again and couldn't. At first, he thought his eyes hurt, but then realized that it was his entire face. And legs and stomach and shoulders and arms. Basically, James hurt all over.

He tried to sit up. Strong hands held him down.

"The elder is up," a voice called out.

For a second, James regretted still being alive and having to deal with the bullshit of the wastelander tribes and ChronoCom and Valta. Then he thought of Elise and panic gripped his chest. He fought past the hands holding him down and sat up, and was instantly hammered with fresh waves of pain. He nearly passed out again as he laid back down on his back.

"Stop moving, you flaming idiot," Titus's voice said from somewhere close by.

James forced his eyes open and saw Titus and Grace hovering over him. Franwil appeared on his other side.

"You're all still alive," he whispered. "Does that mean we won? Where's Elise?"

"One thing at a time. Stop moving doesn't mean keep moving," Titus snapped. "You've got a half-dozen broken bones and possibly a lacerated spleen. Whoever you were fighting kicked your ass really good."

Lead Monitor Pollock appeared next to Franwil. "By the time my men got to him, the securitate had beaten him to within an inch of his life. She killed three more of my men before she fled in the collie."

James grimaced. That had been probably his only chance to avenge his friend. He had come so close, only to fall short. "What about Sasha? And Elise? Are they all right?" he asked.

"Sasha is fine. We're keeping her upstairs so she doesn't have to see you like this," Franwil said. "The girl is asking for you."

"As for Elise . . . ." Grace paused and exchanged weary glances with the others. "Valta has her."

James's heart stopped and he felt as if his head were about to explode. He tried to sit up again. It was a testament to how weak he was that three geriatrics were able to hold him down.

"We have to get her!" he screamed. "How could you let this happen?"

"I'm sorry, chronman," Pollock said, holding him down by the shoulders. "We were barely holding on. My men did not realize her importance until it was too late."

"No!" James screamed again until his voice gave and he fell into a fit of tears and sobs. He had failed her just like Smitt, just like everyone else in his life. He struggled against his friends as his crazed mind lashed out at everything and everyone.

Grace appeared right above him, and with a stern look, she raised her hand in the air and brought it down on his face. Fresh waves of pain shot across his entire body, nearly sending him into shock.

"No," Titus barked. "That's the side with the broken orbital bone. His other side next time."

"Good," she replied. "Maybe he'll stop throwing a tantrum."

A small voice in his head tried to speak over the screaming in his broken heart. *She's right. Take responsibility for yourself. Pull yourself together and do something about it.*

James latched on to those words. Memories of the fight flowed back into his head, and he knew it was his fault. His body had grown weak, and he had allowed it. Whether it was accumulated lag sickness or alcohol abuse, maybe just the years of wear and tear finally catching up to his body, this was all his fault. When Elise and Smitt and everyone else needed him the most, he had checked out, fallen into the bottle and fallen apart. He broke down in tears once again as all hope suddenly escaped him.

"I'm sorry," he said, his voice barely audible.

"Stop saying sorry, James," Grace said. "Nobody cares about your apologies. Figure out how to make things right."

"I don't know if I can . . ."

"I swear I will smack more sense into you if you keep this up," Grace growled. "We need the old James right now."

"She's right," Franwil said. "The Manhattan Nation won a major battle today. We've defeated our invaders, and scouts have reported that the enemy have all left the Mist Isle. Victory is ours, and the people celebrate. However, a lot of chiefs are dead, and with Elise gone, they're looking for someone to lead. Many are looking to you, chronman."

"I can't lead them," he said. "They don't trust me. They never have. Black abyss, I don't trust me."

"I wouldn't be so sure about that," Franwil said. "Everyone is crediting you with taking back the All Galaxy. Eriao has already said the tribe will be better served with you as war chief."

"Eriao has been dying to pass that buck along for months." Grace chuckled.

"You have to think about the larger picture as well," said Franwil. "There's hundreds of wastelander tribes, all part of the Manhattan, looking for guidance. This whole alliance will fall apart without strong leadership."

"I don't care about the alliance," he cried.

Franwil grabbed him by the shoulder and stared into his eyes. "You lie with your mouth, chronman, but not your heart. You do. I know it."

Grace didn't word it so kindly. "I swear I'm going to hit you again, James. Do you want all of Elise's hard work to fall apart because you were too weak, too afraid, and too full of self-pity to step up? Besides, if we're going to get her back from those bastards, we're going to need all the help we can get."

"What's the point of all this if she's not here?" James asked.

Titus put a hand on James's shoulder. "The point, son, is there's a chance we can get her back. Don't let it slip between your fingers."

Those words hit close to home. He did care about everything they'd built more than he was willing to admit. And finding a way to rescue Elise right now was the only thing that pulled him away from total despair. He swore he would do whatever it took to get her back. He took a deep breath and closed his eyes, taking his time to collect his thoughts.

"What do you need me from me?" he asked. "I'll do whatever it takes."

"Take over as the war chief for the Nation and be the figurehead that Elise was. The people need someone to look to and give them confidence and hope." Grace smiled. "The three of us will actually be the ones running everything."

"We will guide you like we did Elise," Franwil said.

She and Grace looked at Titus, who shrugged. "I guess."

James looked at his advisers. Together, they were just shy of three centuries old. "We're going to need more than just the Manhattan Nation if we're going to go up against a megacorporation."

"Auditor Levin from Earth Central has sent word," Pollock added. "He says ChronoCom wishes to ally with the Manhattan Nation. He wants a meeting with your leaders immediately to discuss the defense of the planet as well as continuing pursuit of a cure for the Earth Plague. How should I respond?"

James looked at everyone looking expectantly at him. He finally nodded. "Tell Levin that the war chief of the Nation of the United Tribes of Manhattan looks forward to meeting with him."

Elise woke up in a white room also thinking she was dead. First she noticed the shiny white walls and ceilings, then she looked to her left and saw that the floors, doors, and even the furniture were all the same impossibly pure white. She thought the color was impossible because in all the times she had been in this present, she had not seen anything so . . . not dirty.

Except once. That shiny white building-ship thing back in Chicago.

She sat up. She was in a bed, in a square room, with only a table and two chairs. Nothing else. Everything was snow white, even her clothes, from her pants to her shirt to—she checked—her underwear. For a second, she was ecstatic that she was wearing clean fresh underwear. This pure white room was what she had imagined the future would look like.

Then terror gripped her. Where was she? Who had her? The last thing she remembered was fighting those Valta jerks—those white-uniformed Valta troopers—in Aranea. More memories returned. Her mechanoid was split open and she had lost consciousness. Now she was here.

"Where in Gaia am I?" she said aloud. Her voice felt dead in this windowless room. Dampened. "Hello?" she said louder. "Anyone here?"

A few seconds later, one of the walls hissed, and a tall thin man with an equally long face walked in. He was bald, but in a manicured way. His features were delicate, and he looked almost alien. Like her, he was wearing all white. He moved with an eerie grace. She scooted to the back of her bed as he approached.

The man pulled up a chair and sat next to her. "Hello, Elise Kim. I trust your accommodations are more suitable for you than the horror of what you've experienced the past few months."

"Who are you?" she asked. "What do you want with me?'

The man bowed his head. "I am Sourn, Vice President of Earth Operations of the Valta corporation. We're all terribly excited to have you on board."

Elise's throat sank into her stomach. She tried to cry out, but nothing came. Her hands shook. "You genocidal bastards. You've killed so many of the Elfreth and the Manhattan people. You killed all my friends on the Nutris Platform."

Sourn looked surprised, and then shook his head. "Those fiends and savages have told you lies. It's all right. You're among your own civilized people again. You're safe now."

"What are you talking about?" Elise said. "What do you want with me? Why did you capture me?"

"Capture you?" He looked bemused. "My dear, I think there's been a terrible mistake. You see, ever since we learned about your predicament, we have been doing everything in our power to rescue you from the savages."

"What? Rescue me?" A tinge of doubt crept into her thoughts. She added, "They're not savages."

"Of course they are. Those savages captured and held you for the past year. We're so relieved to have finally mounted a successful rescue."

Elise's jaws dropped. "What are you talking about?"

She knew what she had experienced the past year with James and Grace and Franwil and the Elfreth. That was real. However, what this person Sourn was saying made sense. Could she have somehow misunderstood the situation from the beginning? Was this some strange case of Stockholm syndrome? A very small seed of doubt sprouted inside her. She couldn't be sure anymore.

"What do you want with me?" she asked again, hesitantly.

"We require your expertise, Elise Kim. Valta is trying to cure the Earth of an evil known as Terravira, or what you refer to as the Earth Plague, and we need you to help us do it. Why else do you think we obtained the Nutris machines?" Sourn stood up and offered his hand. "Will you help us heal our planet?"

She pulled back. "Why would I help you?"

"Because," Sourn gave her a warm smile. "We're the good guys."